FRIENDS to LOVERS
One Kiss

FRIENDS TO LOVERS: ONE KISS © 2025 by Harlequin Books S.A.

CRAVING HIS BEST FRIEND'S EX
© 2018 by Katherine Garbera
Australian Copyright 2018
New Zealand Copyright 2018

First Published 2018
Second Australian Paperback Edition 2025
ISBN 978 1 038 94360 6

THE DATING DARE
© 2020 by Barbara Dunlop
Australian Copyright 2020
New Zealand Copyright 2020

First Published 2020
Second Australian Paperback Edition 2025
ISBN 978 1 038 94360 6

FRIEND, FLING, FOREVER?
© 2019 by Janice Lynn
Australian Copyright 2019
New Zealand Copyright 2019

First Published 2019
Third Australian Paperback Edition 2025
ISBN 978 1 038 94360 6

Except for use in any review, the reproduction or utilisation of this work in whole or in part in any form by any electronic, mechanical or other means, now known or hereafter invented, including xerography, photocopying and recording, or in any information storage or retrieval system, is forbidden without the permission of the publisher.

This book is sold subject to the condition that it shall not, by way of trade or otherwise, be lent, resold, hired out or otherwise circulated without the prior consent of the publisher in any form of binding or cover other than that in which it is published and without a similar condition including this condition being imposed on the subsequent purchaser.

All rights reserved including the right of reproduction in whole or in part in any form. This edition is published in arrangement with Harlequin Books S.A. Cover art used by arrangement with Harlequin Books S.A. All rights reserved.

This is a work of fiction. Names, characters, places, and incidents are either the product of the author's imagination or are used fictitiously, and any resemblance to actual persons, living or dead, business establishments, events, or locales is entirely coincidental.

Published by
Mills & Boon
An imprint of Harlequin Enterprises (Australia) Pty Limited
(ABN 47 001 180 918), a subsidiary of HarperCollins
Publishers Australia Pty Limited (ABN 36 009 913 517)
Level 19, 201 Elizabeth Street
SYDNEY NSW 2000
AUSTRALIA

® and ™ (apart from those relating to FSC®) are trademarks of Harlequin Enterprises (Australia) Pty Limited or its corporate affiliates. Trademarks indicated with ® are registered in Australia, New Zealand and in other countries. Contact admin_legal@Harlequin.ca for details.

Printed and bound in Australia by McPherson's Printing Group

FRIENDS to LOVERS

One Kiss

KATHERINE
GARBERA

BARBARA
DUNLOP

JANICE
LYNN

MILLS & BOON

CONTENTS

CRAVING HIS BEST FRIEND'S EX   7
Katherine Garbera

THE DATING DARE   155
Barbara Dunlop

FRIEND, FLING, FOREVER?   359
Janice Lynn

Craving His Best Friend's Ex
Katherine Garbera

USA TODAY bestselling author **Katherine Garbera** writes heartwarming and sensual novels that deal with romance, family and friendship. She's written more than seventy-five novels and is a featured speaker at events all over the world.

She lives in the UK with her husband and Godiva (a very spoiled miniature dachshund), and she's frequently visited by her college-age children, who need home-cooked meals and laundry service. Visit her online at katherinegarbera.com.

Books by Katherine Garbera

Sons of Privilege

The Greek Tycoon's Secret Heir
The Wealthy Frenchman's Proposition
The Spanish Aristocrat's Woman
His Baby Agenda
His Seduction Game Plan

The Wild Caruthers Bachelors

Tycoon Cowboy's Baby Surprise
The Tycoon's Fiancée Deal
Craving His Best Friend's Ex

Visit her Author Profile page at
millsandboon.com.au,
or katherinegarbera.com, for more titles.

Dear Reader,

I grew up in the '80s and loved Rick Springfield and his song "Jessie's Girl." I think it's safe to say that I wanted to be Jessie's girl and have Rick singing about me with such longing in his voice. So when I was thinking about Ethan Caruthers and the woman he lusted after, I had the chance to write about that feeling. Crissanne is Ethan's best friend's ex-girlfriend. Unlike the song, she was never Ethan's but she could have been...if only Ethan had asked her out when he'd first seen her instead of pointing her out to his best friend.

Love is complicated. I think we all know that. Nothing rational dictates whom we fall in love with or don't fall in love with. Sometimes the person who seems so perfect for someone else actually doesn't end up having those feelings. But in Ethan's case, he sort of liked that Crissanne was out of reach. He could have that perfect/ideal love in his head and it wasn't messy or complicated...until she shows up on his doorstep alone and single.

I really had a lot of fun writing this book and I hope you all will enjoy coming back to Cole's Hill, Texas, and catching up with all of the Wild Caruthers men!

Happy reading,

Katherine

To the Zombie Belles for having my
back and making me laugh!
It's hard for me to believe that I've known
some of you more than 20 years!
I love you all.

One

Ethan Caruthers opened the door to find Crissanne Moss standing there, face pale, biting her lower lip the way she did when she was worried. What was she doing here? She had her camera bag flung over one shoulder and a suitcase on the step behind her, and a taxi was pulling away from the curb. She pushed her sunglasses up on her head, and a strand of her silky, straight long blond hair slipped free in the late summer breeze. She parted her lips and blew the strand away. As always, he had to force his eyes away from her mouth.

With some women he'd met, he could easily ignore the fact that they were female. But from the moment he'd been introduced to his best friend's girl, it had been a struggle to control his intense attraction to her.

He had felt so disloyal to Mason yet at the same time had been powerless to control his attraction. He'd wanted her from the moment he'd seen her and he'd hesitated…

"Well, hello there. I wasn't expecting you, was I? I mean, Cole's Hill, Texas, isn't your normal neighborhood," he said, holding the door open for her to enter before going to get her suitcase. She'd been living in LA with his best friend, Mason, for the better part of the last three years.

"No, you weren't expecting me, and when you hear why I'm here I won't blame you if you tell me to hit the road," she said.

Crissanne had a Northwestern twang to her speech that he'd always found endearing. He couldn't imagine anything she could do that would make him send her away. "I'm a lawyer and have heard some pretty outrageous things over the years. I doubt you'll shock me."

She gave him a sweet smile that didn't reach her clear gray eyes and then reached over and hugged him. "You've always been the best, Ethan. Frankly, I didn't know where else to go..."

Intrigued, he put her suitcase against the wall near the front hall table and then closed the front door before turning to face her again. He wanted to ask where Mason was, but also thought he remembered something about his best friend heading to Peru to film his extreme adventure survival show.

And right now, Ethan was pretty sure he was going to hell for lusting after Crissanne, but he'd never been able to look at her and not see the two of them tangled together in a big king-size bed.

He liked to think that he'd hidden his reaction, though; he was always on guard whenever he was around Mason and Crissanne.

"Come into the kitchen. My housekeeper made some sweet tea and chocolate chip cookies before she left for the day," he said. "We can have a snack and you can tell me why you're here."

He gestured for her to precede him down the hall. It was the gentlemanly thing to do, but as his gaze fell to her hips, which swayed gently with each step she took, he knew there wasn't anything polite about his attention. He wanted her. He swallowed hard and knew he had to get himself under control.

He'd broken up with the woman he'd been seeing off and on in Midland a while ago, so he'd been celibate for longer than he liked. "I need to grab my phone from my study. Help yourself to the cookies."

He turned into his study and then stood there for a second, forcing himself to remember everything he'd ever heard in Sunday school about not coveting things that weren't his. He grabbed his smartphone from the desk and then went down the hall, sure he had himself under control, until he saw her standing at the French doors that led to his back porch, resting her head against the glass.

She looked lost.

She needed a friend.

He remembered the hug and it was suddenly easier to shove his lustful thoughts to the back of his mind. She needed him.

"Crissanne?"

She turned and pulled her sunglasses from her head, putting them on the kitchen table. She put her hands in her back pockets, which thrust her breasts forward in the loose, peasant-style top she wore.

Damn.

"Mason and I broke up," she said, her words pouring out in a rush. "We had a really bad fight and he said I could stay in his condo in LA while he's in Peru but I couldn't. I...I just needed to get away. And I don't have any family. When I got to the airport I didn't know where to go, and then I thought of you."

But he was stuck on *Mason and I broke up.*

She was single.

She was hurting and alone. He knew she had no family. She'd grown up in the foster system and had only a few close friends...most of whom she shared with Mason. They'd been a couple since freshman year in college. Clearly, she needed Ethan to be her friend at this moment. Something he'd always been for her. And he buried his desire for her as he always did.

"Of course you are welcome to stay here as long as you need to," Ethan said to put her mind at ease right off the bat.

"Thank you. Honestly, I know this might put you in an awkward position, but I didn't know where else to go."

He shook his head. Of course it was going to be uncomfortable to explain to Mason when his friend called. But turning her away didn't sit well with him. It was easy to say that his dad had raised him to be a gentleman—and it was true. Crissanne was in a tight spot and clearly needed a friend. But the truth was he *wanted* her here and he'd endure anything to have her under his roof. "It won't be awkward. Are you sure this is a permanent breakup? I know Mason gets moody before he goes away to film."

He wanted her to be happy, and until now he'd thought she and Mason were the ideal couple. As much as he wanted Crissanne for himself, her happiness had to come first. And Mason might be an ass when it came to women, but over the years he'd noticed that they seemed good for each other. Mason had been the one to encourage Crissanne to set up her travel vlog, which had turned into a financial boon for her and given her a career she was in control of.

"I'm sure. He and I have grown apart lately. And I know he's your friend so I'm not going to talk smack about him to you, but we want different things out of life."

That was news to him. Obviously. But he'd sort of avoided hanging out with them too much lately because it had become too hard to be around Crissanne and not want her. Business had brought him to the West Coast more frequently and as dinner plans with Mason had fallen through because of his shooting schedule, it had been just Ethan and Crissanne. And he had hated that weakness in himself.

"Do you want to talk about it?"

She shook her head, long strands of hair sliding over her shoulder to rest on the curve of her breast. "Not right now."

"Well, how about I show you to your room and you can clean up, and then I'll treat you to dinner? I didn't have my housekeeper prepare anything."

"That sounds great," Crissanne said. "Are you sure you don't mind?"

"Positive," he said.

"I'll start looking for my own place right away," she said. "LA was always Mason's town and I'd been thinking of living in the center of the country instead of staying on the West Coast...so it's here or Chicago, and since I know you...but I can definitely stay at a hotel. In fact, I should have gone there."

"Stop. You can stay here. There's no hurry for you to find a place. This house is big enough for both of us," he said. And Mason would be out of the country for a few weeks, so Ethan had time to figure out what to say to his best friend when he got back home.

"You really are the best friend a girl could ask for," she said.

He tried to tell himself that he could settle for being friends, but it had been a lie for a while now, and he knew that having her in his home was going to make it even harder.

Crissanne had hoped for this reaction from Ethan. She'd be lying if she said she hadn't noticed that Ethan had always had a little crush on her. She had hoped he'd take her in. She wasn't the kind of woman who made friends easily. Part of it was because she was competitive, but also she'd never really learned to trust. She remembered how the psychologist her last foster family had sent her to when she'd turned eighteen had stressed that this was going to be a barrier to her happiness.

Maybe it was what had driven the wedge between Mason and her. But the truth was, she had nowhere else to go. She'd rung her friend Abby, who lived in San Francisco, but she'd just started a relationship with a new guy and thought it would be weird if Crissanne moved in with them.

She had a good relationship with her brand manager at one of the large luggage brands that sponsored most of her vlogs and gave her most of her work, but she didn't want to call her up and ask to live with her. She had needed a friend and someone who wouldn't judge. And Ethan was that.

Also, he was busy. As an attorney, he was in court a lot so she'd have some quiet time to figure out what was next. She would make this work. Because staying in the house she'd shared with Mason after that horrible fight where things were said that could never be taken back was something she simply hadn't been able to do.

She wanted to be someplace where she felt accepted and Ethan always made her feel like she was someone. Not a girl who had been abandoned by her crack-addicted mother or passed from foster home to foster home because she was too quiet and weirded people out.

"This is your room," Ethan said when they reached the second-floor landing and he opened the third door on the right.

She stood in the doorway of one of the most luxurious bedrooms she'd ever seen. She'd never visited Ethan before; he'd always come to the West Coast. The house had a lot of Spanish design influence, from the tiles in the entryway to the large sweeping arch that led into the great room, but this room had more of a rustic Western feel. The carpet was thick and lush, and as she stepped into the room she wished she'd taken her shoes off so she could feel it on her bare feet. A large four-poster bed with dark navy drapes and a canopy on it dominated the space. The nightstands on either side of the bed each had a lamp. There was a sitting area with two overstuffed leather armchairs, a small table between them, and a landscape painting depicting the Texas Hill Country on the wall.

"This is a gorgeous room," Crissanne said.

"Glad you like it. There's a desk in the alcove over there leading into the walk-in closet and then to your private bath," he said, gesturing toward them. "If you need anything at all just let me know."

"I'm really low-maintenance, so I don't think I'll need anything," she said.

"Hey, you know, I bet once Mason lands in Lima he's going to be on the phone apologizing," Ethan said.

She didn't think so. Mason couldn't get away from her fast enough when she'd suggested maybe they should get married and think about a family. She'd expected him to balk a little, considering their life together was meetings in airports and nights together in the different apartments he owned in major cities around the world. But the outright rejection had stung.

When they'd talked, he'd said he didn't want to have a family…well, that had changed things for her. A family of her own had always been her dream, especially after her rough, lonely childhood.

"I wouldn't count on that," Crissanne said.

"Well, like I said, you're welcome as long as you need to be here," Ethan said. "Take your time settling in. I'm going to be in my study working. I have to be in court early tomorrow and want to go over my notes again."

"We can skip dinner if that would be better for you," she said.

"No. I was planning to eat out. And my daddy would kick my butt if he knew I served you cereal after you came halfway across the country," Ethan said with that crooked grin of his.

"How are things on the Rockin' C?" she asked.

"Not too bad. Dad is retired but that doesn't mean anything to him," Ethan said. "He still sticks his nose in all the time, making Nate crazy."

Ethan was one of four brothers. Nate was the oldest. He'd taken over running the family ranch, the Rockin' C, and was the CEO of the company that had interests in oil and mineral rights. Another of his brothers, Hunter, was a former NFL wide receiver who had recently been exonerated in a scandal that dated back to college. And then there was Derek, who was a surgeon in Cole's Hill.

Ethan was way too sexy to be an attorney. She felt no guilt whatsoever in thinking that. He had thick, dark blond hair that curled onto his forehead despite the fact that he had styled it to stay back. His tailored shirt hugged his frame, showing off his muscled arms and hugging his lean abdomen.

"Does he make you crazy, too?" Crissanne asked, realizing she'd spent too much time staring at Ethan.

"At times," Ethan admitted. "But luckily Nate's daughter, Penny, is a good distraction. Having a granddaughter kind of calms Dad down. So it's not just me here at the house in addition to my housekeeper. I have a...manservant. Saying that makes me feel way too *Downton Abbey*, but *butler* sounds pretentious as well. Anyway, his name is Bart and he lives here and takes care of the house, the pool and the yard."

"You need two helpers to keep your house?" she asked.

"I probably don't need them but I am gone a lot. And Bart needed a job and no one would hire him because he had a record. Mrs. Yarnall used to work for my parents until they moved into the small house and didn't need her anymore. Now that it's just Nate at the Rockin' C, there isn't a need for two housekeepers at the main house. She has five or so more years before she retires, and I could use the help here."

"Weren't you worried about hiring Bart?" she asked.

Ethan shook his head. "He's a good man who just grew up with bad influences. And I've seen a real change in him since he was paroled."

If she needed a good example of the kind of man Ethan was, this was it. He cared about everyone. He saw the person, not all the other junk like upbringing or record or age. Not that many people took that kind of time to really make sure everyone had a purpose the way he did.

Though she'd come here knowing he sort of liked her, she didn't kid herself that it would turn into something more than just curiosity. Mason was his friend, and Ethan was loyal. Not blindly loyal, but the kind of man who lived by his own code.

Then again, he probably had been crushing on her because she was forbidden fruit. And that made her sad, because she wanted Ethan to be the perfect man she always imagined him to be.

He strode toward the door and then hesitated. "The balcony overlooks the pool and grounds. It connects to the other rooms," he said.

"Where is your room?" she asked.

"Two doors down," he said before leaving and closing the door behind him.

She stood there in the nicely appointed room, trying very hard not to feel like she was lost. It had been a long time since she'd had this feeling, but she was flashing back hard to the foster homes of her youth and feeling adrift, like she wasn't sure where she was going next. She was on her own again. She'd gotten used to being part of a family with Mason, and she knew that it had been a false feeling. He'd liked the noncommittal state of the relationship, and she'd been able to fool herself that it was something else. Something more. And she promised herself she wouldn't do that again.

Rubbing the back of his neck, Ethan entered his study and closed the door, leaning back against it. His brothers were all settling down and getting their lives together, but what did he have in his life that mattered? One thing was his job, the career he loved and would never give up. And the other was a woman who thought of him as her friend.

Hell and damn.

He walked to his desk, sat down in the big leather chair his mom had helped him pick out, and glanced down at the photo of him and his brothers that had been taken at Nate's wedding. His life always looked ideal, perfect from the outside. And that had made him struggle.

He knew his weaknesses and never shied away from them. So he knew ignoring this thing with Crissanne wasn't the solution. He had to face it, deal with it and then let it go.

He'd texted Bart earlier to let him know that Crissanne was here. Ethan wondered if they'd met and introduced themselves yet.

He left his office, following the sound of music playing to the kitchen. Not Bart's usual MO, but perhaps he'd been charmed by Crissanne, too. There was something about her, a sadness lurking in her eyes, that had always made Ethan want to cheer her up.

But Bart wasn't in the kitchen. It was just Crissanne, singing to Jack Johnson while she sat at the island typing on her laptop. Her back was to him, and he stood there watching her.

He tried to tell himself it was sweet, that there was nothing remotely sexy about her as she worked. Yet she still tempted him. He decided then and there that the only solution to this was to try to think of her like one of his sisters-in-law.

She glanced up from her work and turned slightly. When she saw him standing in the doorway, she stopped singing.

"Sorry," she said. "I guess I got carried away and was singing out loud."

"You were," he said. "I liked it."

"You did?"

"You don't sound nearly as bad as Hunter. That boy has a lot of talents but singing isn't one of them," Ethan said, thinking of his younger brother, the former NFL football player.

"Your family always sounds so..."

"Big and annoying?" he asked.

"Nice," she said at last. "I don't have any siblings."

Ethan leaned back against the countertop. "They can be a pain in the backside. I can't tell you how many times I wished I were an only child."

"But you don't still feel that way?"

He shook his head. He was glad he had his brothers and that he lived so close to his family.

"I was thinking while you are here, you might want to do a feature on Cole's Hill for one of those travel blogs you write for in addition to doing your vlogs. We have the SpaceNow and NASA Cronus training facility here now. I marked them on a map for you while I was in my office," he said, going over to the desk in the kitchen and picking up the map he'd drawn for her.

He handed it to her and she arched both eyebrows at him. "You seem to have put a lot of time into this."

"It didn't take much time," he said. "I figured you'd want to keep busy. I know that's how I felt in the past when my relationships ended."

She arched an eyebrow at him. "I thought you were the one-night man."

"No need to ask where you heard that," he said. Mason always called him that. "I've had a few relationships that lasted longer."

"I kind of want to dig into that and find out why you never let yourself get involved for longer," she said, then winked at him. "But that would be too prying."

"It would be," he agreed. He'd have to make up something if she did try to probe more deeply, because she was the reason he'd never gotten involved with anyone for the long term. It had never seemed fair to get involved with one woman when he was obsessed with another one.

She gave him one of her sweet smiles and then came around the counter and hugged him. He held himself stiff at first but then put his arms around her and hugged her back, even knowing that he shouldn't. He closed his eyes and breathed in the flowery scent of her hair, and then forced himself to step back.

"I'll let you keep your secrets for now," she said.

"Should I say thank you?" he asked.

"Yes," she said.

"Ready to go to dinner?"

She nodded. "Let me get my bag and phone."

She walked out of the room and again he watched her go, knowing he was fooling himself pretending to be her friend. He was good at arguing a point in court and convincing juries to believe his point of view, but he'd never been able to bluff himself. He had always been very aware of his own weaknesses and if he was being completely honest, Crissanne felt like a dangerous vulnerability. There was no way he was going to ever be able to look at her and not want more, not want to feel her lips under his and not want her body twined with his all night long.

Two

The Peace Creek Steakhouse was conveniently located near the downtown area of Cole's Hill. When Ethan was growing up, his family would rent the wine room in the back to celebrate major accomplishments. As he and Crissanne stood in the foyer waiting to be seated, he remembered how he'd get money from Babs, one of his parents' housekeepers, to get mints from the machine in the front of the restaurant and how he and his brothers would all scramble to be the first one there.

It was in his childhood that Ethan learned to argue with his words and not his fists. He was never going to be stronger than Nate, who was two inches taller than Ethan. But Nate could be distracted by anyone who didn't share his point of view. Of course, some of those early arguments had ended in a broken nose for him. But it had been worth it to be the first to the candy machine.

"What are you thinking about?" Crissanne asked.

He shook his head. "Fighting with my brothers to be the first to get a mint from that candy machine."

"It's so foreign to me that you've lived in the same place

most of your life," she said. "I bet everywhere you go there are memories."

"There are," he said. "Don't you have places where you could go back to?"

"I guess," she said. "The group home I lived in as a kid was torn down a few years ago, and then as a teen I was in a home in Northern California, but I hated it. I felt so…out of place in my Goodwill clothing. I think I'm better at looking to the future," she said.

He started to reach out to squeeze her shoulder but stopped and dropped his hand. Desire had always been such a part of the atmosphere when he was around Crissanne. With Mason as a barrier to anything ever actually happening, he'd allowed himself casual touches that were much more dangerous now. He needed to be careful.

She was still off-limits, but it didn't feel that way.

"That's the best way to look at it," he said. "You can't change the past."

She moved away to look at the pictures on the wall while he gave their name to the hostess, who was the daughter of one his cousins, Liam Shannon. He exchanged small talk with her as she promised him the first table that was available and then moved away from the hostess stand. Ethan had never noticed the framed prints before. They were all images of cowboys that were at least thirty years old, which he knew because there was one of his father when he'd first inherited the Rockin' C, standing in front of his F-150 pickup with the Rockin' C logo. His dad had been the one to take the ranch to the next level of production. The family company had the mineral rights that earned them a large part of their fortune, but Winston Caruthers had made the cattle ranching operation a contender in the portfolio.

"This guy… I love the mixture of confidence and bravado in his eyes," Crissanne said as Ethan joined her.

"That's my dad," Ethan said. "One of his sayings is 'he who

hesitates is lost.' He's always just gone for whatever it is he wants."

She turned to look at him. "You have inherited that. You never hesitate, do you?"

One time.

When he and Mason had both seen Crissanne across the quad and he'd stood there wondering if he should ask her out, while Mason, always willing to take a chance, had stridden over and done just that.

His dad was right.

Again.

He took a deep breath. "I have my ups and downs."

"Seems to me that you have more ups than downs," she said. "Your business is very successful."

"Usually, but I don't like to brag."

She mock-punched him on the shoulder. Damn, her touch sent an electric current through him, even though he realized she was still touching him like a friend. He had hesitated... damn, he'd done it again. She rattled him.

He prided himself on being calm and in control, but she was messing with his restraint. He didn't like it.

If he'd learned anything in his thirty years on this earth, it was that he didn't do well without some sort of limits.

A strand of her hair fell forward, and he lifted his hand to tuck it back behind her ear. Her lips parted and she caught her breath. He couldn't help rubbing his finger down the side of her neck—her skin was so soft—before he dropped his hand.

"Ethan..."

"Yes?"

"Mr. Caruthers," the hostess called. "Your table is ready."

Crissanne swallowed hard and then nodded and stepped around him to follow the hostess into the dining room. The dynamic had changed between the two of them.

He had changed it. He'd tried to be casual about touching

her, but there was no way he could continue to hide the way he felt, especially now that Mason was out of the picture.

And while a part of him knew that caution would be the noble route, another part of him didn't care about that, the selfish part that could only see the woman he'd always wanted walking in front of him to a table set for two. Her hips swayed gently with each step, her blond hair swinging back and forth as he watched.

But they were friends.

At least that much was true. He thought about his brother Derek and his best friend, Bianca, and how they'd somehow managed to turn friendship into love. But that wasn't him and Crissanne. It had never been the two of them in their friendship; it had always been three of them. And it would be ridiculous to think that Mason wasn't going to come to his senses and return for her.

Ethan knew that was what he'd do.

So tonight had to be two old friends catching up...nothing more.

Crissanne fell back as Ethan engaged in a conversation with one of the many people in Cole's Hill who knew him as they walked out of the restaurant. It was safe to say he was a favored son here. She saw in the bones of the streets and its charming historic district that it had been a smallish town but was growing quickly. In fact, the man who was talking to Ethan was discussing a development going in just south of the town limits.

Her fingers itched for her camera. She used the one on her smartphone at times, but she preferred to have the lens at her eye, fiddling with the focus until she could capture whatever it was about her subject that fascinated her.

Maybe if she did that, then she'd be able to understand this attraction to Ethan she was feeling. But she wasn't holding out hope that it would help. The light from the storefront of the Peace Creek Mercantile was throwing shadows on his features, bringing that strong jaw of his into focus. *What the heck.* She took her phone from her pocket and opened the camera app.

The light played over his hair, drawing her eye to the fact that he had some light blond highlights. She tuned out everything, watching Ethan through her camera app and moving to get the right angle for the photo. She zoomed in closer, and saw he had a scar on his left eyebrow...she'd never noticed that before.

His expression was earnest and confident as he focused on the man he was talking to. That was one of the things she really liked about Ethan. He gave his attention 100 percent to whomever he was engaged with. She snapped a few photos, but when she moved around to change her angle, she bumped into someone.

"Sorry."

She glanced up to see a cowboy. Like a legit, thought-they-only-existed-in-the-movies cowboy. He had a leonine mane of brownish-blond hair streaked through with gray, his eyes had sun lines around them, and his skin was tanned. Leathery, she'd say, but he wore his years well. There was something familiar about the set of his eyes and his nose. She knew it would be rude to snap a picture of him, but that face told a story.

"That's okay. I'm sure you could find something prettier to photograph, though."

"Than what?" Crissanne asked.

"That shark over there. You know he's the type to argue," the cowboy said. "He's a lawyer."

"I know," she said. "He's a champion at debating just about anything. One time we spent forty-five minutes arguing the merits of fresh salsa versus that stuff they serve at the fast-food chains."

"Surely there was no competition," the cowboy said.

"Believe it or not, he thought that the fast-food salsa had its place on the salsa scale."

"That boy always was ornerier than a mule," the cowboy said.

"Only someone who knows Ethan well would say that," she replied. "Who are you?"

"Hello, Pa," Ethan said, joining them. Then he turned to Crissanne. "I told you my family could be a pain."

"You did," she admitted.

"Winston Caruthers," the cowboy said, holding out his hand. "You can call me Pa—everyone does."

Crissanne knew it was a casual offer, probably one he made a dozen times a day, but she'd never had a father figure. No man had ever offered for her to call him Pa. And it meant more than she knew it should.

"Thank you," she said, taking his hand. "I'm Crissanne Moss."

"Pleased to meet you, Crissanne," Pa Caruthers said. "Ethan, you'll have to bring your girl out to the house one night soon to meet your ma."

"Pa, uh, we're not a couple. She's Mason's—"

"Ex. I'm Mason's ex and I'm here for a job, so Ethan is letting me stay with him for a few days. We were friends in college," she said, taking control of the conversation. She had no idea what Ethan had been about to say, but Crissanne knew she wasn't Mason's anything anymore.

"Your ma would still like to meet her," Pa Caruthers said in a firm tone.

Ethan's jaw tightened. "Of course."

"As I said, Pa," Crissanne interjected, and it gave her a little thrill to say it, "I'm working here so I'm not sure what my schedule is, but we'll try to get out there."

Winston nodded and put his hat back on. "See you on Saturday, Ethan."

"Yes, sir," Ethan said. His father nodded at Crissanne and then moved on down the sidewalk.

"He still thinks I'm a teenager," Ethan said.

"I think it's sweet," she said.

Ethan arched an eyebrow at her. "Sweet? He's ornery as hell. Everyone says that."

"Do they also say you're just like him?" Crissanne asked, because he sounded just like his father had when he'd been talking about Ethan.

Ethan chuckled. "Yeah, but that doesn't mean they're right."

"Did you get some good pictures of the town?" he asked.

She flushed. She was pretty sure all she'd photographed was Ethan. "I did. Sort of scene shots with the street and the people on it."

"Good."

They continued walking in silence back toward Ethan's Ferrari, which he'd parked at the far end of the historic district on the other side of the Grand Hotel. She thought about how nice this town was, how lovely Ethan's family was and how she really had to be careful about her emotions. This was a stopgap. Cole's Hill was meant to be a place for her to breathe and then figure out her next move.

She couldn't fall for the town or the Carutherses. And she knew that was a distinct possibility. Ethan held her attention—Lord knew, he always had—but seeing him here and not in Los Angeles was bringing him into focus.

And she wished she could say that she was seeing all his scars and his faults, and that was a turnoff. But his scars made her understand him better. Which was dangerous. She could resist perfection. But she was going to have to really stay on her guard to keep the Ethan she knew at arm's length.

Ethan had been in bed for two hours listening to the sound of the wind blowing and the scrape of the tree branches against his window. He really needed to take care of that. But he knew that wasn't what was keeping him awake.

Crissanne was in his house. Sleeping just down the hall in the spare room. He had never slept with her under his roof before. It wouldn't have mattered before, but now he knew it did.

He'd told himself over and over that she was just a friend.

She was still Mason's girl until his best friend told him otherwise.

And of course that just sharpened the ache of desire inside him. His skin had felt too tight for his body all night, except for those few moments when she'd smiled at him, and then he'd forgotten she wasn't his. She was here as a friend. And she was her own person.

She'd come to him for friendship, and he was going to deliver.

He rolled over and saw the empty expanse of the bed next to him. He closed his eyes and swore he smelled the scent of her perfume drifting through the open French doors that led to the balcony.

He got up and walked to the open door and saw the shadow of someone standing at the railing.

Crissanne.

He reached for his jeans and drew them on over his naked body. He carefully pushed his erection out of the way as he buttoned his jeans, and then scrubbed his hand through his hair as he stepped out.

"Couldn't sleep?" he asked, keeping his voice low so he didn't startle her.

"No. Too much in my head," she said, turning to face him. She wore a thin sleeveless nightgown that ended at her knee. The moon was full tonight and it shone down on her, making her look almost as if she wasn't of this world. As if she didn't belong here.

Hell.

He knew she didn't.

"Did I wake you?" she asked, leaning back against the railing. The breeze stirred her hair, catching it and making it flow against her shoulder and then across her face. She tucked it back behind her ear.

"No."

"I'm glad," she said. "But what's keeping you awake? Maybe talking will help."

He doubted it was going to help either of them sleep if he told her he'd been consumed with images of her and that he couldn't stop thinking about her mouth and wondering about her kiss. He rubbed his hand over his chest as his skin started to feel too hot. He needed her. He knew what lust felt like.

But this was Crissanne. Not a stranger, not someone he could simply hook up with and then smile at the next morning.

They had history.

And on his side...attraction.

So much wanting, he thought. In the moonlight with the shape of her body hidden by the flowy nightgown she had on, his imagination was running away from him. He wanted to lift the hem of that gown—

"Ethan?"

"Huh?"

"Do you want to talk about it?"

He shook his head. "No. What about you?"

"I definitely don't," she said.

"Want to play sips and lies?"

She laughed. "The last time we played that I won."

"Only because I let you," he said.

"Uh, sure."

"It's true," he called back over his shoulder as he walked to the wet bar at the end of the balcony. "I'm a gentleman."

"Whatever you say," she said, moving over to the padded lounge chairs that were clustered around a portable fire pit. She sat down and pulled the throw off the back of the chair, drawing it over her shoulders.

He busied himself looking through the bottles searching for the Patrón that he knew was her favorite. And then he sliced a lime and put it on a serving tray next to the shaker of salt and two shot glasses.

He set the tray on the end table between two of the chairs. "Are you cold? I can light the fire."

"I'm okay with the blanket," she said, pouring both of them a shot of tequila.

"Who's going first?" she asked.

"You."

"The gentleman thing again?" she asked.

He shook his head. "Haven't had time to think of a lie that you'll believe."

She started laughing.

He loved the sound of her laughter. He still remembered the first time he'd heard it all those years ago. She'd been sitting on the arm of Mason's chair and someone had said something and she'd started laughing. It was such a joyous sound it always made him smile and at times had cut through the fog he'd allowed himself to live in for a few years.

The game, which they'd played many times in college and since then, was simple. They took turns telling a story and the other players had to guess if it was true or false. If the guess was right, the one telling the story had to drink, and vice versa.

"Topic?" she asked.

"First kiss," he said. It was the first thing that had come to his mind, and as soon as he said it he knew that he was in trouble. He shouldn't be sitting in the moonlight with Crissanne, drinking and talking about kisses. He didn't have the strength that he'd need to keep his distance.

"First kiss? Well, that's an interesting one. It was that time I kissed a frog," she said. "I was at this party at school and I remembered the fairy tale about the kiss turning a frog into a prince. Molly Moore dared me to do it, and I thought what the heck and did it."

He leaned back in his chair. "Was the frog an actual amphibian?"

"What other kind is there?" she said, not really answering his question.

"I'm going to go with lie," he said.

"Truth. I got in trouble for kissing the frog and had to have detention," she said.

"Why?"

"Molly and I were really there to free the frogs from the science lab, so me kissing one was the distraction while she set the others free."

Their eyes met as he licked the back of his hand and shook some salt on it before licking it off again. Then he tossed back the shot, keeping eye contact with Crissanne, before he brought the lime wedge to his mouth and bit it, the tangy juice filling his mouth.

As he tossed the used lime wedge onto the tray, Crissanne reached forward, brushing her thumb over his lower lip and sending a jolt straight through him as she pulled her hand back and licked her thumb.

Yeah, this has bad idea written all over it.

Three

It was August in Texas, so even this late at night it was hot, or at least that was the excuse Crissanne was going to use for the heat sweeping through her. It had nothing to do with the fact that Ethan sat across from her wearing a pair of low-slung faded jeans and nothing else. His chest was bare, and he had more muscles than she'd expected.

He was a lawyer. Surely that meant he spent a lot of time at his desk not working out. But to be fair his muscles weren't overly large...just enticing. He had a flat stomach but no washboard abs, so realistically she knew that there were probably women somewhere in the world who would argue that he wasn't the sexiest man alive. But sitting here in the moonlight with the taste of lime on her tongue and his warm voice telling her a tale that she knew was a lie, she knew she wouldn't agree with those women.

He arched one eyebrow at her and she realized he'd stopped talking.

"Uh...lie?"

"Woman, you are wrong," he said, handing her the bottle

of Patrón. And given the fact that her judgment was already a little off-center, she knew she should call it a night and go back to her bed.

Instead she took the tequila and poured it into her shot glass. Their eyes met as she licked the back of her hand, and she noticed that his pupils dilated. She shook the salt out, then leaned forward as she let her gaze drop and licked the salt, watching him from under her eyelashes. She noticed the muscles of his chest contracting as she tossed back the shot and felt the sting of it before she took the lime and bit it.

She put the lime on the tray as Ethan got out of his chair and walked to the balcony railing. She watched him as he braced his hands on the wrought iron and craned his head forward. His back was long and smooth, his neck strong and sexy. That intense longing rose inside her again.

And all the reasons she thought she had for coming to Texas floated away on the night breeze. She watched Ethan, felt the conflict inside him and knew she should go back into her room.

But instead she got to her feet and went over to him. She wrapped her arms around his waist and then leaned her head against his back right between his shoulder blades. He went tense for a minute before he relaxed.

"This is a bad idea," he said, his voice a low rumble that carried no farther than her ears.

She rubbed her hand over his smooth chest, and she knew he was right as she kept her face buried between his shoulders. But she'd been alone for a long time. Even though she'd only just broken up with Mason, they'd been drifting apart. She hadn't spent more than a few hours with him in the last six months, and she knew a big part of her had already started to move on.

She didn't want to think about that. About how easy it was for her to lock away her hurt and disappointment and just function. She had thought…well, hoped that she'd left that in her past. That the girl who had never connected with any of the families she'd fostered with had grown into a woman who made solid bonds with her boyfriend.

It hurt to realize how wrong she'd been.

"I don't care," she said. Saying it out loud made her realize it was true. "There is something between us."

He took her arms from around him and stepped aside.

"Yeah. Mason."

She shook her head. "That's not what I meant. I always had you pegged as a straight shooter, but I guess you are probably used to saying whatever you have to in order to win an argument."

He shook his head. "Don't do that."

"Do what?"

He closed the gap between them in two long strides and reached for her, his hands briefly brushing over her shoulders before he dropped them to his sides.

"Don't make this impossible," he said.

"It already is," she said. "Or maybe I'm the only one who feels this."

He shook his head. "Dammit. You know you're not."

He stepped closer, and the waves of heat from his body enveloped her as he reached for her waist and drew her closer. She put her hand on his arm, and felt his biceps tense as he lifted her slightly off her feet.

He lowered his head toward hers, and she tipped hers back. Their eyes met. A flash of their entire history went through her mind. All the times they'd sat quietly talking in a corner while Mason had been entertaining their friends with some daring trick.

She knew that this was sudden and was afraid that Ethan would pull back. That he'd let his friendship with Mason keep them from kissing. So she did it.

She initiated the kiss.

His lips were warm and firm, but soft. When they parted, she tasted the lime and tequila on his tongue as it rubbed over hers.

She dug her fingers into his upper arm and lifted her head trying to get closer to him. He tasted good. His kiss was perfect, and so was the way he held her to him. She felt him shift so that he was leaning against the balcony railing, her body resting fully along his.

She felt his hard-on against her lower stomach, and her breasts were nestled against his chest. Just the thin layer of her nightgown kept her from feeling his skin against hers, and she wanted more. She let her thigh fall to one side so that his leg was between hers, and he groaned as his hands roamed down her back to her butt, cupping it and shifting her into a deeper contact with him.

She raised her head to look down at him, and he was watching her. Just staring up at her. She wasn't sure she could read the emotion in his eyes, but it sparked something deep inside her that was more than sexual need.

She started to draw back, aware that she was craving something from him that felt dangerous and edgy, but he tunneled his hands in her hair and drew her head back to his.

Her hair was soft. Way softer than anything he'd touched recently. Her eyes were half-closed, lips wet and swollen from their kiss. Her hands were on his waist, holding him lightly. She tipped her head to the side, their eyes met, and he thought of all the arguments he could make. All the reasons that he could list to make himself drop his hands and walk away from her. But he wanted her.

And he'd been denying it for too long. It had been easy when she lived with Mason, but now that she was here in his house, sitting on his balcony, putting her hands just inches above his groin, he knew he wasn't interested in anything other than following his gut instinct, which was clamoring for him to pick her up and carry her into his bedroom.

"Are you sure?" he asked. He had to. This was Crissanne. She meant more to him than a hookup.

And it didn't matter to him if it wasn't the same for her. She might be looking for sex from him just to forget or to make Mason jealous or for a million other reasons. But for him this was the one woman he'd wanted for over a decade. The one woman he'd thought he'd never touch like this. And he needed to be sure she wanted him, too.

"Yes," she said, her fingers moving up the center of his body until she wrapped them around his neck and kissed his chin and then his jaw.

He stopped thinking. His mind shut down and he turned his head to capture her lips with his. His grip on the back of her head tightened a little bit as he tried to control the passion that was roiling through his veins.

She was unleashing something that he'd forgotten was a part of him. He groaned and then wrapped his arm around her hips, standing up and carrying her into his bedroom without breaking the kiss. He stepped over the threshold, and she pulled her head back.

He let her slide down his body, biting back a moan at how good she felt against him. And then he realized she might change her mind now.

Hell.

He would have to let her go if she did.

But please, God, don't let her change her mind.

He watched as she trailed her fingers down his chest again, and then glanced over her shoulder at the king-size bed that dominated his room. The studded-leather headboard was mounted on the wall and there was a huge pile of pillows that his housekeeper arranged each morning when she made the bed. Above the bed were the horns of the first longhorn bull he'd raised when he was a kid.

"I always forget you're a cowboy," she said, turning to look at the horns.

He shrugged, taking her hand in his and drawing her closer

to his bed. "Not really, but I can put on my boots and cowboy hat if you want me to."

"Only if you lose these jeans first."

"Uh, I don't think any self-respecting cowboy would be seen like that," Ethan said.

"Too bad," she said, raising both eyebrows as she stepped back and let her eyes move slowly over his body. "You'd look damn good in just a hat and boots."

He felt his chest swell and he couldn't keep his pecs from flexing. "You think so?"

She nodded. "Maybe one day..."

"Maybe," he said. He wasn't sure he'd do that. He was a lawyer. He was the serious Caruthers brother. The arguer who was always thinking of the consequences. Which couldn't be said of him tonight, as he stood there in his bedroom next to Crissanne with a raging hard-on.

She turned back to him, her hair swinging around her shoulders as she held her hand out to him. He took it, lacing their fingers together, and she stood on her tiptoes and put her hand in the center of his chest again, spreading her fingers out and rubbing her palm over his skin. A shiver went through him and he drew her closer. He lowered his head, but this time it was just so that their foreheads would meet.

He felt the brush of her exhalation against his neck and closed his eyes.

Crissanne Moss was in his bedroom.

All the feelings he'd been ignoring flooded him, and he realized he wanted this to be more than it could be. He wanted sex, of course; he couldn't deny it. But he wanted her to somehow be his.

And that wasn't what was happening.

This was a hookup. He knew it.

For her, this had to be rebound sex. Something to prove to herself she was still attractive.

He knew because he'd had a dozen hookups like this. Where

he was sleeping with someone else to prove that he was over her. Over Crissanne.

And now she was here, and he knew that he was willing to be whatever she needed him to be tonight. He was done with pretending that he didn't want her.

He cursed under his breath, and she shifted her head to the side, putting her finger over his lips.

"Don't think," she said.

"Is that the only way you can be here with me?" he asked.

She cursed, and he realized that he wasn't going to do this.

She didn't know how to answer Ethan's question. Of course, the whole situation felt like trouble no matter how she sliced it up. She wanted him. She wanted to be with him. She had narrowed down the list of people she could stay with to him. And now she was in his bedroom trying to convince herself that she could get with him and then be cool the next day.

But even with her skill at ignoring her emotions, that sounded like an impossible situation.

"No. Not like you mean," she said. "It's just if we start to think, then we're going to be back to pretending that we don't want each other. And that's a lie. I'm tired of pretending with you, Ethan."

"You say that but you were with my best friend," Ethan said.

"That's over."

"Is it? Or is this about making him jealous?" Ethan asked.

Was it? She hadn't even thought about Mason when she'd gotten on the plane. She'd been thinking of the one person who'd always made her feel better.

"No. Honestly, there are men a lot closer to LA who would have fit the bill if that was my goal. I'm here with you...even though this is what I wanted to avoid. And once we start talking it's going to get complicated."

He sighed and then stepped back from her, walking over to

the bar in the corner of his bedroom and then pouring himself something that looked like whiskey from where she stood.

"It was complicated before we started talking," he said quietly. "We were both just letting our hormones direct us."

"Was that so bad?" she asked.

"I don't know. The thing is, Crissy, I don't want either of us to wake up in the morning with regrets. And as good as tonight would feel I know that we would."

"Why is nothing easy?" she asked out loud. But really she wanted the answer from herself. "I'll leave in the morning. I saw an ad for a B and B in the ladies' room at the restaurant tonight. I should have gone to a hotel or something."

He just watched her, the whiskey glass in his hand. As he stared at her she felt the emotions coming off of him, but she was too turned on to think about how it was impacting him. She was embarrassed that they hadn't just fallen into bed, and dealing with everything else was just beyond her tonight.

What was it that caused these men in her life to pull back? What was it she lacked? She couldn't even get the man who'd looked at her with lust in his eyes when he thought she wasn't paying attention to sleep with her.

She was broken in some way that the world picked up on. She hadn't realized it until this moment, and if she were a different person, one who actually allowed herself to connect to her emotions, she knew she'd be crying.

But instead she just turned and walked out of his bedroom, past the fire pit and the discarded shot glasses and limes, and tried not to think about how the fun they'd had earlier had turned into this mess.

She entered her bedroom and walked over to the bed, sitting down on the edge, rubbing the back of her neck. She couldn't stay here.

Not for another second.

She wondered at the pattern of her life that every time she

ended up in a place she wanted to be, she ruined it and had to leave. This was a new record for her. Not even twenty-four hours.

Stop.

She forced herself to move.

No thinking.

The words that had changed everything in Ethan's bedroom now motivated her to get up and get dressed. She pulled on a pair of jeans and the first T-shirt she touched. Then she got her suitcase from the closet and put it on the foot of her bed.

Her phone vibrated and lit up on the nightstand, but she ignored it. She wasn't in the mood to read her news updates. She had enough on her plate right now.

She went back to the closet but her phone was blowing up with messages, vibrating like crazy. She walked over and glanced down at the screen, seeing they were from a number that wasn't programmed into her phone. But based on the area code, she thought it might be the production company that Mason worked for.

Unlocking her phone, she opened the text messages and began reading them with a mounting sense of disbelief. Then she let the phone fall from her fingers as she sank to the floor, drawing her knees up to her chest.

Mason's plane had crashed.

Oh my God.

She hadn't thought she had anything left to feel, but she hadn't been ready to say goodbye to him. She immediately tried to call Mason. His phone rang, and then a message came on saying that he was out of range and to try her call again later.

She texted the production company back, asking for more information. But there was no immediate response.

She hadn't realized that until this moment a part of her had been holding out hope that he'd come back to her. It made her feel small and stupid, because she'd thought she was over him.

That she'd buried those emotions so deep, pretending she didn't feel them. But they were there.

"Crissanne."

She glanced up to see Ethan standing at the foot of her bed. His phone was in his hand and his face was pale. She stood up and ran over to him.

"Did you get the message?"

"Yeah. I can't get through to Mase or the guy who sent the text," Ethan said.

"Me, either," she admitted. "Do you think he's okay?"

"I don't know. We both know he can survive a lot. He's got skills."

"Yeah. Skills."

Ethan opened his arms and she closed the gap between them, putting her head against his shoulder and just crying. She didn't know what to say. Suddenly she was very glad she hadn't slept with Ethan. Not tonight. Not now when Mason was...

"Do you think he's dead?" she asked.

"I hope not."

Four

The next morning, after a mostly sleepless night when Crissanne had dozed off and on and Ethan had just watched her, they were both in his home office trying to get answers. Sitting in the guest chair, Crissanne looked smaller than he'd ever seen her. All that bravado she usually presented to the world was gone. She had one of the cashmere throws that his housekeeper placed on the back of the chairs over her shoulders.

Ethan was at his desk on his laptop, messaging with the production company and trying to use his contacts in South America to see if they had any local information. So far, all they knew was that Mason's plane had gone down near the summit of the Andes where he had been heading to film his latest series for the production company. There was no information on whether anyone had survived.

Ethan heard voices in the hallway, and a moment later all three of his brothers were in the room. They all glanced over at Crissanne, and Hunter, who had lived in Malibu until recently and had met Crissanne a number of times, went to her and squeezed her shoulder.

"Don't worry. If anyone can find Mason it's Ethan," Hunter said.

"What can we do?" Nate asked.

"I don't know," Ethan said honestly, looking at his oldest brother. "I'm on hold with some officials in Peru. We are communicating but not as well as I'd like since my Spanish is more suited to ordering food or talking about legal matters."

"I've gotten pretty good lately," Derek said. Derek was a surgeon who had just married his best friend, Bianca Velasquez. She and her small son had been living in Spain until last year when she'd moved back to Cole's Hill.

"Do you mind?"

Derek gave him a hard look. "That's why we're here."

Ethan handed the landline phone to his brother, who took it out into the hallway. Hunter was chatting with Crissanne and distracting her from her own fears when Nate nodded to the hallway and Ethan followed him out there.

"What's going on? Dad said he'd seen you two in town last night and it might be a date," Nate said.

"Not now. We have bigger things—"

"No, you don't. You staring at your phone isn't going to make Mason safer or get information here quicker. What's going on?"

Ethan looked at his oldest brother and felt like a kid again. "I don't know. She showed up yesterday with her suitcase, saying things were over with her and Mason and she needed a place to stay."

"She's the one, isn't she? The one you are always visiting out in LA."

"I go to LA for business, not to see Crissanne. Though we usually have dinner, but that's the same thing I did with Hunter and Manu when they lived there." Manu Bennett was the brother of the famed astronaut Hemi Bennett, who was based at the local training center. Manu had been a defensive lineman in the NFL and until this year had been a special teams coach in California. But he'd recently moved to Cole's Hill to coach the high school team and to be closer to his brother and sister-in-law, Jessie, who was pregnant.

"She's not Hunt or Manu. I think you know that."

He shoved his hand through his hair and turned away from his brother before he punched him, though a fight might be what he needed right now. "Stop. I can't do this now. Whatever might have been possible before Mason disappeared is gone."

Nate nodded and then pulled him in for a quick hug. "Whatever happens, I got your back."

"I know and I appreciate it," Ethan said. "Depending on what happens I'll probably take the family jet to LA."

"Of course," Nate said.

Derek finished with the call and walked over to them. "So what they know is the plane went down after a Mayday call and they have dispatched rescue crews, but they aren't hopeful of finding any survivors."

"When will they know something?" Ethan asked, his heart sinking. A part of him still wanted to believe that his friend, who had always been so full of life and was sort of a superman, could survive the crash.

"They hope within twenty-four hours. They have our number and of course the production company's, but I reiterated that you needed to be informed at the same time. No sense getting information secondhand."

"Thanks, Derek," Ethan said. What was he going to tell Crissanne?

"No problem, bro," he said. "I'm bach-ing it this week while Bianca and Beni are in Spain visiting his grandparents. Want me to stay here? I can translate again." His brother had never really been into the bachelor lifestyle but now that he had a family he always referred to his time alone that way.

"Yeah, that'd be great," Ethan said.

Derek stopped smiling as he looked past Ethan's shoulder. He turned to see Crissanne standing there.

"The plane crashed, which we already knew, but Derek found out that the search-and-rescue crew has been dispatched and they are hoping to let us know something within twenty-four hours," he explained.

She nodded. "Okay."

Just that one little word. She looked lost, and he wanted his brothers gone so he could comfort her and talk to her. But he knew that he had to be careful there. He'd almost stepped over that line earlier.

"I guess all we can do is wait," she said.

"Yeah," Ethan agreed.

"Or you could get out of the house," Nate said. "It would be better if you went for a walk."

That was a good idea, Ethan thought. "Want to do it? My brothers will be here in case the Peruvians call back, and we both have our cells."

"Yes, let's do it," she said. "I'll go get my shoes on and be right back."

Ethan watched her run up the stairs from his spot in the hallway and then turned around to notice all three of his brothers watching him.

Hunter raised one eyebrow at him. "Is there—"

"No," Ethan said, brushing past his brothers and walking toward the front door. "Tell Crissanne I'm waiting outside for her."

He didn't hang around and risk an interrogation. He just stepped out into the hot August day. The sun was already high and temperatures were climbing. He threw his head back and looked up at the sky.

He wasn't ready to say goodbye to his best friend. He and Mason had a scuba trip planned for the Caribbean in September. And as much as he wanted Crissanne for his own, as much as he'd been tempted earlier, he knew he wanted his friend back more. He didn't want to lose this extra brother he'd found or the bond of friendship that was so strong between them.

***

Ethan lived in a gated community known as the Five Families. The houses were mansion-sized with well-landscaped lots. There were sidewalks and paved paths large enough to accommodate kids on their bikes and golf carts. There was a golf course, tennis courses and a country club with a sit-down restaurant and a bar, a pool with a snack bar, and several rooms that had private pool tables. She liked it. Ethan had spent the last ten minutes of their walk regaling her with all of those details in a nervous sort of rush.

"I feel it, too," she said at last, coming to a stop and waiting until he did. She had brought her Canon with her because she knew she needed to distract herself, and looking through her viewfinder always gave her distance from the problems in her life.

The problems that had led her to Cole's Hill and Ethan Caruthers. The problems that just kept getting worse.

"I can't stop thinking," he admitted wryly. "Guess I should have followed your advice and never started."

"I think that's impossible for both of us. It's just so odd. He broke up with me," Crissanne said, saying what was in her heart and in her mind to Ethan because he'd get it. "And if he came walking back in the front door this morning I wouldn't feel guilty—at least I don't think I would—but imagining him injured and waiting for help is confusing me."

Ethan nodded. He had his aviator-style Ray-Ban sunglasses on that made it nearly impossible to read his expression. She realized that she felt raw. Not just from the worry and fear about Mason, but from everything that had gone on between them the night before.

"Want to see the lake?" he asked.

"Sure. I didn't know there were many lakes in Texas," she said, pretty sure she'd read that the geology of the state meant that it didn't have many natural ones.

"There aren't. This one is man-made. When they built this

subdivision they wanted it to be idyllic and sort of put in everything that we didn't have on the ranches," he said, resuming his pace. She fell into step beside him as Ethan again started talking nonstop about his family and this place.

She got it. Talking was how he distracted himself. When they were in college, she'd seen him debate with perfect strangers right before midterms and finals. He did it to keep himself from dwelling on whatever it was that worried him.

When they got close to the lake, she saw the beauty of the landscape and realized that she had an idea to get Ethan to stop talking and to distract herself.

"Pose for me," she said.

"What?"

"I need to take some pictures. I need to get my perspective back and I can only do that when I'm looking at the world through my lens. Will you let me take some photos of you?" she asked.

He turned to face her, crossing his arms over his chest, and she remembered how hard his muscles had been under her fingers last night. She swallowed as a rush of awareness went through her. But no guilt.

Just curiosity.

She was upset about Mason, so it was especially surprising that she didn't feel guilty about Ethan.

She took the lens cap off, lifted her camera and took a few photos just to check the light. Even if he didn't pose, she needed this. She wanted to see the land and find her center.

"I didn't say yes," he said, but his lips had quirked as soon as she lifted her camera.

"You didn't say no."

He turned away from her and she caught her breath. His broad shoulders tapered to a lean waist, and his faded jeans, the same ones he'd had on last night, hugged the curves of his butt and his lean thighs. So it hadn't just been tequila and moonlight. It had been Ethan.

She'd sort of suspected that, but it was easy in the clear light of day to pretend that it was something else. Anything else.

Especially when he seemed so nervous around her today.

It was impossible not to see it and feel it as they'd waited tensely for the production company to call with more details. And then there was this walk, where he'd talked about everything but what was between the two of them.

And she got it. Men didn't like to talk. How many times had Mason told her that? But Ethan was a talker...well, sort of.

"I like your boots," she said. He had on a Western-cut pair today. They were in good shape but she could tell they were worn in. They had probably gotten to that comfortable stage.

She moved around to see the different effects of the light and realized that looking through the lens was for her what talking about this place was for him.

"Tell me about the lake," she said.

He glanced at her and she snapped a couple of quick photos. Her camera could capture an unguarded expression that would be too quick for her eye, and she couldn't wait to examine the photos later.

"It was debated for three years before they finally got around to digging it out, according to my papaw. He said that there was some discussion of whether it should be one mixed-use lake or two different lakes—one for swimming and small watercraft and the other for fishing."

He continued to tell her the story as she moved around taking pictures. For a short time, she almost forgot that the man they had in common was missing. But she knew if she wanted to find her own peace with Mason and Ethan, she needed to ensure that she didn't ruin the men's friendship.

"Tell me about how you and Mason became friends," she said.

Surprised, he turned to face her, but she was hidden behind the camera. So many people used the digital display when they took pictures nowadays.

"Why aren't you looking at the screen?" he asked.

"I like the way the world looks when I'm shooting," she said, dropping the camera from her face and looking over at him with a smile.

She was so much more relaxed with the camera in her hands. She seemed like she was breathing more easily now that they were out of the house. It was the same for him. He'd felt the walls closing in even before his brothers had arrived.

"You know how you said that I was lucky to have my brothers?" he asked her.

"Yes. I still think that," she said.

"I do, too. The best part about family is that you don't have to ask for them to be there," he said, not realizing how his words might sound to her until he saw the wistful expression on her face.

"That must be nice."

"It is. It can be a pain in the ass as well. That's sort of how Mason and I became friends. By the time I went to college, Derek had been away for a few years and Nate had just gone to College Station, but I was determined to go to Harvard. So I studied and worked my ass off to get there. My parents, who are very supportive, were determined to make sure that I didn't feel lonely up in Cambridge. So they all went up there with me."

"That doesn't sound so bad," she said.

"I don't mean just my parents. My brothers all came, even Hunter, who was going to college in Northern California," he said. "I had arranged to do a house share. My dad was checking out the locks and my mom was in the kitchen cooking casseroles I could heat up for the week and my brothers were setting up stuff…it was just, I'd picked Cambridge because I had gotten sick of being a Caruthers in Cole's Hill. Everyone knows everything about you here, and I realized that no matter where I went they'd be there."

"You carry them with you," she said. Just like she carried that image in her head of the parents she wished she'd known. She had no idea what they looked like. In her teenage years, she'd spent hours staring at herself in the mirror wondering if she had her mom's eyes or her father's coloring. Finally she'd cut a picture out of a magazine and put it in a cheap plastic frame that one of the other kids at the foster home had thrown out and decided the people in the photo were her parents.

She hadn't thought of that in years. If Mason didn't come back from Peru, she'd really be all alone.

It wasn't like she'd made any other close bonds in the last ten years. There was Ethan and Mason, and to a certain extent Abby in San Francisco, but that was it.

"I do," he said. "That's partly why I ended up back here. Didn't make sense to be out there in the great big world, you know?"

She nodded. "So how did you meet Mason?"

"He didn't have any family, as you know, and all the stuff about my family that made me crazy, he loved. When I got back to the house share from running an errand, he was sitting in the kitchen taking notes as my mom told him how to make tuna casserole."

That made Crissanne laugh. "Oh my God. That's his only dinner dish."

Ethan smiled, too. "He never forgets anything."

"He doesn't," she said. "God, I hope he's okay."

"Me, too," he admitted. "We're supposed to go on vacation in September. Just a week of scuba diving."

"He hadn't mentioned it," she said.

"He didn't?"

"No," she said. "We haven't been in the same room for more than an hour in a long time."

Ethan hadn't realized that. She had said things were over, but he hadn't believed it. Had Mason been avoiding Crissanne?

"I'm sorry."

"You know what, Eth, that was a big part of what pushed me to force him into a relationship discussion. I want a family. I've never had one of my own and we've been together for a long time...so I just waited at home. I turned down a job and waited for him. I had to know."

Ethan moved closer to her.

"What did you have to know?"

"Why he was avoiding me," she said. "And he finally said he liked us the way we had been. The fun stuff. He wasn't ready for a family."

"But you were."

"Yup, and he said that he didn't see himself that way. Not ever."

That sucked. Big-time. For both of them. "I'm sorry."

"Me, too. We fought and then he left and I came here and now his plane has crashed..." She made a broken sound. "The last words I said to him weren't very nice. I have spent the better part of the last twelve years with him and I was just...a bitch."

"No," he said. "I don't know what you said, but I know you weren't a bitch. And I do know one thing about Mason. When things get too close and he needs space, he forces the situation to make the other person react. He did that to me when I was dithering about staying in LA or coming back here."

"Did he?"

"Yes," Ethan said. "Don't feel bad about what you said. Mason knows how you really feel about him. And he's going to be found and you'll have a chance to talk to him again. Soon."

Five

Ethan had never spent a longer day than this one. His brothers had gone home since they weren't expecting any news till tomorrow. Apparently there was a weather system keeping the rescuers from reaching the wreckage. So no news.

Crissanne had gone to her room when they'd returned, and he hadn't seen her in the last eight hours. He was restless, and that was never good. He thought about leaving the house and heading to the Bull Pen, where he'd be sure to find some outlet for the energy inside him. He could ride the mechanical bull or even find one of his frenemies from high school to fight with in the parking lot. But Ethan liked to think he was beyond that.

He heard Bart out by the pool and went outside. The other man was talking to Crissanne.

Ethan stayed where he was in the shadows.

"If you don't check the balances every day they could change. The sun sometimes causes certain ones to burn up quicker than others."

"That sounds a lot like science to me," Crissanne said as

she took photos of the pool. "I've never been one to understand that."

Bart laughed. "Chemistry is my thing. Well, it used to be my downfall, but Ethan helped me find a better way to channel my interests."

"He's good about that," Crissanne said. "He always sees the best in everyone."

Ethan knew he needed to leave or announce himself, but he was interested to hear how Crissanne really saw him and was tempted to stay. His phone pinged, and he glanced at the screen.

Crissanne and Bart both turned toward the noise.

"The production company has news and wants to video chat with us. Do you want to do it out here or in my office?" he asked.

She had gone completely white when he said that they had news. In fact he felt the same way. Good news could have been texted. There was no reason why they couldn't have said *he's alive*.

"Inside." Crissanne's voice was low, gravelly and raw.

He reached for her hand, and she took his. Her grip was tight, as if he were her lifeline to whatever was coming next.

"Let's go."

The hallway to his office just off the foyer was short, but it felt like it took forever to get there. He entered the bookshelf-lined room that his mom had helped him decorate. That had been their thing when he'd been growing up. Books. When they'd traveled, she'd taken him to secondhand shops all over Texas and the country, and they'd collected old leather-bound volumes.

He knew he should be thinking about Mason, about the call. Instead he was trying to comfort himself with thoughts of his mom and their collecting.

"I'm scared."

Crissanne's voice brought him back to the moment. He could deal with his own emotions later; right now he needed to help her through this. She was looking to him to be the one to stay strong, and he would.

Of course he would.

He set his iPad on a console table on one side of the room, and he and Crissanne sat on the leather love seat right across from it.

"Ready?"

She nodded.

He engaged the video call and then sat down next to her. She wrapped her arm through his and hugged it to her chest. He looked down at her, the girl with no family who had given twelve years of her life to a man who then said he didn't want to start one with her, and his heart broke a little bit. But he knew that whatever had happened at the end between her and Mason, there had been love there, and friendship.

And he didn't want to see her lose everything.

The call connected and the screen was clear.

"Uh...thanks for doing this on video. I'm Cam Jones," the man at the production company said.

"Cam, you have news for us?" Ethan asked, getting right to the point.

"I do. There's no easy way to say this. The rescuers got to the wreckage and they didn't find Mason. There was a fire after the plane crashed, and no bodies were recovered."

Crissanne started to cry softly next to him.

Ethan pulled his arm free of hers and wrapped it around her shoulder. He didn't want to believe what Cam was telling them. It was unfathomable that Mason would die in a plane crash.

"Are you sure he's dead?"

Cam nodded. "You know Mason has skills, so we told the rescuers to search the surrounding area of the crash, and nothing...no one was found. Mason Murray is dead."

The words echoed in Ethan's mind. He knew Cam was still talking, but he turned to look at Crissanne, who was sobbing as she buried her face in his chest. All he could do was hold her.

He held his best friend's ex-girlfriend and wondered how he

was going to get through this without Mason to talk sense to him. Mason, who'd always been the one to get that even though to the world Ethan seemed to have all his shit together, he still was treading water.

Every. Damned. Day.

And now he had to help Crissanne.

He would focus on her. That would have to be enough to get him through this. Until she was okay, he'd just keep his own grief bottled up.

But he'd lost a brother today. He'd lost someone he wasn't ready to let go of, and he had no idea how he was going to cope.

"Will you be coming to LA?" Cam asked.

"I'll get back to you later today. But yes, we will be there."

The video call disconnected and he just held Crissanne. It was what he'd always wanted. To have a clear shot at this woman. But now it was all wrong. He'd never wanted to have her at the cost of Mason. For a moment last night, it had almost seemed possible, but then he knew the things he craved the most were always the ones that were just out of his reach.

Crissanne had been alone before. And she and Mason had broken up. So she wasn't sure why she couldn't stop crying.

Ethan was being very sweet. He'd told her to just sit in the sun while his housekeeper packed her bags. Bart had disappeared into the pool house and she sat there, trying to make sense of it all.

Mason gone.

It didn't seem real to her. How had that happened?

The sense of loss she felt was so strong that she just kept crying. Honestly, she'd had no idea she could cry that much. The tears just fell, and when she'd calm down and be able to stop for a moment, they'd just start right back up again.

She wanted Mason back. She didn't want him back in her life as her boyfriend. That had been over long before this breakup.

But she wanted her friend back. He was the only person she had shared so much with over the last twelve years.

And even those memories weren't as full as they could have been. In their last argument, he'd said they were strangers, more like casual friends who slept together when it was convenient for both of them. Not a real couple. But she hadn't understood until this moment. As their life together flashed before her eyes, she realized that most of it was her waiting for him and getting back to him. Not actually spending time with him. She finally got what Mason was saying. Damn him for going to extremes to prove his point.

"You were right," she said out loud. "You win. Come back and I'll tell you to your face."

But he wasn't coming back. He was gone. Lost to her forever like the parents she'd never known. And her weary heart shrank even further in her chest. How many times did she have to see the same message before it sank in?

She drew her knees to her chest on the lounge chair and put her forehead against them. She had always believed deep inside that she was meant for something more. That she'd grow up and make the family she never had. But the truth was she'd never learned to bond with anyone. How was she going to have a family when she couldn't connect?

"Crissy?"

She glanced over at Ethan. Sweet Ethan, who was helping her through something that was horrible for him, too. He always put her first and she just used him...

"Yes."

"Whatever it is that's going through your mind, stop it," he said.

"What?"

"I can see it on your face. The guilt and the loneliness and the sadness, all of it. And the truth is you are entitled to all of those feelings, but you aren't responsible in any way for what happened."

"I know that," she said, but realized that Ethan had nailed it. That was what she was afraid of. "But I told him I never wanted to see him again. Eth, I said that to him. I walked away muttering that it would be better if he were dead."

"You didn't mean it."

"I know that. But I said it. I put that out in the universe."

He came over to her, sat down on the end of her lounge chair and put his hand on her calf.

She looked up and their gazes met, his gray-green eyes so intent and serious. "You're human. We all get mad and say things we don't mean. It happens. And he'd broken up with you. Don't judge yourself by that one moment. You didn't do anything to Mason's plane. You didn't force him to go."

No, she hadn't. And she wouldn't have been able to live with him after what they'd said. Because there was more to the fight than she could share with Ethan. "I wanted him to stay. I didn't want him to take this trip, which is what started our fight."

"Which makes everything that much harder to deal with," Ethan said. "I think he would have done anything to get back to you."

Crissanne nodded. But she knew that wasn't true. And she was still too close to the heartbreak he'd given her to be able to remember just his good parts. That was what Ethan was trying to make her do: remember the best of Mason. "At least he died doing what he loved."

"Yes. He did. He loved going out on his adventures and filming them. He wouldn't have wanted to live any other way," Ethan said.

"He said as much to me when we fought. His life wasn't meant for suburbia."

Ethan nodded. "He told me one time that he'd learned to survive on his own because he knew no one was there for him. He liked being in the wilderness because there was no illusion that anyone was looking out for him. He knew it was just him and nature. And nature didn't allow sentimentality."

Crissanne had to smile at that. "That's so Mason. I'm sure he followed it with his usual mantra...if you depend on yourself you won't be let down."

"He did. And I can only say I'm sure he wasn't," Ethan said.

But Crissanne knew that she was. Of course she'd depended on herself, but she'd always wanted more. She'd always expected to have more and now she was alone. Truly alone again. And though Ethan had been lovely, she couldn't come back to his town, his life, his house after this.

It was time to start living the way she'd always pretended she wasn't going to, by depending on herself.

But as Ethan got to his feet and offered her his hand, she realized just how hard it was going to be to walk away from him.

Ethan wanted to get in his Ferrari and just drive. Go out on the old FM road that went out of town and put the pedal down. Go as fast as he could for as long as he could, scream out his grief and frustration about the ending of Mason's life, but he couldn't.

Instead he'd driven them sedately through town to the private airport that had become bigger and busier since the NASA training facility opened. When they got there, he'd busied himself with talking to the pilot and copilot and texting his assistant.

In fact, he had a list of things that needed to be taken care of. He'd put Crissanne at the top, but he knew he had to pull back and distance himself. He had to give her room to grieve. He had cases he had to refer to other attorneys in his practice. He had to make sure that the oil rights he'd been negotiating for the Rockin' C were taken care of. Hunter had taken care of letting his staff know that Ethan would be staying at his house in Malibu for a few days.

Now he was ready to go, but he paused to take in Crissanne. She stood there on the tarmac looking so damned beautiful that it took his breath away. She had on a pair of large-framed sunglasses that covered half of her face and her blond hair blew in the wind. She'd put on a pair of black skinny jeans that showcased her long legs and a short-sleeved T-shirt.

She looked like she was coping, but he saw her surreptitiously wipe away a tear just then. She was going to be grieving and coming to terms with Mason's loss for a long time.

She looked like...she looked like everything he'd ever wanted, but she was still out of reach.

He had just finished filing the paperwork, paying for the fuel and making sure they were set to go. He walked out of the small airport office toward the waiting G6.

"All set," he said. "I wasn't sure if you'd want to stay with me at Hunter's house or at your place..."

"It's not my place. I already moved out. If you don't mind, I'd like to stay with you."

"That's why I offered," he said.

He cupped her elbow and led her to the stairs up to the plane. When they got inside, she took a seat on one of the large leather chairs.

"Why does your family have a private plane?"

"Why not, right?" Ethan asked.

"I guess, but it doesn't strike me as something you'd all need," she said.

"Well...are you sure you want to talk about this?" he asked.

"Yes. I need to talk about something or I'm going to go crazy just thinking about Mason and what could have been."

What could have been. The words echoed in his mind and he shoved them away.

"Well, as you know, Hunter was accused of a crime he didn't commit," Ethan said. "So while he was playing for the NFL he flew mainly on private jets to avoid possible confrontations. It started the first time he was coming home one year for Thanksgiving and flew commercial. Some people on the plane thought he was guilty and weren't shy about expressing their opinions. They made the flight hell for him, and my father came to me and said we don't fly commercial anymore. So we bought the plane and now we all use it."

Ethan didn't like to talk about that long period of time when Hunter had been living under a cloud of suspicion. In college, a female classmate had died under mysterious circumstances and Hunter and a classmate had been suspects in the investigation. But the Carutherses had all stood by Hunter because the boy who loved God, football and his girlfriend would never have committed a crime like that. But to the outside world, Hunter had looked like a privileged boy who thought that rules didn't apply to him.

"I'm glad we did. It is a nice asset for us to have," he continued, when Crissanne didn't say anything.

"I'm glad, too. I can't believe people. Hunter wasn't even arrested for that crime," Crissanne said. She knew the details because of their years of friendship.

"True. But you know how it is with social media and the court of public opinion," Ethan said. "On the subject of the public, the production company asked me to write a statement for them to release from Mason's family and friends."

"They did?"

"Yes. They were going to ask you, but Cam said he didn't think you'd be in the right frame of mind to write it. He was worried that it would be overwhelming for you."

"Does he know that Mason broke up with me?"

Ethan had no idea. "He said it because of how upset you were by the news on our video call."

She bit her lower lip. "I don't want to be dishonest, but if people are going to treat me like I'm Mason's girlfriend, what am I going to do?"

"Just be honest," Ethan said. "Do what you feel comfortable with."

The pilot leaned his head through the cockpit door and advised them to put their seat belts on and get ready for takeoff.

Ethan sat down across the aisle from Crissanne and put on his seat belt.

She reached out and touched his arm.

"Thank you."

He smiled over at her. She still looked so sad that his heart ached, and he knew he would do everything in his power to make her smile again. He would put all of his resources behind helping her through this.

"That's what friends do," he said.

"You're more than a friend, Ethan. And this means more to me than I can say," she admitted. "I'm used to doing things on my own and just getting through it."

He took her hand in his, laced their fingers together and ignored the tingle that continued to run through him from when he first touched her arm. She needed him.

And that was really all that mattered right now.

Six

After three weeks in Los Angeles, she felt like she was in a fog. She had since they'd first landed here and she'd felt the sun on her face. She'd felt that way the entire time they'd stayed at Ethan's brother's oceanfront house in Malibu, as they handled all kinds of questions and paperwork.

Each day Ethan left her a note with the housekeeper letting her know where he was and what he was doing. He had paid for another team to go to Peru and search for Mason. Today, he'd asked her to come downtown to his firm's LA office. So that was how she found herself standing in the lobby of a high-rise building, wearing her one decent-looking dress and heels. Because she knew that no matter how West Coast casual she was, his law firm wasn't.

When she took the elevator up to the third floor, the receptionist gave her a bottle of sparkling water and directed her to a conference room that overlooked the Fashion District. She had her camera with her and intended to spend some time walking around there when she was done. She hadn't been able to make videos or write at all since the news of Mason's death had reached them, but she'd taken so many pictures and had been publishing them on her blog instead. Just faces of people she met on the beach each day as she walked and searched for answers that were still out of reach.

The door opened and she turned around, feeling a piece of her hair slip from the clip she had it pulled back in. Ethan was wearing nicely tailored suit pants but had taken off his jacket. His hair was mussed. He slipped his phone into his pocket as he walked toward her.

"Sorry to make you come all the way down here. Did you drive?" he asked. He'd also left a car and driver for her use.

"No," she said. "I hate LA traffic so I asked Peter to drive me. I told him I'd catch a ride back with you."

"I might be working late," he said.

Of course he was. He'd been avoiding being alone with her.

"I'm planning to go down to the Fashion District to get some photos for my blog, so I'm not in a hurry."

"Well, okay then. I've had a report from the team we sent," Ethan said, coming farther into the room and holding out a chair at the table for her.

They sat down and Ethan pulled the tablet that had been on the table closer to him. She watched his hands moving on the tablet as he entered the pass code. For a brief moment, she flashed to what those hands could do to her. She had spent a lot of time on her walks on the beach thinking of that one night they'd had before everything had gone so crazy.

"Okay. Did they find anything? Any signs that he might still be alive?" she asked.

He pulled up a file. An image of the burned fuselage of the plane flashed on the screen. He swiped, and the next photo showed six body bags.

Horrified, she turned away. This was it.

It was real. Mason was dead. He was gone.

Really gone, and there was nothing that could bring him back.

She hadn't realized she was crying until Ethan handed her a

handkerchief. She turned away. It was funny how she had been able to reach for him before, but not any longer. The more time they spent together the more distance had grown between them.

She felt the sting of tears, but she'd already known that Mason was gone. It wasn't the sweeping grief it had been the first time. She sighed and reached for the tablet for a closer look at the photo.

"I hate that he died like that," she said at last.

"Me, too," Ethan said. His voice was the same monotone it had been since they'd heard the news.

She didn't think he was fully processing his grief, but because he was always working or taking a call about work she'd had no chance to talk to him about that.

"Are we friends?" she asked him.

"What?"

He turned to look at her, and for a moment she caught a glimpse of the sorrow in his eyes before he masked it with his normal calm expression.

"Are we friends?" she asked again, turning the swivel chair to face him and then putting her hands on the arms of his chair and pivoting it until they were face-to-face. He had to move his legs to either side of hers to ensure they could both sit comfortably.

"Yes. Why do you think we aren't?"

She put her hand on his knee, and he jerked his leg from under her touch. "Since we've been here you've been running away from me. We haven't talked about anything that's important, and I'm sick of your damned notes from the housekeeper. Are you just saying we're friends so that I won't be alone?"

He shook his head.

"What is it? I can't keep doing this. I know that I, out of everyone, should be used to going solo but this isn't what I expect when I'm with you."

"I know," he said, taking her hand in his and turning it over.

He started rubbing his thumb over her palm, which caused a warm sensation throughout her body.

"Okay, so what's going on?"

"I...I..." He dropped her hand and got up, walking to the plate glass windows that looked down on the street.

She waited for him to see what it was he would say, but instead he just put his head against the glass. He looked like she felt inside. So alone.

She got up and went over to him, but was afraid to reach out in case he pushed her away again.

"I can't let out even a moment of what I'm feeling," he said at last, his voice so soft it was barely a gravelly thread. "If I do, I'm not sure I'll be able to control it."

Ethan had been doing his level best to remind himself that Crissanne was vulnerable now. More than she had been when she'd shown up on his doorstep. He wanted to think that it had meant something—her appearing like that—but a part of him suspected it had to be that she'd wanted to make Mason jealous.

Mason.

Ethan had been very careful not to let himself dwell on his friend's death. His best friend. Mason was the one who had truly known him best. Ethan was close with his brothers, but they all had their own lives and careers. It was Mason he called in the middle of the night when he was fighting his own demons, and Mason had always reached out to him when he was in the middle of something he didn't know how to control.

Which was why the breakup with Crissanne had taken him by surprise.

Mason had been quiet about it.

And Ethan would never have the chance to talk to his friend now. He missed him. He could admit that around 2:00 a.m. when he was sitting in his bed not sleeping, but not now. It was the middle of the afternoon in his office building. He had to keep his shit together.

Crissanne put her hand on his shoulder. A comforting gesture to be sure, but at the same time it sent a tingle down his back that he couldn't ignore. He needed something mindless. He wanted sex with a stranger but that wasn't happening. Even if Crissanne weren't staying at Hunter's house with him, she was the only one turning him on these days.

She was so close her body heat was surrounding him, and when he glanced into the plate glass window he saw her reflection. Saw the way she was watching him. And then her fingers moved against his shoulder. He had left his suit jacket in his office, so it was just the two thin layers of his oxford shirt and the T-shirt he had on underneath keeping her from touching his skin.

His blood seemed to flow more heavily through his body and he turned to her, head down, intent on walking away. But she was close, and their foreheads bumped. He felt the startled exhalation of her breath against his lips and then he felt her lips against his.

He grabbed her waist and drew her closer to him, more fully into contact with him, and he knew he wasn't going to let go. Not this time. Not until he was buried between her legs and doing what he should have done that night. That night before—

"Say no and leave," he said, his voice so low and gruff that he hated it. All the trappings of the civilized man he'd learned to be were falling away. "Because if you don't I'm going to lock the conference room door and have you right here on this table."

She chewed her lower lip between her teeth and then nodded. She dropped her hand from his shoulder and turned away from him.

Fuck. He'd known he couldn't let his guard down. That he was throwing away something with Crissanne that had always been hard for him to process and understand. But then she stopped at the door. Instead of opening it, she turned the lock on the handle and then leaned back against it.

"I'm not leaving," she said.

Hell, yeah.

He didn't think anymore. Thinking hadn't done a damned thing except make him hyperaware of how little control he had over any part of his life.

Instead he walked across the room toward her and she stayed right where she was. Watching him with those eyes of hers. He put one hand on the door behind her head and the other on her waist. She tipped her head back as he lowered his toward her, but he didn't want to kiss her again. He wanted to taste that long length of her neck.

He sucked at the skin there. She smelled of strawberries and the ocean. Her skin was tanned and smooth. He wanted to be a gentleman and take his time, but he'd waited a lifetime for her and he knew that wasn't going to happen.

He lifted her off her feet as he turned his head, plunging his tongue deep into her mouth. She wrapped her thighs around his hips and held his face in his hands, angling her head for a deeper kiss as she rubbed her center against him.

He pushed his hand up under her skirt, feeling the coolness of her bare thigh, and then sliding it higher to her butt. He slipped his hand underneath the fabric of her panties and then cupped one cheek in his hand, running his finger along the crack.

She shifted again, pulling her mouth from his and whispering something he couldn't understand. He was beyond listening or thinking. He was focused on her. On having her.

With one hand, he lowered his zipper and shoved his pants and underwear out of the way so that his dick was free. She reached down, brushing his hands aside as she stroked him, her fist wrapping around him and her finger rubbing over the tip of him with each stroke.

He set her on her feet, and she hopped from one foot to the other as she pushed her panties down her legs and then stepped out of them. She glanced up at him and he knew he should say something. Make this seem like it was about more than sex and forgetting, but he couldn't.

Instead, he put his hand on her waist and stepped closer to her. The wall was at her back, and Ethan was pressed along the front of her body. The cloth of her skirt rubbed over his erection and he pulled his hips back, realizing he needed protection.

"Dammit. I don't have a condom."

"It's okay. I'm on the pill," she said.

Ethan lifted his hand, rubbing it over the line of her jaw, and she shivered. She realized she wanted to touch him. She didn't want to settle for half measures, because this might be the only time he dropped his guard enough. She felt his thigh between her legs and shuddered as he cupped her butt with his hand and drew her forward. She undid the buttons on his shirt, but found he was wearing a T-shirt underneath it.

Frustrated, she tugged the shirt up his chest until the hem was right underneath his armpits. Then she bit her lower lip as she drew her fingers over his bare chest and abdomen. His muscles were hard; she knew that from that long-ago night that she'd touched him. But now she felt his heat and realized how much she'd forgotten as she skimmed her fingers over his chest. There was that light dusting of hair that tapered down to his groin and she caressed it, following the line as he continued to fondle her backside.

She was creamy and wet for him, and drawing this out was out of the question. She reached between them and stroked her hand down the length of his shaft, pulling him forward between her legs, rubbing the tip of his dick against herself. She bit her own lip and closed her eyes, letting her head fall back as sensations ran through her.

But it wasn't enough. She wanted him inside her. She needed him deeply filling her, and she wanted it now.

She shifted on his thigh, moving her hips forward and pushing his erection down until he was poised at the entrance of her body. His hands tightened on her ass, and he bit the point where her neck and shoulder met as he drew back his hips and then drove them forward.

She groaned as he filled her, digging her nails into his lean hips and holding on tight.

He muttered her name. "You feel so good."

She nodded. She couldn't think, could only feel. She tightened herself around him, and he groaned against her neck as he pulled out and then plunged back into her again.

She smiled as she rotated her hips to adjust to him inside her. She wanted him deep, filling her completely.

He tightened his hands on her backside as he continued driving himself up and into her, and suddenly everything inside her felt on edge. She was close to her orgasm. He sucked hard on her neck and she threw her head back, calling his name as she came. He tightened his hold on her, driving into her hard and deep until she felt him shudder in her arms and he emptied himself inside her.

She closed her eyes, resting her head on his shoulder as he held her. Her body kept tightening around him and his breath sawed in and out of his mouth. He moved his arms up her back to hold her and she just breathed deeply, realizing it had been too long since she'd had sex.

That had to be the reason why she was holding on to him so tightly and why she felt like crying. She'd been alone for so long, and having him inside her and his arms around her made her realize what it was she wanted in her life.

She needed more of this. More of him. And it had nothing to do with Mason's death. It had to do with Ethan, and what she'd been hiding from herself for too long. She wanted what Ethan had to offer. This quiet intensity.

He shifted, pulling out of her, and he set her on her feet, stepping away. "Uh, I didn't think this through at all. There is a restroom down the hall."

"Ethan?"

"Hmm?"

"Are we okay?" she asked. Because he wasn't looking at her. Hadn't looked at her since he'd shifted out of her body.

He'd turned his back to her, and when he turned back around, his T-shirt was tucked into his pants and his zipper was up. He was doing the buttons up on his shirt, and she felt like the impact of the sex had been stronger for her than for him. Maybe he'd just needed to come and then he could breathe again.

"Yeah. We are," he said. But that flat note was back in his voice again.

She almost turned away. Almost let him force them back to the détente they'd been living in for the last three weeks. But instead she walked over to him, stumbling over her discarded panties. When she glanced up, she caught his unguarded expression.

He wasn't as aloof as he was trying to be.

"Good. Because I'm done with the distance between us. I came to you before Mason's plane crashed because my life was at a crossroads and I thought...I thought I knew what I wanted. Mason's death has made me realize that life is short. None of us is guaranteed a long life and I'm tired of always waiting..."

She stepped back. "I'm not waiting anymore, Ethan. I want more than friendship with you, and I think you want something more from me, too."

He rubbed his hand over his chest and looked at her. For the first time she saw the pain and hope and guilt in his eyes, and she knew that he wanted more than they'd been sharing lately.

"Let's go home. Let's go back to Cole's Hill and figure out if this is just a reaction or something solid," he finally said.

Seven

It had been all well and good to say he wanted to go home, but there was still Mason's memorial to get through. Meanwhile, Crissanne had moved into his bedroom. Not that she took up that much space, but she had a big presence. Everywhere he looked, there were signs of her. Right now, he was in the big en suite bathroom with the double sinks. He didn't even have to turn his head to see her perfume bottle and makeup brushes on the counter. She was in the bedroom singing off-key to Liam Gallagher's "For What It's Worth."

He took a break from doing his black tie in a Windsor knot and put his hands on the sink counter. If there was a song that was more about Mason he'd never heard it. The first one to fly…he'd been that one; he'd always gone above and beyond. He had a temper and he had been brutal in his honesty, and it was only now that he was gone that Ethan could admit even to himself that Mason had been the one to see through his facade.

Fuck.

He'd always been able to see through it. Even when they'd been at school the first year and Ethan was trying to mask the fact that he was using drugs to stay up late and get in all the studying he needed to. Trying to hide that he'd gone beyond just using drugs to study and had started becoming addicted.

But he hadn't fooled Mason.

He saw it and didn't try anything like counseling or talking to him. He had punched Ethan hard in the jaw. He'd been pissed as hell and punched him back, but Mason hadn't stopped. They'd beat the shit out of each other that night and when it was over, Mason explained that he'd never had what Ethan had. No parents who cared or brothers who dropped by. Ethan was a damned lucky fuck, so he needed to stop screwing up his life.

That was it.

Mason had never said another word and Ethan had stopped using. It had been hard, but he always remembered looking into Mason's green eyes in that bruised and bloodied face and hearing the longing in his friend's voice. It had gotten through to him in a way nothing else had been able to.

"Damn, I miss you, brother," he said. The words were drawn out of him and he felt—oh, hell, no, he wasn't going to cry.

He had been strong until this point and he wasn't about to give in now. He had to stay strong. He pushed the heels of his hands into his eye sockets and held them there so tightly he saw stars, breathing in through his nostrils until he felt that need pass. He dropped his hands, cleared his throat and went back to work on his tie.

He needed to do it for himself and for Crissanne, who was coming to be more than he'd expected her to be. He knew a part of him wanted her because she was pretty, with those long legs and her easy smile. Her offbeat sense of humor had caught him off guard more than once. But getting to know the real woman was making him fall for her. Legitimately fall for her, not for the illusion of wanting a girl who was off-limits.

This was different.

She was different.

And he wanted to be different, too.

But he'd always been better on paper than in real life. The third son of a prominent ranching family. The smart lawyer who was good in court. The man who never left any broken hearts because he'd never let himself really care.

He heard her in the doorway and looked over to see her standing there, dressed all in black. The sheath dress hugged her curves and ended just above the knee. She had her hair pulled up and she wore a pair of pearl earrings that he knew Mason had given her. He'd been with him when he'd purchased them.

"You okay?" she asked, but she stayed where she was.

"Yeah. Today is going to be a tough one," he admitted.

She nodded. "It is. But it will be good to say goodbye to him. Now that we know he isn't coming back."

"Did you think he might have been?" Ethan asked.

She shrugged. "Obviously I thought I'd run into him again. You and he are friends and if I stayed with you…"

It was there again, that thought that he'd been careful not to allow to fully form before. "And you were with me to make him jealous?"

She shook her head.

"It wasn't that at all. It was more about you than about Mason. I came to you because when I thought of being alone in the world, and about the one person I knew I could count on, it was you, Ethan."

He finished up his tie and then turned his back to her to undo his trousers and tuck his shirt in. The action was more to give himself time and distance than because he was bashful. He wanted to believe that he hadn't betrayed Mason when he'd kissed Crissanne the first time. Or when he'd taken her in his office. But a part of him couldn't get square with the idea.

He felt her hand on the center of his back and it startled him. As he stood stock-still, she said, "I never meant to be something else you had to regret."

Did she see him that way?

"I don't," he said, turning to face her. She had put on makeup that changed the shape of her eyes. She still looked like herself, but so different from the girl she usually was. The black liner made her eyes look wider and more exotic, but the truth that stared at him from them was the same. She always watched him like she was afraid of something.

The memorial service was held at a funeral home in Malibu. When Crissanne entered with Ethan she was surprised to see his entire family waiting there. His dad came over and gave her a hug, his weathered face full of concern. Ethan's brothers and sisters-in-law were there, too. Two little kids sat quietly in one corner reading a book.

The little girl had red hair that was up in pigtails and wore a black dress that had a horse embroidered on the skirt. The little boy wore a tiny black suit with a bow tie. Both of them couldn't have been more than three or four years old, but they were well behaved and clearly shared a close friendship.

"I hope it's okay that we brought the kids," Kinley Caruthers said as she came over to her. Crissanne knew all of Ethan's sisters-in-law as he'd sent her pictures after each of the weddings. Kinley was married to Ethan's oldest brother, Nate. She and Nate had apparently had a hot Vegas weekend that had resulted in a child. But Nate hadn't found out about his daughter until last year.

"Of course. Thank you for coming," Crissanne said. "I'm surprised at how well behaved they are."

"Benito's father died last year," Ethan's other sister-in-law Bianca said, coming over to them. The former supermodel had married a Formula One driver but he had died in a plane crash. She'd come home to Cole's Hill, where she and Derek Caruthers had rekindled their friendship and that had led to love.

Bianca wrapped her arm around Crissanne's shoulder and gave her a quick hug. "It's sad to say it, but he knows how to behave at a funeral."

It was sad. "Where are you all staying?"

"We are going to be at Hunter's tonight," Kinley said. "There wasn't time to get over there this morning."

"When did you decide to come?" Crissanne asked. Ethan hadn't mentioned to her that his family was going to be at the memorial service.

"I don't think there was a discussion. More like Nate saying let's go," Kinley said. "That man tends to take his big-brother role seriously."

"Derek had to finish surgery before we could leave," Bianca explained. "Hunter and Ferrin were already at the airport."

More people started to file in and Crissanne moved away from the Caruthers family as she recognized the people from the production company and past film shoots that Mason had been on. She talked to them for a few minutes, and then the funeral director came to find her and asked her if she wanted to have a few minutes alone before the service started.

She wasn't sure.

In the end, she nodded because the reception room was getting too full of people she really didn't know. She followed him into a room that was set up like a church. In the spot where a casket would have been if they had the body, there was an easel with a portrait of Mason on it. She walked away from the man and moved toward the front of the room and the picture.

It was one she'd taken. She'd been expecting to see it, but with the flowers around it and the pressure of just being here, suddenly she missed him keenly.

She reached out to touch his face. She remembered the exact day she'd taken the photo. They'd been out on his catamaran sailing between Dana Point and Catalina. He'd been trying to teach her how to sail, but the sun had felt too good on her skin and she'd just lounged around, letting him do all the work, taking photos with her waterproof camera.

He'd been in his element.

That day she'd seen what he looked like when he was in love.

Maybe that was when she had first realized that she was competing with nature and she'd never win when it came to Mason.

The door opened behind her and she glanced around to see Ethan standing there. "I hope you don't mind my joining you."

"Of course not. You need to say your goodbyes privately, too," she said.

"I do," Ethan admitted. "It's hard for me to deal with emotion."

"I know," she said quietly. "I think that's one thing I liked about you and Mason together. He'd lose his temper or jump up and scale a rock face and you'd be sitting there quietly weighing the pros and cons or talking him down from the edge."

Ethan shook his head. "Mason always called me his safety net."

"You were," she agreed. That sounded like Mason. Like what he'd said to her as he'd walked away. She was his chance at normal. But that normal wasn't in the cards for him.

"I was surprised to see your family here," Crissanne said. "It's so nice that they came."

"They knew him, too. And they also know we'll need our support network around us."

"I don't have one," she admitted.

"You do now," he said, putting his arm around her.

As they stood there in front of the color photograph, she looked into Mason's eyes and she thought…he'd want her to be happy with Ethan.

Someone cleared his throat behind them and she turned to see the funeral director waiting there. "Are you ready to start letting everyone in?"

"Yes, sir," Ethan said. "I'd like to go over the details with the minister who'll be conducting the service."

"He's back there," the director said, pointing toward a doorway to the left.

"Are you okay by yourself?" Ethan asked her.

She nodded.

He left and the doors opened. Ethan's family were the first ones to come in. Crissanne noticed that Bianca and Kinley weren't in the crowd, which made sense with the kids. Hunter, whom she'd met a number of times, came over and introduced her to his wife, and Crissanne felt almost normal for a short while. She stood there in a crowd by herself but it was sort of comforting. Hunter had known Mason and reminisced about the times they'd had together, and it comforted her. It made it easier to let him go and helped her realize that she was moving on the way she should be.

As the service started, the sentiment she got out of all the stories everyone shared about Mason was that life was meant to be lived at full throttle.

She promised herself that starting now, she was going to live her life that way. No more hiding and pretending. Staring with Ethan Caruthers.

The walls of his bedroom in the house in Malibu were starting to feel like they were closing in on him. Ethan pushed the sheets off his body and got out of bed. The house was quiet now, but it had been full of people talking about Mason and celebrating his life earlier today.

It had been sobering in a way he hadn't anticipated. He'd spoken to many different people today, all about Mason. His friend had touched the lives of so many. It had humbled Ethan to think of what Mason had left behind. In his will, which Ethan had helped him put together, Mason had left his money to a charity that would fund inner-city kids' tuition to summer camps at the beach or in the mountains. Mason had always said that if he hadn't been sent to the mountains the summer he turned fourteen, he'd never have found his path.

Ethan scrubbed his hand over his chest, grabbed a pair of basketball shorts from the floor and pulled them on. Quietly, because his entire family was here and sleeping. He and Crissanne were sleeping in separate rooms. It had just felt like the right choice, but of course in the middle of the night, he regretted it. He missed her. He opened the door to the hall and made his way through the living room out onto the porch. The sky was bright and clear; the stars seemed to shine more brightly here in Malibu. He grabbed a bottle of Jack and headed down the stairs to the beach.

He hadn't been able to really say goodbye to Mason. Not yet. Not until tonight.

He walked toward an outcropping of rocks and was surprised to see someone already sitting there.

Crissanne.

He hesitated. She'd probably come down here for the same reason. To say goodbye in private. The last thing he wanted to do was disturb her.

He'd been trying to keep his distance, had been doing that odd act of wanting her and needing her close, but also knowing that she needed space. Sex in the conference room had been what they'd both needed but it had felt…like a reaction to Mason's death more than something between the two of them. Sleeping with her in Cole's Hill was one thing but back here in Malibu, where she had been Mason's…

That had felt wrong.

He wanted whatever developed between them to be about them, not a reaction to their friend's passing.

He turned to go back to the house.

"Ethan, don't go."

He stopped and walked over to her where she was sitting on the outcropping. The tide was out so the beach was damp, but there wasn't any water lapping at the rocks.

"I didn't mean to disturb you."

"You're not. Just looking up at the night sky and talking to Mase."

Ethan sat down a respectable distance from her. He held up the bottle of Jack. "I came out here to toast him."

"I'll join you."

He lifted the bottle higher up in the air. "To good friends who will always live in our hearts."

Crissanne nodded. Ethan poured a measure of the whiskey on the ground for Mason before taking a swallow, and then he handed the bottle to her.

"Your turn," he said.

"To always living life on the edge," she said, then splashed a bit on the beach before taking a swallow and giving the bottle back to him.

He had another shot and leaned back on his elbow. They were both hiding from something. The truth was if Mason hadn't died and he'd come back to find that things had changed between Ethan and Crissanne, he might not have liked it.

"I'm not going to apologize to you for what's happening between us," Ethan said.

"Good. I don't want you to," she said.

"I feel guilty," he admitted.

She reached over and put her hand on his leg. "Don't. Mason and I were finished long before you and I kissed in Texas."

"But in my mind you weren't," Ethan said.

She tipped her head to the side, watching him in the moonlight. He wondered what she saw when she looked at him.

"Do you wish we hadn't hooked up?" she asked him.

"No," he said, his answer almost torn from him. "It's guilt, not regret. I want more with you and I wish that I'd been able to clear the air with Mason before we moved on together."

"Together? Are you sure?" she asked. "You've been…well, I wouldn't say running away because you are too smart for that, but there is a distance—"

"I know. I'm sorry. It's hard for me to be the man I want to be and the man I really am. You deserve my best."

"I don't have any complaints."

All of his life he'd had an argument or words for any situation. But with her, he felt like he was a first-year law student who couldn't do anything but quote back stuff he'd read in textbooks. "You should."

She shifted so that she was closer to him, then put her head on his shoulder. He wrapped his arm around her and something that had been tight and tense inside him finally relaxed.

He let out a long sigh and held her closer to him in the moonlight.

"The truth is I might have just moved out at the beginning of August, but Mason and I hadn't been a couple since January. I kept pretending I could just make it work if I stayed, but he kept leaving. I feel guilty, too," she admitted.

"Why?" he asked.

"Was I the reason he kept picking more dangerous places to film?" she admitted.

That hurt Ethan's heart. No one was responsible for Mason's decisions. "That boy was stubborn as the day is long, Crissy. He didn't do anything unless he wanted to."

She didn't say anything. She just put her hands over his wrist and they sat there until dawn sipping on the bottle of Jack and talking about their friend. They said goodbye in a way that had real meaning to the two of them and when dawn came, Ethan realized that he was ready to go back home.

Eight

Crissanne had fallen into a routine as the long summer days lingered in Cole's Hill. It was nearing the end of September and they'd been back from California for almost two weeks. Ethan's family had rallied around her, trying to cheer her up and make her part of the community. She'd even been recruited to the bachelor auction committee at the Five Families Country Club. Kinley had had to step down when her daughter, Penny, had gotten sick with pink eye and given it to her mom. They were both better now, but the end result was that Crissanne was helping with publicity.

And part of that was taking photos of all the bachelors in Cole's Hill. They were very diverse but she noticed one thing about Texas men: the confidence and humor they all brought to the table.

Today she was set up in the main lounge of the country club and was doing a brisk business with the members.

"This room always takes me back to my childhood," Bianca said as she walked in.

Having been a supermodel for years, Bianca was on hand to

style the men, whose photographs would go into a booklet that would be sent to every household in Cole's Hill.

"Does it? Who are all these people?" she asked. "I mean, I read the plaques and I recognize the Caruthers name and the Velasquez name because of you, but the rest I'm not sure of."

"These are the members of the five families who founded Cole's Hill. The man in the middle is Jacob Cole. He gave the town its name. Next to him is Bejamina Little. She's Jacob's stepdaughter. She founded the first school in town. My ancestor Javier Velasquez was a rancher in this area before Jacob came. We had a land grant from the Spanish king. Next to him is Tully Caruthers and his sister Ethel. Jacob built her a house that stood where the clubhouse is now. Then there are the Abernathys. You'll meet Wil when he comes for his photo. He's funny and a bit of a flirt, so be warned. The last of the five families are the Grahams. Their ancestor is Bones Graham. He was the undertaker. His family turned the old homestead into a microbrewery on the outskirts of town. They are all reprobates."

"Talking about me, Bianca?" a man said from the doorway.

Bianca smiled over at him. "Of course not, Diego. Crissanne, this is my brother, Diego. He's harmless."

"Bi. No man wants to hear that. I'm a badass. Don't let my sister tell you any differently."

"A badass?"

"Yes," he said. "And many women find me appealing."

She had to laugh at the brother and sister bantering with each other. And surprisingly, the pang she usually felt when she was around families wasn't there. She had always thought she needed to be married or in a relationship to find a family, but she was slowly coming to realize that friendship was a strong bond.

"I'll reserve judgment until I see your photo," Crissanne said. "The camera always shows me the truth about someone."

"Uh-oh, Diego, you're in trouble now," Bianca said.

He mock-punched her and then moved farther into the room. Bianca's brother ran one of the largest stud programs in the

United States. His horses were known for their speed and agility according to Nate, who had just signed a deal to have some of his mares covered by Diego's studs. She'd heard all about it at dinner a few nights ago.

"Give me a minute to adjust the lighting," she said. Originally, they'd toyed with the idea of having the photos taken at each bachelor's place of work, but it had been too hard to coordinate and Bianca had arranged for them all to come to the clubhouse instead. Crissanne had worked with the high school art department to design canvases to use as backdrops for the different men.

"One of your second cousins did this," Crissanne said. "Julia, I think."

"It's gorgeous," Diego said. "She's so talented. We're all very proud of her."

The five families had really put down roots here. Crissanne had learned as she'd been taking the photos that pretty much everyone—except for the newest residents of Cole's Hill—could trace their ancestry back to one of the five families.

Diego was easy to photograph. He smiled easily and wore his black Stetson well. He chatted with her the entire time, and when he left he winked at her as he walked out the door. She just shook her head and tried not to laugh.

As the day wore on, she was impressed by the wide range of men who came to be photographed. One of her favorites was Wil Abernathy. The rancher was more easygoing than Diego and didn't have the intensity of the other man.

Another bachelor who stood out was Manu Bennett. He had bulging muscles and posed with his shirt off, showing off his Maori tribal tattoos, which were distinctive to his family and covered his entire chest and back. He was tanned and muscled and it was only when he spoke about his brother and sister-in-law that she caught a hint of softness in his face. Otherwise he was intense and serious. She took her time making sure she captured that essence of him.

"Only one more," Bianca said around five thirty. "Then a dinner break and the evening shift."

"I'm looking forward to going over the photos I took today."

"Me, too," Bianca said.

"Who's next?"

"I am," Ethan said from the doorway.

Ethan. She already had more pictures of him than she'd ever admit. But this was for the auction, so she'd be careful to photograph him in a way that would make women want to bid for him.

She felt a pang of jealousy. She knew she didn't want Ethan going to anyone but her. But there continued to be a tentativeness between them, even as she'd begun to find her place in Cole's Hill. Which was why she was looking for her own apartment. They both needed some space to process Mason's death and then she hoped they'd be able to move on together.

"We can grab dinner when you're done," Ethan said.

Dinner.

"Like a date?"

He gave her a smile and she realized how much she'd missed him even though they'd been living together. "Yes, just like a date."

He'd been busy at work. Mason had wanted Ethan to be the director of his memorial foundation, and setting it up required a lot of time. In addition to that, he still had his regular law clients to take care of.

At home, he hadn't been sleeping because he'd reached out to Crissanne and then left the ball in her court. He wanted her in his bed, but he hadn't wanted to pressure her into sleeping with him.

He knew that since they'd come back from Malibu he'd been having a hard time dealing with the new thing with Crissanne and Mason's death. So he'd shut her out.

She was living in his house, trying to come to terms with a new town, and he knew she needed time and space even though she said she was fine. He caught her in moments of sadness when she thought no one was watching.

"What do I need to do?"

Bianca had done her magic, styling his outfit so he looked as good as he could. But he loosened his tie after she left the room.

"Stand over there in front of the backdrop," Crissanne said, directing him to a corner of the room under the lights. She looked through her lens and then stepped back and set the camera down.

She posed him and took a series of photos. He followed her directions, but she soon stopped shooting and gave him a look.

"Relax."

"I am," he said. But really, had there ever been anything more uncomfortable than posing for a photo? He felt stupid. She'd told him to cross his arms and look confident, but instead he felt dumb.

"No, you're not. I've seen you more relaxed in the courtroom going up against a tough judge," she said.

"When?"

"In LA. Judge McConnell when you were doing that corporate case," she said.

"That was like four years ago," he said. He'd been trying to make a go at corporate trial law but it didn't suit him. The arguing did, but he preferred to settle out of court.

"Yeah, we had dinner afterward," she said. "Remember?"

"I do," he said, smiling as he remembered that night. "We ate at In-N-Out Burger because I didn't get out of work until late."

"We did," she said. "Mason was doing that heli-skiing thing in Canada and you said that we were friends, too, so we could hang out if we wanted to."

He noticed she'd started taking photos again. But he didn't really think of himself as her subject. He'd always liked to watch her work. She lost herself in the moment when she did. It was like she became someone else as she moved and talked.

She came over and moved his chin a bit, then kept taking

photos. As he watched her, he realized that he'd been fooling himself for the last few weeks.

He'd been pretending he was giving her space when the truth was more complex. He'd been hiding from himself how much he liked her. Sex was one thing and actually more easily explainable to him. This emotion that he felt for her—well, that scared him. Because he'd never really know if she liked him for himself or if she'd just crashed into him when she'd been falling away from Mason.

"I think I've got something I can work with," she said. "I've never known you to look so tense, though."

"It's the entire bachelor auction thing," he said. "I know I'm not the only guy to feel silly that people are going to be bidding on me."

"I think it's a great idea. You should know that there is a lot of excitement in town about it," she said as she plugged her camera into her laptop and hit a few keys.

"Doesn't make me feel any less silly," he said. "Want to grab dinner now?"

She glanced over at him and smiled. She'd tied her hair back in a ponytail and the lipstick she'd had on earlier had worn off. "I would like that. I have to be back at seven thirty for another session."

"No problem. We can eat here at the club," he said. "In fact if you want to finish up I'll go and order a picnic dinner. I'll show you my favorite spot in this subdivision."

"Sounds good," she said, but her attention was on the photos downloading to her laptop. He approached and looked over her shoulder at his face on the computer screen. He hadn't realized how earnest he looked when he was talking. *What the hell?* He also hoped he was the only one who could see it, but the expression on his face made him look like he cared for Crissanne a lot. He knew that look. And it had been there for too long.

"What do you think?" she asked.

He didn't know what to say. And God, that wasn't like him. "You did the best with the subject matter."

She punched him lightly on the arm. "You're silly. I bet you're going to raise a lot of money. This photo is good. I'm not just saying that because I took it. I think it captures the essence of you."

"What is the essence of me?" he asked.

She tipped her head to the side and a strand of her hair fell forward against her cheek. "Honesty, integrity and a mouth that makes a woman think of long nights together."

Her words sent a shiver down his spine that made him feel every hour since he'd last held her in his arms. Since he'd kissed her and called her his own. It had been hard keeping his distance.

"You might see that," he said. "To everyone else I'm just that odd Caruthers."

"The odd Caruthers?" she asked.

"Well, the one who likes to argue," he added. What was he doing? He never talked about his place in his family. How he'd never really fit in.

She shrugged. "Maybe, but you're my favorite Caruthers."

The tension and the guilt that had been riding him since they returned to Texas fell back, and he knew that this was what he'd needed. Just being alone with Crissanne without the guilt that had been riding him hard. And he'd been afraid he'd pressured her into something but he was coming to realize that he hadn't.

Ethan was different as they walked along the golf course. He had been quiet since he saw the photos she'd taken of him. He had been her favorite to photograph today. Though she'd enjoyed the stories that all the men had told her with either their words or the expressions on their faces, Ethan was always going to be her favorite.

She'd been trying to find a place for herself here. A reason to stay that wasn't about liking Ethan. And she was pretty sure she finally had. She had projects to keep herself busy. She had mentioned to the committee chair of the Daughters of Cole's Hill that she thought they might be able to use some of the bachelors in a calendar. And the committee chair had agreed.

And she was ready to take the next step. Tomorrow she had an appointment to go and look at houses with a Realtor. If she was going to stay, she had to find her own place, not just move into Ethan's. It was something she'd thought about in Malibu as she'd stood by the ocean many a night waiting for Mason to return from one trip or another before they broke up. Before he died. Now she realized that she'd spent her entire life waiting for someone to give her a home and she needed to find one for herself.

"You're quiet," Ethan said as he led her up the steps to a gazebo and they sat down on the bench.

"I was just thinking about Cole's Hill," she said.

"What about it?"

"I like it. I came here...well, I was running to you, not really thinking about the work I'd do. I mean, I knew I could sell a travel piece on the area, but I didn't have a plan. Vlogging wasn't working because I felt so lost," she said. She was rambling.

"You don't need a plan. You were in a bad place," he said.

"That's kind, but I always like to think of myself as an independent woman. When we were in Malibu I reflected a lot on my life with Mason. You know, I wasn't exactly dependent on him but I certainly was always waiting on a signal from him before I decided what I'd do next. I hate that," she said.

Ethan opened the picnic basket and handed her a plastic container and cutlery. "That's part of being in a relationship."

"Have you ever done that?" she asked.

He shrugged.

She'd never really considered it before but she'd never seen Ethan with a serious girlfriend. "Have you ever had a serious relationship?"

"Not really. I work too many hours and travel a lot. That's not really a good combination for a relationship," he said.

And yet that's exactly what she and Mason had had. "You're so right. I don't know why I couldn't see it before. Mason and I were both always leaving."

"It's hard to build something when you are both gone," Ethan said.

"It is. So is that all that's been keeping you back?" she asked.

"Where are you going with this?" he asked. He sounded defensive and a little bit guarded.

"I guess I want to know more about what makes you tick in the romance department," she said. "We've never talked about that."

"Why is that, do you think?"

"Maybe because I didn't want you to have a serious girlfriend," she said, quietly putting down her container and standing up and walking a few feet away from him.

He thought of all the years he'd spent watching her and Mason from the sidelines and the envy that had been hard to manage at times.

"Is that why you've been keeping your distance since we got back here?" he asked.

She shook her head. "I was waiting for a signal from you. See my pattern? I don't know why I do that."

"I didn't want to pressure you," he admitted. "You are just settling in here in town, and then there's everything that happened with Mason. You need time."

"I need you," she said quietly, turning back to him.

Her words went through him, starting a fire that he didn't even try to ignore. He had done the right thing, the gentlemanly thing. He had spent every damned night of the last two weeks awake and aching, alone. Not really sleeping. Listening for any movement from her room and wanting her. Wanting to hold her, make love to her and claim her as his own.

He knew that she needed time. But time had always felt like

an endless abyss to him. He knew that he didn't do well with waiting. Mason had always said it brought out the worst in him, and in honor of his friend's death, he'd tried to be better. But damned if he was.

He saw her standing there in the twilight as the landscape lights came on, and he wanted her. The sun set behind her and the heavy, warm air stirred the fire.

He was tired of waiting. Tired of pretending that he was cool with letting her set the pace.

He stood up, holding his hand out to her, and she stepped forward and took it. "I'm tired of pretending with you," she whispered.

"Good," he said. He pulled her into his arms and kissed her like he'd wanted to since they'd left Los Angeles. She tasted better than he remembered and his arms, which had felt so empty for so long, held her close. He told himself to slow down, to gentle the embrace, but he couldn't. He wanted her and now that he held her he knew he wasn't ever going to let her go.

There were a million reasons to let her go, he thought. Her life was in transition and most likely, so was her heart. His ties were to Texas, but she might find life pulling her somewhere else.

But right now, nothing mattered except the way she felt in his arms and the way her mouth felt under his.

Nine

Crissanne let herself into Ethan's house using the key he'd given her. Bart and Ethan's housekeeper were both out of town for the weekend, and Ethan had needed to leave her at the country club when he got a call that one of his clients had gotten himself in trouble.

The house was quiet except for the subtle whir of the central air-conditioning. But then as she was walking toward the kitchen she heard a curse from Ethan's office and the sound of a glass shattering.

She hesitated, wondering if she should leave and let him have the house to himself tonight. She hadn't even realized he was already home. But then she decided she was done with running. She'd run from Los Angeles to Cole's Hill, from Cole's Hill back to Los Angeles and from Mason to Ethan. And now she was here.

She was staying put. Wasn't that what today had been all about? Setting down roots in the community? She couldn't wait to talk with the Realtor—she'd already seen a listing for a small space in the historic district that she could lease for her office and photography studio.

She knocked on his door and saw him sitting on the large leather love seat between the bookcases with a glass of something that looked like whiskey in one hand and his laptop balanced on his knees.

There was a broken glass near the bookcase next to the wall.

He glanced up at her and smiled, but it didn't reach his eyes. Then he gestured for her to come in and she did, slipping her shoes off at the door. The floor was a beautiful Spanish tile, cool against her bare feet as she walked over to him. The room smelled of books and cigars and Ethan's cologne. As she got closer to him she noticed he had an earpiece in.

He hit a button on his keyboard. "Sorry, Crissy, I'm on a conference call."

"That's okay. You sounded pissed."

He shook his head and lifted his glass to his mouth and took a long swallow. "I work with idiots."

She had to laugh at the way he said it. Ethan was one of the smartest men she knew and normally so even-tempered. But not tonight.

"Can I do anything?" she asked.

He shrugged. "Not really."

She started to leave but got only halfway across the room before she glanced back and saw the way he was sitting there looking at the screen. Looking so alone. She realized that there were all kinds of running and this sort of isolation was Ethan's version.

She turned around, taking the cashmere throw off the back of one of the guest chairs and putting it on the floor at Ethan's feet. She sat down on it next to his legs, putting her hand in his.

He squeezed her fingers, and then put his hand on the side of her head, loosening her braid so that her hair fell around her shoulders. She tipped her head back to look up at him. He pushed a button on his laptop and set it aside.

He ran his finger down the side of her face, taking his time to carefully trace her cheekbones. Then she felt his finger move over her lips. She bit his fingertip and his eyes widened as he licked his lips.

She'd been waiting for him to make a move since they'd gotten back to Texas, but she'd soon realized that Ethan was too much of a gentleman to do that while she was sleeping under his roof and trying to figure out her next move.

But for now they were going to finish what they'd started in the gazebo earlier tonight.

She used his tie to pull him forward and kiss him. She loved the firmness of his mouth and how when it opened for her, the kiss would be soft. She teased him, keeping the kiss light when what she wanted was to straddle his lap and take him deep.

She wanted him but she didn't want to push intimacy on him when she knew he was dealing with guilt and pain at Mason's passing. Still, she ached for this. Being so close to Ethan and not having him was like seeing the...the very thing she wanted but knew she could never have.

She turned her head and rested it on his thigh as he sat back and pushed his hand deeper into her hair. He shifted his legs and she saw the ridge of his erection against his trousers. She stroked him through the fabric of his pants. He was hard and long, getting longer in her hand, and she realized how much she wanted him.

That ache that had been inside her every moment since they'd returned from California finally made sense. She'd wanted something that was almost within her reach. And it was within her reach right now. She drew her finger down the line of the zipper and then back up, watching him grow inside his pants.

He shifted, pushing his legs farther apart, and she moved between them, taking the tab of the zipper and drawing it down until she could reach inside his pants. He wore a pair of boxer briefs underneath his trousers and she found the opening in them, sliding her fingers through until she touched his hot flesh.

She ran her finger up and down his length, taking extra time at the tip. She shifted again so that she was kneeling. She heard him start talking, but she knew it was his call. His voice was a low rumble as she undid the fastening at his waist and pulled his pants down slightly. He freed his erection from his underwear and she took him in her hand, leaning forward, her tongue darting out to touch the tip of his erection. His hand was at the back of her head, urging her forward until she took him in her mouth.

He thrust his hips and she felt him at the back of her throat as she moved her head up and down, her tongue teasing him as his hands moved over her neck and shoulders.

She pulled back and swirled her tongue around the top of his erection, stroking her hand down his length to cup him. He put his hand on her mouth, his thumb rubbing over her lower lip as he tilted her head back and their eyes met. Then he tossed his earpiece aside and lifted her up onto his lap.

She put her hands on his shoulders, pushing her fingers into his thick hair. This time when their lips met, he didn't let her tease him. His hand was on the back of her head, his fingers tangled in her hair, holding her head so that he could thrust his tongue deep into her mouth. She brought her teeth down lightly on his tongue before sucking on it as she rubbed her center against him. He groaned and she felt one of his hands moving down her back, pulling at the fabric of the dress she had on, tugging it up until he could get his hand underneath it. Then she felt his big, warm palm against the small of her back. He held her closer to him, his hips moving between her spread thighs, and she felt the tip of his erection against her center through the fabric of her skirt and her panties.

She pulled back, catching his lower lip between her teeth as she broke the kiss and shifted around in his arms, trying to remove her panties while staying on his lap.

He sort of laughed as she tumbled off his lap and he caught her, lifting her to her feet.

"Get naked, woman."

Yes. This was what she'd needed. This moment between the two of them.

She pulled her dress over her head and felt his hands on her naked breasts as she tossed the dress aside. She pushed her panties down her legs and then she was naked standing next to him. He was still wearing his shirt and tie, and his pants had fallen down to his ankles.

She looked up into his face. Their eyes met and the feelings she'd been trying so hard to bury overwhelmed her.

He was so dear to her.

She put her hands on his jaw and went up on tiptoe, kissing him hard, emotions roiling her like the jagged lightning that sometimes flashed across the big Texas sky. She felt his hands on her butt as he lifted her off her feet and carried her across his office. Then she felt the cold, hard surface of his mahogany desk under her.

Her nipples were rigid points and her breasts felt fuller. He kissed her hard and deep and then lifted his head and started to make his way down her body, biting at the point where her neck and shoulder met. Then he went lower to tongue one of her nipples while he lightly pinched the other one between his thumb and forefinger.

His mouth traveled farther down, until she felt the warmth of his breath against her most intimate flesh. He kept pinching her nipple with one hand while he parted her folds with the other. She felt his tongue flicking over her and she moaned, her head falling back as shivers went through her.

She held his head in her hands and let herself go, closing her eyes as he kept up the pressure.

"Do you like this?" he asked, his voice a low rumble, his lips moving against her body.

"Yes. Don't stop," she said. Her voice was husky and almost unrecognizable to her own ears.

"I'm not planning to until I'm buried deep inside you."

She shivered again as he continued to tease her clit with

his tongue until she couldn't stop her orgasm. She tightened her thighs on either side of his head and held him to her as she arched her back and called his name.

She went limp in his arms as he kissed his way up her body to her stomach, his teeth biting gently into the flesh around her belly button. He continued trailing kisses up her body until he reached her mouth. Attempting to regain the advantage, she reached between the two of them, taking his shaft in her hands and drawing him forward until she felt the tip of him at her entrance.

He brushed his chest over hers, moving his hips to thrust deep inside her. She arched her back, tightening her thighs around his hips as he drove himself up and into her again and again. He held her with one hand in the middle of her back, and the other was braced on the desk beside her, his thrusts relentless, until she felt herself start to come again. She moaned as she felt him driving harder, deeper and faster, and then he came, filling her as he called her name. She wrapped her arms around him and held on to his shoulders as he continued to thrust three more times into her.

He pulled her off the desk and sank to the floor, cradling her on his lap. They were still intimately connected and she wrapped her arms around his shoulders, resting her head against his shoulder and neck.

He swept his hand up and down her back until their breathing quieted. Then he stood up and carried her out of the office up the stairs to his bedroom. Neither of them said a word as he put her on her feet next to his bed.

They took a shower together and then he climbed into his big bed with her and she turned on her side, looking up at him like she was searching for an answer to a question only he could provide.

"Thank you," he said, his voice sounding dry to his own

ears. He said it simply to keep her from saying something real. Something that would remind him that sex with Crissanne—

"No, don't thank me," she said. "I'm not going to keep pretending there isn't this thing between us."

Thing.

Yeah, that was how he wanted their relationship to be referred to by the one woman he'd always wanted.

She shifted around, propping herself up on her elbow. "When I showed up on your doorstep it wasn't only because I had nowhere else to go. I wanted to be with you, Ethan. I was sad and lonely and I tried to think of the one place in the world that would make me feel better..."

She trailed off and his heart started to beat double time. He knew himself. Knew that if he let this woman into his emotions, into his heart, he was never going to be able to let her go. No matter what she said, he knew she wasn't in her right state of mind at this moment. She'd ended a more-than-a-decade-long relationship with her boyfriend, come to him, her boyfriend died, and now they were in bed together. Only a liar could convince himself this could be real.

And he wasn't about lying to himself. Not where she was concerned.

"Ethan?"

"Hmm..."

"What do you think about that? Are you glad I came to you?" she asked.

She needed something from him. Something he should definitely say to her. But what? The truth was he had dreamed of her in this bed with him for a long time. But he wasn't about to tell her that. He'd never thought of himself as a coward. He'd seen things and done things that most would say were brave, but when it came to being honest with Crissanne, something stopped him. Something made him hesitate because if he told her the truth and she rejected him...he'd have nowhere to turn.

Mason was gone.

His brothers had always seen him as the sanest one. The one who had his shit together. And now that they had all settled down and were working on families, he couldn't go to them all crazy.

He had to be smart.

"Ethan."

"Crissanne."

"Don't. Don't do this. I want to know what you're feeling."

"I don't know what I'm feeling," he admitted. "I know that sounds like a cop-out, but you have to remember that you and I have been friends a long time. I don't want to do anything to ruin that."

She shifted back, sitting up next to him and taking the covers with her. Pulling them up around her naked breasts. Which just made him remember how she'd looked naked in his office downstairs.

Hell.

Now he was getting turned on again and she wanted to talk about feelings. He couldn't do it.

He wasn't going to do it.

He wanted her. He liked having her in his house. For now that had to be enough, because he wasn't sure what he'd do if she suddenly woke up and realized that she was ready to move on.

He tugged on the sheet.

She raised both eyebrows at him and scrambled to keep the sheet pressed to her body.

"I can't concentrate on anything but your breasts when you're naked."

She shook her head. "I know. That's why I'm covered up. I wanted to talk."

"We did talk," he said, wrapping his arm around her waist and tugging until she fell into his arms.

"Ethan."

He heard the longing and the insecurity in her voice, and

he buried his head in her neck and took a deep breath. "I can't let you go."

"Really?"

"Yes," he said, pulling back and looking up at her. Their eyes met. "Can that be enough for now?"

She nodded, pulling him closer and hugging him to her. "It won't be enough forever."

"I know," he said, rolling onto his back and taking her with him. She was on top of him with the sheet wedged between them but their naked legs tangled together.

He put his hands on her face and looked up at her with that heartbreaking sadness and need and affection that she wanted to believe was love.

"Oh, Ethan," she said.

He didn't say anything, just kissed her fiercely, his tongue moving into her mouth. She pushed the sheets out from between them and straddled him, taking the only thing he'd freely give to her. She put her hands on his chest and shifted until he was at the entrance of her body, and then she slowly sank down onto him.

Their eyes met and her heart clenched as he wrapped his arms around her, thrusting up inside of her. She rode him not stopping until she felt him shuddering underneath her. She buried her head against his shoulder as her own orgasm washed over her.

It wasn't enough, she thought. She still wanted more. But this physical attraction between them was all he was willing to give her and for now she'd take it.

He held her as their breathing slowed, then rolled to his side, tucking her close. She closed her eyes and drifted off and he held her in his arms, unable to sleep.

He wanted what was best for her. He wanted to see her smiling and happy. If that meant he kept her here in his arms, then that was what he'd do. If that meant he had to let her go when the time came, he'd do it. No matter how hard it would be.

But for tonight she was his. She was here in his arms and he wasn't going to waste a single minute of it.

He stroked his hand down her back and realized how empty he'd been before she came here. In the brief time that she'd been in his life this way, she'd become the one person he needed to see each day. The one person he needed to talk to each day. The one person he needed more than life itself.

Ten

The next morning when she woke up, Ethan was already gone. She sat up in the bed realizing that they still hadn't really found a way to talk about anything important. She loved being in his arms and sleeping with him, but if she'd learned anything in her relationship with Mason it was that there was more to being a couple than hooking up.

She glanced at the nightstand and saw a note. Of course. Ethan liked to leave handwritten notes instead of texting. It was kind of old-fashioned and yet at the same time suited to the man Ethan was.

She pulled the note off the table, rubbing the sleep from her eyes.

Crissanne—
Sorry I couldn't stay with you. I was tempted to call in but I need to get a deposition this morning. My folks want us to come to dinner at the Rockin' C tonight. My entire family will be there. Do you want to go? Call me later.
E

She leaned back against the headboard.

"What am I doing?" she asked the empty room.

But she knew she was going to say yes. Hot sex with Ethan was only part of the reason she liked him. She had to admit in all honesty she loved his family. They were in each other's business a lot of the time and he couldn't go anywhere in Cole's Hill without running into them. And the best part was they were treating her like she was one of their own.

Family had always been out of her reach and by coming here she'd gotten more than she'd bargained for.

But it was dangerous as well. If things didn't go well with Ethan she was going to have to leave. Cole's Hill was his town. The Carutherses were his family. And no matter how nice they were to her she had to remember that.

"Damn."

She got out of his bed and went down the hall to her bedroom to shower and get ready for the day. She was meeting the head of the bachelor auction planning committee to go over the digital proofs she'd shot yesterday, and she had an appointment to meet with the Realtor about that space downtown.

When she was all dressed, she sat down to look through the photos but found herself lingering over the ones of Ethan. He'd been tense when he'd first come into the session but then as he'd relaxed... She reached out to touch his face on her computer screen.

She had to be careful. She didn't want to screw this up the way she had every other relationship she'd ever had. Her heart felt heavy when she thought of hurting him, or even worse, never seeing him again.

She texted him that she'd love to have dinner with him and then mentioned she was looking at a space in town for her studio.

He texted her back that he was busy at work but would try to join her if she wanted a second opinion on the space.

Did she?

No, but seeing Ethan during the day would be nice.

She texted him the address and then put her phone in her purse and left the house.

When she got to the meeting she was surprised to see the room was full of about fifteen women. She hadn't been expecting a crowd, and was reminded that no matter how much goodwill had been given to her as Ethan's friend, she was essentially a stranger.

"Crissanne. Over here."

She looked over to see Bianca waving at her. She was seated next to Ma Caruthers and Kinley. Relieved to see some familiar faces, she made a beeline toward them.

"We saved you a seat," Kinley said.

"Thanks. I had no idea the committee was this large," Crissanne said, sitting down.

"I had the same reaction when I came the first time," Kinley said. "My boss Jacs donated my party-planning skills to the event, so even though I wanted to bolt for the door I didn't."

"I thought you grew up here," Crissanne said. Ethan had told her that Kinley's dad had been the foreman on the Rockin' C when Kinley was growing up and her mom had worked as a housekeeper for the Velasquez family.

"I did. Doesn't mean all these Five Families women don't intimidate me."

Crissanne had to laugh at the thought of Kinley feeling daunted around anyone. The younger woman was a dynamo, one of the most sought-after wedding planners in the country. And until last year, she had been a single mom.

"I can't believe that."

"Well, you should. Some of these women make me feel like I'm still wearing Bianca's hand-me-downs."

"They always looked better on you than on me," Bianca said.

"That's a big fat lie," Kinley said. "But thanks for trying to make me feel better about it."

"That's what friends do," Bianca said. "My mother might be

coming later. She's up for a promotion at work so is spending more time at the station than usual."

"How's it going?" Kinley asked.

Crissanne sat there and realized that the nerves she'd first felt had disappeared. She had never experienced this before. While she'd never met Bianca's mother, the women were kindly including her in the conversation. And when Ma Caruthers turned toward them, she smiled warmly at Crissanne.

"Will we be seeing you for dinner tonight?" she asked around Kinley and Bianca.

"Yes, ma'am. Thank you for including me in the invite," she said.

"Not a problem. How are you adjusting to Cole's Hill? I know Bianca is going to tell us all once again how we live in the fastest-growing small town in the United States, but we're just a blip compared to Los Angeles."

"I love it. There's something so nice about the pace here," Crissanne said.

"Glad to hear it. And my son's not making you crazy yet?" Ma Caruthers asked.

"No, he's not," she said, but a part of her knew that he was making her a little...well, crazy. She wanted this to feel like home, like the place she belonged, and that connection was missing again. Was it her? Was it Ethan?

Ethan had spent the better part of the day working, trying to focus on his clients and not Crissanne. It was harder than he wanted it to be.

But as he headed for the Rockin' C that evening, he had nothing to distract him. Just the local country music station that seemed to be playing songs that made the ache in his gut even stronger.

When Blake Shelton sang about his wife naming the kids while he got to name the dogs, Ethan wanted everything to be clear-cut like that for him. But it wasn't. Yes, he wanted Crissanne. The sex between them was hotter than even he could have imagined, and he'd spent a lot of time over the years imagining it.

But there was something holding him back. He knew that in his mind he'd always believed that if they did get together it would just be perfect. So how did he explain the messy long pauses that he sometimes felt cropping up when they were talking? Or that awkward thing last night where he'd had to turn to sex to distract her?

When he looked at the relationships of other people in his life, they all seemed to go so smoothly. Even his dad, who was probably as close to a stereotypical laconic cowboy as a man could get, still managed to make his mom laugh. Some of Ethan's fondest childhood memories were of listening to the two of them talk on the porch after he'd gone to bed, their voices a low murmur through his open window.

He didn't have that easy rapport with Crissanne. Well, that wasn't precisely true. He felt it at times, but then he felt this crazy excitement at seeing her after a long period apart. This heady cocktail of needing to get her into bed and having her again and again so that maybe she would just get addicted to sleeping with him and that would be enough…for her.

He cursed and pulled off onto the side of the road.

Fear. That's what this was.

He'd always insulated himself from the things that would wound him. He'd used knowledge and arguments to keep anxiety at bay. But with her, there wasn't enough data he could accumulate to make him feel like she was a sure thing.

And why was it that he felt like this when his brothers all seemed to have nailed relationships with relative ease?

Someone honked and Ethan glanced in his rearview mirror as a pickup truck with the Rockin' C logo pulled to a stop behind him.

"Let it be Marcus," Ethan muttered to himself, hoping to see the former ranch foreman who had been recovering over the last year from a heart attack.

But no, it was Nate.

His big brother, who was always good for advice and a fight. He got out of his truck and walked toward Ethan's Ferrari.

He rolled down the window as Nate approached.

"That toy you call a car finally give up the ghost?" Nate asked. His brother had never been able to understand why Ethan had opted for speed and beauty over stability and strength.

"Nah. Just had to take a call and don't like to drive while I'm doing it," Ethan said. The lie was the first thing that had popped into his head.

"Yeah, right," Nate said. "What's really going on?"

"Nothing," Ethan said. "Why do you always do that? Question me?"

"Bro, I'm not trying to start anything. It's just there is absolutely no cell signal out here," Nate said.

Damn.

"Fair enough," Ethan said, putting his head forward on the steering wheel. Crissanne had even taken away some of his ability to be quick-witted when put on the spot.

"Ethan, you okay?" Nate asked.

"Yeah," Ethan said, then got out of the car to stand next to Nate because he wanted to feel less like a little brother at that moment. "I suck at relationships."

There, he'd said it. He knew admitting his faults was always a good place to start.

"Don't feel like the Lone Ranger there," Nate said. "I'm not that great, either. In fact, I'm out here because Kinley told me to take a hike for a while before she lost her temper."

Ethan smiled. "You two fight just to make up."

"Sometimes," Nate admitted. "But this was legit. Relationships are hard and they take a lot of work."

Was that true? "You make it look easy."

"That's because Mom raised us not to air our dirty laundry in public," Nate said. "That's why I'm out here riding the land while Kinley and Penny get ready for dinner. She needs a chance to cool down and so do I, or we'll have it out in front of everyone later on tonight."

"What's going on?"

"I want another kid," Nate said. "I didn't get to see Penny from birth and I think that we should jump right in and have another one before Penny gets too much older."

Kinley had raised Penny by herself until his niece was three because Kinley and Nate had lost touch; he hadn't even known he was a father. "Kinley wants to wait. Did she say why?"

"She wants to give the three of us a chance to really gel as a family, and I get it. I mean, I was a playboy and a douche. But I'm not going anywhere. I feel like she still sees the old Nate and is making me pay for what I said to her."

Ethan put his hand on his brother's shoulder. "She loves you. She might just want a chance for herself to feel secure. It's not always about you."

Nate threw his head back and laughed. "Derek said the same thing to me. Is my ego that big?"

"Sometimes," Ethan said, realizing that talking to his big brother had helped in a way he hadn't expected. "You told Derek?"

"Yeah, and Hunter...just between us, Ferrin is pregnant and he's going to announce it tonight," Nate said. "That's really what got me thinking about another kid."

"When the time is right it will sort itself out," Ethan said, not just to his brother but also to himself.

"I know. I just feel like I missed out on so much, I want it all and I want it now."

"I get that," Ethan said. "That's how it is with Crissanne." Ethan completely understood where his brother was coming from. Part of him felt that way with Crissanne.

Nate looked out at the horizon and then back at him. "I'm

not trying to start anything but are you sure that you should be getting together with her this quick?"

"No."

"Well, hell," Nate said. "I mean, we all suspected you had a thing for her...but she was Mason's girl."

"Except Mason dumped her. Before he left on the trip to Peru. So what does that say? All those years I stayed back so they could be happy..."

"Like I said, no judgment here. I just wanted to make sure you knew what you were doing. Ma said to leave it be. If you wanted to talk you'd come to us."

"Ma was right," Ethan said.

"Fair enough."

As he got back in the car and followed his brother to his parents' smallish two-story ranch house that they'd downsized to from the big house, he realized that he was closer to finding some peace about his feelings for Crissanne.

Ferrin Caruthers was a pretty professor at the University of Texas, the daughter of a famous college football coach. She'd married bad boy Hunter in a lavish wedding that Kinley had come to Cole's Hill to plan. It had been televised and viewed by millions on TV. So Crissanne wasn't sure what to expect when she met her, but Ferrin was down-to-earth and funny.

She was quieter than Kinley and Bianca but just as adamant that Crissanne should be part of their group. She hesitated to remind them that she and Ethan were...well, who knew what they really were. She liked him—a lot. And as soon as he'd walked onto the patio of his parents' house with his brother tonight, she'd felt that tingle go down her spine. She'd wanted to run over to him, but she'd made herself stay put.

She had to admit that the bond between the two of them was strong, but it seemed rooted in sex. Other than that, they had quiet night snippets of real conversations. She knew they were both not used to trusting others. Ethan, because of his career, where he saw people use the minutiae of the law to wiggle out of things. For her, it was thanks to the numerous group homes she'd lived in growing up.

But the truth was, she already trusted him.

She wouldn't have come to Cole's Hill when Mason dumped her if she didn't trust Ethan. And that's where her problems started. Were her feelings for him legit or was he just her safety net?

Could she live with herself if she treated Ethan like her safety net?

She knew that it would be difficult. She liked him and it was starting to feel like…love? She had no idea what love really was and she had no one to ask. She'd thought about bringing it up with Ethan's sisters-in-law, but they were all in solid relationships and seemed so much more together than she ever was. She should ask them for advice but she didn't know how to apply it. She wasn't the same as these women who knew their parents and came from the kind of families she could only dream of having.

Most of her life had been spent behind the camera capturing the important moments in others' lives, but never in her own.

She put the margarita she'd been drinking aside. She felt herself sliding into sad-drunk, which wasn't a good look on anyone and not what she needed to be tonight when she was dealing with Ethan's whole family.

Dinner was a barbecue. Ethan and his brothers stood around the pit with their father and the former ranch foreman, Quinten, who was Kinley's father. Benito and Penny were playing in the pool under the watchful supervision of Penny's British nanny, Pippa. She was a very pretty blonde who had jokingly said she needed to buy sunscreen in buckets.

They ate around a large table set under a pergola. Crissanne had been seated across from Ethan and as their eyes met she knew there were things she should say to him. But it was too much to mention at a family dinner.

For starters, she had to tell him she'd signed the lease on the shop in town and was going to move into the loft apartment above it. He hadn't been able to join her to look at the space after all.

She wanted to tell him before he found out from his mom, who had gone with her to check out the space. Ma Caruthers had treated her...well, in a way that had made Crissanne feel like she was part of the family.

She wanted that. But not at the expense of her friendship with Ethan. Her friendship, and whatever else was developing between them.

"I have an announcement," Hunter said, standing up and lifting his tequila glass.

"*You* have one?" Ferrin asked wryly.

"We have one," Hunter said, drawing his wife up next to him, wrapping his arm around her. As the two of them stared into each other's eyes, Crissanne realized that was what she wanted. She wanted Ethan to look at her the way Hunter was watching Ferrin.

Like she was the beginning and the end of his world. Like she was all that mattered. And Crissanne, who'd always been passed on by prospective adoptive parents and whose more-than-a-decade-long relationship had ended in, well, a crash and burn, really wasn't sure she was worthy of that look. That anyone would have that kind of desire for her.

Especially someone like Ethan. She had always suspected that he was attracted to her but now she knew it was more than attraction.

"Ferrin and I are going to be parents," Hunter said.

There was a whoop of joy and everyone raised their glasses to drink a toast. Crissanne joined everyone else in giving Ferrin and Hunter a hug, but Crissanne felt the reality of her place here when someone asked her to take a photo of the family.

Once again, she was on the outside looking in.

She shook the feeling off and went inside to grab her camera instead of using the smartphone. When she came back, she took several photos.

Looking at the world through her camera balanced out her emotions. Gave her the perspective she needed.

"It's time," Pa Caruthers said when she was done taking pictures.

There was some groaning as the men watched their dad trying to work his smartphone. "Someone come and show me how to make this thing play music."

As Nate helped his father, the women all shook their heads. But then applause came out of the speakers, followed by the low country drawl of Waylon Jennings. It was "Good Hearted Woman."

"Brace yourself," Ferrin said. "This is the Caruthers family song."

Winston Caruthers started singing along with Waylon, and then Hunter came in on Willie Nelson's part. Before too long all five Caruthers men were singing along. Then they all started to come over and claim their women. Ethan reached for Crissanne and for a brief moment, she really felt like she finally had someone she could call her own.

Eleven

Ethan hadn't meant to drink as much as he had or to dance with Crissanne until after midnight, but then, nothing went the way he planned with her. And they were still at it. Now Niall Horan's "This Town" was playing, and unlike earlier on the drive over when Ethan hadn't been able to relate to the song on the radio, this one made him realize exactly what he wanted from Crissanne.

"Why are you watching me like that?" she asked.

"Just figured out the answer to a question that has been bothering me for days," he said.

"What is it?"

"I think...I really care for you," he admitted, dancing her off the patio and toward the garden that was his mom's pride and joy.

The path was illuminated with lights placed every five feet along its length. The smell of jasmine and roses combined in the air and Ethan took a deep breath, looking up at the night sky so clear and wide and full of stars tonight. It seemed like the truth was finally in front of him.

Everything came back to Crissanne.

He'd been afraid to admit it until now.

"I care for you, too," she said softly as he led the way to the bench near the fountain at the center of the garden.

He heard the party still going on behind them but it faded as they moved farther into the garden.

"I'm sorry I missed going with you to see the studio space in town today," Ethan said. He wanted a clean slate to start before he said what was in his heart. It had been there for a while now but he'd been afraid to admit it. But then he dived right in.

"I always think that I have this ordinary life where I'm not very tempted by anything and there is no fear. But with you, Crissy, I question that."

"What do you mean?" she asked.

"I am so unsure of myself with you. I mean, I know I want you and having you live with me over the last six weeks has been, well, better than I expected," he said.

"It's nice for me, too," she said. "But there is something I wanted to talk to you about. I mean, it's hard to really give our relationship the right perspective when we are always together."

What was she getting at?

Had he found his way to her but only too late?

They sat down on the bench. He was silent for a moment as he looked around at the plants and flowers, whose petals were mostly closed for the night. "My parents moved out here a little more than three years ago and my mom started working on this garden."

"That's nice."

"Yeah, she had never had one because she was busy being a ranch wife. Cooking for the hands with our housekeeper, running kids to school and serving on committees in town. But when dad retired and they moved here she said that she realized her entire life had been building toward this."

"It's very pretty. Why are you telling me this?"

"I've never felt that my life was building toward anything," he admitted. "I'm a senior partner in the firm but that's not what Mom was referring to. She's talking about the bigger picture. I've never had that feeling of achieving my dreams in my personal life...until you."

She stared at him without answering. Was that fear in her eyes? Hope?

"I know it's too soon for this. We haven't had a proper courtship or done any of the things that couples should do. But for me when I think about my life and the future I realize I'm picturing you by my side."

"Ethan—"

"Don't say anything. I'm just telling you where I am. I know you're not in the same spot," he said. How could she be? She'd broken up with Mason and then he'd died. And she'd moved her entire life from California to Texas.

"The thing is, I might be," she said. Her voice was soft, and she looked over at him before taking his hands. "I need to tell you something before you find out from someone else."

"What?" he asked, not sure what she had just said. Did she want a relationship with him? Was she happy to just keep things as they had been?

"I signed the lease on the studio in town and the loft apartment above it today. I am going to move into the apartment this weekend," she said.

She was moving out of his house.

"Why? There's plenty of room at my place," he said.

"There is and there isn't," she said. "Everywhere I look it's your house. I feel like I belong there, but I don't know if I do. Does that make any sense?"

"No," he said. "I like having you in my house."

"I like it, too, but I like you more, Ethan. I think I could really care about you and I don't want to let myself get sucked into not believing in us because you are offering me something I've always wanted. I've never had someone to call my own, really my own. Living with you here would be solid and real and that scares me."

"What?" he asked. "What is it that I represent that you are afraid of?"

"Home."

Just one word and he couldn't argue with her anymore. He got it. She needed space to be sure. The same way he needed her in his bed every night and to wake up next to her each morning to feel secure. She needed that apartment of her own.

"Do you want me to give you space?"

"No," she said. "I was hoping we could date and try this like real people."

Real people. He wasn't sure that there was one way that was more real than another, but if she needed to live in town to feel like she had her own space, then he couldn't argue with her. She'd been sharing a home with Mason for a long time and that hadn't brought her the relationship she wanted. He could be the bigger man and give her space.

But he hated it.

He felt that if he let her go now she'd just slip away from him.

"Okay. I'll help you move this weekend," he said.

"I was hoping you'd say that," she said.

Ethan had been as good as his word, even going as far as asking his decorator to use his accounts at the different furniture stores in the area to make sure that she had everything she needed.

Right after moving in, Crissanne had to take a trip to New York to meet with a brand that wanted to work with her, and she'd left with the belief that her apartment would be boxes and a mess until she had a chance to sort it out. But Ethan had taken care of everything.

When her flight arrived today, he'd come to pick her up at the airport and drive her to the apartment. Now, as she opened the door, she was surprised to see that the decorator had gotten everything in place as they'd discussed.

"What do you think?" Ethan asked, carrying in a box of photos that she'd been storing in his garage since she'd moved out of Mason's house.

"I love it. I can't believe how finished it is," she said. She walked farther into the room. It smelled of the ocean and sunny summer days, no doubt thanks to the plug-in air fresheners, she thought as she slowly went from area to area. The only permanent wall in the loft was one that divided the bathroom from the rest of the space. There was a screen that she'd ordered that created a separate bedroom from the living area. And Bart had come out to build a low counter on one edge of the kitchen area. The floors were all hardwood and the window treatments were sumptuous yet modern.

The entire place fit her aesthetic in a way she hadn't realized it would. She'd always had an eye for what went together from framing scenes to be photographed, but this was the first home she'd ever had all to herself. The first place that she could call her own.

She was slightly overwhelmed at it as she looked around.

"Thank you," she said to Ethan.

"All I did was supervise and make sure that everyone followed your instructions," he said. "I like it."

"Thanks. I wasn't sure if it would all come together or be a mess. In my head I saw it one way but this is so much better."

He laughed. "Ellen was very impressed with your skills and suggested if you wanted to stop being a photographer she'd hire you at her interior design company."

Crissanne shook her head. "I don't think I'd like it. This was so personal."

"Where do you want this box?"

"Just put it over there in the living area," she said. "I have to figure out which pictures I want to put on the walls."

"I'll go and get the kitchen stuff while you do that," Ethan said. "Bart said he'll be stopping by later to finish up the island in the kitchen."

"Yes, he is a really good worker," Crissanne said. "I was a little hesitant at first when I heard his story but I should have factored in the Ethan effect."

He shook his head. "I'm not sure I want to know what that is."

"Just how you bring out the best in everyone. I think it has to do with the way that you see people without judging them."

He blushed, which she thought was cute. There was something about having Ethan here in her place that made her realize how much she was going to miss living with him. But they both needed this. She wanted to be sure that what she felt for him wasn't just about having a nice house and good people around her. She wanted to make sure her feelings were for *him*.

She already suspected they were, but this would help.

"Who am I to judge?" Ethan asked. "I'm just a litigator."

"You are a good man," she said.

He shrugged and left the loft, and Crissanne turned back to her box of photos. She sat down on the floor next to it and opened the lid. The first framed photo she pulled out of the box was one of Mason and Ethan that she'd taken while they were all still in college. The two of them were arguing about something while sitting in the quad. They'd been so intent on making their points—both of them—that she'd actually been able to get an entire series of shots before they noticed her.

She leaned the photo against the large square wood coffee table and pulled another photo from the box. Most of them were of Ethan, Mason or shots she'd taken on the job. She'd been nominated for a few awards over the years and would put those photos in her office downstairs along with the awards.

But she'd have to figure out where to place the private ones in the room.

"I remember that day," Ethan said quietly as he came over to where she was.

She glanced at the picture propped against the coffee table. "What were you two fighting about?"

He lifted the framed fifteen-by-seventeen-inch photo off the floor and held it in both of his hands as he looked at it.

"You."

"What? Why?"

"I thought that Mason wasn't giving you what you needed, that he was pushing you toward a career in travel photography because it suited him and his lifestyle more than you," Ethan said.

She just stared up at him. He'd been right, of course, but then again when wasn't Ethan correct? It had been one of the things that she and Mason had fought about over the years. He liked that she worked away from home. Liked that she traveled at least as much as him.

He had said it was so neither one of them was home all alone, but now looking back she realized it was so that they didn't get too used to having the other around.

"I do like my job," she said.

"Do you? I think you like the idea of having the studio here in town," he said. "I'm glad you've settled here in Cole's Hill."

She looked up at him and knew that the reason she'd come to Texas had been more complicated than she'd wanted to admit. But her reason for staying seemed to be centering on Ethan.

Later that afternoon, Ethan's parents, along with Derek, Bianca, Hunter and Ferrin, had all stopped by to bring housewarming gifts and help out with different tasks. Ethan had been dealing with all sorts of emotions since Crissanne told him she wanted to move out, but seeing her in her own place and so happy had just confirmed that it was the right move for her.

And for him.

He'd never talked about Mason in anything but glowing terms. If she'd stayed with him, there would have been no point. Even now, Ethan didn't really want to speak ill of the dead, but there had always been a part of Mason that was focused on what he wanted and what he needed from those around him.

He had one time told Ethan that he pictured his entire day and who he'd run into and what he needed from that person. It was one of the things the two men had in common. They both were able to look at the world and see their own path so clearly.

But while Ethan saw his path now with Crissanne, it was becoming more and more clear to him that Mason had seen a solo path for himself. He just hadn't known how to break free of Crissanne.

When she'd first shown up on Ethan's doorstep, he thought it was temporary. A lover's quarrel that would be resolved in time. But he realized now that would never have happened. Maybe he was making assumptions about Mason's mind-set when he broke up with Crissanne that could never be confirmed now that Mason was gone. But when he really thought about it, Ethan was pretty damned sure that his best friend wouldn't have minded his relationship with Crissanne.

"Got a minute, Eth?" Hunter asked him while they were all in the kitchen making sandwiches for lunch.

"Yeah, what's up?"

"Nothing big. Just wanted to talk to you alone."

"You can use my office downstairs," Crissanne said with a smile.

"Thanks," Ethan said, leading his brother down to the office.

"Sorry to do this today but Ferrin and I have to head back to College Station this afternoon and I thought it would be better to talk in person. I don't know what I have to do to legally protect Ferrin in case something happens to me. Since we got married last year I named her as my beneficiary, but I think I need to do more."

Ethan handled the estate planning for his whole family, not just for their individual accounts but also for the family trust and ranching business. "You're all set up as far as the family trust and the accounts for the Rockin' C Corporation are concerned. She'd get your shares upon your death and I've set up a separate trust for your child when he or she turns eighteen. Do you want to do something different?"

"I don't know," Hunter said. "I hadn't even considered it until Ferrin mentioned how young Mason was when he died and I thought hell, we don't know that we'll be given tomorrow, you know?"

"I do know," Ethan said.

He spent the next hour going over estate planning details with Hunter and reassuring his brother that everything would be taken care of.

"I spent so much of the last few years just focused on the past and clearing my name that this is sort of weird. I never thought I'd have Ferrin or a baby or anything like this," Hunter said.

"I know. But you deserve this happiness and I'll do everything I can legally to keep your worries at bay," he said.

"I know you will, Eth," Hunter said. "What's the deal with you and Crissanne? I like her. I think she's good for you."

"Good for me?"

"She got you dancing the other night instead of just sitting around and drinking or starting a fight with someone," Hunter said.

"I like her, but she's... I think she's at a crossroads," Ethan said, trying to explain something that he wasn't sure he understood. He was doing his best to give her what she needed. To not take anything for himself, which he was only just realizing was his usual mode with her. He always saw her as out of his reach and it wasn't lost on him that the one time she was actually in his arms he'd let her slip away again.

"What crossroads?" Hunter asked.

He took a deep breath and finally admitted what had been swirling around his mind for too long. That his best friend was always going to be between them. No matter that she'd left Mason before the other man had died, a part of Ethan would always feel guilty that he was sleeping with his best friend's girl.

"Somewhere between me and Mason," Ethan admitted.

"That's BS. She was always on her own with Mason. His hold on her was tenuous."

Ethan didn't believe that for a moment. Why would she have stayed with Mason so long if she hadn't wanted it to work out with him?

"Maybe. Whatever. She's here now and we are going to try to date and stuff like that."

"Ha."

"Ha?"

"Yeah, you always try to manage everything, but love isn't like that."

"I didn't say I loved her."

"You don't have to," Hunter said. "When she laughs you smile."

Ethan hadn't realized that. "I…"

"Don't deny it. No one knows more than I do how much falling for a woman can mess with who you think you are. But Ethan, from the other side, let me tell you that it is worth it. Ferrin has brought something to my life that I never dreamed I'd have. And I think Crissanne can do that for you, if you let her."

He didn't know how to respond to that and luckily Hunter let him change the subject. But after his family went home and it was just him and Crissanne, he had to admit that he was falling in love with her.

Twelve

Ethan helped her clean up after the party and then went home. And just like that, she was alone. Suddenly she understood why she'd stayed with Mason for all those years despite the fact that the relationship had been over for a while. She really didn't like being alone, despite the fact that she spent so much time by herself. It didn't matter that the apartment had been decorated by her and was her home now. It felt the same way as whatever small little room she'd been assigned when she'd been growing up and moving from house-to-house.

Too big and too empty.

She had all this space but was once again alone with no one to help her fill it. She wanted someone in her life. Someone she could trust and build a family with. She wanted that man to be Ethan.

She reached for her phone and started to text him. But how could she determine her true feelings for him if she kept leaning on him like a crutch? She got up and went to her laptop on the kitchen table and got back to reviewing the photos she'd taken over the last week.

The faces of Cole's Hill were starting to become so familiar to her. There were little details of people's lives that she had gotten to know through working with the women's group to photograph the bachelors and talking to the people she'd stopped to photograph in the park. Unlike Los Angeles, where everyone was essentially a stranger, these people were her neighbors.

She wanted this to be her home. She'd fought for so long for this that she knew she was going to make it work.

There was a knock on her door and she got up from the table, leaving a photo of Ethan enlarged on the screen.

She looked through the security peephole and caught her breath.

It was him.

"Hello, you," she said, opening the door.

"Hiya," he said, holding up a bottle of chilled Moët. "I know it's your first night alone and everything, but I thought we could have a toast and maybe talk."

"I almost texted you," she admitted, standing back so he could come in. "But then I felt silly because I was the one who moved out. Shouldn't I be able to stand on my own?"

"Who says you're not?" he asked. "I brought you a little something."

She opened the door further and he stepped inside. When he walked over to the kitchen table to put down the bottle of champagne, he looked at his photo on the computer.

"It's for the auction."

He just nodded and grabbed a towel from the kitchen counter to open the champagne. "Aren't you curious about your present?"

"I am."

She went into the kitchen after him, taking a seat at the breakfast bar and drawing the Neiman Marcus box he'd set down toward her. "You have already done so much for me, you didn't need to get me another gift."

"I wanted to," he countered.

He popped open the bottle of champagne and then came over to stand on the other side of the counter from her. "Open it."

She carefully opened the box. Inside there was a pair of champagne glasses with gold leaf on them that spelled out her name.

She stared at them knowing she needed to thank Ethan but unsure if she could. He'd given her something she wouldn't have thought to ask for. It might seem silly to think that as a thirty-year-old woman she'd never really had things that felt like they were part of building a future, but she hadn't. She'd lived in the now with Mason because that was what he liked. And in her childhood, she'd taken nothing with her from the homes where she'd lived. All she had from that time was the Brownie box camera she'd bought at a secondhand shop before leaving for college.

"Ethan..."

"They were supposed to be delivered this morning but of course didn't arrive until tonight. I wanted you to toast your new home with your glasses."

"I'd love that."

Ethan rinsed the glasses and dried them while she sat there on the stool making small talk about the upcoming bachelor auction.

"I was surprised to hear this is your first year participating," she said.

"I almost always plan a trip around this time of the year so I'm not here when it happens. I make a donation and don't have to go up on the stage."

"But not this year?" she asked.

He shook his head. "I had that trip planned but it...got canceled."

With Mason.

"Do you feel like there is ever going to be a moment when Mason isn't between us?" she asked after a long silence.

He tipped his head to the side and arched one eyebrow at her as he poured the champagne.

"No. He's been a part of our lives for too long."

He had been. But she was starting to resent his presence in a way because he was keeping both her and Ethan from letting down their guard. She was tired from traveling today so couldn't analyze it properly, but she knew there had to be a way for them to step out from the long shadow cast by their friend.

"To your first home and the start of your adventure in Cole's Hill," Ethan said, raising his glass toward her.

She clinked her glass against his and took a sip, closing her eyes for a moment.

"To good friends."

"I want to be more than friends," he admitted to her.

She did, too. "I want to be sure, Ethan. I don't want to hurt you. It's only fair to you."

He glanced around the apartment.

"This place?"

"Your town, your family, it's everything I've secretly wanted for so long."

Ethan put his glass down and walked around the counter, not stopping until he turned her on the stool to face him.

"You're all I've secretly wanted. And if it takes you living on your own to convince you that we are meant to be together, then so be it."

They decided to watch a movie with superheroes in it that didn't hold his attention. Every time she reached into the bowl on his lap for some popcorn, his body responded. He wanted her, but she'd moved out and any man with half a brain would realize she needed space to think.

"I guess I should be going," he said when the movie finally ended.

"Not yet," she responded, turning to face him on the couch.

"If I stay we are going to be doing our version of Netflix and chill," he said, lifting his head to meet her stormy gray gaze. "Are you sure you want that?"

"I'm not sure about anything," she admitted quietly, tangling her hands in his hair. "But I want you, Ethan, and being apart hasn't changed that."

A pulse of desire went through him, shaking him to his core. She shifted on the couch, straddling his lap to kiss him. He realized how much he liked her hands on him. Rubbing her back, he slipped one hand under her shirt, loving the feel of her bare skin. She was so natural about everything she did.

That was a turn-on in itself. But then, everything about Crissanne was. He'd wanted her from the first moment they'd met. But he'd been cautious and for once he wondered if that wasn't the way he should be. She was bold, taking chances and reaching for him even though she wasn't sure. He wanted to have every detail locked down and secured before he gave her any more of his heart. But maybe that wasn't the way to go.

All he knew was that right now, he was glad to have her in his arms.

"I think I want you to spend the night here," she said. "Will you do that?"

"Sure."

"And since tomorrow is Sunday that means I don't have to wake up to a note," she added.

She meant for him to stay in bed with her, wake up with her lazy-Sunday style, and he wasn't sure he could do it.

"Uh, of course," he said.

"What?" she asked, and as she straddled his lap and looked straight into his eyes there was no place for him to hide.

"If I stay it's going to be even harder for me to give you space," he answered. "Already I hate that you moved into town without me."

She chewed her lower lip and sat back on his thighs, shifting away from him. "Me, too. But I needed to do it. I had to prove to myself that I am strong without you."

"Did you do that?" he asked.

She shook her head. "Not yet. All I proved is that I am stubborn and won't give in to things that tempt me. You tempt me, Ethan Caruthers, but I don't want to push you away."

"Me, either."

She stood up and held her hand out to him and he followed her across the loft to her bed. It was queen-size with a plain cream-colored bedspread. She stopped there next to it and he pulled her close, singing under his breath the words to Eric Clapton's "Layla," because if ever there was a woman who'd been his obsession for his entire adult life it was Crissanne.

Even having had her in his bed, he still felt like she was just out of his reach. His Layla. And he didn't want that anymore. Sure it would be smart and sensible to give her space and let her make her own way back to him, but as Hunter and Nate had both warned, love didn't follow the sensible path.

She wrapped her arms around his back and rested her head on his chest as he sang and danced her around the room. And he knew that he loved her. He might have been trying to play it like he just really liked her, but the truth was, he loved this woman.

She stumbled on the bedside rug and they tumbled back onto the bed, both of them laughing.

"Dang it, woman, all you had to do was ask and I'd have gotten in your bed."

"My way worked," she said, still giggling. "Now get naked."

"Get naked?"

"Yeah, it feels like forever since I've seen you naked," she said.

"Only if you get naked, too," he said.

"Deal."

She hopped off the bed, shimmying out of her skirt and pulling her tunic over her head, and all he could do was lie there and watch. She was tanned and her waist was nipped in, her hips full and her legs so long. She glanced over at him.

"Uh, nothing else is coming off until I see some skin, Caruthers."

He pulled his T-shirt over his head and tossed it aside. "How's this?"

"Not bad," she said, reaching over to caress his chest. "But keep going."

He sat up and snaked his arm around her waist, drawing her forward between his legs and then falling back on the bed so she was on top of him. He found her mouth with his and kissed her long and hard and deep. Using one hand, he undid the back of her bra. Feeling it come free, he slid the straps down her arms until it was caught between their bodies.

He felt the tight beads of her nipples against his chest and groaned as she tore her mouth from his and used her hands on either side of his head on the bed to push herself up, grinding her crotch against his. She started to shift away but he put both hands in the back of her panties, cupping her butt and holding her to him.

"That's cheating," she said.

"Objection," he said. "Now we are both topless."

"Counselor, that is pushing it," she said. "I want you out of those jeans."

"I'm holding something I don't want to let go of," he argued.

"I'll make it easier for you," she said, rolling to her side. He let her go, slowly drawing his hands up her back and caressing her breasts as she shifted away from him.

He got to his feet and pushed his jeans and underwear down his legs, completely forgetting about his shoes, which he toed off last. Then he turned back to her, completely naked.

"I think you need to take those panties off," he said.

He glanced up to see her watching him. She pushed her panties down her legs and then stepped out of them. She took him in her hand, stroking him, until he was pretty sure he couldn't get any harder.

He tumbled her onto the bed again, careful to make sure that his weight didn't come down on her. Then he shifted around on the bed until he leaned back against the headboard, putting his hands on her waist, lifting her onto his lap.

She shifted backward on his thighs, stroking her hand up and down the length of his erection. If he got any harder he thought he might explode, and he didn't want to do that until he was buried inside her sleek body.

He brought her hand to his mouth and pressed a hot kiss in the center of it before nibbling his way up her arm to her shoulder. Then, cupping her breasts, he lowered his head.

Her breasts were full and pretty with their pink nipples that stood out against her tanned skin. He plumped them up and rubbed his thumbs over them until they peaked and hardened under his touch. Then he leaned forward and sucked one of them. She put her hands on his shoulders, her nails digging into his skin.

Her fingers caressed the back of his neck in a light teasing pattern that sent shivers down his spine and made his hips jerk forward. But he was determined to make this night last. This was the first time he was making love to her when he knew he loved her. Admitting it to himself had been a long time coming, and he wanted this to last.

But Crissanne was the only argument he had when he thought about defending his life. Slow might be what his mind wanted, but his body had different ideas. She shredded his self-control and left him desperate for more. More of her mouth. More of her body. More of her touch.

She moved over him, her warm center rubbing the tip of his erection as she shifted position.

He lifted his head from her breast and looked up at her. She stared at him for a long time and then leaned forward to kiss him as he slowly entered her body.

He gave over control, letting her slide down on him until he was fully inside her. He reached between their bodies and flicked his finger over her clit, feeling her surprise as she tightened on him. Then as he continued to caress her, she started to rock against him.

He put his hands on her waist and slowed the movement, trying to draw it out, but she buried her fingers in his hair again, forcing his head back as her mouth took his. Damn, he loved the way that felt. She bit his lower lip and sucked it, then followed that with her tongue in his mouth. The kiss was carnal and raw, and he stopped thinking of anything but the way she felt in his arms.

He thrust his hips forward, driving himself deeper inside her. And still it wasn't enough. Tearing his mouth from hers, he noticed that she'd braced her arms on the headboard and her breasts were right in front of his face in that position. He turned his head and sucked her nipple, while simultaneously putting his hands on her hips and urging her to ride him harder and faster.

Still he couldn't get deep enough, couldn't take her fast enough or hard enough, the way his gut was churning for him to do. She threw her head back, gripping his shoulders as she moved on him with more urgency. He felt a jolt in his body and suddenly he came. He'd wanted to wait but as he thrust up into her one last time, he felt empty. He couldn't help it.

Then she tightened on him. Her inner core gripped him, her nails biting into his shoulders and his name a loud cry on her lips as she shuddered in his arms and then fell forward to his shoulder. Her breath brushed over his neck and chest.

He stroked his hands down her back, tracing the length of her spine. She turned her head, looking up at him with those big storm-gray eyes of hers, and he felt a punch near his heart. Tonight, everything was different. Making love to her in this strange apartment confirmed what he'd been afraid to admit until tonight.

He rolled to his side, holding her close to him.

"So we're sleeping in tomorrow?" he asked. Trying to talk when he felt like he wanted to confess his feelings was hard.

"Yes," she said.

"I'll try," he said. Staying here with her was at once the only thing he wanted and the very thing he was afraid of. What if he told her he loved her and she wasn't ready? What if...

She curled up on her side and put her hand over his heart, dropping a kiss on his chest and sleepily saying good-night.

His fears receded as he held her.

Thirteen

Crissanne's phone rang at 2:00 a.m., which made them both groan. She reached for it and knocked the alarm clock off the nightstand instead. Nothing was where she remembered it being.

"It's your phone," Ethan said, getting out of bed and padding naked across the loft to where she'd left her phone charging on the kitchen counter. He turned off the TV as he brought the phone back to her. It had stopped ringing and he handed it to her without a word.

As she hit the unlock button, Ethan's phone pinged with a text message, too.

But that barely registered. Because when she looked at hers, she saw that the missed call was from Mason.

His picture was on her screen, and she couldn't help the tears that burned her eyes as she lifted the phone to her ear and listened to the voice mail. Someone had probably found his phone and was trying to get back in touch with whomever had lost it.

"Shit," Ethan said, reading his text.

The voice mail started at the same moment he cursed. There

was static, followed by a man's voice. "Cris, it's me. I'm alive. We need to talk. Call me."

She dropped the phone on the bed. Mason? Mason alive? She shook as she wrapped her arms around her body and then glanced over at Ethan.

"Mason is alive," Ethan said.

"I know. He left me a voice mail," she said.

Oh. My. God.

"I can't be here," Ethan said.

"Why not?" she asked. She didn't like the panic she saw on Ethan's face. And the guilt.

"It's not right. He's been injured. His text said he's still got a cast on his left leg and his ribs aren't healed yet," Ethan said. "You need time to figure out things with him. Without me in the middle."

Crissanne stared at the man who'd come to mean more to her in six weeks than Mason had meant to her in twelve years. And he was telling her he needed to give her space.

"No. Ethan, I don't think running from my place in the middle of the night will help anything."

"He's on his way to see me," Ethan said.

"What?"

"That's what his text said."

"Okay. Let's both go and see him. I can't believe he's alive."

"Me, either."

"I'm glad," she said. "He was too young to die."

"He was—is," Ethan said, moving around and gathering his clothes.

And in that moment, all the joy and affection that had been between them before was gone.

There was a flatness in her apartment that hadn't been there before. She felt uncomfortable being naked, so she got out of bed and went to her dresser to pull on jeans and a sweatshirt. When she turned back around, Ethan was standing in the living area of her loft on his phone texting.

This didn't feel right.

"We need to talk before we go to meet him."

"You're right but I don't know if this is the right time," Ethan said. There was that look on his face that she'd seen before when she'd watched him in court. It was closed off and not showing any emotion. Not at all the man she'd gone to bed with.

"Too bad," she said. She wasn't going to lose Ethan now that she'd found him. She was so close to having the happiness that had always been just out of her reach, and she knew it was centered on him.

She might not understand her feelings for Ethan, but she knew she couldn't just let him walk out the door. She'd waited for years for Mason to come around and he never had. Now it seemed as though he was back from the dead, but that to Crissanne felt like a separate issue. She'd deal with Mason on her own. But first, Ethan.

"I can't do this," Ethan said. "It was one thing to think you'd broken up with him. Then he died, and everything changed. But now he's back...I just feel guilty."

His words cut through her. "Did you never want to be with me for me?"

"What?"

"Is that what you are saying?" she asked. "That it was just sympathy that drove you into my arms? I mean, if that's true then we should have stopped after that day in the conference room."

"That's not what I said," Ethan said, pushing his hands through his hair.

"But is it what you meant? You are way better with words than I am so when you don't say something straight out I have to believe there is a reason for it."

"There is a reason." Ethan turned and almost shouted at her. "I don't want to talk about this. We need to go and see Mason. He's back from the dead. That should be our focus."

"It's not mine," she admitted quietly. "He and I broke up before he died...or was presumed dead. That part of my life was over, and I have to admit being here with you helped me see what was missing between us. I think Mason saw it before I did."

"Great. I'm glad that you are in that place," Ethan said. "I'm not. He knew I always wanted you. He knew that for years I watched you when you were with him."

"That doesn't matter," she said. But she hadn't realized the true extent of how Ethan felt about her while she'd been dating Mason. It changed things in her mind. Had he been with her because she'd been forbidden fruit?

No wonder he didn't want to talk.

But she needed to hear him say that. Ethan had never used her in all the years she'd known him. She didn't want to think that he'd suddenly turned into the kind of man who would now.

"Was I just some tail you'd always wanted?"

"No! You know it's not like that," he said.

But she didn't know anything. The last time she'd made assumptions she lost twelve years of her life to a man who had walked away from her. "What is it like?"

Ethan didn't want to do this. Not now. He was happy Mason wasn't dead, but his timing could have been better. Ethan had finally decided to let his guard down. But now his friend was back and Ethan knew he had to step back and let Mason and Crissanne sort out whatever was between them. No matter what she said.

And she was angling for a fight? What was motivating her here? He tried to see it but with Crissanne his perspective was skewed, as always. He wanted her, he wanted to see what he needed to in her, and that had always made him see her differently.

Now she wanted to know if he thought she was some piece of ass he'd been chasing for twelve years.

"This isn't the time for this kind of discussion," he said. He needed a shower so he could wash the smell of sex and Crissanne off his body, and maybe then he'd be able to think and figure out how to keep her and not betray his friend.

Because every way he sliced this, it looked like a betrayal of Mason.

"This is the only time we have. Mason is on his way to Texas. You want to leave and I don't want you to go without settling this."

"Why?"

She screamed and turned away from him in frustration.

He didn't want to make this night harder on her than it already was. "He's like my brother. He's going to need everyone around him to help him get better. You and I can't go in there all holding hands and whatnot. It's not fair to him."

Crissanne turned back around. She just stared at him for so long that he felt the full weight of her disappointment. "What about what's fair to us?"

"We can talk about that—"

"No. If you can't discuss this with me before... Wait a minute. Do you want to get his approval before you tell him about us?" she asked.

When she put it that way it sounded...well, not like the answer he should be giving her. But the truth was he'd never talked to Mason and gotten his side of the story about the breakup. What if Mason wasn't over Crissanne and would be hurt? They had to figure these things out before they took the next step.

Because what Ethan wanted with Crissanne wasn't just temporary. He had admitted to himself last night that he loved her. But Mason was like a brother, not a man he could just push from his life.

"It's not like that. But it is true he and I never discussed your breakup and he died not knowing you'd come here," Ethan said. "I'm just saying it might be better to ease him into this."

"I agree. I don't want to go in there acting like a couple and make him feel worse than he already does, but I need to know you're by my side," she said. "Are you?"

Was he?

"I am."

"Great," she said, coming to him, putting her arms around him and looking into his eyes.

But he still had that feeling that she was Mason's.

"You can't, can you?" she finally said.

"It's not that I can't be with you, it's that I hate betraying him. Mason saved me when I was heading down a path—"

"You saved yourself, Ethan. You've always been stronger than you gave yourself credit for. Even Mason would say you did it yourself," she said. "You would never have become a drug addict. We both know that."

"I don't know that," Ethan said.

"Why?"

"Because I have an addictive personality."

"Give me an example of this supposed addiction," she said.

"You."

There, he'd said it. "You are the one that I can't forget. That I've watched and wanted for so long. And I think that if I claim you as my own, if I don't give you the space to figure out if Mason's near-death experience has changed him, you might regret it. And then I'd have what I wanted but at a cost I'm not willing to pay."

She put her hands to her hips and took a step back.

"What cost?"

"Your happiness," he said.

He turned away from her and moved a few feet toward the door. He needed to do this not just for Mason but for Crissanne, who very likely might find her feelings for her ex-boyfriend changed now that he was back from the dead.

"I don't think that will happen," she said.

"Neither of us can say for sure what we are going to feel

when we see him," Ethan said. His phone pinged and he glanced down at the screen.

"He's at my house. Bart has let him in and set him up in the guest bedroom. Apparently he's in bad shape but is sleeping for now. We need to go," Ethan said.

"Okay then. Let's go. My car was delivered this week while I was away," she said. "I'll follow you."

He nodded. There was nothing else to say. Not right now. They both needed to go and see Mason. To make sure his friend was okay. And then Ethan could see about this woman who had changed him in a way he hadn't expected to be changed. But he knew if he had to step aside for her to be happy, he would.

That was what love was about, he thought. He remembered his mom reading them a poem when they were young about letting things go and waiting for them to come back. Nate had been sure she meant one of the wild horses that he'd seen on their summer vacation. Ethan hadn't really thought that it made any sense at all. Until this moment, as he followed Crissanne down the stairs out to the parking lot at the end of the block.

It was the wrong time to tell her that he loved her; he knew that. She needed to be able to make her decision unencumbered by that knowledge.

He'd have to let her go and see if she came back.

As Crissanne followed Ethan through town in her new car, she couldn't help thinking that it was all so surreal. She had no idea what had happened, but Mason was back.

She was so happy about the news but didn't see how it had to change things between her and Ethan. And from how Ethan was acting, she had to wonder if he was more concerned about Mason's happiness than theirs. He'd said he had her feelings front and center at heart, but she wasn't too sure about that.

It felt more like...

She didn't know.

Her radio was playing quietly in the background and when

she glanced down to find the volume button, she realized she was crying. What was she going to do?

Mason was alive. Who knew if his crash had changed anything about him? She certainly doubted that after twelve years of her trying to make him into a forever man one crash would be enough to do it. But he'd been through a lot. He may have changed his mind. But so had she. She knew he wasn't the same man who'd left her back in Los Angeles and she had to admit she wasn't the same woman. She'd been afraid to ask him to stay, afraid she wasn't worthy of having a family with him or anyone else. But being with Ethan had given her the strength and the courage to admit that she did want—and deserve—those things.

But she wouldn't know until she saw him. She wiped her nose on the back of her hand as she turned into Ethan's circular drive and parked her car behind his. She took a deep breath, used the hem of her sweatshirt to wipe her entire face dry and then got out of the car, taking the keys with her.

Ethan waited at the top of the stairs on the porch by the front door. Looking at him, she realized she resented him. How he could keep them waiting for a life together even after all they'd built while Mason had supposedly been dead.

She didn't say a word to him when she got to the front door. He looked like he was going to talk, but she just glared him into silence.

The problem with Ethan was that he thought he could explain everything until she just accepted it. And the truth was, that wasn't going to work. Not tonight.

They stepped into the hallway and she had an intense sense of déjà vu from the moment she'd come to Texas after she and Mason had broken up. She'd been looking for a safe place and had found it, not just in this house but in Ethan.

Mason more than likely was thinking the same thing. He was here for Ethan and not for her. She realized that now.

She caught Ethan's arm before he took another step.

"I don't think Mason is here for me," she said at last, her voice sounding thready and raw from the crying she'd done in the car. Mason had already shoved her from his life, and though Ethan thought the three of them would be friends, she just didn't know.

She also didn't know if she could hide the way she felt about him.

She didn't want Ethan to see her the way Mason saw her. As undesirable. Unlovable.

"We won't know until we talk to him," Ethan said.

She nodded. "I just don't want you to see me the way he does. He never wanted me."

Ethan pulled her close and hugged her, and this time she felt a bit of hope that things would sort themselves out. She knew she should step away from him in case Mason got up from the bedroom where Bart had told them he was sleeping. Ethan kissed her temple softly. "I would never see you and not want you."

"How sweet," Mason said from the open doorway of the bedroom downstairs. "I'm left for dead and my girl and my best friend hook up."

Crissanne pulled back and Ethan dropped his arms, turning toward Mason. He had a crutch and one leg in a cast, a sling on his arm, and his nose looked as if it had been broken. His eyes were bloodshot and out of focus.

And she felt her heart take a punch. This man was broken. She finally understood what Ethan had meant. What Mason needed. She and Ethan went to him at the same time and he just swayed between the two of them.

"I'm so glad you're alive," she said, tears burning her eyes again. God, how had he survived? He looked like he had barely recovered, and this was six weeks after the crash.

"Didn't look like it from where I was," he said.

"Mase, we thought you were dead. Did you really think that the two people who loved you most in this world wouldn't come together to share our grief?" Ethan said, gingerly putting his arm around Mason's middle and leading him back into the bedroom.

"Is that all it was?" Mason asked.

Ethan looked at her and she shrugged. "How did you survive? The production company's people thought you were dead. Everyone assured us that no one survived the crash."

Crissanne rushed ahead to fix the covers. It seemed like Mason had gotten out of the bed in a hurry. Ethan helped him back into it and they got him settled. She took a seat on the end of the bed.

"I was buried under a piece of the wreckage," he said. "I think. I was in and out of consciousness and when I finally woke up I was in a village. They nursed me until I was well enough to be taken down the mountain and transported to a hospital in Lima."

"I'm so glad the villagers found you."

Mason nodded. But his head fell back against the pillows and Crissanne could tell he was far from recovered. This wasn't going to be a quick visit. He'd come to Ethan to recover and she knew that she'd be in the way if she stayed.

"Are they announcing your return in the news?" Ethan asked.

He got the conversation moving on to things they had to discuss.

"Yes. The production company will be sending out the announcement later this morning. They want me to do some press but I wanted to come and find you first... You were like a brother to me," Mason said.

"I still am."

"Doesn't feel like that right now, bro."

"Why did you come here?" Ethan asked. "It's because we are family, right? And you wanted to be with family and not on your own. That hasn't changed."

The two of them were like brothers, and she'd at times realized that her bond with Mason wasn't as strong as the one he shared with Ethan.

Mason seemed to drift to sleep and Ethan looked over at her. She nodded.

He'd been right. They'd have to wait until Mason was at least more himself before they did anything else.

Crissanne couldn't help feeling that once again the family she'd always craved had been stolen from her.

"I'll take the first watch," he said.

Fourteen

The next two weeks passed slowly for Ethan. October brought with it some fall days, but mostly it stayed warm since it was Texas. The bachelor auction loomed in one week and Mason was starting to recover a bit more. He hadn't said anything to Ethan about Crissanne since that night when he'd first arrived.

Crissanne had been to see Mason several times, and she came over and stayed with him when Ethan had to work long hours. But Ethan and Crissanne had barely had a chance to talk. As glad as he was to have his friend back, he missed Crissanne. He'd run into her at the coffee shop in town one morning and she'd looked tired and so pretty he hadn't been able to think of anything but kissing her and holding her in his arms.

Mason had gone to Houston for a day to do a satellite uplink and interviews with all of the morning news shows. Otherwise he was lying low in Cole's Hill until he finished healing and figured out his next move.

Ethan didn't know where that left Mason and Crissanne so he had been giving her space. But he wanted her back in his life. And he had no idea how to ask if she and Mason were back together.

So he'd stared at her awkwardly before turning and leaving the shop without his coffee. At work his assistant said he'd turned into a tyrant and had assured him that unless he changed his attitude he wasn't going to get any bids at the bachelor auction.

Carlene had a point. Ethan knew that he had to figure out how to go back to the old way he'd always been around Mason and Crissanne. But he couldn't. Back then, he'd never held her in his arms, let alone kissed her or made love to her.

"Dude, did you hear a thing I said?" Mason asked, interrupting his thoughts. They were sitting at the table near Ethan's pool playing twenty-one. They were supposed to be figuring out how to legally bring Mason back from the dead. It wasn't easy. There was a lot of paperwork. Ethan was still working to get everything filed and then expedited.

"Sorry. My mind was elsewhere," he replied. "What'd you say?"

"What's up with you and Crissanne?"

"Nothing," Ethan said.

"Did Derek tell you that lying to me would speed up my recovery?" Mason asked as he put his cards on the table and leaned forward, putting his arms on the table.

"Derek is a cardiologist. Even if he had I wouldn't believe him," Ethan said.

"Well, I'm not blind," Mason said. "You two are damned awkward around each other, and that's telling."

Ethan shrugged. "I don't want to talk about her."

"You never have," Mason agreed. "Even when I asked her out to make you jealous."

"Is that why you asked her out?" Ethan asked. He'd never thought much about it. Why wouldn't Mason want Crissanne? From the moment he'd seen her with her blond hair and her stormy gray eyes, Ethan had wanted her.

"Maybe. I mean, that's not why I stayed with her for twelve years," Mason said.

"But you broke up, right? That's what she said."

Mason rubbed his hand over his chest and shifted back in his chair. "We did. I...I wasn't ready to commit the way she wanted. She wants kids and a family."

Ethan felt the sharp sting of jealousy at the thought of Crissanne and Mason having kids together. He wasn't going to be able to save his friendship with Mason. He just wasn't. And as much as he loved the other man like a brother, if he and Crissanne got back together it would be torture for Ethan. He had thought he could be noble and put her happiness first, but that would be the end of this.

"She deserves it," Ethan said. "She'd never even had her own place until she leased the studio and apartment in Cole's Hill."

"I know. I thought...we're so similar, Cris and I. But she grew up holding on to dreams of what might be and I grew up secure in the knowledge that family was the kind of messed-up tie I never wanted."

For the first time since he'd come back to Cole's Hill, Mason sounded like his old self.

"I thought my mom had changed your mind."

He shook his head. "Nah, your family is the exception that proves the rule. But Cris never saw that."

"Do you want her back?" he asked.

"She's not yours to give," Mason said. "Or mine to take. I think we both know she'd light into us but good if she heard us discussing her like this."

"I know," Ethan said. "But you changed after almost dying... in a lot of ways. I've never seen you this mellow before."

Mason took off his sunglasses and Ethan searched his green gaze for an answer to the question he didn't want to ask. Had Mason decided that he wanted a family now that he'd almost died? But there was no answer in his eyes.

"That might be the drugs I'm using to manage my pain," Mason said.

But Ethan knew his friend better than that. He had changed in a fundamental way. He'd been very clear about wanting to live here in Cole's Hill instead of going back to Los Angeles. That was a huge change, and Ethan suspected it had a lot to do with him wanting to be closer to family. His family, and of course, Crissanne.

If Mason tried to get her back, hell, he would win. Ethan couldn't take a chance at happiness from him or Crissanne after they'd waited twelve years for it.

"I hurt her, Eth. I said things that I knew would hurt her and I don't think she could ever forgive that."

"Why did you do it?"

"Because she deserved more than me. You asked if I'd changed and the truth is sort of a vague maybe. I don't know yet. When I see you and Crissanne together I want her, but that's because I'm selfish and don't want you to have everything. I've always been jealous of you because of your brothers and your family, even this town you live in. If you had the woman you always wanted…well, I won't say any more and show you just how much of a bastard I can be."

Mason's honesty humbled him and he got up and went around the table to hug his friend. "You have all of this. My family is yours. My town is yours."

"And Crissanne?"

"Is her own woman," Crissanne said, startling the both of them as she walked out onto the patio.

Crissanne had been in town buying some clothes and shaving items for Mason that he'd asked her to get for him. It had become clear over the last two weeks that she and Mason had fallen into a new pattern. The spark that had once flared between them was gone. It had been gone for a while; that's why they'd broken up. But in its place there was something new.

More of a friendship, and she liked it. She was getting closer to thinking that she might be able to find her way back to Ethan with each day that Mason spent in recovery. She knew she'd fallen fast for Ethan, given that she'd been with Mason for a dog's age and hadn't ever felt like this.

"Mason, you and I were over as a couple long before I forced the confrontation and we broke up. Thinking you were dead made me realize how much I care for you but I have to be honest, those feelings aren't the same as what I feel for Ethan."

"Fair enough," Mason said. "But I know that neither of you has mentioned the thing that I said that first night. That you two are clearly more than friends now."

Ethan stood up. "The time hasn't been right to discuss anything. Your recovery is the top priority."

"That's very nice of you," he said, sounding slightly sarcastic.

"It's the truth," Crissanne insisted.

Mason looked at her and his expression softened. "I know. I was jealous and also a little sad because we never had what I saw between you two," he said to her. "I know that I've thrown everything up in the air between you and that's the last thing I'd want for the two people who matter the most to me in this world."

Mason stood up and walked to Ethan, using his crutch. "I know that neither of you is mine to give away to the other but I'm taking myself out of this equation. Just know we're always going to be friends no matter what happens."

He walked by them and into the house. Ethan turned toward Crissanne, who just watched him go. Ethan had no idea what to say. And when he looked at Crissanne he realized that she didn't know, either. She stood there with one arm around her waist, her sunglasses pushed up on the top of her head.

"I love you," he said. "Before we say anything else I need you to know that. I thought I could step aside and do whatever I need to in order to make sure you were happy, but I realized that I can't. I want you in my life. I want to start a family with you."

"Ethan—"

"Let me finish," he said. "I know that I was pushing to give us time to figure this out but if I'm being honest, being apart from you has just made me realize how clear my feelings are. All the doubts I had are gone. I know it's not fair to throw this at you right now. That Mason is still recovering and no matter what he said, you have a right to your feelings. I'll wait but you should know that I'm not going to be standing on the sidelines while you figure out what you want. I'm going to do everything I can to show you how much I love you and how perfect our life together can be."

She walked toward him. "Perfect is an illusion. In real life, there aren't filters to blur away the rough edges, and you know what, Ethan? I'm so glad. Because I love you, too. I mean, I never in my entire life felt anything for a person close to what I feel for you. I've been trying to give you the space you needed to work things out with Mason, but I miss you.

"Every night I hug that pillow you slept on at my loft close to my chest and pretend it's you. Every morning I'm at the coffee shop in town hoping you'll stop in for a cup before work just to see you, because even if we don't talk it makes my day a little better to simply see you."

"Really?" he asked.

"Truly," she said.

He pulled her into his arms and kissed her because the only other words he had to say were jumbled in his head. He didn't want to start babbling like an idiot and was very much afraid he would.

"I want to marry you," he said.

"Yes. I want that, too."

"Good. We can start with you moving back in with me," he said.

"Okay," she said. Her heart was so full of love and happiness that she was almost afraid to trust it, but then Ethan lifted her in his arms and carried her toward the house, and she knew that she'd found safety with him. He was the one person she could trust to always be there for her.

Epilogue

With the bachelor auction in full swing, Crissanne left her position backstage to make her way to the front of the ballroom. Mason was saving her a seat at the Caruthers family table; it was funny how the two of them had realized that they had the family they both had always been seeking. She sat between Kinley's nanny and Mason, ready to bid on her man.

Crissanne was wearing a simple engagement ring that Ethan had given her the night before at a family dinner at his parents' house. She glanced at it as she sat down and Mason winked at her. "You two are perfect together. Almost makes me think about finding someone of my own."

She doubted that would ever happen. "What woman could compete with the wildness of a mountain path you have yet to climb?"

"Touché."

Pa Caruthers said something to Mason and he turned away. Pippa flipped through the catalog as if she were looking for someone.

"Are you bidding tonight?" Crissanne asked her.

"I am. I've had my eye on this Texan for a while," she said, pointing to Diego Velasquez. "And since it's my birthday I've decided to treat myself."

Crissanne laughed at the way the other woman said it. "He's certainly a treat. And flirty as all get out. I think you'll have fun with him."

"Good," Pippa said. "I need some fun in my life."

Before she could respond, Nate, who was emceeing the event, announced Ethan's name. Crissanne turned toward the front of the room as her fiancé walked out toward the center of the stage. The emcee was reading a bio about Ethan, and Crissanne noticed it wasn't the one that had been in the brochure.

"Ethan Caruthers was the last of the wild Caruthers boys to remain single, and some say it was because he was waiting for the right woman to come along. Of course, the bidding is open to anyone, but Ethan has warned us that his heart and soul belong to only one woman and his wild days are behind him. So he's made a large contribution to make up for the bids and has asked that we offer him up only to the one who truly loves him and wants to spend the rest of her life with him."

"I do!" Crissanne said, jumping up and raising her hand.

"Come and claim your bachelor," Nate said.

Ethan met her halfway to the stage, pulling her into his arms and kissing her. There was applause and whoops of joy. She put her hand on his face as he lifted his head. "You're mine."

"Always," he said.

"And now for our next bachelor," the emcee persisted from the stage. "Ladies, prepare to be tempted by the untamable Diego Velasquez."

* * * * *

The Dating Dare
Barbara Dunlop

New York Times and *USA TODAY* bestselling author **Barbara Dunlop** has written more than forty novels for Harlequin, including the acclaimed Chicago Sons series for Harlequin Desire. Her sexy, lighthearted stories regularly hit bestseller lists. Barbara is a three-time finalist for the Romance Writers of America's RITA® Award.

Books by Barbara Dunlop

Chicago Sons

Sex, Lies and the CEO
Seduced by the CEO
A Bargain with the Boss
His Stolen Bride

Gambling Men

The Twin Switch
The Dating Dare

Visit her Author Profile page at
millsandboon.com.au,
or barbaradunlop.com, for more titles.

Dear Reader,

Welcome to *The Dating Dare*, book two of the Gambling Men series.

When economist James Gillen was left at the altar in book one of the series, I knew he needed his own happy ending. Serendipitously, bridesmaid and librarian Natasha Remington was also recently jilted and available to share empathy.

Together, James and Nat decide they each need an image upgrade to attract the opposite sex. They change their names to Jamie and Tasha, upgrade their appearances, take chances on the stock market and make a ton of money. They also take on new and exciting adventures. Their efforts work—better than either of them ever expected.

I hope you enjoy the story!

Barbara

For all my friends at the office.

One

It wasn't like I was completely alone.

I had friends at work. Well, acquaintances really. But some of us exchanged Christmas gifts. We went to lunch. We even stopped for drinks in the evening before heading home.

My lifelong friends Layla and Brooklyn might have moved out of Seattle, but I'd rebound from that. People rebounded from absent friendships all the time. They filled their lives with other things, new experiences and new companions.

The companions didn't even have to be people.

I liked cats. I especially liked kittens. I'd heard once that kittens should be adopted in pairs, littermates if you could get them. That way, they kept themselves company when you were away.

A librarian with two cats.

Perfect.

Exactly how I hoped my life would end up.

I was at the Harbor Tennis Club in downtown Seattle contemplating the latest text message from Sophie Crush, the fourth close friend in our circle. Several games were underway on the indoor courts below me. The frequent sound of balls popping hollowly against the painted surface faded into the background while my herbal tea cooled on a round polished beech wood table in the lounge.

I liked herbal tea. It was a comfort drink, and I didn't want to give it up. All the same, I was thinking I might have to choose between tea and cats to keep from becoming a cliché.

I had acquaintances here at the Harbor Club, too. I'd been a member since I was a teenager. I'd taken lessons and played matches over the years with most of the other members in my age range.

But acquaintances weren't close friends. They weren't the people you could call up to spend a lazy Saturday afternoon with dressed in yoga pants, eating gourmet ice cream and loaded nachos, adding wine as soon as the clocked ticked over to four o'clock. They weren't the people you could count on when you were feeling down.

I was feeling down.

I told myself it was normal. And it was. I didn't begrudge Layla and Brooklyn their happily-ever-afters. I was happy for them. But it was hard to be happy for me right now.

I checked my cell phone screen again. The text from Sophie stared back at me.

Her lunch was running late—her lunch with her new guy was running late.

I surmised from the grinning emoji that lunch with the new guy was going great.

I was happy for her, too. Again, just not for me.

She'd canceled our Saturday tennis game at the last minute, so here I was sitting alone in my tennis shorts, my racket by my side, with no plans for the afternoon and none for the evening, either. I found myself wondering how late the animal shelter was open on weekends.

It felt pathetic again, the cat thing. I did like cats. What I didn't like was what they represented, like I'd given up and started that long, long journey through stoic mediocrity to... I don't know...retirement or death.

Wow.

I tried to laugh at myself. I'd just gone from a canceled tennis date to death in under thirty minutes. Maybe I needed tequila instead of tea.

One of the games below me ended. Two men shook hands and walked off the court.

I recognized James Gillen—Layla Kendrick's, née Gillen's, older brother. If I had to say, he was the one person in the club worse off than me.

I didn't know if that made me feel worse or better. Better for me, I suppose, since I'm human and not a saint. But worse for him—I definitely felt worse for him. Again, since I was human and capable of empathy.

I wouldn't wish his life on anyone.

James had been high-school sweethearts with my gorgeous and much sought-after friend Brooklyn. And up until this July, they'd been blissfully engaged.

They'd spent a full year planning one of the greatest weddings in the history of weddings. It would have been magnificent. In fact, it was magnificent—at least at the start, right up to the moment Brooklyn left James at the altar in front of five hundred guests and a stringer for the local newspaper.

I didn't blame Brooklyn, at least not completely. By all accounts her handsome, successful new husband, Colton Kendrick, was a real catch.

It hadn't surprised me at all that Brooklyn would have two great guys competing to marry her. Brooklyn sparkled. She always had, and I expected she always would. And that sparkle drew men—flies to honey and all that. It was a gift.

I wished I had that gift.

I pretended for a second that I did. I gave a Brooklynesque smile at my faint reflection in the tennis court viewing window. I tried to toss my hair the way she did, but it was fastened back in a tight braid, so my toss didn't work out.

I gave a real smile then, a laughing-at-myself smile. I took a sip of the lukewarm tea, wishing it really was tequila.

Librarians didn't sparkle. We weren't supposed to sparkle. We were practical and dependable, admirable qualities for sure. But there were no flies coming to my honey.

I removed my sports glasses and reached for my everyday pair as a couple strolled into the lounge. With my glasses back in place, I recognized them. My besieged heart sank another big notch.

It was Henry Reginald Paulson III with his pretty, bubbly girlfriend clinging to his arm.

She was tall, thin and blonde, with shiny white teeth and luscious eyelashes that seemed to blink too often. I thought her name was Kaylee or Candi or something. I'd never seen her play tennis, but nobody cared about her tennis skills. Athletic ability was obviously not on the top of Henry's wish list for a girlfriend.

The Paulson family, with Henry's parents at the center, practically ran the Harbor Club, hosting fund-raisers and sitting on the board. They were third- and fourth-generation members of the private club. Henry was the crown prince.

He was also my ex. He'd unceremoniously dumped me back in May, May 25 to be exact. It was the same day the Northridge Library had celebrated my fifth anniversary as an employee. It meant I was entitled to an extra week's holiday leave, and I moved up to parking lot B—two blocks closer to the civic building. I'd looked forward to those perks, and I'd been excited to meet Henry to cap off the day.

But our celebratory dinner at the Tidal Rush Restaurant turned into a lonely cab ride home in my blue crepe dress before the appetizers had even been served. I'd tossed the Northridge plaque into my bottom drawer and left it there.

Henry had said that night we'd stay friends. He told me I had many good qualities. He said he admired me and that one day I was going to make some man very happy.

He hadn't complained about my plain brown hair, my glasses, my understated wardrobe or my modest height. But since he'd replaced me with my physical and stylistic opposite, I could draw my own conclusions.

Henry spotted me from across the lounge.

He smiled and waved as if we had, in fact, remained friends. We hadn't even spoken since the breakup.

I wished I wasn't sitting alone right now.

I wished I was out on the court playing tennis with Sophie.

I wished I was anywhere or anything but—

"Hi, Nat." It was a man's voice directly beside my table.

I looked up to see James.

Thank you, James.

If James would only stand still and chat for a minute or two, then I wouldn't have to look completely pathetic while Henry and Kaylee joined a boisterous clique of members at a central table.

"Hi, James," I said.

"Waiting for someone?" he asked, with a glance around the expansive room.

I lifted my phone as evidence. "Sophie just canceled. I'll have to give up our court time."

"Is she okay?"

"She's fine. Something came up." Something better than me.

"Mind if I sit down?"

"No, please." I pointed to one of the other chairs at the table for four. I honestly could have kissed him right there and then.

"I'm dying of thirst," he said. He signaled to the waiter and glanced at my little teapot. "You want something else?"

The waiter promptly arrived.

"A beer," James said to him. "Whichever local one you have on tap today."

Then James looked to me, raising his brows in a question.

"Sounds good," I said.

It wasn't four o'clock yet, but on a day like this, I was in.

It took him a second to get settled into his chair.

"Good game?" I asked.

"Caleb's a strong player. I got a serious workout."

James had obviously taken a quick shower. His hair was slightly damp and he'd changed into a pair of charcoal slacks and a white dress shirt with the sleeves rolled up.

He was a good-looking man, tall and fit. He didn't have Henry's flamboyance or gregariousness. He wasn't tennis-club royalty. But he'd always been respected for his playing skills.

Now...well, now he had to contend with the tactless gossip over Brooklyn running from St. Fidelis in her wedding gown. Consensus had it that James had been marrying up, and it came as no huge surprise to some that Brooklyn had dumped him for a better offer.

I could only imagine they were saying similar things about me. My relationship with Henry had only lasted a few months, but people probably assumed I was a quick fling for him, a roll in the hay, a temporary detour to the short and mousy side.

I wondered when it would stop feeling so humiliating.

I hoped James hadn't heard the worst of the Brooklyn gossip. I really didn't subscribe to the misery-loves-company school of thought. Nope, the fewer people in the world who felt the way I did right now, the better.

"I might have to do some biking later to make up for the lost game," I said, switching my thoughts to something more productive.

I wasn't a fitness freak by any stretch, but I did count on my Saturday tennis games for a weekly workout.

"Where do you ride?" he asked.

"Along the Cadman lakeshore, mostly. My apartment's only a few blocks from Green Gardens."

"I've ridden there," he said. "It's nice in the fall."

The waiter arrived with two frosty mugs of beer.

"Can you cancel Ms. Remington's court time?" James asked as the waiter put coasters under the mugs.

"Certainly, sir."

I thanked them both with a smile. Then I gripped the handle of the generous mug. "It might not be a very long bike ride after I finish this."

James smiled at my joke and held his own beer in a toast.

I bargained with myself out loud. "Maybe I'll go tomorrow morning instead."

Then as I clinked my glass to his, I caught sight of Henry, his arm around Kaylee as he regaled the four other people at their table with some kind of a story.

"Something wrong?" James asked me.

I realized I was frowning. "No. Nothing." I turned my attention back to James.

But he looked over his shoulder and saw Henry.

"Ahhh, Paulson. That's got to be aggravating."

Aggravating wasn't exactly the word I'd use.

"It is," I said.

James's dark blue eyes turned sympathetic.

I didn't want his pity. And I didn't want him to think I was wallowing in my own misery, either—even though I was. To be fair, I was wallowing in more than just my breakup with Henry. I liked to think I'd made a bit of progress from the breakup. But on aggregate, there was a lot to wallow in about my life right now.

I tried to shake it off. "It's nothing compared to you."

The words were out before I realized how they were going to sound. I'd managed to be both tactless and insensitive all in one fell swoop. I tried to backtrack. "I mean... I didn't... I'm sorry."

"I'd rather you blurted it out than silently thought it—or whispered it like everybody else around here." He scanned the room. "And it *is* nothing compared to me. I was dumped on a much grander scale, an epic scale, the scale to end all scales here at the Harbor Club."

I wanted to disagree. I should probably disagree. But he was right, and if I said anything other than that, I'd be lying.

"How are you holding up?" I asked in a quieter tone.

"It's weird," he said. Then he took another drink. "I keep finding her stuff in my apartment. I don't know what to do with it. Do I send it to her? Do I store it for her? Do I burn it?"

"Burn it." The words had popped out. "Wait, I shouldn't have said that."

But James chuckled. "I like your style."

Brooklyn was my close friend. But even close friends did bad things. And James deserved to be angry with Brooklyn. He deserved to light something on fire.

"Then can you explain your gender to me?" I asked James. Somehow one beer had turned into two.

"I doubt it," he said.

"Are they just shallow?"

"Mostly."

"I mean, look at Candi over there."

"I think her name is Callie."

"Not Kaylee?"

"Should we ask?"

"No!"

James chuckled at my panicked-sounding tone. I wasn't really panicked. I was just…well, self-conscious about even caring who Henry-the-cad was dating now.

I lowered my voice and leaned in. "Is she really what all men want?"

James slid a surreptitious glance to their table. "Some do."

"Some or most?"

"Okay, lots."

I heaved a sigh. I wasn't exactly disappointed, since I'd known the answer all along. Still, it didn't renew my faith in men in any way.

"Women are no better," James said.

"We're not obsessed with looks."

"You're pretty obsessed with looks, but you're even more obsessed with power and prestige."

I couldn't completely disagree. "We also want compassion and a sense of humor."

"A sense of humor is pretty hard to quantify."

"I suppose. And you can't exactly see it coming from across the room."

James tapped his mug on the table as if for emphasis. "See? Women are just like men. It's human nature to start with looks. Maybe it's because they're the easiest benchmark when you first meet."

"I wish I had them." The minute I made the admission, I wanted to call it back.

James wasn't my best friend, and this wasn't a heart-to-heart Saturday afternoon talk in yoga pants.

Now he was scrutinizing me, and I wished the floor would open right up and swallow me whole.

"Why do you say that?" he asked.

The answer was painfully obvious. "Because it *would* be nice. You must get it. You were with Brooklyn all those years."

Anybody who fell for Brooklyn understood the appeal of a beautiful woman.

"I mean, why do you think you don't have them?"

It was my turn to stare back at him.

"Hello?" I said. I pointed to my chin. "Plain Jane librarian here."

"Well, you're not exactly glamorous," he said.

"Thank you for making my point." I tamped down the ego pinch. I hadn't really expected James to insist I was beautiful. Still, blunt honesty was hard to take sometimes.

"But you're pretty."

I shook my head. "Oh, no. You can't backpedal now. Your first reaction is your true reaction."

"My first reaction was that you have the raw material."

"Be still my beating heart."

He grinned at me.

I had been joking. Well, I was mostly joking. I could make light of my looks or I could get depressed about them. I wasn't going to get depressed.

Plain was fine. It was ordinary and normal, and people led perfectly happy lives with plain looks. In fact, most did—the vast, overwhelming majority of people had looks that were plain in some way or another. The bombshells among us were few and far between.

"You did get a look at the guy Brooklyn married, right?" James asked.

I definitely got a look at him. I hadn't attended Brooklyn's wedding to Colton Kendrick, but I'd gone to Layla's wedding right after when she married Colton's twin brother, Max. Colton and Max were rich, rugged and handsome. They also seemed to be truly great guys.

I nodded to James.

He made a sweeping gesture down his chest. "Then you can guess how I feel."

"You have the raw material," I said.

I tried not to smile. I knew heartbreak wasn't funny.

James shook his head and seemed to fight his own smile. "Are we going to sit here and wallow in it?"

"That's the opposite of what I want to do," I said.

"What do you want to do?" he asked.

I gave my racket a pointed look. "I wanted to play tennis."

"Not this minute. I mean more broadly, in life, going forward?"

"I was thinking about getting a cat."

"Seriously?"

"No. Not really."

"A cat's a big commitment."

"You don't like cats?"

He seemed to ponder the question. "I'd probably go for a dog. But I'd have to get a house first."

I knew he and Brooklyn had planned to go house shopping right after the wedding. I wasn't going to touch that one.

"A dog does need a yard," I said instead.

"Maybe I'll buy a house," he said. But he didn't look enthusiastic about it.

I wished I could afford a house. It would be years before I had a down payment saved up for even a condo. I'd be staying in my loft apartment for the foreseeable future.

"Real estate is a good investment," I said.

James was an economist. I didn't exactly know what he did on a day-to-day basis in his job, but it seemed to me economists would be interested in good investments.

"It's definitely a good time to lock in an interest rate."

"But?" I could hear the *but* in his sentence.

"It's hard to know what to look for when you can't picture your future."

The statement seemed particularly sad.

While I searched for the right response, my phone rang.

"Go ahead," James said, lifting his beer and sitting back in his chair.

"It's Sophie." I was curious about her lunch date, but I wasn't about to have an in-depth conversation here in front of James. I swiped to accept the call. "I'll tell her I'll call her back."

"You want privacy?" He made to leave.

"No." I shook my head. I didn't want to chase him away. "It's fine."

"Hi, Sophie," I said into the phone.

"Bryce has a friend," she said.

"Uh...that's nice. Listen, can I call you—"

"As in *a friend*," she said. She was talking fast, enthusiasm lighting her voice. "A friend for you, a guy who wants to meet you. We can go on a double date. Dinner tonight. Does tonight work for you?"

I found myself meeting James's gaze.

"Nat?" Sophie asked. "Are you there?"

"Yes, I'm here."

I didn't know why I was hesitating. No, I didn't have plans for Saturday night, and of course I wanted to meet a new guy. What single girl wouldn't want to meet a new guy?

It seemed like Bryce and Sophie were hitting it off. I knew Sophie had good taste in men. If Bryce was a good guy, it stood to reason that his friend would be a good guy. I'd like to meet a good guy.

"What time?" I asked.

"Seven. We'll swing by your place. You might want to meet us downstairs. I mean…you know…"

Sophie was not a fan of my utilitarian loft apartment. She bugged me about fixing it up all the time.

Myself, I didn't see the point in spending a lot of money on cosmetics. The place was perfectly functional. Then again, if the guy thought like her, I didn't want to put him off straightaway because of my questionable taste in decorating.

"Sure," I said. "Seven o'clock downstairs."

"Perfect!" She sounded really happy.

I ended the call.

"Sorry about that," I said.

James waved away my apology. "Girls' night out?"

"Not exactly. Double date."

James sat forward again. "Blind date?"

"Yes." I took a sip of my beer "I haven't been on one of those in a while."

"I guess your dry spell is over."

I didn't particularly like calling it a dry spell. It made me sound desperate—like I was thirsty for a man.

All I really wanted was to move completely and permanently on from Henry. I supposed that made me thirsty enough. There wasn't much point in dressing it up.

"That's one way to put it," I said to James.

He lifted his mug in another toast. "Well, congratulations."
I touched my mug to his again and laughed at myself. I'd just been moaning about my loneliness. I should be thrilled about having plans for tonight. I would be thrilled. I was thrilled.
"That's better," James said. "Smile and be happy."

Two

Since I hadn't thought to ask Sophie where we were going for dinner, I went middle of the road on an outfit—a pair of gray slacks and a monochrome animal print blouse. The blouse was V-necked, with long sleeves, and the rayon fabric was loose and comfortable. I liked the way it draped over my hips, asymmetrical from front to back.

I put my hair into a loose braid with a long tassel. My hair grew fast, and it had been a while since my last trim. If I left it completely loose, it felt wayward and messy, making it hard to relax while I ate. This way, it was up out of the way but still wispy around my face, so I didn't look too severe.

I wore a little more makeup than usual—though it was always disappointing when the carefully applied mascara got lost behind my glasses. I put in some dangling gold earrings Layla had given me for my last birthday, and went with a pair of medium heel, charcoal boots.

I threw a sweater over my arm since September weather was unpredictable, and I hooked my trusty brown leather tote over my shoulder. It was heavy. I often thought I should streamline the contents. But the truth was I liked to be prepared—wallet, keys, sunglasses, comb, lotion, tissues and wipes, hair elastics in case of unexpected wind, a couple of coins in each denomination, enough hidden cash for a taxi home within a twenty-five-mile radius, credit cards, my phone, a flash drive—because, well, these days you never knew when you might need to unexpectedly download data—and self-defense spray because, well, these days you just never knew.

When I met Sophie at the street entrance, I rethought my look. Then again, I usually rethought my look as soon as I saw how Sophie had dressed.

She was wearing a short black scooped-neck A-line dress with just enough swish to make it fun. Over top, she'd put a faded jean jacket with a few scattered rhinestones on the collar and shoulders. The sparkling gems echoed her choker and earrings. She carried a little clutch purse, and wore strappy black platform sandals.

Her highlighted light brown hair was thick and lustrous, framing her dark brown eyes and full lips.

"Hi, Nat," she said. "You look terrific."

I didn't feel terrific. Then again, I hadn't been going for terrific. So, there was that.

"You look fantastic," I said.

She linked her arm with mine. "Bryce is a super good guy. He got us a sedan instead of a taxi. Classy or what?"

"Classy," I said. "Where are we going?"

"Russo's on the waterfront."

"Nice," I said. Russo's was a very trendy Italian restaurant. "Do we have reservations?" Saturday nights were crowded everywhere downtown.

"You don't need to worry about that. Bryce can worry about that."

"So, you don't know if he made them or not." I wasn't being obsessive, merely practical.

"We're on a *date*, Nat. Let the guys do the planning."

"Okay." I was still curious, but I wasn't going to belabor the point.

Two men were standing in front of a black sedan parked at the curb.

"This is Bryce," Sophie said of the taller one.

Bryce was easily over six feet. His hair was thick and near jet-black. He had a classically handsome face with brown eyes and a nice smile. His shoulders were square beneath a sport jacket and a white shirt.

"Bryce is head chef at The Blue Fern," Sophie said.

"I didn't know you worked together," I said to Sophie.

She supervised food and beverage service at the local high-end restaurant. I'd had the impression Bryce was a customer she'd met while working.

"I'm sure I told you," Sophie said.

She hadn't. But I decided disputing her memory was pointless.

"Nice to meet you," I said to Bryce, offering to shake hands.

His grip was gentle, his hand broad. "Sophie talks a lot about you to me, but obviously not the other way around."

I couldn't tell if he was offended or not. I decided to take countermeasures just in case. "Our jobs are so different we really don't talk about work very much."

"Nice save," Bryce said, telling me he'd been at least slightly offended.

Sophie and I really didn't talk much about our work. But belaboring the point would only make things worse. I stopped talking.

"And this is Ethan," Sophie said, gesturing to the other man.

If she noticed she'd offended Bryce, she didn't seem particularly worried about it.

Ethan was shorter than Bryce, about Sophie's height in her high-heeled shoes—still a good bit taller than me.

His hair was a sandy blond with a copper hue. His face was on the round side, his eyes a pale blue.

"Nice to meet you too, Ethan," I said, giving him my best smile, since he was my date, and since a woman never knew when she might meet "the one." I tried to imagine Ethan as "the one." I wasn't quite seeing it, but the evening was young.

"Hi, Nat." His grip was firmer than Bryce's.

His mouth was shaped in a smile, but his eyes didn't quite seem to meet mine—odd. It looked like he was focused on my eyebrows.

It made me wonder when I'd last plucked them. Did they look messy? Bushy? I sure hoped those little blond hairs hadn't grown out in between them. That would be embarrassing.

"Do you work at The Blue Fern, too?" I asked him.

"Ethan is a computer engineer," Sophie said. "He has his own business."

"That's impressive," I said.

I'd never been strong in science and technology. Layla had always been the brainy one of the group.

"Our focus is robotics," Ethan said.

"He's a genius," Sophie said.

Ethan gave Sophie a warm smile at the compliment. "The team turns big ideas into reality. And Bryce and Sophie have presented some very exciting concepts."

I didn't understand, so I looked to Sophie for an explanation.

"We're technologically revolutionizing the food service industry," she said with a wide grin.

The way she said it sounded like she was joking, though I didn't completely get what was funny about a technological revolution of the food industry. In my mind I pictured robotic salad tossing.

The image was a little bit funny, so I smiled back at her. "You're turning The Blue Fern into *The Jetsons*? Jet packs and robot waiters?"

Their silence told me I'd got it wrong.

"You're mocking her?" Ethan asked.

I sobered. "No. I didn't... I mean..."

"It's a brave new world," Sophie said, clearly disappointed by my reaction. "You have to progress with the times."

I felt terrible.

"We should get going," Ethan said, his expression telling me I hadn't made a good first impression. So much for judging him. He was judging me.

If Sophie was serious about orchestrating a technological revolution, you'd think she might have mentioned it to her best friend.

Ethan took the front passenger seat while Sophie climbed into the back and pushed to the middle. Bryce made to climb in behind her, so I went around to the opposite door, feeling awkward and self-conscious.

"Bryce and Ethan went to high school together," Sophie said to me while I wrangled my seat belt into the clasp.

"You've been friends all this time?" I was happy to have the conversation move along.

"We weren't friends," Bryce said.

"Oh." I left it at that.

I decided to keep my responses short and sweet from here on in.

"Ethan was a nerd. I was more of a jock," Bryce said. "He went off to university, and I went to culinary school."

"You must have done well," I said. "I mean, if you're a head chef already."

"It's a small place," Bryce said.

"But we have really big plans," Sophie said.

"It sounds like," I said, leaving her an opening to elaborate.

"You've heard about 3-D printing?" she asked me.

I nodded. I didn't know a whole lot about it, library materials not normally being 3-D. Our printers were 2-D. We had color for a price, but that was as high-tech as we got.

The excitement level in Sophie's voice grew as she spoke. "The three of us are partnering on a tech start-up."

"Our patents are pending," Bryce said.

Patents?

"We've got a prototype," Ethan said from the front seat.

"You should see it, Nat," Sophie said.

"It's too big," Bryce said.

"I have some ideas on that," Ethan said.

"But you can't fault the quality," Bryce said.

"We'll need investors," Sophie said. "We need to scale up."

"Once it's perfected," Bryce said.

"We're very close," Ethan said.

I had about a thousand questions for her, starting with: *What the heck?*

"How long have you been at this?" I asked instead.

"A few months," Sophie replied. "I didn't want to jinx it, so I've kept really quiet."

"Even from me?" I felt even more isolated than I had this morning.

It looked like Bryce wasn't such a new guy in Sophie's life, after all. I felt like I was at a business meeting instead of on a date.

"I did," Sophie said. "Sorry about that."

"Just so I'm clear," I said. "You are dating Bryce?"

Bryce threaded his arm through Sophie's. "We started off as colleagues, then friends, and now, well...we've discovered something very special."

"And Ethan brought the tech side," Sophie said.

I assumed Ethan brought the tech side to the business venture and not to the romantic relationship.

"Baker's confectionary is our domain," Ethan piped in. "We're upping the level of precision and sophistication with which restaurants, even small establishments, can conceive, refine, create and serve desserts of every variety."

"You're 3-D printing desserts?" I wasn't exactly wrapping my head around that.

I'd seen a news report once on 3-D printing action figures.

They took a scan of a person's face, cartooned it, and created a personalized action figure.

I got how a printer could squirt colored plastic in a specific pattern. I wasn't seeing how it baked a cake.

"We couldn't even be thinking about this without Ethan," Sophie said. "Bryce brings the culinary expertise, and I'm bringing the business know-how. We're an awesome team."

She reached forward and squeezed Ethan's shoulder.

He put his hand over hers for a second.

"So, like cakes and pies?" I asked, still skeptical.

"Oh, so much more than that," Ethan said.

"You should see how beautiful they are." Sophie smiled and sat back.

"And delicious," Bryce added, looping his arm around her shoulders. "You can build in a level of precision for incredible consistency."

Sophie nodded, looking excited. I was happy for her. She'd always had boundless energy and enthusiasm, and an impressive sense of adventure. Growing up, it was always Sophie who came up with the ideas for our adventures.

It seemed she'd gotten bored at work—but in a good way. She was branching out to a brand-new venture, and it even came with a romance.

The driver pulled to a stop at the curb and I shifted my attention to Russo's front patio. It was a lovely building, decorated with tiny white lights on clusters of potted trees. The walkway and stairs were red cobblestones, and the front door was made of thick oak planks with gold embossed hinges and handles.

Bryce opened the car door and stepped out and turned to help Sophie.

I went out my side and walked over the uneven cobblestones around the back of the car, glad for the moment that I'd gone with sturdy boots.

In her spike high heels, Sophie hung on to Bryce's arm.

Ethan and I fell in behind them.

I felt awkward walking silently beside Ethan.

"You grew up in Seattle?" I asked to break the ice.

"I was three when we moved out from Boston."

"I was born here," I said, keeping the conversational ball rolling. "We lived in Queen Anne."

"Wallingford. My parents are university faculty members."

"His mom's a renowned chemistry professor," Sophie said over her shoulder.

Bryce opened the big door and we all walked into the dim interior of Russo's.

"That's very impressive," I said to Ethan.

"Professor Mary Quinn." He sounded quite proud. "She's published over thirty articles in technical journals. Perhaps you've read some of them?"

I didn't have an immediate response. I wasn't sure why he thought I'd be reading chemistry articles.

"Since you're a librarian," he prompted.

"I'm in the public library. We don't catalog many scientific journals."

He seemed surprised by that. "Really? Have you considered the importance of STEM to young readers? And, really, to any readers?" He took a beat. "STEM stands for science, technology, engineering and mathematics."

I knew what STEM stood for. "It's a matter of capacity. For technical works, I'd refer people to the university library, or maybe the State Association of Chemists."

We'd stopped in front of the reception desk.

"Do you have a reservation?" the hostess asked Bryce.

"Brookside for four," Bryce said.

Sophie turned to us, a little sigh in her voice. "I wish I was that smart."

"You are smart," I said to her.

She had a business degree. She was only twenty-six, and she was already a manager at one of the best boutique restaurants in the city.

"I'm not science smart."

"You're real-world smart, and that's much more practical."

Silence followed my words.

Again.

"There's nothing more practical than science," Ethan said.

"It takes a team," Bryce said.

Ethan kept talking. "Science is responsible for everything from advanced agriculture to green mining techniques to fabric dyes for fashion shows, and all the obvious technologies. Take your cell phone, for instance. It took generations of highly trained scientists to develop the concepts that make a smartphone run."

"And we're grateful for that," Bryce put in.

"Right this way," the hostess said to us.

"I do enjoy my cell phone." I took Bryce's lead and tried to lighten the conversation.

Bryce followed the hostess. Sophie went behind him as we wound our way through the tables.

I took up the rear.

The friendly woman showed us to a booth with a half-circle bench. It was on the second floor overlooking the harbor. After a bit of fumbling over the seating arrangements, I ended up on one end of the bench next to Ethan. Bryce took the other end, and Sophie was sandwiched between the two men.

"Drinks?" Bryce asked, opening the cocktail menu.

"Oh, a cranberry martini for me," Sophie said.

"I'll take one of those," Ethan said.

"I'm having a Canadian whiskey," Bryce said, looking to me.

"A glass of cabernet sauvignon," I said.

A glass now and a glass with dinner, I decided. Then I'd be nicely relaxed.

"This whole thing started when we lost our pastry chef," Sophie said. "And we were having trouble finding a new one with the skills and expertise."

"The ante keeps going up and up," Bryce said.

"Enter technology," Ethan said.

"I did an informal poll of our customers," Sophie explained. "And dessert was the number one determiner of restaurant choice among women. It was only number three for men. They like steak and seafood."

Ethan jumped back in. "Studies show that on a date, especially the first few dates, men go where women want to go."

"And the business world is drastically changing," Sophie said. "There are more women executives."

"They want great dessert on their expense accounts," Ethan said.

"Studies show?" I asked him.

"That's just logic," he said.

"The skill level, the prep area, the prep time," Bryce listed off on his fingers. "There's a reason most restaurants have limited dessert menus, especially the small establishments."

"We knew technology could help," Ethan said. "Hence, the inception of BRT Innovations."

"Our company," Sophie said, pointing to all three of them.

"I see." I didn't see everything yet. But I had a feeling I was going to learn a whole lot more before the night was through.

As a date, the evening hadn't gone particularly well. As a business meeting, it had gone quite a bit better.

I hadn't exactly kept up, but I'd learned how much time, thought and energy had gone into the idea for Sweet Tech. If everything they said came to fruition, my friend Sophie really was going to technologically revolutionize desserts.

They'd dropped me off at ten thirty.

Ethan had dutifully walked me to the lobby door. He hadn't kissed me, just said good-night and that he'd had a nice time.

I said I'd had a nice time, too. I suspected our level of enthusiasm for each other was about equal.

On the upside, the restaurant had been lovely, the food delicious.

I'd had the grilled sole with a spring greens salad, opting for a brandy instead of dessert. A good decision since, on top of the wine, it had lulled me into a lovely deep sleep.

I felt rested this morning, ready for my bike ride along the lakeshore.

No more jealousy over Sophie's adventure, I decided. No more moaning about being stood up for yesterday's tennis game. I felt like an independent woman in the morning sunshine, pedaling along the paved bike path, up little rises and down small hills, the wind whistling past my ears.

"Good on you." A voice came up on my left side.

I looked sideways and realized my glasses were sliding down my nose.

I pushed them into place and saw James coming up to pedal alongside me.

"I wasn't sure if you were serious," he said.

"I was serious. I like bike riding."

"I can see that."

I smiled. I was happy to see him. We'd joked quite a lot yesterday, and I'd had fun.

"I prefer rowing," he said.

I knew he'd been on a championship team in college. "Yet, here you are."

"Here I am. You inspired me."

The idea of inspiring James amused me. "Like your own personal trainer? 'Get your butt out of that bed, Gillen! Gear up! Outside! Give me twenty!'"

James laughed at my imitation of a drill sergeant. "Twenty laps of the lake? That seems a bit ambitious."

"We probably should have packed a lunch," I said, feeling lighthearted in the fresh air and sunshine.

A woman and two children approached us riding the other way, a boy and a girl looking about ten years old. The kids had flushed cheeks and windblown hair and were pedaling hard to keep up with their mother.

James shifted in behind me to give them space to pass. We both stayed tight to the right side of the path.

"How was your date?" he asked after the family passed.

A man was throwing a ball for his dog on the grass beside us, and I kept a watch in front of me as the animal ran close to the path.

"It was fine," I answered.

"Fine as in good, or fine as in meh?"

"Fine as in…mediocre, I guess." Sophie's business plans were secret for now, so I wasn't going to talk about them.

It would have been nice if the date part had gone better. I'd wanted to like Ethan. I mean, he wasn't that bad. Other women might like him just fine.

"Sorry to hear that," James said. "Where did you go?"

"Russo's."

"That sounds nice. Did you have the prime rib?"

"The grilled sole."

"Their prime rib is to die for."

"I'll try that next time."

"Is there going to be a next time?"

"I hope so." Then I realized he meant a next date. "I don't know about a next date. But I'll definitely go back to Russo's."

"Nix the guy, stick with the restaurant. I do like your style, Nat."

"The guy seemed fine." I felt guilty dissing him. "His name was Ethan. He's a tech guy. He seems very smart."

"But no second date? Are you one of those picky women with a long list of qualities you want in a man?"

"What? No. I'm not like that. I don't have a list."

At least, I didn't have one that was written down. But I'd admit there were certain things I was looking for—a sense of humor, for example, a progressive worldview, maybe somewhat more humble than Ethan. And I wouldn't be wild about someone who smoked or drank to excess or who, say, had a gambling addiction.

"You're listing it off now," James said with a tone of amazement.

"I'm not..." But I was.

He'd caught me.

"It's not a long list," I said defensively.

"What's on it?"

"What's on yours?" I asked.

"Are you thirsty?" he asked.

We were coming to a snack bar near a sandy beach and a play area.

"Are you changing the subject?" I asked.

"No, I'm just thirsty."

"Okay. I'll take a sparkling water. But then I want to hear what's on your list."

We both slowed our bikes, coasting to the dark green bike rack set next to a scattered group of picnic tables.

I pushed my bike tire between two bars.

"Spill," I said, smoothing my windblown hair.

I'd pulled it back into a ponytail, but some strands had come loose around my face. I tried not to imagine what I looked like. Some women looked cute when they were all disheveled. I looked messy. On me, messy wasn't cute or sexy or anything other than messy.

"It's a short list," he said, dismounting.

"That should make it easy."

"Not Brooklyn."

I felt a lurch of guilt. I probably should have kept my big mouth shut about relationships. James didn't need this on a leisurely Sunday morning bike ride. I felt terrible.

"Now you give me something," he said.

He didn't sound sad or upset.

I was grateful for that. Maybe I hadn't completely spoiled the morning.

"No gambling addiction," I said.

"Seriously?" he asked as we walked to the counter. "You felt the need to include that on a list?"

"You think I should date a guy with a gambling addiction?" I asked.

The teenage girl behind the counter gave us an odd look.

I thought about clarifying the statement, but it seemed silly to launch into an explanation for a stranger whose life would only intersect with mine for a matter of minutes.

"Two Sparkletts," James said to her. "Plain."

The teenager turned and moved to the cooler.

"I don't think you should date a serial killer, either," he said to me. "But you don't need to put that on a list anywhere. It's obvious."

"I'd rather date an addicted gambler than a serial killer."

The teenager heard that one too, and gave us another puzzled look. "That'll be seven fifty."

James handed her a ten. "No need for change. Thanks."

"Thank you," she said with an appreciative smile.

We each took one of the bottles. I couldn't help but wonder what the clerk thought as we walked away.

"That girl back there thinks I'm dating a gambling addict," I said, twisting off the bottle cap.

"She really doesn't care."

"I suppose not. Still, I hope I didn't accidently set a bad example."

"I think you're safe." James took a long drink. "Now, give me a real one."

"A real what."

"A real item on your list."

I wanted to tell him to give me a real item, too. I didn't think "not Brooklyn" was legitimate. But I didn't want to risk upsetting him.

"Good sense of humor," I said.

"Too generic," he said.

"It's legitimate."

"What else?"

"A progressive worldview."

"What does that mean?"

"It means you're progressive." I kept my expression deadpan. "You know, in your worldview."

James grinned. "Touché."

"You give me one."

"Me? But I'm a sad sack recovering from utter heartbreak."

I took in his überinnocent expression. "I *knew* that was a ruse." I shoved him with my upper arm.

"Not buying it?" he asked.

"Dish."

"Okay, let me see...hardworking."

"And you say *I'm* too generic."

"You think I should date a lazy woman?"

"Depends. Exactly how good does she look eating bonbons in front of daytime television?"

"Nobody looks good doing that."

We came to our bikes and stood there while we finished our drinks.

"I don't know what I'm looking for," I said.

"Love?" James asked.

"Now, *that's* the generic answer."

"But true." He took my empty bottle from me.

I knew he was right. "But how do you find it?"

I was serious. I felt like it had always eluded me. I mean, I'd liked Henry a lot, but with him, even when things were going well, it sure didn't feel like the poems and stories said it would.

James headed for the recycle bin. "You look really hard," he called back over his shoulder.

He tossed the bottles and started back. "Meet a lot of people, I guess. Statistically speaking, that'll give you the best shot at falling in love."

We mounted up.

"There are people everywhere," James said as we continued down the path.

He pointed to the beach. "There's one, and another, and another. Take your pick."

I chuckled as I pedaled beside him. It was silly, and it was funny, and it felt good to laugh at life.

"What about her?" I asked as we came up on a pretty woman in a white bathing suit cover-up.

"Mommy, Mommy." A two-year-old boy threw himself in her arms.

"Taken," James said.

"Either of them?" I joked about two women in their sixties chatting in matching lawn chairs.

"Wrong era," he said.

"You're so fussy."

"Him?" James nodded to a shirtless jogger with a tiny dog on a leash.

The twentysomething man's chest was shaved, and his bulging pecs were shiny with oil.

"Too self-obsessed," I said.

"You can tell that just by looking?"

"You can't? How many hours a week at the gym do you suppose that takes?"

"I guess," James said.

"When would he mow the lawn or clean the gutters, or play with the children, or plan date night?"

"You *do* have a long list."

"I'm a practical woman. It's not like I won't help around the house. But I'm not cleaning the gutters all by myself."

"I can respect that," James said.

We pedaled along in our own thoughts until we reached the far end of the lake where the path curved sharply over a wooden bridge that cut across a burbling creek.

"You want to take a rest?" James asked.

A wooden bench was positioned on a concrete pier that jutted out into the lake.

"Sure."

We pulled our bikes onto a grassy patch and took the empty bench.

"I think we're coming at this all wrong," James said.

"Coming at what?" My first thought was the bike ride. Did he not like the lakeshore path?

"It really is a numbers game."

"Riding?"

"No, meeting the opposite sex. You need to meet a lot of eligible people to up your odds."

"Sure."

Who would argue with that? Not me. I might not be a science nerd, but I understood the law of large numbers.

"And we need to bring them to us."

"The eligible people?" I wasn't exactly seeing what he meant. Were we going back to the crowded beach?

"Think about Callie."

My face pinched up. "What about her? And are you sure it's not Kaylee?"

"We can call her whatever you want."

"I always thought she looked like a Candi."

"Candi." He paused in thought. "She does sort of look like a Candi."

"Don't drool," I said.

"I didn't mean it like that."

"Yes, you did."

James grinned unrepentantly. "Okay, we both agree most men would point at her from across the room."

"We do."

He was right. Candi was gorgeous and glamorous and eminently desirable.

"And we agree that most women would point at the Kendrick twins from across the room."

I was surprised he brought them up. "Yes."

Separate or together Colton and Max Kendrick were definitely pointworthy.

"Let's do that," James said.

I was really puzzled now. "Point at people from across the room?"

"No." James shook his head. "Get people to point at us."

Three

"Explain to me again how this works?" I said to James.

We'd finished our ride, locked up our bikes, and found ourselves a table on a deck overlooking the Orchid Club courtyard at the edge of the park.

"The view is perfect," James said. "Are you ready to take notes?"

"I can take notes." I had my phone. It had apps.

He glanced at his watch. "There'll be an event at the club tonight."

"What's the event?"

A waiter came by with a platter of nachos and two beers with quarters of lime stuck in the necks of the bottles. I'd also been eyeing the mini éclairs pictured on the menu. But I'd decide on that later. I was holding out hope the nachos would fill me up enough to take the éclairs off my mind.

"I don't know the event," James said. "It doesn't matter. Whatever it is, it'll be posh. People will be dressed up, looking fine. We're going to pick out our favorites."

"Please tell me we're not going to talk to them."

I was still wearing my yoga pants and an oversize T-shirt. And I was still slightly damp with sweat. The sun was going down, and I was grateful for the propane heater stationed next to our table.

"Were you not paying attention?" James asked, looking stern.

I looked to the club entrance. "Did I miss something?"

"*We're* not approaching them. *They're* going to approach us."

"Dressed like *this*?" I gestured to my chest.

"Not these people. Other people. Future people. Tonight, we pick out the pointworthy people and take notes on what makes them pointworthy. Then, we replicate it."

"What if it's genetics? I'm not getting plastic surgery."

A new hairstyle and a fancy dress were only going to get me so far. It's not like I'd never dressed up before. I'd dressed up plenty of times. Dressing up didn't turn me into Brooklyn or Sophie or anyone else.

James was giving me a horrified look. "Who said anything about plastic surgery?"

"What if we decide I need a new nose? Or..." I glanced down at my chest. "Upgraded breasts?"

"You don't need upgraded breasts!"

He gave a glance around at the other tables and moved his chair closer in, lowering his voice. "I told you, you already have the raw material."

"I'm not so sure about that. Wait. Look. There's a limo."

I pulled out my phone and hit the notes app. "Who is it?"

A man got out of the back seat.

He looked about fifty.

"Nice tux," I said.

"Formal wear gets your attention?" James asked.

"Formal wear is good, depending on the occasion. I wonder if this is a wedding."

"Could be the father of the bride," James said.

The man extended his hand and helped a middle-aged woman out of the limo.

She was followed by two younger men in business suits.

"Which one attracts your attention?" James asked. "Don't think, just blurt it out."

"The guy with dark hair."

"Why?"

"He's tall."

"I could put lifts in my shoes," James said.

"You're tall," I said to him.

"Other men are taller."

"You're tall enough."

James was well over six feet. I'd say six-two. A whole lot taller than that and the height started to be a detractor. There was a perfect sweet spot. He was in it.

"What else?" he asked me.

"His shoulders," I said. "They're broad, but it's more than that. There's something to the set of his shoulders. It makes him look confident. Confident is good."

"Confident shoulders." James flexed his.

I chuckled. "Yes. Confident shoulders."

Another vehicle pulled up. This was a big white SUV.

Four girls piled out wearing identical aquamarine dresses.

"Wedding," James said.

"Definitely."

We were both silent for a moment while they settled themselves into a group.

James munched on a nacho.

"So, which one?" I asked.

"Auburn hair," he said.

"You like auburn hair?"

He shook his head. "It's not the hair color. It's... I would say the shape of her figure and the brightness of her smile."

I jotted down "bright smile."

I found myself running my tongue over my teeth. I'd whitened them a few months ago. But maybe it was time to have it professionally done. I needed a dental checkup soon. I could easily get some whitening at the same time.

It couldn't hurt.

"She has a graceful walk," James said.

"I could practice that," I said.

He looked at me. "I never paid any attention to your walk. Walk somewhere and let me look."

The request made me super self-conscious. "No."

He pointed. "Over to the exit and back."

"I'm not going to walk for you."

"How can I help you if you won't let me assess you?"

Assess me? "I'd feel ridiculous."

"Well, get the heck over that. I'm going to do whatever you want."

I couldn't let that opportunity stay hanging. "What*ever* I want?"

"You know what I mean. I'll walk. I'll talk. I'll make confident shoulders. Come on, Nat. If this is going to work, we have to trust each other."

I realized he was right. Everything he'd said and done so far made me believe he was sincere. I should get over myself and take his help.

It was either that or cats, cats and tea, tea and cats until I was old and gray and alone.

I stood. "Don't you dare tell anyone about this, especially not Layla."

I'd be mortified if he told his sister that I was on a self-improvement binge.

"You think I want Layla to know what we're doing? You think I want *anyone* to know?"

"So, our secret?"

"Yes."

"To the grave?"

"You want me to pinky swear?"

"That would be good."

He solemnly held up his pinky.

I hooked mine around it, and we both broke into twin grins.

"I pinky swear," he said.

"So do I."

His hand was warm and strong, his skin rougher than mine. It felt odd to touch him, and I realized how rarely it happened.

I'd seen James hug Brooklyn countless times. He hugged Layla, of course. And I'd even seen him hug Sophie—who pulled pretty much everybody into hugs at one point or another.

James and I, on the other hand, had always kept a respectful distance.

I hadn't thought about it until now.

But now I was thinking about it.

He dropped his hand from mine.

"Walk," he said.

I turned, took a breath and walked straight to the exit. There I turned and walked back, trying really hard not to feel utterly stupid.

"More glide," he said when I got back to the table.

"What do you mean?"

"Smoother, don't clunk when you walk, and keep your feet closer together, more like you're walking on a line than on the two sides of a railroad track."

"A *railroad track*?" Just how unattractive was my walk?

"Do it again," he said.

It was on the tip of my tongue to refuse.

But I told myself to buck up. Maybe my ugly walk had been the problem all these years. I wondered why nobody had said anything before now.

I glanced around to make sure the people at the other tables weren't paying attention. They weren't.

I breathed again, really deep this time.

I turned and walked—glided, I hoped. I pretended I was on a balance beam, moving my feet together with each step.

I turned.

I couldn't look at James.

I picked a spot in the trees above his head and I did my best to glide back.

"Hmm," he said.

Embarrassed, I sat down before he could tell me to do it again.

"Hmm?" I mimicked. "I get a hmm?"

"It was better. I think."

"You *think*?"

"You seemed a bit stiff."

"Well, of *course* I was stiff. I could feel you watching me."

"We'll practice."

"We?"

"I'll do the shoulder thing."

I looked back down at the courtyard to see that three more vehicles had arrived. "Oh, I'm going to find something way better than the shoulder thing for you to practice."

I was definitely not going to be in this alone.

"Bring it on," he said.

I watched two more couples get out of their cars.

Valets had arrived and were moving the cars away as more people turned up.

"That guy," I said to James. "The one in the blue blazer."

"You like him?" James squinted. "Next time we should bring binoculars."

"We're going to be stalkers?"

"Private eyes. Investigators. We're investigators investigating beautiful people."

"It seems a bit invasive to me."

"What do you like about blue blazer guy?"

"He looks relaxed." I gazed at James to contrast the two men. "You look uptight."

"I do?"

I nodded. "You do. You look critical, like the world isn't quite measuring up to your standards and you're about to tell it why.

That guy down there, he looks like he loves the world and can't wait to meet it and have fun with it."

James gazed at the courtyard. "Interesting. I'm not sure how I practice that."

"Tequila." The suggestion jumped out of my brain.

"I'm game." He munched on another nacho. "But I'm not sure how much tequila will help with your walking problem."

I smiled and reached for a nacho myself. "Are we really going to do this?"

He met my gaze. "I think we are."

"Embark on a secret mission to make ourselves irresistible to the opposite sex?" I bit down on the nacho. It was delicious, and I was hungry.

"Law of large numbers until we fall in love."

"Okay," I said.

This was by far the oddest thing I'd ever done. But however it turned out, it was going to be way better than cats.

"You *have* to come with us." Sophie shut the heavy door of my apartment behind her.

I lived in what was once an elementary school and had been converted to thirty apartments. I was on the third of three floors in a high-ceilinged loft under what were now murky skylights, with an aging wood floor partially covered in scattered worn rugs. The walls were gray-painted cinder blocks, enclosing a single big room, plus a bathroom.

I'd added a freestanding wooden divider to cordon off the bed. I didn't like making beds, and I didn't want the world to see my failing.

"Nat," Sophie said with an urgency to her tone.

"Did Ethan specifically ask you to invite me?" I was having a hard time believing Ethan wanted another date with me.

Sophie paced to the cluster of sofas and armchairs on one side of the room. "Of *course* he wants you to come. That's the whole point, that the four of us would have fun together again."

"I didn't think he had fun last time." I went to the kitchen area to get a pitcher of iced tea from the fridge.

"Sure he did. Didn't you?"

"I felt a little out of place." I dropped ice cubes into two glasses.

"Why?"

I turned to look at her. "Because all you talked about was the dessert project."

"We talked about other stuff."

I had to grin at that. "A little bit. But it was mostly about Sweet Tech."

"I'm sorry." She dropped down on the arm of one chair. "Are you mad at me?"

I poured the iced tea. "I'm not mad. I didn't say I was mad."

"We didn't mean to be boring. I'm sure Ethan didn't mean to be boring."

"You weren't boring." I crossed the room and handed her a glass. "You were excited. And I'm excited for you. I just don't think Ethan and I are going to work."

"You didn't really give him a chance."

"I didn't feel a spark." I sat down in my favorite burgundy armchair.

I'd moved it and the matching burgundy sofa from my parents' basement on the other side of the city. I bought my brown sofa and the two leather contour chairs from an online reseller. They all surrounded a square glass-topped coffee table.

Sophie took an end of the sofa cornerwise from mine.

"You barely had a chance to get to know him."

That might be true. But I was pretty confident in my impression.

"Did it take a long time with you and Bryce? Could you tell right away that you liked him?"

"We were always friendly," she said. Then she seemed to give it some thought. "I never disliked him. Do you dislike Ethan?"

"I don't know him well enough to dislike him."

She made a mock toast with her iced tea. "Thank you for making my point."

I sighed. I didn't feel like having this argument.

I'd only been home from work for about twenty minutes. But I'd already slipped into a loose cotton T-shirt and a pair of worn blue jeans. I was planning to make a bowl of soup, then putter around in my sundeck garden for a while. The heather was still nice, and the pansies and chrysanthemums would last a few more weeks. I wanted to enjoy my little patch of outdoors as long as the weather held.

Afterward, I was thinking I might search for a video on graceful walking. Surely, I wasn't the only woman in the world with that particular challenge. I didn't want James to frown at me and say *hmm* the next time I tried walking for him.

"My car's out front," Sophie said. "I'll tell Bryce we're going to meet them there. That way you don't have to rush to get ready, and we can come home whenever you want."

"I wasn't planning to celebrate Technology Week," I said.

"This is a fun event. It's not nerdy at all. It's the Things Festival—phones and tablets and home alarm systems. It's stuff you should be learning about anyway. Don't you want to see the hologram exhibit?"

"I was planning to garden after dinner." I knew there was a whine in my voice, but I was feeling a little whiny at the thought of going back out again tonight.

"Come on, Nat. You can garden any old time. And it's way more fun when you're there."

Now I felt selfish. Sophie obviously liked Bryce a lot. She wanted my support, and I should buck up and give it to her.

I glanced at my torn jeans. "Do I have to change?"

"It's definitely come-as-you-are. Flats are better for walking around."

"I haven't eaten yet."

"There'll be vendors."

"With 3-D printed food?" I joked.

She looked worried. "I sure hope not. We're trying to be ahead of the curve."

"That was a joke," I said.

"Oh. Good. It'll be more like burgers and nachos."

"I can live with that," I said, forcing myself to stand up and show some enthusiasm. "Give me a minute."

Leaving Sophie to finish her iced tea, I cut past my bed to the bathroom, freshened my face and tossed my hair into a ponytail.

Then I hoisted my shoulder bag from the bed. I hesitated, testing its weight in my hand for a moment. Deciding to play the odds and be more comfortable, I stuffed the essentials into my jeans pockets—my phone, a credit card, a little bit of money, a mini comb and a couple sticks of gum.

Back in the living area, I laced up my runners and tied a sweater around my waist. "I'm ready."

"You're fast," Sophie said, coming to her feet.

"Do you have to stop and change?" I asked.

She was wearing blue jeans and heeled black boots with a burgundy tunic sweater that had a loose cowl neck and a row of oversize buttons. Her hair was airy and fluffy and framed her face.

"I'll just go like this."

Once again, she looked chic to my utilitarian.

I wasn't going to let myself worry about that. It wasn't like I wanted to impress Ethan.

I locked up and we headed down the central staircase.

My phone buzzed against my butt and I retrieved it from my pocket.

It was James.

For some reason, my chest gave a little lift at the sight of his name.

I didn't want to answer in front of Sophie, but I didn't want to not answer, either. So I slowed my steps and let her get ahead.

"Hi," I said into the phone, sounding more breathless than I'd expected.

"Are you biking?" he asked.

"Heading down the stairs."

"Doing stairs. Good for you." He sounded impressed.

"No, not *doing* stairs, just going down them. I'm with Sophie."

"Oh. I misunderstood. Girls' night out?"

"No, another double date."

There was a pause on the line. "Oh… With mediocre guy?"

I hung back even farther. "I don't think you should call him that. But, yes, with Ethan again." I listened for a second. "James?"

"I shouldn't bother you, then."

"It's no bother. We're just heading out. What's up?"

"I was thinking about the weekend. But you probably have a date."

"I don't have a date." I didn't expect to have a date. I was going along tonight to support Sophie.

I came to the bottom of the stairs as Sophie was on her way out the door.

"What were you thinking?" I asked James.

I wouldn't mind having some plans for the weekend. I wouldn't mind it at all. If nothing else, it would give me a good answer on Friday when people asked what I was doing.

"That we could shop for some new clothes. I don't know anything about the right places or the right designers, but we could look that up. We have to start somewhere."

"We do," I agreed.

I'd never gone clothes shopping with a guy before. I usually went with Sophie and Brooklyn. Which, now that I thought about it, was usually about their clothes and not mine.

I pretty much had a set style: Miles Carerra for blazers and skirts, Nordin for slacks and Mistress Hinkle for blouses. I rarely bought dresses. I stuck with my classic standbys that I'd had for a few years now.

I picked up jeans, yoga pants and T-shirts at the outlet mall. I didn't much care who made them, as long as they fit.

"So?" James prompted.

Sophie had stopped. Holding the door open, she waited, watching me with a puzzled expression.

I tried to look like I was having a business conversation. "What time?"

"I'll text Saturday morning. Around nine?"

"That'll work. I better go. Sophie's waiting."

"Have a mediocre time."

I couldn't help but smile as I started walking. "That's kind of what I'm expecting."

"Who was that?" Sophie asked. "What are you expecting?"

"I'm expecting the Things Festival to be interesting," I said.

"That's the spirit."

She didn't press me for more information on the phone call, and I didn't volunteer. The James and Nat self-improvement project was going to stay a closely guarded secret.

As we climbed into Sophie's car, my phone pinged.

I checked to see the message was from James.

Enjoying the mediocrity?

I sent a smiley face back, because he'd made me smile.

"What's going on?" Sophie asked as she pulled into traffic.

"Work," I said.

I didn't explain what kind of work. And creating a whole new me was going to take a lot of work. It was going to take a *whole* lot of work.

So I reasoned that I wasn't lying. I was misdirecting. Misdirecting wasn't exactly noble, but it wasn't the worst sin in the world, either.

And I was being Sophie's wingman tonight—reluctantly but with good humor, I was helping a friend. I hoped the two things balanced each other out.

* * *

On Saturday morning, James picked me up in a low-slung red convertible.

It shone bright under the sunshine, looking out of place against the dusty curb.

"Is this new?" I asked, shading my eyes. My clip-on sunglasses were in my purse, and I decided I was going to need them.

As usual, I was glad to be prepared.

"I bought it yesterday," James said. "What do you think?"

I didn't know what I thought. Mostly I thought, *Holy cow!* "It's very red."

"Isn't it?"

"Yes."

"I went to the dealer at lunchtime."

"Uh-huh." I was trying to think of something positive to say.

The car was pretty ugly, low to the ground, a bit boxy. The black interior was harsh. It looked like something a gangster might have owned in the '70s. And I wasn't sure about owning a convertible in Seattle. We had plenty of nice days in the summer, I supposed. But we had plenty of rain, too. And the winters were a mixture of slush and ice. It was hard to tell how well the car would stay heated.

"I took a good look at everything they had," James said.

"And you picked this?"

"You hate it."

"I... It's... It definitely doesn't seem like something you'd pick."

"I know. That's the point. I picked the one I wouldn't have picked. It's a *new me* car." He opened the passenger door to let me in.

"I suppose."

If we were changing who we were, I guessed what you drove was part of that.

I had a ten-year-old crossover, hunter green. It was serviceable if not beautiful. It definitely wasn't flashy.

I held on to the back of the bucket seat as I lowered myself inside. It was low, really low. If we had to hide under the trailer of a semi, we were going to fit just fine.

James shut the door, and I felt like I was sitting on the sidewalk.

He rounded the back and got in on the driver's side.

He popped a pair of sunglasses on his face and adjusted the rearview mirror.

"Do you like the way it drives?" I asked.

He started the engine, and it throbbed beneath us, roaring under the hood.

Since the top was down, I could hear every piston.

"It corners like a supercar," he said.

"I take it that's good?"

"It's very good."

"Okay," I said.

"Buckle up."

I snapped myself in.

The tires chirped as we jolted away. James wound out the engine in first, then grabbed second gear and we lurched forward.

I was sucked back against my seat.

He quickly braked, since we were coming to a red light.

"Comfortable?" he called to me above the noise and the wind.

"The seat's nice," I said.

"What?" He cupped his ear.

"The seat's nice!" I called out.

He nodded.

The light turned green and we lurched forward again.

It had good acceleration, I'd give it that.

We slowed and turned onto the I-5 on-ramp, and James pressed on the gas.

We were going faster than traffic and easily merged.

Something hit me in the forehead. It stung, and I flinched.

"What?" he asked me.

I reached up to find a smashed bug on my forehead.

I held it out to him. "I'm not crazy about having the top down."

He laughed at me.

The cad.

Okay, I'd admit it was kind of funny.

"You'd think the windshield would be a little higher," he said.

Then he flinched, and I saw a black spot on his cheek.

This time I laughed at him.

He geared down. He flipped on his signal and took an exit.

"This sucks," he said.

"It's a little bit funny," I said.

"This is a stupid car."

"You don't like it?" I wanted to ask if he'd even test-driven it before he bought it. It seemed like an awfully impulsive purchase.

"You hate it," he said.

"It's not about what I like."

"Okay, I hate it."

We were slowing down now, and the noise wasn't quite so oppressive.

"So why did you buy it?"

"Like I said, I didn't want to buy something I liked."

"Like a practical sedan?"

He turned onto a side street. "I've had one of those for years."

"Maybe you went too far the other way."

"Maybe."

"You know." I was thinking this through as I spoke. "We're going to have to like the people we turn into."

He turned into the empty lot of a small park. "The danger in that is that we'll stay exactly as we are. We have to expand."

"We can choose the direction we expand in."

"We can't trust our own instincts. Our own instincts are what brought us to where we are."

I had to admit, he had a point.

He brought the car to a halt in a parking spot facing a baseball diamond.

"How about this," I said. "I'll trust your instincts, and you trust mine. That way we change it up, but we don't..." I gestured to the dashboard. "We don't do something completely stupid."

"Are you calling me stupid?"

"I'm calling this car stupid. It's going to be freezing in the winter, if you don't lose it in the first snowfall. I feel like a kindergarten kid sitting down so low. The black leather looks like something a gangster would own. And it's butt ugly, James. Fire-engine red? What, are you having a midlife crisis?"

James started to laugh.

"I'm just saying..."

"The dealership's only about five miles from here."

"Can you take it back?" That seemed like the best course of action to me—the very best course of action.

"I can probably exchange it for something else."

I breathed a sigh. "I think you should."

"I think I should, too. And I think you're picking the next one."

"What?"

He couldn't be serious.

He put it in Reverse. "We've determined we can't trust my taste."

"But... I can't pick you out a car. A pair of blue jeans, sure. Maybe a tux. Maybe even a hat."

"You think I need a hat."

"No. I'm not saying you need a hat. You don't need a hat. You have very nice hair."

He did have very nice hair, thick and dark, classically cut in a way that showed off his square jaw and gorgeous blue eyes.

He headed for the parking lot exit. "You're picking the new one, Nat."

I tried to be helpful. "You just have to go... I don't know...a little less...flamboyant."

"I'm sure you will."

"I'm not doing it alone, James."

"Ah, but you are. You volunteered."

"I did not."

"And I quote—*you* trust *my* instincts."

He looked completely serious.

I considered for a moment the strategy of choosing something completely ridiculous, like a superlifted pickup truck. Then he'd have to overrule me. That could work.

"I can hear what you're thinking," he said as we tooled along a main road.

"You cannot."

"You're thinking if you botch it, I'll have to take over. I'm not going to take over. This one's on you."

"You've lost your mind."

"Nope. I've gained yours. I think I got the good end of that trade."

I couldn't help but smile. "Then are you going to pick *me* out a new car?"

He glanced over at me. "Absolutely."

I'd been joking. "I can't afford a new car."

"It doesn't have to be brand-new. But cars are like clothes. They introduce us to the world."

I gestured to the dashboard again. "And *this* is what you wanted to say?"

"I plead temporary insanity."

Four

I chose a gunmetal-gray SUV. It had sleek curves, a tough-looking black grille, diamond-shaped headlights, big durable wheels that would stand up to any weather conditions, and comfortable seats that made you feel like you were sitting on a cloud.

I didn't analyze my choice too closely. I just knew that if three men drove up, one in a sports car, one in a sedan and one in an SUV, I'd be most interested in the SUV guy.

Maybe it projected strength, or maybe there was room in the back for my eventual kids. It could easily have been anthropology and my primal brain influencing my decision. But I picked it, and James bought it, and we left a very happy salesman behind.

"This is way better," James said as we drove along I-5 and he fiddled with the controls on the dashboard.

"I can hear every word you say," I said. "It's like a miracle."

"Yeah, yeah. I get it. Your taste is better than my taste."

I felt a moment of doubt. "As long as you truly like it."

"I like it a lot." His smile turned warm and his tone was sincere.

I liked how his voice sounded in my ears. I liked how the warmth made me feel—like I'd done something right and he was happy about it.

"We're going downtown," he said. "I researched the 'it' places to buy a tux."

"You're seriously buying a tux? You can rent those, you know."

"Be honest, Nat. Do you go for the guy in an off-the-rack rented tux, or for the one in a perfectly cut, perfectly fitting *owned* tuxedo?"

"You can't just—"

"Answer the question, partner."

"Owned," I admitted. "But I'm not falling for a bankrupt guy, either."

James grinned. "I'm not going bankrupt."

"Bold words from a man spending like a drunken sailor."

"I don't need to cash in the 401(k) just yet."

"You have a 401(k)?"

"Why? Is that sexy?"

I batted my eyelashes at him. "Depends on the size. Women like a man who can provide."

"Should I have my tax status tattooed on my forehead?"

"A little too showy, I'd say. You'll have to work it into conversation."

"And that won't be showy?"

I patted the dashboard. "If you show up in this baby wearing your new tux, you won't have to brag about money."

"And you say men are shallow."

"I didn't say you were shallow. I said you were obsessed with looks."

He exited the interstate onto the downtown streets. "Fair enough. We pretty much are. But your gender seems all about money."

"It's not so much the money."

"Ha."

"It's the power, all the power things—good height, broad shoulders, confident stance, intelligent, good career and, as it turns out, a really nice SUV."

He deepened his tone to übersexy. "That's because it has tall tires and deep treads."

I raised my fingertips to my chest. "Be still my beating heart."

He grinned along with me.

We made our way into downtown and found a spot in an underground parkade. From there, James led the way to Brookswood, a high-end store near the waterfront. I'd never been inside it. I'd sure never planned to shop here.

"I assume they sell tuxes here," I said as we passed through a tall glass doorway into what felt like a rarefied environment.

It was nearly silent. The lighting was muted. The floor was a plush carpet. The displays and stands were placed far apart. It was clear to me that successful people came here to buy very expensive things.

We'd entered into the purse and shoe section.

I didn't see any price tags on the nearby merchandise. It was probably just as well. The prices would likely freak me out. Good thing we were shopping for James and not for me.

"I think they sell most things," he said.

We stopped and took in the lay of the store.

"How did you pick this place?" I asked.

"Fashion bloggers."

"Seriously?" It was hard to picture James browsing fashion blogs.

"They're pretty obsessive about shoes," he said. "And I have to say, I'm not about to wear any of those tight leather pants."

"I think you'd look awesome in tight leather pants," I said with a straight face.

"Bright red," he said with disgust. "Bright red leather, decorated with steel studs. I'd feel like it was Halloween."

"And you were going as a disco vampire?"

James shuddered.

A well-dressed man approached us.

We turned to greet him, and he offhandedly but obviously took in our outfits.

I was wearing black slacks, a green pullover and a pair of comfortable black flats.

James was dressed in a blue-and-white-striped dress shirt over dark gray slacks.

The store clerk didn't seem impressed by us.

"May I help you, sir?" he asked James.

The expression on the man's face said he thought we'd wandered into the wrong store.

"I hope so," James said. "I'd like to look at a tux."

"Bold start," I muttered under my breath.

James gave me a little shove with his arm.

I took it to mean I wasn't being serious enough.

"A tux?" the clerk echoed. He still seemed skeptical.

"A tux," James said with conviction.

"Then, right this way, sir." The man turned to lead us farther into the store.

"This is making me nervous," I said to James in a low tone.

Like the clerk, I couldn't shake the feeling we didn't belong here. At least, I didn't belong here. I shouldn't speak for James.

It was possible that he shopped at stores like this all the time.

I doubted it—based on what I'd seen of his wardrobe. But I didn't know for sure.

"You need to roll with it," James whispered to me.

"It's your credit card," I said back.

"You think you're getting away unscathed?" he asked, amusement coming into his tone.

"I—"

"They have a ladies' section."

I shook my head. "I can't afford a place like this."

"Think of it as an investment."

"An investment in what?" It wasn't like used clothing appreciated over time.

Vintage dresses in some cases, sure. But I'd have to be royalty or a movie star to have a realistic expectation of that happening.

I was neither.

I was very far from being either.

"In your future," James said.

We stepped onto an escalator.

"I don't need *this* much of an image upgrade," I said.

I thought about the balance in my savings account. I had some money, not a ton, but I'd rather spend it on a new car or a vacation. I knew I wouldn't get the same level of enjoyment out of new clothes.

"Go big or go home," James said.

"In that case, I might have to go home."

He frowned at me. "You bailing on me already, Nat?"

I felt bad about that. "I wasn't..." I tried to frame my thoughts. "I didn't mean it literally. I just didn't expect to drain my savings account on day one."

He seemed to think about that.

We stepped off the escalator and found ourselves in the men's clothing section.

"I'll buy you something," he said.

"Oh, no you won't." That wasn't where I'd been going at all.

I was trying to be realistic. I could change styles, but I couldn't drastically change price ranges like this.

"I didn't think about the cost," he said. "Don't get me wrong, I'm not floating in money. But my salary's got to be higher than yours, plus I get bonuses."

"There's no way you're buying me clothes," I said. "We'll find another way. We'll go to an outlet mall or something. If you do it right, you can get bargains on good stuff."

"You have to know what you're doing," James said.

When I didn't say anything back, he kept talking. "Face it, Nat, we don't know what we're doing."

I couldn't disagree with him on that. We each had zero clues about what we were doing. And zero plus zero was still zero.

"One outfit," he said.

I shook my head but he pretended not to see it.

"One outfit," he repeated. "Something we can take on a test-drive to decide if it's worth the investment."

The clerk stopped and turned to face us, looking rather bored. "In this section we have Remaldi. To the left is Dan Goldenberg. And over there is Mende and Saturday Sweet. Do you have a preference for a designer?"

"I wasn't thinking off-the-rack," James said.

He sounded so posh that I felt a burst of pride.

The clerk's expression faltered, and he seemed to reevaluate the situation.

At least, it seemed to me that he was reevaluating the situation.

If I was him, I'd be reevaluating the situation.

He'd written James off.

That was a mistake.

Okay, this was kind of fun.

"Of course, sir." The man's tone had changed. His shoulders squared, and his expression became more welcoming.

I was right.

I could tell by the amused twinkle in James's eyes that he saw it, too.

"Right this way," the clerk said. "I'll show you to our tailor. I'm Charles, by the way. Is your purchase for a specific event?"

"My firm has a number of formal and charitable events coming up this fall," James said as we fell into step with Charles.

It was my turn to elbow him.

He was getting a little carried away.

He looked down at me. "What?" he mouthed.

I shook my head and gave him a censorious look.

He just grinned.

* * *

The lack of price tags was making me nervous.

I was on my fifth, or maybe it was my sixth dress.

They were all pretty. Some of them fit better than others, but nothing I'd tried on so far was butt ugly.

I realized now as I stared into the mirror just how much I normally factored price into my buying decisions.

"Let's see it," James called to me from outside the fitting room.

We were separated by a heavy blue velvet curtain that hung in a semicircle from big wooden rings.

I stood on a soft carpet in a cubicle with a three-way mirror, a padded chair, and a set of six hooks along the curved wall.

A salesclerk named Naomi had picked out a dozen dresses for me to try.

I hadn't been allowed to pick my own. Oh, no. James insisted we couldn't trust my taste.

He reminded me that I got to pick out his new SUV. It was his turn to choose something for me.

We'd let Charles run wild with the tux.

Once Charles realized James was a serious customer, his enthusiasm level had risen to impressive heights. Along with the tailor, they'd measured every inch of James, consulted me on fabrics and cuts and accessories, until they finally seemed satisfied with the order.

James had remained stoic throughout the process.

I knew he'd spent a fortune. But he'd assured me he could afford it, and he insisted it was my turn next.

I told myself to forget about the prices. For once in my life, I was going to indulge without guilt.

I drew back the curtain.

James stood nearby. Naomi had offered him a chair and a drink, but he'd refused both.

"Well?" I asked, trying to gauge his expression.

"It's better than the last one."

"I liked the last one."

It had been black with a pretty lace bodice, a V-neck and an A-line skirt that draped to midcalf. You could dress it up or dress it down. It would be very versatile.

"That one was too librarian." There was a glint of humor in James's eyes.

"Ha ha," I said, grimacing in his direction.

"This one has more drama," Naomi said.

"You have to match my tux," James said.

"Match your tux?" I asked.

"For the test-drive."

"Your tux is coming with me?"

I don't know what I'd expected in a test-drive. But it wasn't a date with James.

But now I was thinking about a date with James.

I couldn't stop thinking about a date with James—tall, striking, handsome James, with the new shoulder set in his custom-fit tux, and his great new SUV.

The image was sexy.

He was sexy.

I found my gaze stuck on his sexiness.

It was more potent than I'd ever imagined.

How had I missed that?

"And me in the tux," he said, his deep tone only reinforcing my attraction to him.

Uh-oh. I was attracted to James. This was not good.

"Turn," he said to me.

I was happy to do it. It hid my expression. I didn't want him to figure out what I was thinking.

I couldn't be attracted to James.

James was Brooklyn's. Or at least, he used to be Brooklyn's. From the time we were teenagers, he had dated one of my best friends. And now we were buddies, pals, wing-persons for each other.

I didn't dare let attraction into the mix.

"That's nice," he said from behind me. "I like the crisscross, very sexy."

I felt my skin heat in reaction to his words.

He thought I was sexy.

No, no, no, a little voice said inside my head.

He thought the dress was sexy. It was the dress, not me.

It was shimmering green, with a scooped neckline and spaghetti straps that melded into a crisscross pattern over my bare back. It was fitted over my hips, the ankle-length skirt gently flaring out at my thighs. The fabric was light, and I liked the way it moved when I walked.

"Does it come in purple?" James asked.

I turned back to him. "Purple? Really?"

I wouldn't say I was a purple kind of person. I felt exotic enough going with the emerald green. I was already out of my comfort zone.

"A dark plum or maybe boysenberry," he said.

I stared at him in silence for a moment.

"We can have one made through our supplier," Naomi said. "It'll only take a couple of days."

"Boysenberry?" I asked. "That's a very specific color."

"I read," he said. "I learn from all those blogs. And boysenberry will look good with your eyes."

I got a little shiver, maybe a little thrill at the idea that James had been studying my eyes.

I was staring into his right now.

I was staring deeply into his. They were dark deep midnight blue, and they were making me warm all over.

"It'll bring out the highlights in her hair, too," Naomi said.

"I don't have highlights in my hair." All I really did with my hair was grow it.

"But you do," she said. "It's chestnut and gold and copper. You have great hair."

"Really?" I pulled the ends of my hair in front of my eyes.

"You have really great hair," Naomi said. "You should think about doing some layers around your face. Do you put it up?"

"Not really." I didn't think the looped ponytail I used during yoga class would count.

"Don't get rid of the length at the back," Naomi said, scrutinizing me as she talked. "You can do pretty much anything you want with it now. But soften it around your face a bit. It'll look awesome."

I'd never thought much about my hair, my plain brown straight hair. I'd never imagined someone would call it awesome.

"You could stand to lighten it a bit," James said.

I turned my attention back to him. "You don't like my hair."

"I like it a lot," he said. "But I thought you wanted something different."

He was right. I did.

"Go with something semipermanent," Naomi said. "That way you'll keep all the complexity and natural highlights. Just lighten it a shade or two."

"How do you know so much about hair?" I asked her.

"My sister's a hairdresser. Do you have contact lenses?"

I shook my head. I'd tried contacts once, but my eyes couldn't seem to get used to them. It hadn't seemed worth it at the time.

"Too bad," Naomi said. She leaned a little closer to me so James wouldn't hear. "You might want to think about getting some." She canted her head in James's direction. "He likes your eyes."

I opened my mouth to explain the situation, but James jumped in.

"We should probably get your sister's name," he said to Naomi.

Sophie swung open her apartment door and froze.

Her eyes went wide as she stared at me. "What did you *do*?"

"You don't like it?" I was feeling incredibly self-conscious about my new hair and really weird about my contacts.

I got the haircut just this afternoon. Nobody but me and Naomi's sister had seen it so far. I'd been practicing with the contacts for three days now, but I still felt like I was blinking way too often. And I was fighting a constant urge to rub my eyes.

"Are you kidding?" Sophie asked. "I *love* the new you!"

She pulled me into a hug and she whispered in my ear. "Ethan's going to love it, too. Great move, Nat."

"Ethan?" I asked.

I didn't think I'd given Ethan a single thought since the end of our second "date," where he seemed about as interested in me as I was in him.

"Nice to see you again, Nat." It was Bryce's voice.

"Bryce is here?" I asked, pulling from Sophie's hug.

This was supposed to be girls' pizza night at Sophie's apartment.

"Surprise," Sophie said. "I knew it would be more fun with all four of us."

"All four?" Then I spotted Ethan.

He was sitting on one end of Sophie's cream-colored sofa.

Bryce had stood up from the love seat and was looking at me.

"Hi, Bryce," I said. "Hi, Ethan." I smiled to cover my disappointment.

I liked Bryce quite a lot. And Ethan was okay, too. But it was a strain to carry on a conversation with them. And I really wasn't excited about another deep dive into the ongoing adventures of BRT Innovations.

I loved Sophie, I truly did. But hanging out for hours on end with three people who were working on the same all-encompassing project grew tiring.

I wanted to talk to Sophie, just Sophie. I had a lot going on in my life, too.

Not that I would tell her the reasons behind my makeover, or my deal with James, or my weird feelings about James. Still, I wanted girl talk, generic talk about men and relationships, maybe clothes and jewelry. I didn't know.

I did know that 3-D printed desserts wasn't where my head was at tonight.

I dropped my bag on her entry table and headed for the sofa. I would have kicked off my shoes, but everyone else still wore theirs.

I gave an inward sigh as I sat down.

Sophie and I had planned on making mango margaritas tonight, our secret recipe. I supposed that was off, too.

Bryce took his seat again.

"A Hawaiian and a pepperoni?" Sophie asked all three of us.

"Sounds good," Bryce said.

"I prefer vegetarian if nobody minds," Ethan said.

"I'm easy." The last thing I was worried about was the pizza toppings.

Sophie took out her phone. "Don't you love Nat's hair?" she asked as she pulled up the number.

Ethan looked at me, taking in my hair.

I resisted the urge to fluff it or toss my head. The actions seemed appropriate, but too lighthearted for the expression on his face.

"You changed it?" he asked.

"I like it," Bryce said.

"It's lighter," I said to Ethan. "Thanks," I said to Bryce.

"She cut it, too," Sophie said. "Where did you have it done?" Then she got distracted by something on her screen.

Bryce rose and pulled his wallet from his back pocket, extracting a credit card and handing it to Sophie.

I had to admit, it struck me as gentlemanly.

It reminded me of James and how we'd argued but he'd insisted on buying a pair of shoes to go with my dress.

The upshot was that I never did find out the prices. I probably never would.

"I don't know why women insist on doing that to their hair," Ethan said to no one in particular. "Ammonia, peroxide, p-phenylenediamine, diaminobenzene, toluene-2, 5-diamine, resorcinol. It's not exactly a healthy brew."

"Beauty," Sophie said without looking up.

Now I felt like my hair might just blanket the entire Pacific Northwest in a fog of noxious gas.

"If nobody did it," Ethan countered, "if you all went natural, all with the lowest common denominator, then nobody would have to put toxic chemicals on their head."

"I'll tweet that out," Sophie said. "Likely nobody's ever thought about it."

She made me smile.

"Did you hear back from North Capital?" Bryce asked.

"Nothing yet," Ethan said.

"It's after five. I thought the committee was deciding today."

"That was the schedule," Ethan said.

"That's not good," Bryce said.

I was curious, but I wasn't about to ask a naive question about their business, not after my experiences the last couple of times I'd tried.

"It's just one fund," Sophie said. "We shouldn't let it discourage us."

"If we don't get the investment ball rolling soon…" Bryce shook his head.

A light went on inside mine. North Capital was an investment firm. Ethan had said they were looking for investors into BRT Innovations.

There, I had it.

I felt better.

Wait. No. It didn't sound like it was good news.

"Maybe we'll hear tomorrow," Sophie said, obviously trying to be upbeat. "They would have been meeting all afternoon, right? They could have finished after business hours."

"I suppose," Bryce said. He paused. "You're right. Worrying is premature."

I was glad to hear that. I wanted Sophie to be successful. I might not want to hear every single detail of their progress, but I'd sure be her biggest cheerleader if their invention got traction.

"It's the same thing with shoes," Ethan said.

I looked at him in confusion along with everyone else.

He didn't seem to notice. "Do you know the physiological damage done by wearing high heels?"

I had a feeling he was going to explain it to us.

"Dude," Bryce said. "Don't talk them out of high heels."

"You're willing to risk permanent ankle injury so your girlfriend looks sexy?"

Bryce didn't seem to know how to answer that.

"It's okay," Sophie said to Bryce, patting his arm. "We can risk the ankle damage."

I didn't exactly disagree with Ethan. But as a woman who'd only just jumped into the sexy shoe world, I wasn't thrilled with the idea of having them suddenly go out of fashion.

"I'm just saying—" Ethan began.

"That looks don't matter," Sophie said. "Well, I don't believe you. If looks didn't matter to men, women wouldn't go to all the trouble."

"You dress for each other," Ethan said.

"That's not true," I said.

I had it on good authority, James's authority, that men liked glamorous women.

"Studies have confirmed it," Ethan said.

"You'll have to show me those studies," Sophie said. "Pizza will be here in twenty minutes."

I was glad of that, too.

I was hungry, and I was hoping we'd break out some kind of alcoholic beverage.

Ethan turned his attention to his phone.

"Are we making margaritas?" I asked Sophie.

She looked regretful. "Do you mind beer? Bryce brought some imported beer."

"Sure," I said.

Beer didn't strike me as strong enough, since I was pretty certain Ethan was looking up the studies that showed women dressed for each other.

I wasn't going through all this to impress other women.

I wanted to impress men, men like James.

I wanted to impress James.

Oh, man. This was getting bad.

I really needed that margarita.

Five

I felt like a movie star.

The feeling lasted for about thirty seconds. And then I felt like an impostor.

I'd never had my hair professionally styled before. I mean, sure, I'd had it cut plenty of times. But I'd never gone to a hairstylist to get it put up for a special event—not even the day I was supposed to be Brooklyn's bridesmaid.

I'd found myself liking Naomi's sister Madeline. She was upbeat and positive, and she pushed me just enough to be adventurous without completely freaking me out.

I'd gone back to her a second time, and she'd done an amazing job on my hair. It was soft around my face and gathered in a loose braid that somehow swirled into a messy bun at the back of my head. The new highlights really showed up under my bathroom lights and seemed to give it added texture.

Madeline had talked me into a mani-pedi—a new experience for me.

I'd thought about pedicures on a few spa days. But I preferred a good deep-tissue massage to almost anything else. I once had a facial, but I wasn't wild about them.

Now my finger- and toenails were perfectly shaped, perfectly even, and shimmering with a subtle purple Madeline had called oyster mauve. I was almost afraid to use my hands.

I didn't have a lot of jewelry to choose from, and the outfit seemed to need something more dramatic than my usual studs or hoops. I searched the bottom of my jewelry box and found a set of long dangling crystal chain earrings with a matching necklace. They worked, and I was set.

Thank goodness.

I only had five minutes to spare.

I carefully strapped on the exotic shoes James had bought for me. I'd never owned four-inch heels before. They were sharp black on the soles, silver on the inner heel, with silver straps dotted with white and purple crystals.

They were wild.

I stood up in them and practiced my new walking style. For a few seconds, I felt wild.

Then I was back to impostor again.

I took one last glimpse in my full-length mirror, telling myself I could do this. I could go out in public and nobody would guess this wasn't really me.

My stomach started jumping in protest, but there was a knock on my door, and I had no choice but to go.

I opened the door to James.

His eyes widened a bit and he sucked in a breath. It was hard to tell what that meant.

First I wondered if he was reacting to me. And then I wondered if he was actually looking past me into my apartment. He'd never been here before. And Sophie told me all the time that "early industrial" was not going to impress people.

Brooklyn's place had always been tasteful, up-to-date and immaculate. It stood to reason that James would prefer elegance to utilitarianism.

"Hi," I finally said to break the awkward silence.

"You..."

I glanced over my shoulder. "I know it's a bit unusual. But it's quite functional."

"Huh?" he asked.

"My place," I said, gesturing. "I know it's ugly."

He looked over my shoulder for a beat. Then he looked directly at me.

"You did it," he said.

"Did what?"

He gestured up and down. "That is *some* transformation."

Oh, we weren't talking about my apartment. That was probably good.

"Where are your glasses?" He moved closer. "You got contacts?" He broke into a smile. "That a girl. I'm impressed."

"They feel weird in my eyes." I would admit it wasn't as bad today as the first few days.

"Well, they look great."

"Thanks. You look good, too." I shook myself out of my self-absorption.

He looked fantastic.

His hair was different, too.

I took it in, did a walk-around, and came back to face him.

"The hair looks good." It was shorter on the sides, looking updated instead of classic.

And he'd let the stubble grow out on his chin, giving him a more rakish look, a dangerous look. I found myself wanting to reach out and stroke his face to see what it felt like.

I resisted the urge.

He held out his arms. "The haircut cost a lot less than the tux."

"The tux is off the charts."

His shirt was crisp white. His tie was straight, black with subtle inlaid gray diamonds. We'd gone with my choice on the suit fabric, onyx rather than jet-black. The style looked even better on James than it had on the model in the picture.

James had a perfect physique, tall with broad shoulders, a deep chest and what looked certain to be washboard abs.

I felt a rush of attraction. It felt unnervingly like arousal. I feared my face might be getting flushed with it.

"So, worth the money?" he asked, gesturing to the tux.

"I don't know what you paid, but I see a long lineup of eligible ladies in your future." I didn't like the picture, but I was more than sure it would be true.

He grinned. "Let's hope so. Do you need to get a coat?"

I shook my head. "I don't have anything that'll go with this dress. I'll have to hope the ballroom is heated."

"There'll be five hundred people there. I think you can count on it being warm. And I'll tell the driver to turn up the heat."

"You're not driving your new baby tonight?"

"The theme tonight is Mardi Gras. I see some drinks in my future."

"I could get into a hurricane," I said.

I was definitely partial to fruit juices, rum and blended ice.

I stepped into the hall and locked the door behind him.

"Love the shoes," James said.

"You better."

He'd given me some say in the shoes, but he'd definitely been the one to push for higher heels and the sparkle look.

"I have very good taste." He gazed down for a moment. "And you have even better feet."

"I had professional help," I said. "With the hair, too."

"It all looks good, very chic, very swanky. I predict a lineup of men wanting to dance with you."

We started for the staircase.

"I just hope I don't fall off the shoes," I said.

"A gentleman would hold you up." As he spoke, we came to the top of the staircase.

He offered me his arm.

I took it.

I had no desire to ruin the evening by falling down a flight of stairs.

His arm was strong and warm and reassuring. It felt like I was steadying myself against an immovable plank of wood.

I slid my opposite hand along the railing and felt completely secure all the way down.

We started across the foyer, but he stopped in the middle.

"Do you mind?" he asked.

"Mind what?"

"Just standing there for a minute."

I wondered for a second if he'd brought me a corsage. Then I wondered if it would ruin the line of my dress. Then I told myself I was being ungrateful.

If James had gone to the trouble to bring me a corsage, I was going to smile and thank him, then pin it on my dress no matter what color it might be.

He stepped away from me.

I wondered where he might have hidden the florist box.

But to my surprise, he walked around me in a circle, looking, watching, making me feel incredibly self-conscious.

"Well?" I asked as he completed the circle. I felt stupidly nervous and impatient.

"I hate to say it."

"Just spit it out."

If the outfit wasn't working, there was nothing I could do about it now. It wasn't like I had a closet of clothes back upstairs that I could wear to the ball. Like Cinderella, I only had one gown.

"We might be finished."

"For the night?" Maybe I didn't look perfect, but I thought I looked pretty good. I wasn't wild about undoing it all before anybody else even saw the effort.

"Finished making you over." He came closer. His voice went sexy low. "You're absolutely perfect."

I opened my mouth to say I didn't want the evening to be over this soon, but then his words penetrated.

"Wait, what?"

"You," he repeated. "Are perfect. Even your walk. The law of large numbers is going to be massively in your favor tonight. You'll probably fall in love."

I coughed out a laugh. "That's *really* not what I thought you were going to say."

"Well, that's what's true."

"It's a huge exaggeration. But it's nice of you to say so."

"We'll see," he said.

He offered me his arm again.

I took it.

I didn't need it anymore. But I liked holding on to him. I liked the feeling of connection.

He was my partner in crime, after all. He shared my secret, and he was helping me make my life better. It stood to reason those things would make me feel close to him.

"Wow," I said.

"You do go well with the room," James said.

"I'm afraid I might disappear."

Perimeter lights in the hotel ballroom glowed purple. Icicles of glass crystal hung in streamers from the ceiling. The cloths on stand-up tables were mauve, while tall, bulbous arrangements of white roses picked up the surrounding colors.

A quintet played on a low stage at one end, jazzy piano music wafting over the voices in the big room. Hundreds of people were already there, mixing and mingling, looking impressive in their formal clothes.

"Do you do this a lot?" I asked.

I would have stopped and stared, probably with my mouth hanging open.

But James kept walking. "Me?"

"Yes, you. Does your firm send you to parties like this all the time?"

"Never," he said.

My steps faltered for a moment. "Are we crashing?"

James stopped. "What? *No.* I bought tickets. But I don't usually like this kind of thing."

"I never do this kind of thing."

"Buck up, Nat. It's good as a test-drive."

I silently reminded myself why we were here and what we were doing.

I'd started feeling like this was a date.

It wasn't a date. I was James's wing-person, and he was mine.

I glanced around as we walked and noticed how many women were surreptitiously checking him out.

"Do you see that?" he asked.

"I sure do."

"They're impressed."

"They are definitely impressed." More and more women turned to watch him.

I leaned in closer to his ear. "It's the tux."

"The tux?"

"Yes." I knew it was more than just the tux. It was absolutely the man inside the tux. But I wanted James to know he was getting his money's worth on the purchase.

"They're not looking at me," he said.

"They're absolutely looking at you—all of you, the whole package of you."

"The *men*?"

"What men?"

"The men who are staring at you."

"Nobody's staring at me. I'm talking about the women. There are a dozen women looking at you right now."

"Well, there are two dozen men looking at you. One of them just pointed."

I threw James a subtle elbow. "Ha ha."

"I wasn't joking."

I moved my attention from the women to the men in the area. It was true. A few of them were looking my way.

I didn't buy the pointing thing, but it was gratifying to know my dress was working.

"You're getting your money's worth out of the dress, too," I said.

"I'm not getting my money's worth. It's them who are getting my money's worth. Which, when I think about it, isn't really fair, it is?"

I could hear the smile in his voice.

"You want to stand back and point at me?" I asked in an equally teasing tone.

"I think I should abandon you."

I didn't know how to take that. "What? Are you annoyed about something?"

"So they can approach you, Nat. None of them are going to ask you to dance with me standing here."

I could see his point. But I wasn't exactly ready to be left alone here.

"Maybe in a few minutes," I said.

"You can do it."

"No. I can't. I really don't think I—"

He was walking away.

"James." I didn't want to shout.

No, scratch that. I did want to shout. I wanted to shout at him to get back here and help me. This wasn't our deal. My wingman wasn't supposed to fly off in the first thirty seconds.

But he was gone, swallowed by the crowd of people.

I stood still for a few minutes, wondering how not to look like an interloper.

Conversational groups surrounded me, two and three, some groups of up to six people. They seemed to know each other. They were chatting and laughing.

I wanted to sprint for the exit.

I thought about taking temporary refuge in the ladies' room. But then I ordered myself to buck up. I couldn't hide and meet men at the same time.

The law of large numbers. That's why I was here.

I caught sight of a bar lineup and decided it was a halfway measure. Lining up for a drink wasn't the same as hiding, and it would give me something to do other than standing here looking pathetically lonely.

I joined the longest line, hoping it would take a while.

The man in front of me turned.

He was about five-ten, dark blond hair, a very nice suit and a friendly face.

I smiled at him. "Hello."

He nodded. "Hi. Are you from the hospital?"

I wondered if I looked like a nurse. "The hospital?"

"St. Michaels...the recipient of tonight's fundraising."

"Oh."

Well, didn't I feel stupid. It hadn't occurred to me to ask James about the event. I was too focused on my dress and shoes.

"My date is with O'Neil Nybecker," I said.

Then I realized I'd just told him I had a date. Perfect. I was really starting off with a bang here.

"You haven't made it very far," a woman said to him, arriving to link arms with him.

"You were fast, sweetheart," he said to her.

He turned to me. "This is..."

"I'm Nat Remington. I was just saying my date is with O'Neil Nybecker."

Since he wasn't single, I was definitely glad to have claim to a date. I didn't want this man's date to get the wrong idea about me. I wasn't poaching.

"Nice to meet you," the woman said with a friendly smile. "Harold is on the St. Michaels board."

The man held his hand out to me. "Harold Schmidt."

I shook his hand. "Hello, Harold."

The line moved.

"Here we go," I said.

"Ah, yes. This is better," he said.

They both turned to move a few steps.

A man in line directly behind me spoke up. "Did I hear you say O'Neil Nybecker?"

I turned to look at him.

He was younger, maybe in his early twenties. He was clean-shaven, tall and fit. His hair was close cropped on the sides, shaved almost bald, while it was long at the top, thick and fluffed up.

He looked cocky and confident.

"I did," I answered.

The line moved again, and I moved with it.

"I'm from O'Neil Nybecker. Just started a couple of weeks ago. Do you work there, too?"

"I don't. I work in the public library."

He gave a winning smile. "So you came with someone from the firm. Do I dare hope you're here with a friend and not a lover?"

I wanted to tell him it was none of his business. The question was almost rudely blunt.

Then I told myself to chill. It might have been awkwardly phrased, but he was only trying to decide if I was attached. Probably so he didn't make the same mistake I'd just made and have my date show up all of a sudden.

Not that I'd been flirting with the guy in front of me. I was only making chitchat. Still, his "sweetheart" showing up like that had taken me by surprise.

"A friend," I said.

The man held out his hand to shake. "Aaron Simms. I'm an economist."

I shook. "Nat Remington."

"Nat is short for Natalie?"

"Natasha."

"Ohhhh." He made a point of looking impressed. "A beautiful name for a beautiful woman."

"Are you here with a date?" I asked in return.

If he was with a date, he probably shouldn't be flirting with me.

"I'm here on my own. It's a corporate thing. I want to impress the brass."

"The brass cares about this kind of thing, do they?" I couldn't help remembering that James said he never went to functions like this.

Aaron leaned in and lowered his voice. "I'm showing enthusiasm for the firm. You want to get ahead, you play all the angles."

"And this is an angle?" I had to admit, I was intrigued.

I'd never been one for office politics. Not that there were many politics in the public library. Then again, the last promotion I'd been in line for had unexpectedly gone to someone else. She was very socially astute, organizing outings and events for the staff.

Maybe I should pay more attention.

The line moved again, and I kept pace.

"I'm young, eager, a good conversationalist and dancer. I know which fork to use, and I know how to get the O'Neil Nybecker name out there. Why do you think they donate to the hospital?"

It seemed like a trick question. "To help sick people get well?"

Aaron chuckled as if I was delightfully naive. "Corporate reputation, darlin'."

Darlin'? Seriously, *darlin'*?

He kept talking. "They throw their money at prominent causes, especially those near and dear to the mayor's heart. It makes them look like they care, softens the edges of their hard-nosed corporate focus. Did you see the mayor? He's here with his wife. She's a big supporter of the arts center. Guess which cause O'Neil Nybecker's supporting next?"

Okay, I could get this one. "The arts center?" I asked, half-sarcastically.

"Now you're catching on."

I grimaced.

Luckily, the Schmidt couple were the only ones left in line in front of me. I'd be out of here soon.

"What are you drinking?" Aaron asked.

I truly did not want him to order my drink.

"I haven't decided yet."

"They do a great Sazerac."

"Oh." I wasn't sure what to say back.

I wasn't about to agree to his recommendation. I was having a hurricane. But I didn't want to disclose that, either. I could be wrong, but I was guessing his plan was to order our drinks together and use it as an excuse to walk away with me.

I didn't want my hair, dress and shoes to work on this guy. No thanks.

"*There* you are." James arrived and looped his arm around my waist.

I gave him a surprised look.

My first impression of Aaron might not have been great, but James couldn't know that.

It surprised me that he was breaking up the conversation.

"Hi, James," I said, framing a what-are-you-doing? question with my expression.

"Simms." James nodded to Aaron.

They knew each other. I guess that should have occurred to me. O'Neil Nybecker was a very big firm with a twenty-story office building, but I supposed there were meetings and a lunch room. People would pass each other in the halls.

"Hi, James." Aaron took in James's arm at my waist. Then he looked back at me. "Friends?" he asked, looking a little bit annoyed.

"Good friends," James said.

The Schmidts took their drinks and moved on.

"What would you like?" James asked me.

"A hurricane, please," I said.

"Coming up," James said.

"Was it what you hoped for?" I asked James as we made our way through the hotel lobby at the end of the evening.

"It was about what I expected." He didn't sound thrilled. "You?"

"It was fun walking in."

After James had rescued me from Aaron, I'd mixed and mingled some more. I'd even danced a few times. But I hadn't met anyone interesting. The law of large numbers seemed to have let me down tonight.

James smiled as we approached the front door of the hotel. "You caused a bit of a ripple with your entrance."

I agreed that I'd attracted a bit of attention. But James was the one who had women craning their necks.

"You caused a bigger ripple. Did those women approach you?"

"A few did. They seemed nice."

"But nothing to write home about?" I asked.

He pushed open the door for me. "Definitely nothing to write home about."

"Do you think we were doing something wrong? Or maybe my expectations were too high. I mean, we definitely look good and all."

"We look great," he said.

"Yeah, I think we do." I couldn't imagine any woman not falling all over James the way he looked tonight, that was for sure.

I'd fall all over him myself if I thought there was any chance he'd reciprocate. And that wasn't just the two hurricanes talking. He was hot.

"We'll have to try again," he said.

He looked both ways on the hotel driveway and signaled for our car.

"Try the same thing?" I asked.

"There'll be different people at a different event. I don't think we should abandon this approach just yet. O'Neil Nybecker is a sponsor of the arts-center fund-raiser coming up."

"Aaron mentioned that," I said.

James's brow went up. "Oh?"

"Uh-huh," I said.

There was a bit of an edge to James's voice. "What else did he say?"

"Is there something you don't like about Aaron?"

"There are a few things I don't like about Aaron. What did he say to you?"

I realized Aaron wasn't the most appealing person in the world. "He said he attended events like this to impress the brass."

James gave a cool laugh as the car pulled up in front of us. "That sounds like Aaron."

"He seemed harmless enough," I said. "A bit annoying maybe. A bit young."

James opened the back door. "A bit nakedly ambitious."

"Is ambitious bad?" I asked as I climbed into the car.

Aaron had been clear about wanting to climb the corporate ladder. But lots of people wanted to get ahead.

"Depends on how you do it." James closed my door and went around to the other side.

"How is Aaron doing it?" I asked while James got settled.

I remembered I was thinking about my own lost promotion while Aaron had been talking about his approach to his career development.

"Well, he's got a big leg up, that's for sure."

"Because he's smart? Hardworking? Ambitious?"

The car pulled smoothly away from the curb.

"Because he's a Simms."

"That's a good thing?" I guessed.

"His uncle is Horatio Simms, senior partner at O'Neil Nybecker. Word on the street is that it may soon become O'Neil Nybecker Simms."

"Ahhh," I said. *Ahhh* was how I felt hearing that information.

"Aaron is entitled and cavalier," James said with a frown. "And last week he became my special problem."

That piqued my curiosity. "Why? What did he do?"

"I've been asked to show him the ropes. He's an intern."

"He didn't tell me he was an intern."

Aaron hadn't sounded at all like he was in a training position.

"I'm not surprised," James said. "But let's stop talking about Aaron. I'll worry about him Monday morning."

"One last question?" I asked.

James frowned. "About Aaron?"

"Let's call it Aaron adjacent."

"All right. I'll give you one more. But only since you look so gorgeous."

I tried not to smile, but I couldn't help it. His teasing compliment made me feel good.

I should stop letting James make me feel good. I should at least try to stop it.

"He said the brass is impressed if you attend functions like this. But you said you never attend them. I wondered why not."

There was an edge to James's voice when he spoke. "Maybe I don't care about impressing the brass."

It was clear I'd asked the wrong question. But we'd pledged to be honest with each other. And I had to wonder if James's instincts might not be leading him astray on this one. Women were definitely attracted to money and power, and moving up in a firm like O'Neil Nybecker would only increase James's power and therefore his desirability to large numbers of women.

We were going after large numbers here.

"What would it hurt?" I pressed. "You went tonight. I mean, I know it wasn't the success we'd hoped for, but it wasn't exactly painful, either. Your bosses saw you there. If they liked it—"

"I'm an economist, not a show pony." His sharp response

took me by surprise. "There are people who get ahead by playing games, and those who get ahead through solid, hard work. Maybe I don't want to compromise."

His reaction threw me.

"I thought that was the point of all this? I thought we were playing the image game. All we're doing here is compromising."

"In our personal lives," he said. "Not in our professional lives."

"I was thinking it might work for both. And maybe it only works if we do both. Maybe we need to change all the way through, not just on the surface, not just on the weekends or when we're together playing dress up."

"You want us to compromise all the way through?"

"I'm not saying we compromise our ethics or anything." I wasn't sure where I was going with this, but so far, it sounded okay. "I'm saying where's the harm in being more exciting on all levels? Look at me."

He did.

I gestured to the outfit. "I'm all dressed up. But I'm still librarian Nat Remington. I have her opinions. I have her hobbies. I have her attitude. I have her plain old name. Aaron said Natasha was a pretty name."

"Aaron again?"

"Stop. Seriously. Don't let Aaron mess with your mood. Natasha is a pretty name. But I went with Nat. Why did I go with Nat? Tasha is the better nickname. It's gorgeous. It's exotic. It's the name of someone who leads a wild and glamorous life."

"So change it," James said.

"I might."

"You should."

"I will." I felt empowered just making the pledge.

"Good."

"You change yours, too."

He gave me a look of skepticism. "How can you change James?"

"Jamie. You can be Jamie."

"I don't—"

I reached out and touched his arm. "You promised to trust my judgment. You need a new name, something less uptight than James."

"Seriously?"

"Yes."

"Okay."

"Really?" I couldn't help but feel excited.

"Yes, really. So, tell me, what are Jamie and Tasha going to do next?"

Six

We decided on a popular dance club.

James picked out my dress again, but this time I paid for it.

I kind of loved it. It was a shimmery gold-and-black geometric pattern, sleeveless, with a scoop neck. Tight to the waist, it had a gold metal belt over a pleated skirt. The soft skirt hung to my midthigh and swirled when I danced.

The following Friday, I left my hair down and found some dangling gold earrings that looked flashy enough for the occasion.

James argued for gold sandals, but we settled on black cut-out ankle boots with tapered heels. They were easier to wear, but still had a funky, avant-garde appeal. I never would have considered them before now.

We stood in line for half an hour. The club was loud and crowded, with lots of techno music, flashing laser lights and haze from a fog machine behind the DJ.

It wasn't to my taste, but I danced a lot. I couldn't talk to any of my partners, so I had no idea if I liked them or not. Mostly, they grinned at me while we danced, then they bid me a silent adieu with a wave of their hand before moving on to another partner.

Finally, James touched my arm and pointed to the exit.

My ears were throbbing, the music following us outside as we found our way into the fresh air. It was misty, and a skiff of wet from some earlier rain made the black pavement shine under the lights.

He asked me a question, but I couldn't hear.

"What?" I asked in what I hoped was a loud voice. I couldn't hear myself very well, either.

He leaned into my ear. "What did you think?"

I gave him a shrug while we passed the lineup of more people crowding the sidewalk, waiting to go inside.

Some of the outfits made mine look tame.

"Not my thing," he said.

"Mine, either," I admitted, although it had been my suggestion.

We made our way down the block to the brighter lights of First Avenue.

"Let's scratch it off the list," he said.

"Consider it scratched."

My feet hurt, but I liked walking.

"Hungry?" he asked.

"Starving." I was.

He pointed to a brick café with big awnings and glowing lights. "Try that?"

"Yes, please."

The sooner I sat down, the happier I'd be.

A hostess showed us to a booth beside the window. It looked out on a patio that was empty now since rain was beginning to sprinkle down again.

"This is nice," I said, settling into the cushy seat and opening a big menu on the table in front of me.

James did the same. "So, did Tasha meet anyone?"

I grinned as I read my way through the burger selection,

thinking a chocolate milkshake sounded awesome. "Tasha met a whole bunch of people."

"Did she like any of them?"

I glanced up to see his gaze on me.

"She couldn't tell. I didn't have a single conversation. What about Jamie? Anyone interesting for you?"

He shook his head. "Same thing. Lots of inanely grinning maniac dancers."

"Is Jamie being judgmental?"

"Jamie is being realistic. Dance clubs are *so* scratched off our list."

"I do like the outfit," I said, making a point of taking in his distressed jeans, white-and-gold foil-patterned T-shirt and short leather jacket.

"Never going to wear this shirt again," he said. "What are you having?"

"Maybe you could do yard work or paint in it or something."

"You're too practical for your own good."

"If you don't want it, I'll take it."

"You think it's girlie?"

"I didn't say that."

"It'll be way too big for you."

"I can sleep in it." As the words left my mouth, our gazes met.

They meshed and melded and the air seemed to sizzle between us.

I didn't think I was imagining it.

"What can I get for you?" a waitress asked, stopping beside the table.

James broke the look.

He moved his attention to the menu. "I'll take a bacon mushroom burger with fries."

"Anything to drink?"

"Cola," he said.

I willed my heart rate to slow down.

I wished my skin didn't prickle. I knew I had goose bumps,

and I knew exactly why. There was no point in even pretending I didn't have a crush on James… Jamie. It was Jamie now, and he was hot.

"And for you?" the waitress asked.

"Cheeseburger," I said. "With fries and a chocolate shake." I definitely needed the shake to cool me down. And drowning my arousal in delicious calories seemed like a really great idea right now.

"A shake sounds good," Jamie said. "Can I switch?"

"Certainly," the woman said. "Coming right up."

"Thanks," Jamie said, handing her his menu.

I did the same.

"We have to come up with something else," I said before we could take the conversation back to me sleeping in his shirt. Even though I was staring at the shirt, thinking of how it would feel skimming over my skin and how Jamie would look without it.

Whoa.

"Something else?" he asked.

"Another exciting activity for Jamie and Tasha." I forced a light note into my voice. "Exactly how brave are we? Are we going bungee jumping or skydiving?"

"Is that what you want to do?" He looked serious.

I'd been joking.

"Nah," I said, thinking it through. "It would be over so fast, and we wouldn't meet anyone on the way down."

He didn't answer, and his gaze focused outside the window.

The rain was increasing, bouncing off the tables and chairs on the patio and streaking through the bands from the streetlights.

Jamie frowned, and I wondered if he was worried about flagging a cab.

"Don't worry," I said.

He looked back at me. "About jumping out of a plane? I'll jump out of a plane if that's what you want."

"I thought you were worried about getting a cab."

He looked confused. "Why would I worry about that?"

"The rain," I offered.

"It's Seattle," he said. "The system can handle rain."

"Then why are you frowning?"

"I'm not frowning."

"You were. You frowned when you looked out the window just now."

"Oh, that frown."

"Did I say something wrong?" I went over the past couple of minutes inside my head, trying to figure out what it could have been.

"It wasn't you. I thought I saw someone out there."

I was relieved, but only a little bit. I didn't want Jamie to feel upset about something I said or about anyone else.

"Who was it?" I asked, hoping to make it better.

"It doesn't matter. It wasn't them."

I knew I shouldn't press, but I couldn't help but be curious. "You can talk to me. Remember, we're going to be honest with each other. You said it was the only way this was going to work."

"Fine," he said. "Sure. Why not."

I braced myself, not sure what to expect.

"I thought I saw Aaron."

Okay, that wasn't at all what I'd expected. "From your office Aaron?"

"That Aaron."

I'd met Aaron a second time on a night Jamie and I went shopping. It was clear he and Jamie didn't get along particularly well. But I didn't understand why merely seeing Aaron would annoy Jamie.

"We're not that far from O'Neil Nybecker," I said. "Maybe he was working late."

"I *wish* he was working late. He cut out early today...again."

I still wasn't seeing why Jamie cared. I tried to make a joke. "I take it you don't have flexible hours?"

"Not for interns. And not after the stunt he pulled this week."

Again, I was curious, but I didn't know if the incident would be confidential.

I waited, but Jamie didn't elaborate.

The waitress dropped off our milkshakes.

He was still frowning, and he didn't take a drink.

I sipped through the straw, and the milkshake was delicious.

"Do you want to talk about it?" I asked.

"I don't want to bore you."

"Go ahead. I'll tell you if I get bored."

Jamie tried his own milkshake.

"Good, huh?" I prompted.

"It is."

"So?" I wanted to know what had the power to make him frown like that.

"It sounds minor, but it's not. In a meeting with one of our biggest clients, where, as an intern, he's supposed to sit quietly and learn, Aaron pops up with a *suggestion*."

Jamie paused, and I waited.

I stirred my milkshake with the straw, pretending I wasn't dying of curiosity.

"He says," Jamie finally continued, "and I quote, 'Take the company public.'" Jamie's expression told me he was disgusted.

"And that's a bad idea?" I was guessing, of course. I didn't know anything about it.

"It's a risky idea," Jamie said. "Worse, it's a knee-jerk idea. It's a gut reaction. We don't do gut reactions. We do thoughtful and thorough analysis. Even if it was the best idea in the world, even if we'd done the research, you don't blurt it out in front of the client without a plan. The team had no plan."

"Would you ever go with your gut?" I asked. "Make a risky decision based on your instincts?"

"Never."

I'd never do that, either. At least Nat would never do that. I wasn't sure about Tasha. Tasha just might.

"What about Jamie?" I asked.

Jamie looked confused.

"I get that James is careful, but would Jamie take a flier on something?"

Jamie's eyes narrowed and the corners of his mouth went white. "Are you suggesting Jamie should be more like Aaron?"

I tried to figure out how to call the question back.

But the waitress appeared with two laden plates.

"One cheeseburger," she said, putting a plate down in front of me. "One bacon mushroom." She set Jamie's plate down. "Will there be anything else?"

I shook my head to answer her. I wasn't hungry anymore. I was feeling a little sick.

"We're good," Jamie said to her. "Thanks."

She walked away.

"I didn't mean that," I said.

"Jamie's not careless," he said.

"I'm sorry."

"Don't worry about it. Let's just eat."

But I was worried about it.

I took a bite of my burger and forced myself to eat some fries. But my heart wasn't in it.

Jamie might not be careless. But I was beginning to worry Tasha was.

I didn't hear from Jamie all week.

Sophie called to see if I would meet up Friday night. But I was afraid she'd bring Bryce and Ethan along, so I lied and said I had plans with the girls from work.

By Thursday, I couldn't bring myself to look at my new clothes. After work, I stuffed them to the back of my closet and changed into my oldest and most Nat-like outfit, deciding to garden until I was ready to go to sleep.

I pulled back my hair and tied it up in a scarf. Then I propped open the patio doors to let in the fresh air and tucked my hands into my floral-print garden gloves.

There was a knock on my door.

I ignored it at first, thinking it was probably Sophie. She might be frustrated that I'd turned down her invitation and decided to bring Bryce and Ethan directly to me.

Wouldn't she be surprised to have me greet them all like this? Ha. Ethan would be well and truly cured of any lingering desire to date me then.

The knock sounded again, this time more forcefully.

Fine.

If she wanted to surprise me, I would surprise her right back. For better or worse, this was Natasha Remington. I wear old clothes. I garden. I'm plain and boring, and I like it that way.

It would have been perfect if I already had a cat.

I went for the door, wrenching it open.

It was Jamie.

"Hey, Tasha." He breezed past me. "I have an idea."

I stood with the door wide-open, staring at him.

He glanced around at the decor but didn't react. He turned back to me. He didn't react to my outfit, either.

"I don't understand," I said.

"That's because I haven't told you yet."

"Told me what?"

"My idea. Didn't I just say I had an idea? That's why I'm here."

"But..."

"Rock climbing," he said.

I didn't have a response.

"Wait." He seemed to notice what I was wearing. "Are you... renovating?"

That I could answer. "Gardening. What do you mean rock climbing?"

"Want some help?"

I took in his slacks and dress shirt. "You don't look dressed to get dirty."

He glanced down at himself. "I suppose."

I closed the door behind me. "What are you saying about rock climbing?"

"You and me. Instead of jumping out of a plane, we take some training and go climbing. It'll be exciting and adventurous. And it'll get us out to meet regular people, not the club or ballroom set."

"Have you ever done it before?" I asked.

"Never. You?"

I shook my head.

"I saw a beginners class advertised. It starts on Saturday over near Ballard. We could sign up."

I took my gloves off. "Did I miss something?"

"Miss what?"

"I thought you were ticked off at me."

He looked puzzled. "Why?"

I really didn't want to bring it up again. "The argument... last weekend...at the café."

"I told you not to worry about that."

"You didn't sound sincere."

"Well, I was. Are you that thin-skinned?"

I felt my back go up. "Excuse me?"

"Do you want me to apologize for disagreeing with you?"

"No." I tossed the gloves down. "And I'm not thin-skinned. But you were clearly annoyed with me, and then you didn't call."

"Should I have called?"

"You're missing my point."

He moved a little closer. "I'm sorry. What's your point?"

"You got mad, and then you went silent, and I didn't know what to think."

"You're forgetting the 'don't worry about it' that came in between those two things."

"You can't just toss something off like that and expect it to land. I thought our project was over. I thought you were giving up."

"Are *you* giving up?"

"No." Well, I was. At least, I had been. But I didn't want to. He gently took my hands. "I'm not giving up."

I felt his touch all the way up my arms and into my chest.

I had an overpowering urge to lean forward, to press my chest against his and to wrap my arms around him. I wanted to hug him. I wanted to kiss him. I wanted to... Oh, boy.

I swallowed.

"So, what do you say?" he asked.

Yes! I almost shouted.

"Shall we learn how to rock climb?" he asked.

"Yes," I said out loud. "Let's learn how to rock climb."

He hugged me.

He pulled me against his chest and wrapped his strong arms around me and hugged me to him.

My body sighed. It sang. I hugged him back, leaned my cheek against his chest, closed my eyes and absorbed the heat and the energy pulsing from him into me.

Time seemed to stop.

I felt his breath on my hair.

His chest expanded with a deep breath. Then his arms pulled more tightly around me.

I pretended it was attraction.

I let myself fantasize that he liked the feel of me, the scent of me, that he wanted to taste my lips the way I was dying to taste his.

Too soon, he drew back.

He turned away and cleared his throat.

I was mortified to think he could tell how I felt.

Had I hugged him too tight? The way my body had gone boneless and molded to his had to be a dead giveaway. He was embarrassed. He probably pitied me.

I pitied myself.

I had to get over this infatuation.

"Is there a website or something?" I asked, trying desperately to sound normal. "Where we sign up?"

His shoulders were tense, and he didn't turn. "I'll take care of it."

"I don't mind—"

"I'll take care of it."

"Okay." I waited for him to look at me, but he didn't.

"Uh, Jamie?"

"Yes."

I *so* didn't want to have this conversation, but I wouldn't be able to stand another two days of guessing his mood. I'd just done that, and it was awful.

"Is everything okay?" I asked, bracing myself.

"You bet." He turned then, and he smiled. He looked almost normal. "I'm glad you're willing to give it a try."

I was willing to give a whole lot of things a try right now.

But I couldn't tell him that.

Instead, I fought the lingering hum of attraction. I wished mind over matter worked better than it did. But it didn't. Despite logic, reason and my honest-to-goodness best efforts, I couldn't shake the desire to hurl myself into his arms.

"I'm glad you thought of it," I managed to say.

"The class starts at nine on Saturday. Can I pick you up at eight?"

"Yes. Sure. I'll be ready. Is there anything I need to bring?"

"There's a list of suggested attire on the website. I'll send you the link."

"Good. That sounds good." I felt like we were making small talk.

"See you Saturday." He headed for the door.

I stepped out of the way.

When the door closed behind him, I blew out a breath.

I knew I had to get gardening. I had to do something normal. But my feet didn't want to move.

My phone pinged with a text.

It was Jamie, and my heart lurched ridiculously at the sight of his name.

He was sending the link to the climbing website.

I felt like a foolish teenager mooning over that cute boy in math class.

I was way too old for this.

I took a vacation day on Friday.

I didn't really need the day off, and Nat would never take a sudden, random day off work on a lark. But it felt like something Tasha would do. So I did it. And I was glad.

I was a little restless, but I was still glad.

I sat staring at my gray cinder block walls. I'd lived here three years now, and they were the same color as when I'd first moved in. I'd hung two pictures on them, both in the spots where a previous tenant had drilled a hook.

They were watercolor portraits of four young girls—in one they were smiling, in the other they were thoughtful. Sophie had bought them for me as a housewarming present. She said they reminded her of the four of us: Layla, Brooklyn, her and me.

It was obvious that Brooklyn was the pretty, pink-cheeked blonde. Layla was the intent girl with auburn hair. I was the short brunette with glasses, always the glasses. That was me, always shorter, always a little mousier than the rest.

Sophie had been right. The paintings did look like a peaceful, rather angelic version of the four of us.

I wondered for a minute if actual photos might be even better. I thought I'd like to look at the real us instead of the paintings.

Maybe that was what I would do.

Something Jamie had said was ticking through my mind today.

It had been innocent enough.

I didn't think he meant it as a criticism.

But when he walked into my apartment last night, he'd asked if I was renovating. He clearly thought my apartment needed renovating.

It shouldn't have been a huge surprise to me. Pretty much

everyone who knew me had advised renovating at one point or another.

But back then, they'd suggested it to Nat. Nobody had suggested it to Tasha before. I was thinking this morning that Tasha might like to renovate.

Not that Tasha had the slightest idea of where to start.

But painting the walls seemed reasonable. With the right color of paint, you could make a huge difference without spending a lot of money.

I had hundreds of photos on my computer. I liked some of them a lot.

If I painted the wall, say, a nice cream or pale gold.

"Shut up, Nat," I said out loud.

Tasha, Tasha, Tasha, I thought inside my head. *What color do you like?*

It occurred to me to ask Jamie. After all, we'd agreed that he would trust my judgment and I would trust his. But after last night, I felt really weird about contacting him.

Then again, how better to make the first contact after our awkwardness than over something an innocuous as paint color? It was probably the perfect question: bland, lightweight, easy to answer.

I picked up my phone to type the text.

I'm painting my walls. What color should I use? Tasha.

Before I could talk myself out of it, I hit Send.

His text came back.

Your apartment?

I wasn't sure what other walls he thought I might be talking about.

Yes.

Shouldn't you be at work?

"Reasonable question," I muttered to myself as I typed.

I took a vacation day.

And you decided to paint?

Tasha is impulsive.

He sent a smiley face.

I'll have to come by and take a look.

The smiley face was nice. I felt like we'd made it past the awkwardness. But the rest was disappointing.

I'd hoped he'd tell me mauve or burgundy or blue. I was all set to head out to buy paint, brushes and a drop sheet. I didn't want to sit here for the rest of the day and think about redecorating. I wanted to get started.

I told myself I could clear the decks. Painting was messy. I'd have to move the furniture to the middle of the room. I should roll up the rugs. If I was moving the furniture, I'd definitely need to vacuum underneath.

There was plenty I could do to get going.

I rose from the sofa, cleaned up the few breakfast dishes and changed into some old jeans and a battered sweatshirt.

The rugs were easy. I rolled them up and made a pile.

I decided I'd need about five feet in front of each wall. That meant moving one sofa up against the coffee table. It wouldn't be usable while I painted, but I wasn't planning on entertaining or anything.

I discovered I was right. Beneath the sofa there was quite an accumulation of dust and grit. I plugged in the vacuum and went to work. As it sucked up the debris, I studied the floor. It was in worse shape than the walls, all scratched and scuffed by about fifty years of students. If you looked closely, you could see the pattern of the desk rows, the little round dents from the desk legs and the worn paths where students trod in between.

I found myself smiling when I thought of all the kids that had learned in this room. When you thought about it, it was a nice provenance to have in a home. Maybe some of them had grown up to be doctors or pilots; maybe they were artists or athletes. I would bet a whole lot of them had kids and grandkids by now, Sunday barbecues and family baseball games.

I heard a noise and shut down the vacuum.

I waited, and it came again—a knock on the door.

My first thought was the downstairs neighbor. They were a young family with twin toddlers and a baby. My noise could be disturbing nap time.

I crossed to the door and opened it.

I was startled to see Jamie in the hall.

"What?" I asked, somehow not able to be more specific. "Weren't you downtown at the office?"

"I came to check out your walls."

"In the middle of the day?"

"You're playing hooky."

I found myself insulted at the accusation. "I put in for vacation leave. It's legit."

"I'm on an early lunch."

"It's ten thirty."

"Hence the word *early*. Are you going to let me in?"

"Sure." I stepped back. "Of course."

It occurred to me then how I looked. Not pretty, that was for sure. I hadn't bothered with makeup. I hadn't even showered yet today. My hair was in a quick knot on the top of my head. My gray sweatshirt was stained and boxy, and I had holes in the knees of my jeans.

I resisted the urge to smooth my hair or check my cheeks for streaks of dust. If Jamie was going to show up out of the blue, he got what he got. Tasha might dress up for a night on the town, but she dressed down for painting her apartment.

And, hey, I was painting my apartment. There should be points for that effort.

"I figured Jamie would duck out of the office if he had a good excuse."

"Jamie thinks picking my paint color is a good excuse?"

"I'm here to support you, Tasha," he said in a smooth, silky voice that trickled all the way through me.

I was *not* going to let things get awkward again.

I put some space between us.

"In that case, Jamie, what color should I use?"

He looked around for a long minute. He took a step, changed his angle, turned around.

"This really is..." he said.

"Utilitarian," I said.

He nodded. "That and a few other adjectives."

"Are you going to insult my apartment?"

He fought a smile. "I'm going to say Tasha's instincts are right. Paint is a good idea. Along with..." He looked around some more.

"I was wondering what to do with the floors," I said.

He looked down. "Fresh paint on the walls will definitely make the floors look tacky."

"I'd be offended, but I agree with you. It's high time I did something with this place."

I pictured Sophie for a moment. I had a feeling I was quoting her. She was going to be over the moon when she heard I was redecorating.

Trouble was, she'd want a hand in it. And she had very strong opinions.

I wanted this to be Tasha's apartment, not something tasteful and lovely that was inspired by Sophie.

I'd have to move fast. I wanted to be past the point of no return before Sophie dropped by and caught me.

"So," I said. "How adventurous do you think Tasha is feeling today?"

"Butter yellow with a russet-brown feature wall and some tangerine trim to make it pop."

"That sounds delicious," I said, trying to picture it.

"Maybe not tangerine," he said. "Maybe pumpkin. It's a bit darker."

"Do I want to know how you know all this?"

"I confess, I've wandered from the fashion blogs into home decorating a time or two."

I broke into a grin.

"It'll look great. I'm stealing it from a design I saw last week. I'll send it to you."

I did like the sounds of butter yellow. And given the size of the room and the walls, a contrasting wall seemed to make sense. I didn't know what pumpkin orange looked like, so who was I to say no?

"You could put stone laminate on the floor and pick up the colors."

I looked down.

I really liked the idea of a new floor. But I doubted I could afford it.

"I was thinking about something you said," Jamie said into the silence.

His words piqued my curiosity, and I looked up.

"You asked if Jamie would go with his gut, make a risky decision based on instinct."

I didn't want to argue again, so I didn't say anything.

"He would," Jamie said. "Oh, not on behalf of a client, that would be irresponsible. But he'd take a risk for himself. I'm sure of it."

He had me intrigued. "You're going to take a risk?"

"I think I should."

I saw the chance for a joke. "And you've thought this through."

He grinned at me. "Yes, I'm going to thoroughly analyze my instinctive, impulsive action."

"Do tell," I said. I backed up a little and folded myself into one of the armchairs, motioning for him to do the same.

He sat down across from me. "Short-term trading. High-risk, short-term trading with the potential for large financial gains."

"You're going to play the stock market."

It made sense for an economist, I supposed.

"*We're* going to play the stock market," he said.

I felt an immediate sinking sensation. "I don't have any money to lose."

"I'll stake us," he said. "We can share the profits."

That wasn't fair. "But—"

"No buts, Tasha."

"You're the one with the money. You're the one with the know-how." I would be dead weight in this.

"We'll make the decisions together. I'll explain my thinking to you, but we'll decide together. If it goes well, you'll be able to afford a new floor."

I looked to the ugly floor again. "I don't feel right about this."

Jamie came to his feet. "No, Nat doesn't feel right about this. Tasha thinks it's a great idea."

He was right, and I could tell by his expression he knew it.

Tasha, me, *I* was excited at the prospect of buying and selling stocks with Jamie, of having more secrets with Jamie, of spending more time with handsome, sexy, desirable Jamie.

Nat yelled stop. She recognized the danger.

But Tasha said go. She didn't need a reason.

Tasha won.

Seven

Rock wall climbing wasn't nearly as hard as I'd expected.

I'd have to learn the knots, and I'd have to learn how to put on a harness, and I'd have to learn a whole bunch of technical things before I'd be anywhere near ready to go out on my own. But the actual climbing, finding a handhold, finding a foothold, pulling myself toward the ceiling on the big vertical wall so far was a whole lot of fun.

I'd thought Jamie would be way, way better than me. Oh, he was definitely good, really good. But while he had bigger muscles, he also had a higher body mass to lift. Thanks to my short stature and relatively lean frame, I could hold my own.

I couldn't help but feel proud of that.

It also turned out that I had no fear of heights. I'd never given it much thought before, but quite a few of the people in the class got nervous as they climbed higher. As long as my harness was tight, I just enjoyed the view.

"You're a natural," Jamie said as my feet came down on the mat.

I was facing the wall, and he put his hands on my hips, obviously to make sure I stayed steady.

His touch felt good. It felt strong and secure. I didn't really want him to let me go.

"Your girlfriend's impressive," the instructor, Paul, said to Jamie.

Jamie abruptly let go. He seemed to realize how the gesture had looked.

I was glad my face was warm from exertion, or I might have worried about blushing. It wasn't such a huge mistake, thinking I was Jamie's girlfriend. After all, we'd signed up together. That would be perfectly natural.

As it was, Paul's suggestion embarrassed me. I might secretly want to be Jamie's girlfriend. In fact, I was starting to fantasize about it.

But that wasn't the point. The point here was to make Jamie attractive to other women. I was his sidekick, his means to an end, the person helping him replace Brooklyn with someone equally glamorous and exciting.

"Thanks," Jamie said to Paul.

I couldn't help but note that Jamie made no correction, offered no explanation, and was simply appreciative.

I felt stupidly good about that.

It didn't change anything. But for a second there, I felt more important to Jamie than just a pal. I liked that.

It would hurt later, I knew. But for the moment I was going to bask in the idea that someone, or maybe more than just Paul, considered Jamie and me a couple.

"Want to go up once more?" Paul asked me.

"Is there time for that?"

The clock was inching toward noon.

"Only for one of you," Paul said.

"Go ahead," Jamie said.

"You don't want to?" I didn't want to be greedy.

We'd each had three climbs this morning, after sitting through a presentation on theory and practicing some basic knots. I could see there was a whole lot to learn about the sport.

"Go ahead," Jamie said. "I'll watch Paul on belay."

I waited while Paul double-checked my ropes and equipment. Then I set off again, with Paul on the ground holding the rope to anchor me in case I slipped. To change things up, I started from a different point.

There were three climbers on the wall with me, each working with a different instructor.

Paul had told me to watch my feet. My feet were way more important than my hands. It made sense to me. And since I didn't have a ton of strength in my arms and shoulders—not being a regular at the gym or anything—I was more than happy to depend on my leg muscles. All that bike riding and running around on the tennis court was serving me well.

"Keep your arms straight," Paul called from below.

I reminded myself of that one, looking for a handhold farther away.

I saw one and took it, then I concentrated on my feet, finding the next step.

By the time I made it back down, my legs and arms were quivering. I knew I'd be sore tomorrow, but in a good way. This morning had been a whole lot of fun, and very satisfying.

Now, when I met new people at parties or anywhere really, and they asked my hobbies, I could sound daring and exciting. Who wouldn't be impressed with the answer *rock climbing* if they asked me what I did for fun? It was better than *tennis*, and sounded a whole lot more impressive than *reading*.

"Hungry?" Jamie asked as we drove from the parking lot in his SUV.

"I am. That really works up an appetite."

"Should we go watch some pretty people while we eat?"

"Where?"

"Northland Country Club. Have you ever been there?"

I had, but only once.

It was the high-end clubhouse at a private golf course. The restaurant was open to the public, but the prices were sky-high.

"Dressed like this?" I asked, knowing we'd never fit in.
"You look awesome."
"I look casual and sweaty."
He waved a dismissive hand as we pulled into traffic. "It's only lunchtime. Think of it as being incognito."
"No one will ever suspect we're spies?"
"Exactly. And it's on the way home."
"Sure," I said. "That sounds great."
There was no doubt that successful, stylish people frequented the Northland Country Club. It attracted business tycoons, politicians and millionaires from around the state and beyond.
"I hope our stock portfolio is rising," I said as we made our way through midday traffic. "I hear a cup of coffee costs sixteen dollars in that place."
Jamie tossed me his phone. "Check it out. The password is 8596."
I took a second to absorb the idea of Jamie giving me his password.
"You'll probably have to swipe over one screen. Open the Tracker app."
I entered the password, feeling like his girlfriend and telling myself to stop it already.
I swiped and tapped the app. Six lines came up with codes and numbers.
"What does it say?" he asked.
"CPW 27.32, LNN 2.06, QPP 32.17."
"Read that one again," he said.
"QPP?"
"Yes."
"QPP 32.17"
"Click on it."
I did.
"What do you see?"
"There's a graph."
"What does the trajectory look like?"

I didn't exactly understand the question.

"Long, slow start and sudden spike?" he asked.

"That's right."

"Hit the sell button."

I was kind of intimidated by the request. "Are you serious?"

"Completely. Go ahead."

"I'm selling stock?" I asked.

He grinned. "You are selling stock, Tasha."

"Okay." If he was sure, then I was game. I touched the sell button. "It's asking me to confirm."

"Confirm," he said.

I did. "Wow. That was exciting."

Jamie laughed.

"What did I just do?"

"You just paid for lunch."

"Really?" It felt pretty amazing.

"Lunch and a whole lot more," he said.

"How much did we make?"

"Ten percent."

"How much did we invest?"

"Ten thousand dollars."

I was speechless for a second. "That's... Jamie, we just made a thousand dollars?"

"I'm thinking champagne with lunch."

I looked back down at the phone. "But how...? It can't be that easy."

"It's not easy."

I felt like I'd insulted him, belittled his expertise and experience. "I know... I mean..."

The phone pinged in my hand and a text message came up. I automatically read it. "I'm sorry," I quickly said. "I didn't mean to pry."

"Who's it from?" he asked.

"Aaron."

"What did he say?"

"Are you sure you want me to—"

"You've already read it."

I couldn't tell if he was annoyed or not. "I didn't read it on purpose."

"I know that. What does it say?"

"It says Bernard postponed the IPO."

"Thank goodness," Jamie said.

"It's good?" I was glad it wasn't something to upset Jamie. I wanted to go have lunch. I wanted to analyze beautiful people. I didn't want Jamie rushing off in a bad mood because of a problem at work.

"It means I talked them off the ledge. Aaron had their heads filled with ideas of quick riches and smooth sailing. It wasn't going to work that way."

"Maybe they should have thrown it all into QPP."

"There's nothing wrong with high risk when you're prepared to lose—whether it's a stock or an equity investment. I was prepared to lose on QPP. I doubt Bernard wants to risk losing control of his company."

"You were prepared to lose ten thousand dollars?" I couldn't wrap my head around that.

"We wouldn't have lost it all. Probably not. Likely not. But we could have lost some of it."

"You want me to read the rest of the numbers?" I asked, worried that we could be losing money on something else while we sat here talking.

"I'll check at lunch," he said. "For now, let's just bask in the win."

"Basking," I said as he swung into the country-club parking lot.

Once we'd cut in the edges, the painting went fast. Jamie was great with the roller, putting on an even coat. And with the roller extension, he could stand on the floor and paint all the way up to the high ceiling.

"What are we going to do up there?" he asked, looking at the ceiling.

I held on to the ladder and tipped my head. From up here, I could see more detail than I wanted to know about. "The skylights are really getting grungy."

"They definitely need to be replaced. Are they leaking?"

"No, thank goodness. Construction is way beyond my budget. I don't think the landlord would let me do it anyway."

"He would if it increased the value of his building."

"I suppose," I said.

"But he'd probably up your rent."

I went back to edging the russet-brown wall. I was on the last section cutting in the ceiling line.

"I'd have to get an agreement in advance," I said, thinking out loud.

"You should ask for a decrease in rent proportional with the amount you're putting into repairs."

"Would anyone go for that?"

It seemed like a good idea. But since I'd already started the work, I didn't see where I'd have leverage.

I could ask. I would ask. Maybe I wouldn't mention that I'd already done the painting.

"We should stop for the day," Jamie said.

I was tired, too. I met up with the final corner.

"I can't believe you did all this," I said, looking around.

The room looked brighter and fresher already.

We'd picked up the supplies after climbing yesterday, and Jamie had insisted on coming back to help me this morning.

I felt guilty then, and I felt even worse now, especially when I looked at my watch and saw that it was after six.

"We've been working for hours," I said.

He crossed the room and reached up toward me. "Hand me the paint can."

I bent over to get it to him. "I'm sorry I kept you all day."

He smiled, and his blue eyes warmed. At least, they warmed me. They warmed me a lot.

I had no idea whether or not he could tell.

Our hands brushed as I handed off the can, and the familiar charge of energy sped up my arm.

He looked sexy in his worn jeans, his faded T-shirt and scuffed work boots. I really liked the new scruffy look he seemed to have landed on. It emphasized his square chin, his strong, straight nose, his eyes that were honestly the most beautiful shade of blue. They were bright in the sun, midnight indoors, always startling, always striking.

His shoulders were broad under the snug shirt, his biceps taut and solid. Under a tux, he looked great. Dressed for construction, he looked spectacular.

"The brush," he prompted, pulling me out of my thoughts.

He was staring right at me, into my expression, into my eyes, and for a terrible second I thought he could read my mind. If he could see my thoughts, he'd know I was compromised. I wasn't his buddy, his pal, his wingman.

I was falling for him. And that wasn't even remotely what he'd signed up for here. He'd be disappointed if he knew. He might even be amused if he knew. Mousy little Nat Remington thought a veneer of makeup and a few new clothes would turn her into Brooklyn.

Sure.

Could happen.

In my dreams.

I leaned down to give him the paintbrush.

The ladder shifted. The brush slipped from my fingers.

The russet-brown end caught Jamie in the forehead. "Crap!" I cried out. The brush bounced to the floor. Jamie grasped the ladder, righting it, but dislodging me.

I lost my balance and fell into his arms, and he caught me, pulling me tight before my feet hit the floor.

The ladder wasn't so fortunate. It teetered, then tipped, then banged on the linoleum, the sound reverberating.

"Good thing we moved the paint can," he said.

I blew out a sigh of relief. "You caught me."

"I caught you," he said.

He shifted, and our gazes met.

They locked.

His arms flexed tight around me.

We stared at each other in silence while time suspended.

"Tasha," he whispered.

I wanted him.

I wanted to breathe him, to taste him, to feel him touch me anywhere and everywhere.

I was about to make a fool of myself.

If he didn't let me go, I was going to kiss him hard and long, and he'd know exactly how I'd been feeling all these days.

He kissed me.

Okay, that was unexpected.

I hadn't seen it going that way at all.

But there it was.

His lips were on mine. They were firm and tender and delicious, and this was the best kiss of my life, possibly the best kiss ever in the history of mankind.

I didn't want it to stop.

I cupped his cheeks, feeling the stubble like I'd been dying to do since he'd grown it out.

It felt rough and rugged, adding to my sensory overload.

My breasts were pressed against his chest, my thighs against his, my belly, his belly, his sex.

A roaring sound came up in my ears, as the kiss went on and on and on.

He pulled off my T-shirt, revealing my lacy bra.

We stared at each other, breathing hard. I think we were trying to figure out which of us was more shocked.

Only I wasn't shocked. Okay, I was shocked. But I was aroused more than shocked. I was aroused more than anything.

He removed my glasses. I peeled off his shirt, for the first time getting a look—though it was blurry—at his magnificent pecs, his bare shoulders, what I knew were gorgeous abs.

He reached for the clasp of my bra, and I knew we were gone. This was right out of control, and we weren't stopping for anything.

My doorknob rattled.

We simultaneously whipped our heads in that direction.

"Nat?" It was Sophie.

She knocked. "Nat? I can hear your music. Is everything okay?"

"She has a key," I hissed to Jamie.

He set me down.

I grabbed my T-shirt from the tipped ladder and threw it over my head.

"I'm coming," I called to her.

Jamie threw on his own T-shirt and ran his fingers through his hair.

We stared at each other for a second.

I had no idea what to say or do or even think.

We'd almost had sex.

I gave myself a shake and went for the door.

"What took you so long?" Sophie said as she marched in.

"I was up on the ladder," I said.

She saw Jamie first. Then she saw the ladder and the painted walls.

I could almost hear her brain humming as she took everything in.

"Hi, Sophie," Jamie said.

"What?" Sophie seemed at a loss for words as she looked around.

"James was helping me paint."

Sophie looked completely confused. "Why would he do that?"

As far as Sophie knew, Jamie and I barely talked to each other—which had always been true in the past.

"We were talking, uh, the other day," I said, my mind scrambling for something logical.

"At the tennis club," Jamie put in.

"Yes," I said. "At the tennis club. And I was asking, well, you know, all the stuff you and Bryce and Ethan told me." I went with the first and only thing that came into my mind—Sophie's new business. "And with James's job and all. Well, it got me to thinking, maybe, and I didn't want to say anything to you, because it wouldn't be fair. You know, if it didn't work out."

Sophie and Jamie were both staring at me as if I'd lost my mind.

Which I had. I apparently had completely lost my mind.

To be fair, my brain had overheated from Jamie's kiss.

After a kiss like that, a woman shouldn't be required to think anything coherent for at least a couple of hours, maybe all night long.

"Ethan was saying you needed investors," I plowed on. "James sometimes invests in things. So, I asked him." I looked at Jamie, trying to apologize with my eyes. "I asked him about your 3-D printer dessert thing, if it was maybe something that he could invest in."

"You did?" Sophie looked amazed and hopeful at the same time.

"But I don't think it's going to work out," I quickly said. "It's not the kind of thing that—"

"I'm going to need more information," Jamie said.

I gave him a warning look. My story was only a way to get us through this awkward moment. We couldn't let it go any further.

Sophie moved closer to where Jamie was standing. "We can give you anything you want."

"James usually makes short-term investments," I said from

behind her, trying to shut it down. "Yours is at a really early stage. And it's going to take a long, long time."

"We're going to revolutionize the food service industry," Sophie said.

My gaze hit Jamie's, half apology, half warning.

"We're upping the level of precision and sophistication with which restaurants," Sophie said before I could slow her down, "even small establishments, can conceive, refine, create and serve desserts of all kinds with our technology."

What had I done?

"That was amazing," Sophie said, dropping down on the single sofa that wasn't covered by the painting drop sheets. "But why was James here? And why are you renovating? And why didn't you tell me?"

I decided to answer the easiest question. "It was a sudden decision."

"I could have helped. I can still help. What's your color scheme? What else are you doing besides the walls?"

I said a silent thank-you that we'd moved past James.

I pushed the passionate kiss from my mind. Could I call it a kiss? It was a whole lot more than a kiss—even if we hadn't technically gone any further than a kiss.

"Butter yellow." I did a circle point to the painted walls. "Plus a russet-brown feature wall. And we're... I'm thinking of adding some pumpkin accents."

Sophie stared unblinking at me. "Who are you and what have you done with my friend Nat?"

I wanted to say I was Tasha. But I kept the thought inside my head.

I did smile.

Sophie smiled back. "This is going to be fun."

I'd known that one would be coming.

"Have you thought about furniture?" she asked. "It would be so much fun shopping. This stuff is pretty tatty."

"I'll have to check my budget before I decide."

"It doesn't have to be right away. I mean, not all of it anyway. We can start with some small pieces. Honestly, Nat, anything would be an improvement."

"You keep telling me that."

"And you're finally *doing* it." She grinned. "We need to celebrate."

Then she went quiet for a moment, looking thoughtful.

I braced myself for another question about James. I hoped I could keep a straight face and that I wouldn't have to lie too much. I wasn't going to betray Jamie's confidence. But I was thinking I could talk a little bit about the changes I'd made to my own image—my hair, my contacts, my apartment.

People upgraded their lives all the time. It wasn't so weird.

"Do you think he'll do it?" Sophie asked.

I was guessing she meant Jamie.

"He said he'd talk to people," she continued. "I guess he must know those kinds of people. He works in a financial place, right?"

"He does." I didn't want to say more. I didn't want to get her hopes up.

It was impossible to tell if Jamie was being polite and trying to protect my cover story, or if he really did know people he could talk to about angel investment into a tech start-up company.

I would have liked to ask him—about the money, about the kiss. At least, I thought I'd like to ask him about the kiss.

It had been one incredible kiss. We'd practically torn off each other's clothes. We had chemistry together. That was for sure.

But I was nervous because this wasn't what Jamie had signed up for. And it could have been a momentary impulse. Physical attraction could take you by surprise, and he might regret it already.

The best thing to do was to take his lead. That made sense to me. If he wanted to talk about it, we'd talk about it. If he wanted to pretend it never happened, I'd go along with that.

I didn't want to mess up our friendship or our deal to help each other. Both had become too important to me.

"Nat?" Sophie said. "What do you think?"

I ordered myself to stop obsessing. It was a kiss. It was over. Life was moving on.

"I don't want you to be disappointed," I said to her. It was my honest answer.

"I can't help but be hopeful. I should really call Ethan."

I was surprised Ethan was her first thought. "What about Bryce?"

"Oh, him, too. Of course, him, too. But Ethan's put his heart and soul into this. Bryce is a little bit on the sidelines with the recipes and all."

That hadn't been my impression. Bryce had seemed quite passionate about the project.

"We should meet them somewhere," Sophie said.

"It's Sunday night."

"It's not even eight o'clock. We can grab dinner and talk about the possibilities. Whatever happens, we should be prepared for it."

If I had to make a bet, I'd say nothing was going to come of this. And I really didn't feel like going out right now.

I made a show of looking down at myself. "I'm a mess."

"We won't go anywhere fancy. Comb you hair, put on some makeup, change your clothes."

That all sounded like a whole lot of work to me. I was exhausted.

"Angelo's at the Lake would be perfect. It's only five minutes from here."

"I'm really tired," I said. "And I have to work tomorrow."

"Come on, Nat. This is huge. I mean, I know it's not a sure thing. But I want to see Ethan's face when I tell him the news."

"There's no news yet," I pointed out.

"You have to eat," she said. "Summon up that peppy new gal who did all this redecorating and come out for dinner with your best friend."

When she put it that way, I felt like a cad saying no.

"Fine," I said.

Her grin made me feel a little more energized.

I pushed myself from the depths of the comfy armchair, telling myself I'd perk up once I got out in the fresh air.

While I got myself ready, Sophie texted Ethan and Bryce.

I combed out my hair, fighting a few globs of stubborn paint. It occurred to me that I should have worn a hat while I painted. I'd definitely do that next time.

I washed my face, brushed my teeth, and put on a little makeup before changing into black jeans and a dove-gray sweater with a silver thread running through the weave. The jeans were a gift from Brooklyn. They were tighter than the ones I usually bought, so I hadn't worn them often. But I was feeling very Tasha-y right now.

"They'll meet us there," Sophie called out.

"Okay," I called back.

I put a pair of silver hoops in my ears and decided I was ready.

I did feel a little more energized. And I was really hungry. Angelo's made fantastic seafood lasagna. I was going to treat myself to that.

I felt bad that I hadn't fed Jamie. I'd planned on ordering something in once we'd cleaned up. As it was, all I'd done was close the paint can and put the brushes and roller to soak while Jamie had talked to Sophie about investments.

"I'm all set," I said as I walked around the divider.

"That was fast." Sophie did a double take of me and then stared.

"What?" I asked, looking down at myself and craning my neck to see the back.

"You look great," she said.

"Thanks."

"No really... I mean...you look... Wow."

"I'm going to assume that's good."

Sophie took in her own outfit of blue jeans and a multicolored blouse. "I feel like I should change."

Her hair was windblown, and her makeup wasn't as fresh as it usually was, but she looked perfectly good.

"Don't be silly," I said. "You look awesome. It's not like you need to impress Bryce. He's impressed already."

I wasn't an expert on long-term relationships. My romance with Henry Paulson didn't qualify, since it had crashed and burned. But it seemed to me that at some point you could start relaxing your look around your boyfriend.

I thought about how I'd looked today with Jamie. I'd looked pretty casual, beyond casual. I'd looked downright functional— probably because I *was* downright functional.

Not that Jamie and I had anything romantic going.

Even that kiss hadn't been romantic. It had been passionate and erotic and exciting. But I wasn't foolish enough to equate those things with romantic.

Sophie still looked uncertain.

"You want to borrow some makeup?" I asked. "I'd offer my wardrobe, but you know what my clothes are like."

Sophie laughed at that. "That's a cute outfit, though."

"These are the jeans Brooklyn gave me last year."

"Oh, yeah. I remember. Why don't you wear them more often?"

"They're a bit snug."

"They fit perfect. You've got to get away from the early-matron look."

"I think you mean the early-librarian look." I was trying to get away from it.

It occurred to me that I should do some more shopping. Maybe Jamie would like to come with me. Maybe I was obsessing about Jamie. Maybe I should get a grip.

"Either." Sophie paused. "I think I will borrow a little mascara or something."

"Help yourself." I gestured to the bathroom.

While she was gone, I opened the closet and took in my shoe choices.

The black cutout ankle boots I'd bought for the dance club would go great with the jeans. I hesitated, knowing I would have to explain them to Sophie.

But I couldn't resist.

I put them on. Then I stood in front of my full-length mirror.

I looked sharp. I had that casual, "I don't really care about it, but I look pretty great" appearance that Brooklyn seemed to so effortlessly achieve.

Part of me was excited, and part of me couldn't truly believe it was me staring back from the mirror.

Eight

Jamie agreed to another shopping trip.

But there was something off in his texts. They were so brief and to the point. He seemed more formal somehow than usual. And then I thought I was imagining it. And then I thought I was still obsessing about the kiss—which I was—and I was reading things into his seven-word texts that simply weren't there.

After work on Wednesday, one of my coworkers dropped me off downtown. Jamie and I had agreed to meet at Brookswood. We'd barely scratched the surface of its ten floors when we bought his tux and my dress.

I'd decided to blow the clothing budget today. Our investment account profits were still climbing. I'd told Jamie quite a few times that it felt wrong for me to share in the profits, since he'd provided the seed money, and since it was his expertise making the trades.

But he wouldn't listen. He said he'd already made back the seed money and a deal was a deal. I was getting my half.

I'd given up fighting.

If he was going to insist, then I supposed I'd accept it. I pictured myself Christmas shopping this year with a lavish budget and so many choices to surprise my family and friends.

And maybe I'd buy a couple of fancy outfits. Or maybe some not-so-fancy outfits. I could buy some of those deceptively casual clothes that were high quality and well made. To other people, they simply looked good. The secret was that they made *you* look good.

I was beginning to realize that Brooklyn and Sophie were onto something. There was a difference in quality and flair as you moved up the price range. Sometimes it seemed subtle, but it was real.

Last Sunday when I wore the black jeans to Angelo's, a dozen guys turned their heads when I walked to the ladies' room. Nobody had pointed, at least not that I saw. But many of them had followed me along, appreciative gazes on their faces.

Ironically, Ethan hadn't been one of them. Although Sophie kept trying, Ethan and I were never going to connect.

He connected better with Sophie than he did with me. I supposed that had a lot to do with their business venture. But still, his expression lit up for her and stayed flat for me.

Sometimes I thought Bryce saw that. Sometimes I thought Bryce got annoyed.

Sophie seemed like the only one who didn't notice.

After the outing at Angelo's, I vowed that if she suggested another double date, I was going to be frank with her and refuse. I wanted to spend girl time with Sophie. I wanted to hear more about her business venture. It was obvious she was really excited about that. But I hoped I could do it without spending another uncomfortable evening with Ethan.

I could tell Ethan had a crush on her. But I didn't want to throw that kind of a grenade into the Sweet Tech business venture. If Bryce didn't want to address it, there was no value in me addressing it. I would probably make things worse by telling her.

Jamie beat me to Brookswood and was waiting outside the main door.

"Hi," I said, feeling suddenly breathless.

He looked sexy, handsome and aloof.

"Hi," he said back and immediately turned for the door.

He held it open for me and I once again entered the rarefied environment of high-end shopping.

After a few steps, I opened the conversation. "Did you have a nice day?"

"It was fine." His strides were long and I had to hurry to keep up.

"So was mine."

"Good. Do you want to start with office wear, casual wear, a jacket? The weather's going to turn soon."

The weather? We were going to talk about the weather?

"Jamie?"

"Hmm?"

"What's going on?"

He looked down at me. But he wasn't seeing me, not really.

"What?" he asked.

"Something's wrong. What's wrong?"

"Nothing. We're shopping. You're right. We both need a more extensive new wardrobe. I hope you're not planning to bargain hunt."

"I'm not. You've convinced me to spend the investment profits. At least, you've convinced Tasha to spend the investment profits. Turns out she's not as scrupulous as me."

I expected him to laugh at my joke, but he didn't.

"You are Tasha," he said.

"You know what I mean."

"And it's not unscrupulous to spend money that belongs to you. What about shirtdresses? I read they're a thing."

"Jamie, stop."

He clamped his jaw, but he stopped.

"Look at me."

He turned, the aloof expression firmly in place.

"Is it the kiss?" I asked, tired of feeling jumpy, tired of trying to guess how he felt about it.

From the way he was acting, I could definitely guess he regretted it.

I pushed myself forward. "Are you being like this because we kissed each other?"

He didn't answer. And he sure didn't look happy that I'd brought it up.

I wanted to let him off the hook, to show him it was no big deal and I hadn't been obsessing about it—which, of course, I had, like every second since it happened.

"It was a kiss," I said. "A simple kiss. People do that. We were working together. We were happy. Plus, we've been, you know, turning each other into the image we think will attract the opposite sex." As I framed up my explanation, I decided it was pretty good. "All that kiss meant was that it's working. It's working, and that's a good thing. Hey, you should have seen the guys react to me at Angelo's on Sunday night."

Jamie sucked in a breath.

So did I. I needed oxygen to keep on talking. "They liked my look. A lot of them liked my look. As for you and me, well, it would be weird if we weren't a little bit attracted to each other. Don't you think that's true? And we were. And we kissed. And it's over. It doesn't have to mean a thing. It doesn't have to make you go all..." I gestured up and down at his posture. "I don't know, James-the-uptight on me."

"I'm not uptight." But he said it through teeth that were kind of clenched.

"I doesn't have to mean anything," I repeated. "It doesn't have to change anything. I don't want it to change anything."

I really, really didn't want anything to change between us, and I was afraid that I'd already blown it. These past few weeks had been the most enlightening, exciting and downright fun of my life. I didn't want to lose Jamie, and I desperately hoped my unbridled reaction to his kiss hadn't done just that.

He stayed silent for a moment. "It didn't change anything."

I felt a tiny hint of relief. "Then smile or something."

He tried, but it didn't come off.

I decided to keep it light and hope against hope that tactic would work. "Well, that's pathetic. The Jamie I know would blow past a little kiss in a heartbeat."

"You call that a little kiss?" he asked.

"I do."

We stared at each other for a moment.

He seemed to be daring me to do something or say something. But I couldn't tell what he wanted.

I took a stab. "I want to stay friends, Jamie. I really don't want to lose what we have."

His expression finally relaxed just a little bit. "Neither do I."

"Good." I was relieved, and I was glad. I didn't dare say anything more.

Instead, I glanced past him to the racks behind. "I don't really want a shirtdress."

"No shirtdress then," he said. "How about a jacket?"

I wouldn't say the shopping trip was the best time we'd ever had. We were still tippy-toeing around each other. But at least it was successful. We both left the store with armloads of new clothes, shoes and some jewelry for me.

Jamie got a text while we were paying and asked if I minded stopping at his office.

I easily agreed, not yet feeling like we were back on normal ground.

We drove over and parked in the company garage in a spot labeled for Jamie.

His key fob opened the doors, and an elevator whisked us to the thirty-second floor.

Aaron was sitting at a desk in the open office area.

There were a couple of other people in the distance, but otherwise the office was empty and quiet.

"Tell me exactly what Bernard said," Jamie said to Aaron.

"You didn't have to come all the way in," Aaron said.

"I assume it was you who changed his mind."

"A lot of things changed his mind. He thought about it, and he decided he's willing to take the chance."

"He never should have been put in this predicament in the first place. Watch and learn, Aaron. How hard is it to understand the concept of watch and learn?"

Jamie was angry.

I didn't know what to do with myself.

I felt awful just standing here listening to the argument, but there wasn't an easy way for me to escape. It was a long walk back to the elevators, and I wasn't sure where I would go from there. All the offices around the periphery of the space were closed. Not that I'd randomly walk into somebody's office.

"Rehashing it isn't going to help," Aaron said in obvious frustration.

Jamie clenched his jaw. "Then give me a path forward. You set this up. What's your solution?"

Aaron stood. "It's done, so we roll with it."

Jamie coughed out a laugh. "Go public on Monday without doing due diligence?"

"It's going to work, James." Aaron's tone was emphatic now. "I know in my gut that it's going to work."

"We're not trusting your gut. Your gut's only two months old."

"What about your gut?" Aaron asked.

The question seemed to throw Jamie.

"What does your gut tell you?"

I could see that Jamie didn't want to answer. I had to wonder if it was because he disagreed with Aaron or because he agreed with Aaron.

For some reason, he looked at me.

I tried to give him an encouraging smile, even though I had no idea what he was thinking.

The last thing he might want is for me to be happy when he was so obviously frustrated.

I wasn't happy about his frustration, of course.

But I was curious about the obvious struggle going on inside his head.

"I'm not recording this," Aaron said.

Jamie glared at him.

"Gut reaction." Aaron shrugged. "What could it hurt to say it out loud?"

"It'll work," Jamie said.

"There we go." Aaron smiled.

"No, there we *don't* go."

"Do you want me to explain gut reactions to you?" Aaron asked.

"No," Jamie drawled. "I do *not* want you to explain gut reactions to me."

"They're made up of subtle signals, information that you don't even know you know. It happens deep in your subconscious."

"What part of *no* did you miss?"

"It's not your gut working, James. It's your brain, your whole brain, the deep recesses of your entire brain. You know the answer. You just don't like working without the data on paper, driving without a seat belt."

"Jumping without a parachute," Jamie said. "And I change my mind all the time based on the data on paper."

"How do you do the short-term stuff?" I asked.

I thought I was being helpful, but Jamie shot me the same glare as he'd shot Aaron.

I wasn't being helpful.

"That's completely different," he said. "You know that. I explained that."

He had.

But I didn't see it being completely different. Then again, what did I know? I was a librarian, not an economist.

"Sorry," I said. I was.

"Bernard will ask for our recommendation in the morning," Aaron said.

Seconds ticked by.

"What do we say?" Aaron asked.

More seconds ticked by. I thought Jamie wasn't going to answer.

"Recommend the IPO," he said. His tone made the words sound painful.

"All right!" Aaron shouted and made a fist.

"Don't get cocky," Jamie said. "And if this goes bad…"

"It's on me." Aaron nodded.

"No, it's on me. Because that's the way it works."

Now I was nervous. I hated to think I might have pushed Jamie toward a decision he wasn't comfortable with.

"Jamie, if you're not—"

"Relax, Tasha. You didn't talk me into anything."

I swallowed.

Aaron spoke up. "The mighty James Gillen isn't one to take his girlfriend's advice."

Jamie's tone was cutting. "You don't know whose advice I'll take."

Then he turned to me. He looked tired, and his voice lost its edge. "Come on, Tasha. I'll drive you home."

Rock climbing training was uneventful on Saturday. It felt like our relationship was somewhat back on an even keel, and I told myself to be happy about that.

I didn't have any plans for Saturday night. I was disappointed that I wouldn't get to take any of my new, new clothes out for a test-drive. I'd bought this dusty blue tufted blouse and a short, blotchy, dusty-blue-and-pink-patterned skirt that I was dying to wear somewhere. It was set off with a wide black satin sash, and I'd bought oversize pearl earrings and a necklace to go with it.

It was softly romantic, and totally not me. I wasn't completely sure it was Tasha either, but I was willing to give it a shot. Both the salesclerk at Brookswood and Jamie had said it was a "must."

Who was I to say no to a "must"?

But it wasn't going to be this weekend.

I told myself it was just as well. I still had a lot of work to do on my apartment. If I pushed myself I could get the pumpkin—it turned out that was a very popular color—trim done today. Then I could put my furniture back and feel normal again.

Well, the new normal, of course.

I really did like the way the paint was turning out. It felt fresh and alive. I found it energizing to be at home.

If I worked hard, I'd be ready to start on the floors. I'd already picked up samples of stone and wood laminate. Not all of the brands were expensive, especially if you shopped carefully.

I liked the stone patterns best. It gave you the greatest range of color options.

So, Sunday morning, I dressed in paint clothes. I'd picked up a white cap at the hardware store, and I folded my hair underneath. I wasn't going to risk globs of pumpkin orange in my hair.

I'd masked stripes on the top and bottom of the walls, plus a wide box around each window.

I shook the paint bucket, pried it open, gave it a stir and then held my breath.

The butter yellow and russet brown were pretty low-risk colors. The orange on the other hand was going to pop. I felt like that first stroke was a momentous decision.

There was a knock on my door.

I gave myself a split second to wonder if it was a sign. Maybe I wasn't supposed to paint bright orange on my walls.

The knock came again.

I balanced the brush across the top of the open can, half-relieved by the interruption and half-annoyed that I was being given a chance to change my mind. I didn't want to change my mind. I wanted to dive wholeheartedly into my new bright orange life.

I opened the door to find Jamie standing there with two coffees and a paper bag from Penelope's Bakery.

His appearance took me by surprise. When he'd said goodbye yesterday he didn't say anything about helping me again. Not that I wouldn't say yes to the help. I'd really appreciate it.

Then again, he might not be here to help at all. He could be here for something completely unrelated to my apartment renovations. I shouldn't be so presumptuous.

"Hungry?" he asked.

"Why are you here?" I sounded rude. "I mean, sure, yes, I'm hungry."

He rattled the bag. "Fresh bagels."

I realized I hadn't eaten breakfast.

"I was just starting to paint," I said.

"Then I'm right on time." He moved forward, and I got out of the way.

"I didn't know you were coming," I said as I closed the door.

I was positive he hadn't said anything yesterday.

"Spur-of-the-moment. I stopped by Penelope's. The blueberry bagels made me think of you."

"Blueberry bagels? Really?" I couldn't for the life of me see the connection.

"Okay, it was the giant éclair in the refrigerated case. It reminded me of that time at the Orchid Club."

I remembered the decadent dessert we'd shared on that first reconnaissance foray outside the Orchid Club. We'd ordered mini cream puffs drizzled with chocolate and caramel sauce. I'd eaten the lion's share, and Jamie had teased me about my enthusiasm.

"But I thought it might be a bit much for breakfast, so I went with the bagels."

"Too bad," I said, only half joking.

Chocolate and pastry cream was my weakness.

"I can go back," he said.

"No, probably a good call. I don't want to go into a sugar coma before I finish painting."

Jamie handed me one of the coffee cups and looked around. "Seems like you're all set to go."

I decided coffee and fresh bagels would be worth the delay in starting. I took one end of the uncovered sofa that was angled in the middle of the room.

Jamie sat on the other end and put the bag of bagels between us.

"I'm hoping to finish today," I said.

Then I remembered the flooring samples and hopped back up, going to the kitchen counter where I'd left them.

"Take a look at these," I said as I carried them over to him.

Jamie had opened the bag and extracted a bagel. Both his hands were occupied.

"After you finish," I said and helped myself to a bagel.

"You've inspired me," he said.

"With flooring samples?" I grinned as I took a bite. It was awesome. "Mmm."

"With your willingness to change your life," he said.

It wasn't all me. It was far from all me.

I swallowed. "You're changing yours just as much."

He shook his head. "Not as much. Not everything."

"What do you mean?"

"I mean I need a new house."

I gave another big swallow. Okay, that was pretty huge.

"Are you sure? I mean, we only paid a couple hundred dollars for the paint." As commitments went, sweat equity wasn't nearly as serious as a mortgage.

"I'm moving up," Jamie said. "Or I'm moving sideways. I mean, I'm moving to where Jamie wants to live."

"Do we know where Jamie wants to live?" I asked.

"We're going to find out."

"Wow. That's huge."

"I'm counting on your help."

The statement, along with his expression, made me nervous. My head started to shake all on its own. "I'm not picking out your house."

"You did a terrific job with my car."

My head shaking continued. "That's crazy. It's nuts. A house is a major life decision, maybe *the* major life decision. It's a huge, long-term commitment. You have to pick it out yourself."

"I checked our stock portfolio this morning." He paused. It seemed like he was going for dramatic effect.

I wasn't sure if I should take that as a good or a bad thing. Good, I had to think, if he was talking about it in conjunction with buying a house.

Then again, I didn't want to get my hopes up. He'd come up with the investment seed money without too much trouble. He probably also had a decent down payment waiting in the wings. The two things might have nothing to do with each other.

"And..." I prompted.

"And it's up."

"Good." I was relieved—more for Jamie than for me.

I didn't really have anything at stake in it. We'd already taken out the money for our clothes-buying binge. But Jamie still had his capital at risk. I knew that stocks could fall just as easily as they could rise. And we'd had an awfully good run of it lately.

"Way up," he said.

I could tell he was toying with me.

"Are we going to play this game all morning?" I asked.

He grinned. "Remember Street Wrangle, the wireless company?"

I did. "Yes."

"Remember how I said they'd inexplicably bought that property next to Newmister?"

I remembered that, too. Jamie had speculated that the companies might be talking about a merger.

"They merged?" I asked.

There was a light in Jamie's eyes that said this was big.

I lost interest in my bagel.

"They merged. The stock spiked. It's set to split first thing Monday morning. Traders are lining up to get in. I've never seen buzz like this."

"But we're already in."

Jamie held his coffee cup up in a toast. "We're already in."

"Did we invest a lot?"

"We were bold. We went with our gut."

My grin grew, feeling like it might split my cheeks. "Oh, I *do* like Jamie's audacity."

"Will you help me find a house?"

"I'm scared." This situation called for me to be completely honest.

"Don't be scared."

"I don't know the first thing about real estate. I'll screw it up."

"You won't screw it up."

I gave a chopped laugh of disbelief. There were a thousand ways for me to screw up a choice like this—from location to plumbing to the foundation to…well, everything.

"Don't be scared, Tasha," he said in the gentlest of tones. "You're smart and methodical. And you have great instincts. You have gut instincts that are incredibly impressive. Run with them. Be audacious." He paused and seemed to be thinking. "Plus, I love your taste. You know you found me a great vehicle. Look at it this way, I just moved into a whole new housing bracket." He smiled and reached out to give my hand a quick squeeze. "This is going to be *fun*."

I considered his words. They were heartwarming.

I was on my way to being convinced, but I wasn't quite there. "You have a warped idea of fun. This is going to be *stressful*."

"No, stressful is slapping pumpkin on a freshly painted wall and hoping it looks okay."

"Wait a minute. You were the one who picked out the orange paint."

"And you let me. That was very trusting of you."

"This is on you," I said.

I took a last bite of bagel.

"I'll take that risk." Jamie finished his bagel and tipped back his coffee.

We stowed the trash. Then we crouched down at opposite ends of a wall and started painting orange.

Four hours later, our paintbrushes met in the middle of the last window.

We both straightened up. We took a few backward steps and gazed around.

I was amazed.

It looked fantastic.

"How did you know?" I asked him.

"Know what?"

"That it would look this good?"

"I cheated," he said.

"Cheated how?"

"I stole the idea from a decorating website, remember?"

"Nice steal." I couldn't believe this stylish, sophisticated apartment was mine. Now I couldn't wait to get going on the flooring.

Nine

"If you can do this without flinching," Jamie said to me as we stared up the thirty-foot rock face, "then you can definitely pick me out a house."

We'd looked at three different houses on Thursday night. While I'd tried to drag Jamie's opinion out of him, he kept insisting it was my choice to make. I'd been afraid to say I liked anything for fear he'd pull out his checkbook right then and there.

"I can do *this* without flinching," I said. I was excited about our climb, not frightened.

Spending hundreds of thousands of someone else's dollars? Now, *that* was frightening.

We were on a field trip with Paul, the other instructors and the rest of our class. It was a graduation ceremony of sorts, although Jamie and I had already signed up for the next level of climbing class, as had most of the rest of the class. We weren't qualified to undertake more than an uphill hike or a scramble by ourselves at this point.

"Great," Jamie said.

"But you really do have to weigh in on the house."

We'd seen two more houses last night with the Realtor Emily-Ann. I'd liked the last one quite a lot.

"Go through your safety check," the head instructor called out.

I made sure my watch was zipped into my pocket. I checked my harness buckles, my leg loops, rope orientation and carabiner. Jamie and I double-checked each other's knots, then we waited for Paul to give us a thumbs-up. We both passed his check, and we were ready to go.

I was going first with Jamie on belay.

Each of three teams had chosen a different section of the rock face.

I was ready.

I was excited.

"On belay?" I called back to Jamie.

"On belay," he confirmed.

"Climbing," I called.

"Climb on," he answered.

I found my first foothold, flexing my toe. I'd learned most of the patterns on the climbing wall, and it was exciting to be trying something completely new.

I was connected by a top rope that looped from the top of the climb back to Jamie. I trusted Jamie, and Paul was supervising, so I focused on the foot- and handholds.

I dead-ended once and had to back down a few steps, but otherwise, I made it up without any mistakes.

When I looked back down, Jamie was beaming and giving me a clap.

He lowered me down, and I took belay while he climbed.

By the end of the morning, we were all stripping off our windbreakers under the beaming sun. Paul and the other instructors had brought along a light picnic and some celebratory champagne.

Jamie and I toasted each other in the fresh air, laughing at our accomplishments.

He pulled me into an unexpected hug.

I felt arousal buzz through me.

"Now, that was adventure," he whispered in my ear.

"We are wild and exciting," I whispered back.

"Who wouldn't want to point at us across a room?" he asked.

"Or fall madly in love with us?"

His hug tightened for a second.

"Anyone who wants to take the long way home..." the head instructor said in a loud voice. Then he pointed. "There's a trail from here that goes around the face. It leads to a viewpoint lookout. Farther up, you can get into Pebble Pond. Then the main trail loops around back to the parking lot."

"It's all about the views," Paul said.

Most people were shaking their heads. Everyone was already hot and tired.

Jamie drew back to look at me.

"Game?" he asked.

I was.

In the end, six of us changed into hiking shoes and walked the two miles to the viewpoint.

As Paul had said, the view was spectacular, sweeping green hillsides, spikes of evergreens, and snowcapped peaks surrounding a deep blue lake in the valley bottom.

The rest of the group turned around there.

Jamie wanted to keep going, and my exhilaration was giving me energy. I felt like I could hike all day.

My exhilaration was ebbing by the time we made it along the narrow path to Pebble Pond.

The picturesque and isolated spot was worth the hike, but I'd admit I was glad we'd be going downhill on the way back.

"I like this," Jamie said, gazing out at the blue-green water surrounded by towering rocks and lush grasses and shrubs. A few cedars clustered near one shore with a group of crows circling the tops, calling to one another in the silent wind.

We were on a tiny stretch of pebble-covered beach. The

smooth little rocks were quite a pretty mix of white, blue gray, amber, green and black. Some were solid colors. Some were striped. And some were mottled. It was easy to see how the pond got its name.

It felt like we were all alone in the world.

Above us, an eagle took flight from the cedar trees, then another followed, chasing off the crows.

"Nature in the raw," I said, quoting something I'd once heard.

"My money's on the eagles," Jamie said.

"They must have a nest up there. Chicks do you think?"

"It seems late in the season. But they look like they're guarding something."

The eagles swooped in tandem, and the crows scattered.

The world fell silent again with the barest of breezes lifting the leaves around us.

"I'm sweltering," Jamie said.

I guessed the sun was reflecting off the surrounding rock faces. We did seem to be in a pocket of still heat.

Jamie stripped off his shirt.

My mouth went dry, and my brain paused for a beat. To be fair, I was dying of thirst. But the brain seize was all Jamie—his abs looked like they'd been sculpted from marble. His pecs and shoulders were firm, smooth and rounded. His biceps bulged, and his forearms were thick and sturdy.

I knew he had strong hands. I'd watched him work. But they looked stronger against the backdrop of nature.

Then he reached for the button of his khakis.

"Wh-what are you doing?" My stutter was mortifying.

"Taking a dip," he said, and dragged down his zipper. "Aren't you hot?"

I was hot. I was very hot. I was a whole lot hotter than I'd been two minutes ago.

"Don't look so worried," he said. "I'm not getting naked or anything. Come in with me. You're wearing underwear, aren't you?"

I was wearing underwear.

I was wearing Tasha underwear, sexy but very beautiful underwear. I wouldn't mind people seeing it.

Person, I corrected. I wouldn't mind a person seeing it. And that person was Jamie.

Oh, boy.

He kicked off his shoes, pulled off his socks and stripped down to a pair of black boxers.

This was Jamie all right. It was all Jamie. There wasn't an ounce of James left in this man.

My hands twitched with an urge to reach out and touch him.

But he started for the pond.

I had a ridiculous desire to call Brooklyn and ask her what on earth she thought she was doing. If Jamie had been waiting to marry me in the nave of St. Fidelis, I'd have been sprinting down the aisle, desperate to get going on the honeymoon.

"Come on, Tasha," he called over his shoulder. "Live a little."

I was living.

In this moment, I felt like I was *really* living.

I pulled my T-shirt over my head. I kicked off my runners, peeled off my sweaty socks and stepped out of my pants.

The pebbles were warm on my feet. They shifted as I walked to the shore.

Jamie dived under, resurfacing with a whoop that echoed off the cliff walls. He sent ripples across the surface of the pond.

"Cold?" I asked.

"Refreshing." He swiped his hand across his wet hair as he turned to look at me. He went still then, scanning me from my head to my toes.

I was acutely conscious of my burgundy bra and panties set. It covered everything that needed to be covered. But it covered it all in sexy, stylish satin and lace.

Jamie was definitely all Jamie today. And I was sure all Tasha underneath my climbing clothes.

I waded determinedly into the water, ignoring the cold, acutely conscious of Jamie watching me.

"Refreshing," I said as the water hit my shoulders.

Goose bumps came up on my skin.

He cleared his throat. "You'll get used to it in a second."

"I think you oversold the experience," I said.

He grinned. "Wimp."

"Hey, I just climbed a rock face."

"Want to climb another?" He looked meaningfully above us.

"Dressed like this? Without equipment? I don't think so."

"Live a little," he whispered.

"This *is* living a little."

In fact, it was living a lot. I was leading a hugely exciting Tasha life here. A month ago, I couldn't have even imagined a Saturday like this.

"Up there," he said, pointing to a flat ledge about ten feet in the air. "I'm going to jump."

"Have fun."

"Come, too?"

"Scramble up that little goat track in bare feet just to jump off a rock?" I winced.

"Tasha..." he said, in the most cajoling tone I'd ever heard. He moved closer to me. "I know deep down inside your little heart is a wild woman trying to get out."

I looked around us. "This isn't wild enough?"

I was swimming in my underwear in early October.

"Not wild enough for the two of us." He waggled his brow. "It's not going to kill you."

I looked up at the ledge.

He was right. Jumping ten feet wasn't going to kill me.

I wasn't scared. And it would probably be fun. I honestly didn't know why I was so reluctant. Reflex, I supposed. Nat was used to saying no to anything that seemed weird or offbeat, anything she knew she didn't know how to do, anything that seemed frivolous or silly or without purpose.

Jumping off a rock ledge into a mountain pond was arguably silly and without purpose. But it was also arguably fun.

"Fine," I said.

Jamie looked surprised. Then he grinned. "Come on, Crazy Tasha." He started paddling to the edge of the pond.

"First I'm not wild enough, now I'm crazy? There's no pleasing you." But I followed him.

"I'm crazy, too," he called back. "In a good way."

He hoisted himself onto a space at the bottom of the rock face.

He stood and turned, offering his hand to me.

"There's a foothold about two feet under the water," he said.

I reached for his hand and found the foothold with my right foot.

His grip was strong around my hand. "Ready?"

I nodded.

Jamie hoisted. I pushed with my left. I pulled up with my free hand on the ledge, and in seconds I was out of the water standing beside him.

Our wet bodies brushed together.

I felt the glow of the contact right through to my bones.

Our gazes hit each other. They held for a sizzling moment. But then Jamie looked away, up the side of the rock, finding a path.

He marched away from me, then scrambled to the top.

"It's easy," he called back.

It looked easy. And he was right. It was easy.

In minutes we stood on the edge of the face looking down at the deep, blue-green water.

"Are you scared?" he asked.

"Not really." I might be a little nervous. Or maybe I was excited. Or maybe I was so fixated on the beauty of the man standing beside me, that I didn't really care about the long plunge into the water.

"By the way, did I tell you the latest on our stock account?" he asked.

"What happened?" I couldn't tell if it was good news or bad.

"September Innovations posted their R & D results."

"Good?" I asked cautiously.

We could stand to lose some money at this point. We could easily stand to lose some money. I knew Jamie hadn't dumped our entire portfolio into September Innovations, a wireless technology company. But he had made a substantive gamble on them.

"Come Monday morning, we'll be able to watch the graph go up and up. You should think about buying a condo."

The suggestion took me by surprise. "We just redecorated my apartment."

"You've built up a serious down payment," he said. "You should start setting up some equity now."

It was probably good advice. But my brain didn't want to delve into equity and interest rates at the moment. I'd think about it later, when I was alone, when a half-naked Jamie wasn't crowding out all the logic inside my head.

"I'll think about it," I managed between processing the images of his rugged face, his sexy body and his clinging boxers.

"Good." He reached for my hand and squeezed it in his.

I loved the strength of his grip. His energy flowed up my arm and into my chest, and nothing else in the world mattered, not one little bit.

He nodded to the pond. "On three?"

I was thinking on ten, or maybe twenty, or maybe thirty. Or maybe we could just stand here in the sunshine forever holding hands on this perfect wild and wonderful Saturday afternoon. I didn't think life could get any better.

"On three," I said.

Jamie counted. "One…"

I joined him, and together we said. "Two…three."

We jumped.

I squeezed his hand tight as we flew through the air.

It felt like a long time, but it was only seconds before my feet hit the water, then my hips, my hands, and my head went under.

Cold engulfed my senses, and I lost hold of Jamie's hand.

I bobbed down a few feet, and then buoyancy took over, pushing me back up.

I broke the surface and blinked the water from my eyes to see Jamie grinning beside me.

"I like you, Tasha," he said, his warm gaze holding mine.

"I like you too, Jamie." I meant it in ways he couldn't possibly understand.

I bicycled my feet to stay afloat in the deep water, veering toward the shore.

He kicked toward me.

His expression sobered.

He touched my shoulder, and my whole body lit with desire.

"You are beautiful," he said.

I didn't know what to say to that.

The way he was looking at me made me feel beautiful.

He feathered his hand from my shoulder to the middle of my back.

His other arm went around my waist, anchoring me, and I realized he was standing on the bottom.

I stopped moving my legs.

"Tasha," he said.

"Jamie," I answered.

He tipped his head and slowly leaned in.

His lips touched mine, cool from the water. But they heated quickly.

His kiss sent waves of wanting through my arms, my legs, to my belly and breasts. My body tightened and quickened. Passion amped up as our kiss deepened.

I wrapped my arms around him, sliding them from his firm shoulders across his back, up to his neck. My fingers tangled in the base of his hairline as I held him to me.

My lips parted farther and his tongue touched mine.

Fireworks flashed behind my eyes. Under the water, my legs wrapped around him.

Somewhere deep in my brain stem, I understood what I was doing, the intimacy of the move, what I was signaling. But my conscious mind didn't care about that.

I wanted to get closer to Jamie. I needed to get closer to Jamie. Every inch of space between us should be erased and eradicated.

His hand closed over my breast, the wet fabric making no barrier at all. I moaned with the pleasure of his touch.

I tipped my head back to give him access.

His kissed his way along my neck.

I knew where this was going. I loved where this was going. I couldn't wait to get there.

He cupped my behind, holding me to him, pressing against me, spreading pulses of heat and power in all directions.

Then he quit the kiss and gave a chopped exclamation. "We can't."

He pulled back from me. "Tasha." He took a couple of deep breaths. "I don't—"

"It's fine," I managed. I was as mortified as I'd ever been in my life. "It's nothing."

"It's not—"

"You said it yourself." I disentangled my arms and legs and put some space between us. "I'm completely refreshed."

"Tasha, wait."

"Let's get back to the car." My feet found the bottom of the pond, so I was able to propel myself even faster toward the pebble shore.

"That's not what I meant," he called from behind me. "Tasha, stop."

I wasn't stopping. The last thing I was doing was stopping.

I'd made a colossal mistake. We'd both made a colossal mistake. There was still time to correct it, and that was good.

We'd gotten over the kiss. We'd get over this.

I felt his hand on my arm.

I tried to shake it off, but he refused to let go.

He turned me, and I nearly stumbled over in the waist-high water.

"I only meant—"

"Will you let me go?" I demanded.

Maybe his precious Tasha didn't care about dignity, but Nat still did. There was still enough Nat in me to want to get the heck out of this situation.

"I don't have anything." He stared meaningfully at me, moving close up. "I don't have a condom, Tasha. I wasn't saying we shouldn't, I was saying we couldn't, not here, not now, not without protection."

His words dropped to silence.

It was a very uncomfortable silence.

"Oh." My voice was tiny. I swallowed.

He raked a hand through his hair. "What is with you?"

I didn't have a ready answer for that.

He kept talking. "Do you think I behave like that when I *don't* want to make love?"

I found my voice again. "I don't know. I couldn't tell."

"Well, *tell* already. That's what raw, unbridled lust and passion look like. You're hot, Tasha. Any guy within fifty yards of you probably wants you. And none of them, definitely not me, is going to shut it down without a damn good reason."

"Oh," I said again, struggling to shift the emotional gears inside my head.

"We should go," he said.

"Okay." I had no idea where this left us.

He moved closer. His expression changed. And my uncertainty dropped a notch.

"To your place," he said with meaning. "As fast as we can get there."

* * *

I opened my apartment door to find Sophie inside.

We both stared at each other in shock, me on finding her in my apartment—which was not unheard of, but pretty unusual—and her likely wondering why my hair was wet and why Jamie was with me.

What on earth was I going to say about that?

"Oh, good," she said before I could form any kind of a coherent sentence. "You brought Jamie. I guess you heard?" Her eyes were alight with joy.

"Uh…"

"Aaron called. Bryce and Ethan are on their way over. I can't believe it." She started to pace. "I just can't believe it. How long have you two known?"

I looked at Jamie.

We must have had identical expressions of bafflement.

"I wish you'd told me yourself," Sophie said to me. She closed the space and wrapped me in a tight hug.

Then she seemed to notice my wet hair.

She looked at Jamie, then back at me. I could see it all unraveling right here in front of us.

"Were you at the club?" she asked us.

"Yes," Jamie said.

Sophie took a step back and put her hand on her forehead. She grinned and turned away. "We need champagne."

I gave Jamie a panicked look and mouthed the word *what?*

He shrugged his shoulders.

"When Aaron told me it was five hundred thousand, I made him say it again. I couldn't believe it."

Five hundred thousand? Dollars? Did she mean *dollars*?

She turned back. "We need champagne."

"Aaron talked to you about five hundred thousand dollars?" Jamie asked.

His tone was tense, his expression worried.

"Did I get the number wrong? Oh, I hope I didn't get it

wrong because I told Bryce and Ethan. Did you talk to Horatio Simms?" Her question was directed at Jamie. "Did he say that was his investment? Oh, I sure hope I didn't mess up."

"Horatio Simms is investing five hundred thousand dollars in Sweet Tech?" Jamie asked.

"I know I have you to thank for that. I don't know what you did, but—"

"I didn't talk to Horatio," Jamie said.

Sophie looked confused.

"But Aaron told me..."

"I did talk to Aaron," Jamie said. I could hear the annoyance in his voice. "Aaron must have talked to Horatio."

Sophie breathed a sigh of relief. "Oh, then that makes sense."

Jamie went to his phone.

I didn't know what was happening, but I could tell we had a big problem. There was a knock on the door.

"That'll be Bryce and Ethan." Sophie brushed past me.

"Simms?" Jamie said into the phone. "I'm at Tasha's with Sophie and her crew."

I glanced to Sophie to see if she'd noticed Jamie calling me Tasha.

She hadn't.

"When you get this," Jamie said. "Call me. Or better still, get your butt over here and tell me *what is going on*."

Jamie disconnected.

"What?" I whispered to him.

Jamie came close to my ear. "I specifically told Aaron that Sweet Tech wasn't ready for investment. It's way too high risk and we don't have a proper prospectus. I waved him off, and he pulled in his uncle instead? This is going to go *so* bad."

I didn't know what to say. I was awash with both guilt and worry. I hated the thought that I'd caused problems at work for Jamie.

"Bryce brought champagne!" Sophie said. "Get some glasses, Nat."

I forced a smile on my face. "Sure." I didn't know what else to do, so I started for the kitchen. "Can you tell me more about the deal?"

Maybe, at the very least, I could arm Jamie with some information before he talked to Aaron.

I found my champagne flutes in a high cupboard, and I passed them around.

Jamie tried to refuse, but I gave him a glare that told him to play along. There was no point in getting angry right now.

Sophie and her friends were oblivious to any problems. To them, Jamie was the hero who'd saved their fledgling business. All she could see was a bright and beautiful future of success and riches.

If it had to come crashing down, it had to come crashing down. But we should figure out exactly why before we gave her the bad news.

"To success," Sophie said, raising her glass. "And to James for all of his help."

For a second I thought Jamie might blurt something out. But he didn't, just took a drink of his champagne.

Sophie, Bryce and Ethan all started talking, fast and with plenty of emotion and excitement. I heard them say *scale up* and *distribution* and *markets*.

Before I could take Jamie aside again, there was another knock on the door.

I opened it to find Aaron.

He was grinning. "Hi, Natasha."

I could feel Jamie's presence right behind me. "Start talking, Simms."

"You heard."

"Of course I heard. Why, *why* would you tell Horatio about Sweet Tech?"

"Because I knew you were holding out on us, keeping it all to yourself."

Jamie shook his head. "That wasn't it. You knew that wasn't what was going on."

Aaron shot back, "No. I know that you told me it wasn't ready for investment."

"It wasn't. It isn't. And Horatio should know that. This isn't his kind of deal. How did you convince him to invest so much money?"

Aaron didn't answer.

"How?" Jamie repeated.

"I told him it was your recommendation."

"You *what*?" Jamie bellowed.

"I'm not an idiot, Gillen. You were going to invest. You might have wanted to dot the *i*'s and cross the *t*'s, but you know you were going to invest."

"I was *not* going to invest."

"Then why spend all that time, effort and energy on it?"

"I was doing a favor for a friend."

Aaron looked at me. "A *friend*."

His inference was clear.

"You've set your uncle up to lose money. And he's going to think I suggested it. You overconfident, cavalier little jerk."

"Nat?" Sophie's voice sounded shaky behind us.

My heart sank.

"What's going on?" Sophie asked.

There was a brittle silence. Finally, Jamie turned.

"Aaron made a mistake," Jamie said to Sophie.

"There's no mistake," Ethan said. "We have a handshake deal for five hundred thousand dollars."

Jamie shot Aaron a brief glare. "I need to talk to Horatio. He didn't have all the facts when he made that deal."

"You don't have faith in us?" Sophie asked Jamie.

Jamie didn't answer.

"It's not that," I said, trying to help.

"Tasha, don't," Jamie said.

Sophie gave him a puzzled look at the name Tasha.

"You're right," Jamie said to Sophie in a clipped, professional voice. "I don't have faith in you. The reason I don't have faith is that I'm a realist. You're at a very early stage. You need patient capital. Horatio is looking for a faster return on his investment. You're not going to be able to give it to him."

Ethan took a step forward. "Who says?"

"I say... Ethan, is it?"

"Ethan Tumble. I'm the technical brains behind this, and I know a good idea when I see one. This thing's got legs."

"I'm not saying it's not a good idea."

"We should close the door," I said.

I didn't have a lot of neighbors, but I didn't think this was a conversation we wanted people to overhear.

Jamie looked frustrated, but he stepped aside and Aaron came in.

I closed the door.

Jamie spoke again. "You may have the best idea in the world. Over the long term, you might all be headed for stellar success. And I hope you are. I really do. But it was presented to Horatio in a ridiculously irresponsible way. Aaron has to answer for that. And I have to answer for Aaron. And I will. *We* will. We'll tell Horatio the truth and take it from there."

"We're not getting the money," Sophie said, sounding completely dejected.

I didn't blame her, and I hated that I'd had a hand in setting up this debacle.

"Simms," Jamie said as he reopened the door. He gestured for Aaron to leave.

Aaron left, and Jamie followed him out.

Sophie looked like she might cry, and I realized Jamie had left me alone.

I mean, Sophie, Bryce and Ethan were still there. But Jamie was gone.

I'd come home from the hike with such high expectations for Jamie and me. This wasn't how the day was supposed to go.

The day was supposed to end with the two of us alone, together, in my bed with a condom and our pent-up passion for each other.

Ten

I wished I could have done a better job consoling Sophie. But I was fumbling in the dark. I had no idea what was going to happen next.

We speculated on the potential for Horatio's investment, and we talked about other investments that might replace it. I reminded her that she still had a good job. I told her she was young, just starting out. Things were going to go up, and things were going to go down. And I truly believed that.

Trouble was, she'd gotten her hopes way up. I knew it was hard to go from the top of the world to the depth of disappointment. It really sucked.

Privately, I wondered what Jamie and Aaron were going to say to Horatio—Aaron in favor of the investment and Jamie opposed was the best I could guess. And I really couldn't see how Horatio would be willing to invest in Sweet Tech by the end of that conversation.

A handshake deal was all well and good, but I doubted it would stand up in court. I honestly couldn't imagine Sophie suing anyone anyway.

She left at about ten thirty, after a couple of glasses of wine. We didn't have the heart to finish the champagne.

I showered the dried pond water out of my hair, using extra conditioner to get the softness back into it. Then I changed into the worn cotton shorts and T-shirt I usually wore to bed.

But I wasn't tired. I wasn't hungry. I didn't feel like watching a movie or reading a book. I wasn't even thirsty.

I prowled the apartment for a few minutes before I decided to surf around online.

I thought back on what Jamie had said about me buying a condo. I was feeling like I should get my life in order. This windfall from our investments might or might not last. I should put it to good use while I had the chance.

I'd be thirty in a couple of years. I should own my own real estate by then. That's what people did when they became full-fledged adults. They invested. They settled down. They started to build their lives.

I looked around my apartment and thought about moving. I really liked the work we'd done, the colors and the style. But it wasn't mine. It was a temporary stop for me. I considered how I could duplicate the colors and style if I bought my own condo.

Maybe I could get something on a ground floor. It would be nice not to have to lug groceries up the stairs every week. Not that it wasn't good exercise. It was very good exercise. But if I could find a place near the park, I could keep my bike handy and get exercise that way. Riding through the park would be more fun than lugging groceries up the stairs.

There was a knock on the door.

I got up to answer, my first thought being that Sophie was back. Like me, she was probably feeling way too blue to sleep. I hoped she hadn't driven her car after we'd had the wine.

Then I hesitated before opening the door.

It was really late, well after eleven. And why hadn't she texted me? She would have texted me if she was coming back.

I glanced to the dead bolt to make sure it was locked.

"Hello?" I said through the door.

"It's Jamie."

At the sound of his voice, my chest tightened with anticipation. I was glad that he'd come back, way too glad.

I quickly unlocked and opened the door.

"What happened?" I asked him, drinking in his handsome face but forcing my thoughts to Sophie. "Is it bad? Is it good? Have you talked to Sophie yet?"

He came inside. "I haven't talked to Sophie. It's too late to call her."

He was right about that. And bad news could always wait until morning. If Sophie was already asleep, it seemed cruel to wake her up only to make her more miserable.

"What happened?" I asked, hesitant to know, but knowing that not knowing wouldn't change a thing. I knew that much.

"Aaron and I talked to Horatio."

"And?" I backed away a little and braced myself.

I was pretty sure the outcome was inevitable. But once I heard the words, there was no more hope for Sophie. I felt terrible for being a part of boosting then dashing her dreams.

"It turned out badly for me," Jamie said, looking grim.

It wasn't the answer I'd expected. "I don't understand." I struggled to figure out what it might mean. "Oh, Jamie, what did Horatio do? Did you get fired"

"No. It wasn't that."

I felt a small measure of relief.

"But he won't walk away from the investment."

It took me a second to have the words make sense inside my head.

Jamie's expression was at odds with his words.

"But that's good," I said. "That means Sophie will get the money."

"No, that's bad. Yes, they'll get the money. And if they lose it, Aaron and I will be in big trouble."

I was confused. "You told Horatio the whole story, right? He knows you think it's risky. If he decided to stay in anyway—"

"Sure, I told him the whole story. Problem was, he didn't believe me."

I lowered myself into an armchair. "Why didn't he believe you?"

"He thinks I want the investment for myself."

"He thinks you'd lie to him?"

"Horatio is not exactly the trusting type. Aaron had him convinced he'd beaten me to the punch. He thinks the minute he pulls out, I'll jump in."

"Would you?" Even as I asked the question, it sounded silly.

Jamie didn't have five hundred thousand dollars to risk. And why would he put his money where it would be locked up for a long time, and where he thought he might lose it?

Why would anyone do that?

They wouldn't.

"It's still a risky investment," he said. "And if it goes bad on him, Horatio will save his reputation by putting the blame on us."

"I'm so sorry." I stood again. I was feeling worse by the minute.

"I hope I can help them. They need to get out of R & D, bring it to market and scale up."

"I'm sure you can," I said. Everything I'd seen Jamie touch had turned out well.

"Even if I can think of something, Ethan doesn't seem like the kind of guy to listen."

"You're a lot smarter than Ethan. And Sophie will listen to you."

Jamie gave a cool smile at that. "I appreciate the vote of confidence."

I didn't think Jamie needed me to tell him what he already knew. He was amazing, in so many ways. I thought it had to be obvious to the world.

We gazed at each other in silence.

Memories of our swim bloomed to life in my brain.

I wondered if he was remembering, too. I didn't know how to ask. I didn't know how to bring up the subject—the fact that I was sitting here wishing I could throw myself into his arms and pick up where we left off.

I didn't have any experience with this.

How did people tell a friend they wanted to sleep with them?

I was pretty sure they did it all the time. Friends with benefits was a thing. It was a big thing. People seemed quite taken with the concept.

It seemed like the kind of concept Tasha would like. Tasha would definitely like an arrangement like that—all the benefits and a friendship, too. Why wouldn't she want that?

And she'd ask. She'd just outright ask: *Hey, Jamie, how about we sleep together tonight?*

I snickered at myself.

"What's funny?" Jamie asked.

"Me," I said. "Tasha me."

His gaze went soft as he studied my face. "You are Tasha."

"Sometimes," I said.

I'd been very Tasha this afternoon when I jumped off that rock, then nearly jumped Jamie's bones. That had been very Tasha.

"Why is Tasha smiling?" he asked. "I'm assuming she's not amused by my predicament."

"Not at all. I'm really sorry about that."

He waved my words away. "Let's get back to the smile."

I stepped forward, bringing myself closer. It felt easier to say the words when there was some intimacy between us.

"You remember this afternoon?" I asked.

He moved too, closing the distance between us. "Is that a joke?"

"It's an opening line."

"Yes, I remember this afternoon."

I gathered every ounce of my courage and dived into the deep end. "Do you want to sleep with me?"

"Did I not make that obvious?"

"Because I want to sleep with you. There, I said it." I paused. "Okay, you probably already knew that." I recalibrated in my brain. "I'm thinking Tasha would just say it out loud. And so would Jamie. You know that Jamie would say it. If Tasha and Jamie wanted to be friends with benefits, they'd say so. They'd say it. They'd own it. They'd do it. And they'd enjoy it. No big thing. No big deal. They wouldn't dwell on whether or not it was a good idea. They're exciting. They're risk takers. They embrace life and enjoy every single moment of it. And there's no reason, none at all, why we shouldn't do exactly that. I have condoms, you know."

Jamie cracked a sudden smile. "Are you done?"

I took a breath.

Part of me couldn't believe I'd just blurted all that out.

Another part of me was darn proud for having done it. "I think so...yeah... I think that about does it."

"Yes," Jamie said.

I waited for more.

He didn't say anything else.

"That's it?" I asked.

"That's it. A solid, definitive, exciting, risk-taking yes."

I reached for his shirt.

He reached for mine.

We all but tore off each other's clothes.

Then we stopped. We stared at each other. We were mostly naked, both breathing deeply.

"I want to do this fast," Jamie said.

I was fine with fast. I was more than fine with fast. We had two perfectly good sofas within a few feet of where we were standing. And there were the armchairs. I'd make love on an armchair.

Or the floor. I'd happily make love with Jamie on the floor, too.

"But I want it to go slow." He reached out and feathered a touch on the tip of my bare shoulder.

Oh, yeah. Slow sounded marvelous.

His palm cupped my shoulder, and he drew me into a kiss.

It was long and deep and sexy sweet.

I stepped into him, my nipples brushing his chest. Tendrils of passion were winding through me, heating me straight to my core.

I wrapped my arms around his neck, leaning into the strength of him.

He cupped my rear with both hands, pulling me against him.

"But I can't do slow," he growled against my lip.

"Okay," I said.

"Slow later," he said and scooped me into his arms.

I didn't know where we were going, and I sure didn't care.

He rounded the divider in less than five seconds. Deposited me on the bed and followed me down, covering my body with his heat.

He kept up his kisses, and I molded my lips to his, thinking that he tasted good, really good, extraordinarily good. I didn't think a man's lips could taste so sweet.

His palm stroked its way up my side, over my ribs, onto my breast, settling there.

I arched my back, and a moan vibrated my lips.

His fingers wrapped my nipple, and the tingle told me it was beading in response.

"Tasha," he whispered, then stroked his tongue against mine.

I loved my name on his lips, my special, secret name that meant everything I was doing was okay. It was better than okay. It was fantastic and fun, and there wasn't a reason in the world I shouldn't be enjoying sex with Jamie.

We'd made a deal. And it was a good deal. It was a marvelous deal, and all I had to do was lie back and enjoy it.

I parted my legs to cradle him, and I stroked my hands down the length of his back, feeling the satin of his skin, the definition of his muscle, marveling at the texture and the masculine contours of his body.

I broke from his mouth to kiss his shoulder. I wanted to see if his skin tasted as good as his lips.

It did.

I kissed my way across his chest.

He threw his head back and groaned.

His fingers tightened on my nipple, sending quivers of desire rocketing down my body. I arched into him, my legs going around his waist.

"Condom," he whispered.

Good call. For a second I'd forgotten.

I would have remembered, I told myself as I reached out and pulled open the drawer of my bedside table.

The interruption was brief, and I watched his expression until he was done and met my eyes. His were dark blue, deep and intent.

"You're gorgeous," I said.

He smiled. "You're the gorgeous one." His arms slid back around me, and he held me so tenderly close that I felt a random tear slip from the corner of my eye.

I wasn't crying. I wasn't sad. I was very, very far from sad. If anything, I wanted to whoop with joy.

"You ready?" he asked.

I'd been ready for quite a few days now.

"Yes," I said and angled toward him.

He pressed into me.

I closed my eyes, savoring every inch and every second, until we were together and desire was rocketing through my body.

He pulled, and I gasped.

His voice was a groan again near my ear. "This is *so* not going to be slow."

"Good," I said.

Slow could come later. At least, I hoped slow would come

later. If making love with Jamie felt like this all the time, I didn't know how we'd ever stop.

His body met mine, and I synced our rhythm. His hands were everywhere, plucking my passion, drawing out sensations I hadn't known existed.

A colored haze took over my brain, green then blue then yellow and orange. We flew high and crested fast.

I cried out. I dived into the sun. Waves of pure ecstasy all but lifted me from the bed.

Jamie groaned, and our bodies pulsed together for long minutes.

Then I felt the tension drain from him. I melted into every touch, every sensation. My skin was slick against his. The air finally felt cool on my limbs.

"Wow," Jamie said.

"Wow," I said back.

"That was fantastic."

"It was," I agreed wholeheartedly.

"We have to do that again."

I smiled at that. I loved the conviction in his voice. "Right this second?"

"Tonight. Definitely again tonight."

His words made me think about tomorrow.

But I wasn't going to think about tomorrow. I was Tasha, and I was daring and confident, and I was going to take this moment, this night for what it was. A supergood time with a man who was becoming a supergood friend. There was absolutely no value in worrying beyond that.

It was Sunday, and I opened my apartment door to Sophie.

I was expecting Jamie in an hour, and until I saw her standing there I'd hoped the knock meant he was early. I'd hoped he was as anxious to see me as I was to see him. Then I hoped Sophie couldn't see the disappointment on my face.

She didn't.

She looked tired and frustrated.

"It's hard trying to get rich," she said and moved past me.

She was dressed in jeans and flats. Her light brown hair was swooped up in a ponytail that looked hasty. And her sparkly T-shirt hung lose over her jeans—no half tuck, no saucy knot, no nothing. This wasn't like Sophie.

"No orders yet?" I knew they'd all been contacting potential customers.

I told myself I was sympathetic. And I reminded myself how important the success of BRT Innovations was to Sophie and everyone else, including Jamie. I reminded myself that sex with Jamie was secondary to his own career and to Sophie's future.

Still, I couldn't stop thinking about his arrival. And I couldn't help hoping Sophie would be gone by then. Most of all, I couldn't help picturing Jamie naked.

"We've been at it for *months*," she said. "We're all working doubly hard now, and Jamie is helping, but there's no interest from the market. I'm talking zero interest, Nat. And it's starting to terrify me."

I closed the door. "These things take time." I knew that had to be true.

She took a couple of steps and then turned to face me. "It would be different if we had some maybes, if people liked the idea but maybe couldn't afford Sweet Tech. If they thought they might want to buy one in the future. But nobody wants to buy one in the future. They won't even consider the possibilities."

I knew I'd be a terrible salesperson. I couldn't even imagine how demoralizing it must be to face so much rejection.

"We're moving pretty fast, spending, spending, spending," she said, looking even more worried as she said it. "Ethan's put together ten more prototypes."

"You need those for sure," I said, trying to sound optimistic but feeling as worried as Sophie looked.

She gave a nervous laugh. "You have to spend money to make money?"

"I've heard that." I didn't have much else to offer.

"We're spending Horatio's money now. And the things Aaron's said about his uncle make me feel like we're indebted to a criminal—like he'll break our legs or something if we don't pay it back."

"Nobody's breaking anyone's legs." I thought about my half of the money Jamie and I had amassed and wondered if contributing it would help.

I could wait for a condo. I could be happy in my apartment for a few more years. At least it looked great now. It wasn't ugly anymore. I had that going for me.

Another knock came on the door.

My brain and my heart rooted for it to be Jamie. I couldn't help the feelings, even though I knew they were selfish.

"Aaron was going to meet me here," Sophie said.

More disappointment for me.

As I walked to the door, I told myself to stop being so self-absorbed.

Last night with Jamie had been beyond amazing, and I couldn't wait to be alone with him again, to kiss him, make love with him, to talk, to laugh, to whatever with him. I was greedy for every second we could have together.

I was greedy. And I needed to stop. Sophie needed my support right now.

I opened the door, and it was Jamie.

My heart lifted.

"Hi, Tasha," he said, his eyes warm, his lips breaking into a smile.

"Why do you call her that?" Sophie appeared at my right shoulder.

Jamie was obviously surprised to see her.

"It's short for Natasha," he said.

"So is Nat." She looked from him to me and back again. "And what are you doing here?"

Jamie didn't answer.

I opened my mouth, hoping something logical would come out of it. No reasonable explanation was forming inside my head.

Then Aaron appeared in the hallway.

"Did Aaron call you?" Sophie asked Jamie.

"He didn't have to call me," Jamie said, brushing past the awkward moment. "We work in the same office. What's going on?"

As Jamie moved past me, he purposefully brushed his hand against mine.

My skin tingled and my heart thudded.

It had been a busy week, and I was impatient to get to the benefits part of our friendship again. I was feeling *really* impatient. Clearly, I wasn't a very good friend to Sophie.

"We have to get this under control," Aaron said as he walked in the door. "We can't keep bleeding money with nothing to show for it. We need a plan to get some orders under our belt."

Bryce and Ethan arrived behind him, and my apartment filled up with the entire gang.

"We need to open some doors," Aaron said. "Nobody is taking us seriously."

"Because Sweet Tech has no track record," Jamie said, sounding impatient. "BRT Innovations has no track record. That's been my point all along."

"An 'I told you so' isn't going to help," Aaron said.

"Even if it makes you feel like the big man," Ethan tossed in.

"Ethan," I snapped.

Aaron was right. But Jamie was right, too. And Ethan being rude wasn't going to help any of it.

Jamie's eyes were annoyed, but his voice was calm. "Who have you been targeting, and where have you gone so far?"

I was impressed with his apparent self-control. Then again, I was pretty biased when it came to Jamie. I knew he had flaws, but I was hard-pressed to see any of them. He was one incredible package of a man.

I realized we'd turned him into exactly what he'd wanted—the guy that women pointed to from across the room, the guy every woman wanted to meet. And now that we'd succeeded, I didn't want it at all.

Why hadn't I just spoken up way back then, way back when no other women were looking? Why hadn't I just said, "Hey, James, date me, let's see what happens?"

I could tell myself that Nat would never have done that. But she should have done that. I should have done that. Now I felt like our time together was ticking down.

"Suppliers," Sophie said. "We've done trade shows from LA to New York. Bryce and I have taken two weeks' vacation to focus."

I was surprised to hear that. Sophie hadn't said anything to me about using up her vacation time.

"I've been through a Rolodex of suppliers," Bryce said.

"Have you tried individual restaurants?" Jamie asked. "Who are the trendsetters?"

"They can't get a return going retail," Aaron said.

"They can prove the concept," Jamie said. "And trendsetters move things on social media."

"I've tried that approach," Bryce said. "I made appointments during my downtime in New York City. I couldn't get any takers. I'd try locally, but nobody in Seattle has a big enough national profile."

Jamie paced to the kitchen corner and then turned. "Give me your elevator pitch again?"

"Perfection," Bryce said. "Zero labor, no waste, consistency and perfection."

"Who likes perfection?" Jamie asked.

Everybody looked at each other, but nobody answered.

"High-end places," Ethan suggested.

"That's where I've been *trying*," Bryce said.

"This is getting us nowhere." Aaron frowned and dropped onto a sofa.

"Nationally," Jamie said.

I could tell by his quirk of a smile that he'd thought of something.

He kept talking. "Our focus is too narrow. What about international? Who likes perfection? The French? Food is a really big deal in Paris."

"The French are all about taste," Bryce said. "They cater to sophisticated palates. The look isn't so important."

"Italy?" Jamie asked. "Asia?"

"I see what you're thinking," Bryce said. Then he gave a chopped laugh. "Japan."

"That's good," Jamie said.

"Japan?" Aaron mocked. "Your solution is to try doing business in Japan?"

"They're technology leaders themselves," Ethan said, though he looked skeptical.

"Has a Japanese company come out with a comparable product?" Jamie asked.

Ethan looked uncomfortable. "I don't know."

"Well, find out," Jamie said. "If New York doesn't want to be a trendsetter, maybe Tokyo does."

"I don't have a single contact in Japan." Sophie looked like she was close to tears.

"I have a few," Jamie said.

I couldn't help but look at him in surprise again, and maybe in awe, and maybe with an even bigger crush than I'd had ten minutes ago.

Was there anything he couldn't do?

Jamie had his phone out and was pressing buttons. "Ethan, you need to get a prototype packed and ready to ship with us. Bryce, keep working on individual restaurants. They may end up being our only hope. Try LA next. They must have trendsetters in LA. Sophie?"

Sophie glanced at him. "Yes?"

"Want to go to New York with me?"

"Me?" she asked, looking surprised, beautiful and surprised.

I was surprised, too. Not that I didn't trust Sophie's business acumen. I did. But Bryce was the chef and Ethan was the tech specialist.

"Rina Nanami is in New York City right now. The Nanami family is a client, and they own a chain of high-end restaurants in Japan. Our best bet is for her to meet one of the owners in person. It has to be Sophie because Rina will like that she's a woman entrepreneur. That's our ticket in through the door."

I fought a lump in my throat.

I was glad that Jamie had an idea. I was excited for Sophie and for everyone.

And I wouldn't be jealous of Sophie going to New York with Jamie. I got that she was the business owner and not me. Besides, Sophie wasn't interested in Jamie. She was with Bryce.

And, anyway, Jamie and I were just friends. I didn't have the right to be jealous of him with anyone.

But I wanted it to be me in New York, me with Jamie, me on a cross-country flight in his company.

He looked at me then.

I could tell what he was thinking. At least, I hoped I could tell what he was thinking. What I wanted him to be thinking was that he'd miss me. Better still, I wanted him to be thinking he'd stay here tonight, that he'd wait until everyone else left and then he and I could have benefits again.

I wanted him to spend the night this time. I wanted to watch the dawn break in his arms, share coffee in my little rooftop garden, laugh together over toast or eggs or blueberry bagels.

I wanted Jamie to myself.

I didn't want him to fly off with Sophie.

The countdown on our relationship felt like it was ticking louder than ever.

"It'll be a whirlwind trip," he said to me. "I'm..." After a second, he clamped his jaw, seeming to become aware that all gazes were on him.

"Good luck," I said in the brightest voice I could muster.

"I want to be there by morning," he said. "It'll give us the best chance of catching Rina."

He was talking to everyone, but his gaze was still on me.

I thought he was apologizing. At least, I hoped he was apologizing. I wanted him to be as disappointed about tonight as I was. But I couldn't be sure that was happening. It was impossible to know.

It was bad enough to be jealous of Sophie.

I'd spent two days being jealous of Sophie.

But as I walked into the O'Neil Nybecker offices, I had a whole new reason to be jealous.

I'd felt good leaving home to drive over here. Jamie was back, and he'd asked me to meet him at the office. I assumed we were going out for dinner, maybe we'd do a little downtown shopping, or maybe we'd look at houses again. Whatever it was, I'd like being back on track.

As long as we ended up back at my place later on, or maybe his place this time. Friends with benefits was way more fun when you found time for the benefits.

I'd put on a pale blue crepe dress with a flowing gray speckled sweater over top. Both hung to midthigh, leaving a length of bare leg to show off my shimmery, dusty-blue ankle boots. They weren't perfect for walking, but they were better than spike-heeled sandals or pumps. I'd topped the dress off with a chunky bright blue necklace.

I'd felt chic and funky, quite pretty, really. That is, until I spotted Sophie laughing next to Jamie in a royal blue cocktail dress. It was fitted and sleek, with a straight neckline and wide shoulder straps. Sophie looked ready for a night on the town.

Worse, on the other side of Jamie was a lovely, petite Japanese woman. She wore a short, jewel-encrusted jacket over a pleated white skirt. Her dark hair was swooped up, and her jewels looked like real diamonds. She had her hand on Jamie's arm, and he was whispering something in her ear.

They looked fantastic together, a power couple out to conquer the world.

I tried to capture the feeling I'd had when I gazed in the mirror earlier. But it was gone. The sweater that had seemed so fashion forward then felt dowdy now.

"Natasha." It was Aaron who spotted me first. "Did you hear the good news?"

I hadn't heard any news. Although Jamie had definitely sounded upbeat when he'd called and asked me to meet him at the office.

"What's going on?" I asked Aaron.

"We're about to pop the champagne."

"For?" I prompted.

"The contract, of course."

"Of course," I said.

"And all the rest," he said with a grin.

Sophie spotted me then and rushed forward. "Nat. There you are!"

I was grateful for her enthusiastic greeting, but I couldn't help wanting Jamie to notice me, too. So far he was still absorbed in conversation with the pretty woman who still had her hand on his arm.

"Isn't it fantastic?" Sophie asked.

"I don't know what's going on," I told her.

"We got a deal. Rina Nanami, well, her family, the Nanami Corporation, have put in an order for Sweet Tech. A *big* order for their restaurant equipment distribution company in Tokyo. They have customers all over Asia, their own restaurants and a bunch of others. James is thrilled. He says Horatio is thrilled."

Aaron reappeared and handed Sophie and I each a flute of champagne.

I was a little surprised that O'Neil Nybecker would pull out the stops like this to celebrate the sale. I mean, it was fantastic for Sophie and BRT Innovations. But it couldn't be that big of a deal to O'Neil Nybecker. I mean, in the greater scheme of things.

Just then, an older man appeared from a corner office. He was quickly handed a glass of champagne, and the attention all turned to him.

"That's Horatio," Sophie whispered to me.

When I compared him to Aaron, I could see the family resemblance.

Everyone went quiet.

"Thank you all for helping us to celebrate today," he said to the assembled crowd.

I glanced around at executives of all ages in suits, skirt suits and classic dresses.

"To O'Neil Nybecker's newly expanded relationship with Nanami Corporation. Thank you to James Gillen and Rina Nanami for getting the ball rolling. We look forward to our firms' future together in technology and beyond. Ms. Nanami, please extend my sincerest thank-you to your grandfather. We look forward to visiting Tokyo soon."

Horatio held up his glass.

Everyone followed suit and took a drink.

It took me a second to remember to take a sip.

Clearly, there was more going on here than a contract for Sweet Tech.

"Good trip?" I asked Sophie. My tone sounded darker than I'd intended.

She gave me an odd look. "Fantastic, of course."

Jamie still hadn't looked at me. Rina Nanami had all of his attention. I was wishing I'd stayed home.

"I take it James did more than the Sweet Tech contract?"

"Is something wrong?" Sophie asked.

"No. Why would anything be wrong?"

"You tell me. Are you jealous?"

I almost spilled my champagne. I couldn't believe Sophie had pegged me so fast. What had I said? How had I given away my feelings? This was mortifying.

"I'm not a millionaire yet or anything," Sophie said. There was a teasing tone to her voice. "It was a good sale, but you and I are still friends." She gave me a nudge on the arm. "And, anyway, I'll still hang out with you when I'm filthy rich."

I managed a smile. It was a smile of relief. My secret was still safe.

"I'm not jealous," I told her. "And I don't want to be filthy rich."

"I'll take us on a cruise," she said. "You and me in the South Pacific, hanging out on the beach, barefoot waiters bringing us blender drinks."

"You just used up all your vacation." I ordered myself not to look at Jamie.

"After we make the first million, I'm quitting my job."

I managed a chuckle at that. "What about Bryce? Won't he want to go on a cruise with you?"

She waved a dismissive hand. "Oh, that's not going anywhere."

"What? I thought it was a thing. He seems really nice." I couldn't help it. My thoughts went to Jamie again. Was it Sophie I needed to worry about and not Rina Nanami?

I hated myself for thinking that way.

"We decided not to mix business and a relationship," Sophie said.

"You didn't meet someone else?" I hated to ask, but I didn't want to have to wonder. Wondering would be painful.

The alternative was asking Jamie. And I didn't think I could bring myself to do that.

"*When* would I have met someone else?" she asked.

"Oh. Okay." I felt worse. No, I felt better. No, I felt stupidly selfish and suspicious. "Are you okay about it?" Remembering I was her best friend, I checked her expression for signs of heartbreak.

"I'm fine. It was a mutual decision."

"How mutual?" Like me, Sophie had bemoaned her single status after Layla and Brooklyn each got married.

"*Very* mutual. I'll be more than happy to go on a girlfriend cruise. I won't mope around."

My gaze moved to Jamie. I was afraid I might mope around without him.

He caught my eye then, and he smiled. A big, not-a-care-in-the-world smile as if he hadn't been standing there flirting with Rina Nanami and ignoring me for the past fifteen minutes.

He said something to her, maybe excusing himself, maybe telling her he'd be right back, maybe setting a time to meet up with her later…at his place…for wild and crazy sex in his king-size bed.

I knew my imagination was out of control. And I knew I was being stupid, stupid, stupid about my friend with benefits. My job was to help him become attractive to women. If the past few minutes were anything to go by, I could check that one as a success.

But I couldn't help but wonder what had happened between them in New York. They'd been together there for two whole days and seemed to have made the business deal of the year. Clearly, they respected each other. Maybe they admired each other. Obviously they liked each other, quite a lot I had to imagine.

You didn't make the business deal of the year with someone unless you liked them a lot. And Rina Nanami seemed perfect for the new Jamie. She was worldly, successful, sophisticated, exciting. Men definitely pointed at her from across the room. They'd be jealous of Jamie if she was by his side.

They might have had a whirlwind romance in New York. Maybe there'd be no more benefits for me. Maybe Jamie was now taken.

I knew I could ask Sophie if something had happened between Jamie and Rina, but I'd give myself away for sure if I started quizzing her on that.

"Hi, Tasha," he said.

He didn't hug me. He didn't kiss me. He didn't even shake my hand.

I didn't like that.

"Did Sophie tell you we're all going to dinner?"

"All of us?" I asked.

Jamie paused for a second. "Yes. All of us. It's a celebration."

"Great," I said, forcing a note of cheer into my voice. "That's great."

Sophie motioned to Bryce and Ethan.

What? Jamie mouthed to me.

"Nice trip?" I asked him.

I tried to stop myself, but my gaze went to Rina Nanami.

Jamie followed my gaze.

"Sophie told you?" he asked.

The bottom fell right out of my stomach. I was stunned for a moment. I wanted to ask him why he'd bothered inviting me here. Did he want to show off Rina Nanami? Was she proof that our little experiment worked, that our little game together was over?

"I didn't think she'd do that," he said.

"No reason not to," I said.

Sophie didn't know I was falling for Jamie. Heck, Jamie didn't know I was falling for Jamie. I was completely alone here in my heartbreak.

"It's really my news," he said.

"Okay." I waited for him to give it to me with both barrels. I told myself I'd take it well. I'd congratulate him and make an excuse to go home. Maybe I had a headache. I did have a headache. At least, I was developing a headache. I'd have one soon, I could tell.

"Head office is a huge step," he said. "Guys wait decades for an offer like the one they gave me."

I blinked at him.

I might have also cocked my head sideways in confusion.

I dropped my mouth open, hoping for logical words to come out. Nothing did.

Eleven

I sat next to Sophie at dinner.

It was an oversize round table that made it feel like we were slightly too far apart. Aaron was on the other side of Sophie, then Bryce, Jamie, Rina around to Ethan next to me.

Sophie leaned close, keeping her voice low. "Tell me again why Brooklyn didn't marry James."

The question made me look at Jamie. Looking at Jamie made me want him.

After hearing Jamie's big news was a promotion to the head office in LA, I wasn't as jealous of Rina. But it was still clear she liked him. She liked him a lot. As did both waitresses, and I thought the hostess might try to give him her number before we left.

"She met Colton," I said to Sophie, my voice equally low. "She fell in love with Colton."

"I suppose," Sophie said. "But why she'd go looking, I'll never understand."

I didn't want to be jealous of Sophie again. I hated that feeling.

I told myself admiring Jamie was a long way from making

a serious play for him. I didn't think Sophie would do that, not given his history with Brooklyn.

I shouldn't be doing it, either.

I wasn't doing it. Not really.

I was just mooning over him, wishing I could sleep with him again and trying to keep my feelings under control. That wasn't the same as making a serious play for him.

"I don't know why she did, either," I said to Sophie.

It wasn't the first time I'd wondered about Brooklyn's decision.

If I was with Jamie, really with Jamie, not a friend, not a coconspirator on a life-improvement quest, but with him like Brooklyn had been with him, I'd never look at another man.

"Do you think he dates?" Sophie said.

I was pretty sure he didn't. At least, he'd never said anything about dates he'd had since Brooklyn. I knew he'd like to date. That was the whole point of everything we'd been doing.

I wished right then I could tell Sophie about me and Jamie. I wanted to share my confusion and fear, and the thrill I'd felt sleeping with him. Those were the kinds of things best friends shared.

"I expect he wants to move on," I said to her instead.

"I'd date him," she said.

My fork dropped from my hand.

"I mean," she continued, "if he asked, and if there was a spark, if I could stop thinking of him as a brother." She heaved a sigh. "Man, I wish I could stop thinking about him as a brother."

Relief washed over me. At least I didn't have to worry about Sophie.

I picked up my fork.

"Why do you suppose you feel that way?" I was curious. Especially since it turned out I didn't think of Jamie as a brother at all.

"I've known him since I was four, I suppose. And he's kind of always been there in the background, helping us build that playhouse, driving us to the movies, moving our stuff into the college dorms. You know, brother stuff."

I also thought it was all-around great guy stuff. But I wasn't about to start waxing poetic about him.

I caught his gaze across the table. But it only lasted for a split second. Rina was talking, and his attention went back to her.

"Does she seem like his type?" I asked Sophie.

"She's pretty," Sophie said.

"Brooklyn's pretty, too."

Both Rina and Brooklyn were ultrafeminine. I couldn't help wondering how my athletic rock climbing and practical apartment renovation pursuits came across to him. Did he think of me as feminine, or maybe sturdy...sturdy and plain? It occurred to me that, when all was said and done, Tasha might not be all that far from Nat.

"He's a great-looking guy. Great-looking guys date pretty women."

I wanted to change the subject now. "Bryce is a good-looking guy," I said in a low tone.

"Are you interested in Bryce?"

Sophie's response took me aback. I hadn't been thinking that at all. Bryce seemed nice. He seemed fine. He seemed, well, brotherly really when I thought about it. I had no romantic interest in Bryce whatsoever.

"That wasn't what I meant," I said.

"Well, you didn't warm up to Ethan."

"Are you saying I'm picky?"

Sophie grinned. "Very picky. But in a good way. You should be picky. You're wonderful."

I wished I felt wonderful. But this wasn't a wonderful-feeling kind of evening.

Jamie laughed at something Rina said. On her other side, Ethan laughed, too.

"I'm going to the ladies' room," I said to Sophie.

I felt like I needed to stretch my legs and breathe for a minute.

"Do you want dessert?" Sophie asked. "Should I order you something if the waitress asks?"

"Sure," I said. "Pick something decadent."

I'd seen a few desserts go by, destined for other tables, and they looked fantastic. I wasn't above consoling myself with sugar.

I left the table and retreated to the elegant quiet of the ladies' room. In the powder area I took my time, washing my hands, combing my hair, taking my sweater off for a minute to see if I liked the look better in just the dress. It was different, but I wouldn't say better. I should have gone with a more fitted dress, and maybe jazzier earrings. Strappy sandals wouldn't have been the worst idea, either.

When I'd dressed, I'd thought we might be going house shopping for Jamie. I'd thought I might be walking a lot. I didn't want to walk through houses in spike heels. But I could have done spike heels across a restaurant, easy.

When I decided I couldn't put it off any longer, I left the powder room, coming into the hallway back to the dining room.

Jamie suddenly appeared.

He grasped my hand and pulled me against him, stepping back into a small alcove.

He kissed me there. It was a deep, long, tender kiss that had my entire body sighing with joy.

His arms went around me, and mine went around him. I molded myself to the breadth of his chest and his sturdy thighs.

He cradled my hair and tucked my face into the crook of his shoulder.

"This isn't what I wanted," he said.

I really hoped he didn't mean the kiss.

He kept talking. "Nanami is a huge, huge account."

"I got that." I had.

There was nothing Jamie could have done to get out of this dinner. And he shouldn't have done anything. He'd made huge strides for Sweet Tech and for O'Neil Nybecker. He'd done everything right.

I felt a little guilty for sulking.

He kissed me again, and I felt nothing but wonderful.

But then we heard voices and footsteps.

We broke apart. We weren't alone in the hallway anymore.

I went one way, back to the table. And Jamie went the other toward the men's room.

"You okay?" Sophie asked as I sat back down.

"Fine," I said, assuming she was worried about how long I'd been gone.

"You look flushed."

I felt flushed. "It's a bit hot in here. Plus the glass of wine. You know."

She was still peering closely at my face.

"Did you order dessert?" I asked to change the subject.

"Raspberry chocolate mousse."

"Sounds perfect."

I watched Jamie sit back down.

The waiter put a beautifully decorated plate in front of me. But I knew the mousse wouldn't be anywhere near as sweet as Jamie's kiss.

I wished I could have left the restaurant with Jamie. But I had my car, and he had his. It made the most sense for me to drop off Sophie and Ethan. And Jamie was acting as host for Rina.

I told myself not to be jealous. Jamie's kiss in the hallway had gone a long way to making me feel desirable. It was a fantastic kiss. It showed me how much I'd missed him.

If I wanted to worry about something, I should worry about that.

He wasn't mine to miss, but my heart had started pretending he was.

I'd have to watch that. I'd have to watch it very closely. Maybe not Rina, but someday, likely someday soon, Jamie was going to meet Brooklyn's replacement, and I was going to be collateral damage when that happened.

It was good that I'd come home alone.

Good, I told myself as I came to the top of the staircase in my building. So good. "Really frickin' good," I muttered.

Something moved in the shadows of the hall.

I froze.

"I hope I wasn't too presumptuous," Jamie said, stepping into view from my doorway.

My heart nearly thumped from my chest. "You scared me half to death."

"Sorry," he said.

My fear was turning to joy, but my feet stayed plastered to the floor.

He moved toward me. "I needed to see you. It was driving me crazy, you sitting there, us not being able to talk about anything."

"It did feel like an awfully huge secret," I said.

Concern flashed across his face. "It's nobody's business."

"I know." I agreed with that. At least, conceptually, I agreed with that. But Sophie was a pretty close friend.

He framed my face with his hands. "We don't owe anyone an explanation."

"I know," I said again.

His smile was tender. "Tasha doesn't explain."

I reached for my Tasha-ness. "Tasha does whatever she wants."

He gave me a slow kiss that curled my toes.

He moved his lips half an inch from mine. "What does Tasha want to do?"

"You," I said with bald honesty.

I wrapped my arms around his neck and put my pent-up desire into a kiss.

"Oh, yeah," he whispered, wrapping me tight and propelling us to the door.

I fumbled for my key, struggling to slide it into the lock until Jamie's hand closed over mine to steady it.

"You okay?" he asked.

I nodded. "Fine."

"Nervous?"

The very last thing I felt was nervous—excited, energized, aroused. I felt all of those things.

"I'm not nervous," I said.

"Good."

The key slipped into the lock and the sound of the tumblers turning seemed to echo.

Jamie turned the knob and pushed the door open.

"I'm not nervous, either," he said as he closed it behind us.

I couldn't help but smile at that.

"What are you?" I asked.

"Happy."

"Me, too."

"I missed you," he said.

"So did I."

He smoothed back my hair and gazed into my eyes. "I missed this."

He kissed me tenderly.

A sigh coursed all the way through me.

He pushed the sweater from my shoulders and tossed it on a chair.

I did the same with his suit jacket.

"But not just this," he said between kisses. "I don't want you to think—"

"That it's all about sex?"

"It's not."

"I know. We've had sex exactly once."

"Twice," he said. "Did you forget?"

"I meant one night."

We'd definitely made love twice that night. The second had taken a long time, a really, really long and wonderful time.

"Okay," he said.

I pushed the buttons of his dress shirt through the holes, gradually revealing his bare chest.

He stood still and let me work.

I parted the two sides. I kissed his chest, tasting the salt of his skin.

He sucked in a breath.

"I really want to go slow this time," he said.

"Me, too." I pushed his shirt from his shoulders and let it drop to the floor.

"I'm not just saying that," he said.

"Neither am I."

I lifted the front of my dress and drew it over my head. I tossed it aside and stood in my bra and panties. They were a pretty set, translucent white lace with shiny silver details.

"Don't move," he said.

I stilled.

He took a step back, and his gaze traveled from my boots to my eyes.

"My work here is most definitely done," he whispered.

Judging by the glow in his eyes, he didn't mean the sex was over, so I smiled.

He moved in and smoothed back my hair. "You are hands down the first and only woman who men will point at from across the room."

"If I'm dressed like this, they probably will."

"If you're dressed like anything."

"I think your judgment is clouded right now."

I was thrilled Jamie was so sexually attracted to me. I was absolutely attracted to him.

"Take off your pants," I said to him.

"Demanding."

"If you get to check me out, I want equal time."

"Yes, ma'am," he said.

He kicked off his shoes and stripped out of his pants and socks. He was down to his black boxers.

I pretended to consider him for a moment.

"And?" he prompted.

"I'd point," I said.

"Good to know."

"Other women would point, too."

"I think I need to flash a fancy car and a big credit card to guarantee their interest."

"Oh, no, you don't."

I came close enough to trail my fingers down his chest. "You've got pecs and a six-pack."

"Lots of guys have that."

I came closer still, setting my hands on his shoulders. "And really broad shoulders with that confident stance."

"I have been practicing."

I touched his chin, moving it to one side and then the other.

"Why do I feel like livestock at an auction?"

"Strong, square chin," I said. "You can't buy that."

"With the right plastic surgeon, you can."

"Not like yours. And your eyes..." I felt myself falling into their depths.

"What about my eyes?"

"*Best* blue eyes ever. They show off your intelligence, and they glow when you smile or when you make a joke. Women like a sense of humor."

I meant all of it. I meant everything I was saying, and the power of my emotions scared me.

"My lips?" he asked on a whisper.

I set aside my fear. "Kissable."

"That's exactly what I was going for." He kissed me.

He pulled me close.

Our bodies meshed together, every bulge met with a corresponding hollow. We fit. We fit so perfectly.

His hands roamed my body, arousing every inch, igniting

passion along every trail they took. He peeled off my bra and cupped my breasts, sending tiny shock waves through my core, making my limbs twitch in anticipation.

He stripped off my panties and then his boxers.

He lifted me to perch on the back of the sofa, easing between my thighs.

"Condom," I said.

"Got it."

I hugged him close, surrounded him, absorbed his kisses, took his caresses and gave back with my own.

Our bodies were slick as we moved together.

I was hot. His skin was hotter.

His scent surrounded me. His kisses enveloped me. His caresses made me gasp with pent-up desire and burning anticipation.

"Now," I finally groaned, completely out of patience.

"Slow," he said, but his hand kneaded hard on my lower back.

"Too slow."

"Okay." He shifted me. He moved. He eased inside.

I felt the world stop. Every molecule of me was focused on him.

He pressed deep, and I spiraled upward. Again and again and again, until I lost track of time and space.

I kissed him over and over. I clung to his shoulders, ran my hands down his back, pulled him against me and into me, climbing to the top and then finding more.

When I hit the edge and fell, I called out his name.

"Tasha," he groaned. "Tasha, Tasha, Tasha."

I was limp, and he carried me to my bed, flipping back the covers and climbing inside.

We made love again. Slower this time, more sweetly, less passionately, a soft and satisfying echo.

Later, when I felt Jamie move, I realized I'd fallen asleep in his arms.

I opened my eyes to see dawn barely filtering into the sky beyond the window.

His body was warm, wrapped around mine from behind. He put a featherlight kiss on the back of my neck.

"Again?" I muttered.

That would make three.

"I wish," he said, a low chuckle in his voice.

I shifted, settling to a more comfortable position.

"Maybe," he said with a teasing lilt.

"Optimist."

He was quiet for a moment, his breath caressing the hairline at the back of my neck.

I savored the feeling, clung to the moment. I wanted to stop time and never leave this place.

"You should come with me," he said, his voice a low rumble.

My first thought was no. I didn't want either of us to move, ever, not even an inch.

"Where are you going?" I asked after a minute.

He rose onto his elbow and rolled me so he could look at my face. "Los Angeles, remember?"

I did.

He'd been offered a job in O'Neil Nybecker's head office. Their head office was in Los Angeles. I knew that. It just hadn't been foremost in my mind.

Right now, I thought he'd meant breakfast. But he didn't. Jamie was leaving Seattle.

"Come," he said, an eager light in his eyes.

The single-word invitation swirled through my brain, hitting synapses, gathering data, analyzing and comparing to known information, seeking meaning.

I was afraid to hope. But my blooming heart colored my thoughts.

Was he saying…?

Could he possibly be suggesting…?

Did I dare hope he was asking for something more than

friendship, something romantic? Was it possible that of all the adoring women in the world, Jamie might be interested in me?

My head was nodding before I thought it all through.

His grin went wide. "Great. We can carry right on with the house hunting."

I hesitated. Wait. What?

"I want a wild and exciting Tasha-and-Jamie type house."

A house? He wanted me to help him find real estate? Like any good friend would do? I would have laughed if it didn't hurt so much.

"You up for that?" he asked.

"Sure," I said, trying desperately to match his smile. Then I eased away from him.

His arm went quickly around my stomach. "Where are you going?"

"It's almost morning." Cuddling with my friend-with-benefits had suddenly lost its appeal.

"What time do you usually get up?"

"It takes me a while to shower," I said.

He kissed me again.

I kissed him back, and it felt good. But it was a bittersweet good. Last night we'd reached the pinnacle, and there was nowhere to go but down.

I didn't want to give up our friendship. But I knew it would never be the same.

And that was my fault.

It was all my fault.

Jamie had stuck to the rules of the game. I was the one who had broken them.

On the plane to Los Angeles, Jamie showed me our latest stock portfolio numbers.

I was surprised to find we were flying first-class. Not that I didn't like it. I liked it a lot. But it seemed like an extravagant waste of money.

So he'd pulled out his phone.

I'd stared at the numbers, thinking there had to be a mistake.

He'd laughed at my astonishment. Then he'd teased me about having too little faith in Jamie's instincts for trading.

Then he'd given me a half hug and told me he'd booked a five-star hotel.

So here we were at the Chatham-Brix Downtown, checked into a suite with a sweeping view of the city.

I had mixed feelings about sleeping with Jamie again.

Oh, I wanted to sleep with Jamie again. No matter what else was going on in our relationship, the sex was off the charts. And I hadn't had a lot of off-the-charts sex in my life. I'd really never had much at all.

I'd certainly never had any that came close to Jamie.

But the friends thing was hard. I was lying now when I called us friends. My feelings for him had gone way beyond friendship. And when the sex stopped, when everything stopped, as it would as soon as he moved to LA, it was going to hurt so much.

I'd done heartbreak once, and I had no desire to do it again.

I told myself Tasha could handle it better than Nat. But myself didn't really believe it. It was going to be even worse this time because what I'd felt for Henry was nothing, nothing compared to what I felt for Jamie.

"Marnie arranged all three viewings for this afternoon," Jamie said, coming in from the wraparound balcony. "Traffic looks busy, so we better get going."

I knew the houses we were going to see. I'd helped Jamie pick them out on the real estate website before we'd left Seattle. They were all in Santa Monica. One was even on the beach.

We ended up going to the beach home first. It was a sleek modern condo on the ground floor with a patio walkway to the lush green lawn across the road from a sandy beach. It had a lot of white walls, glass features and stark marble countertops, both in the kitchen and bathrooms.

The master bedroom had a gas fireplace, which I loved. And

the patio had a fun wraparound sofa and gas fire pit. I could see it would be cozy on cool evenings. But the neighbors were pretty close, as was the traffic noise.

When we saw the second house, I thought I understood the real estate agent Marnie's strategy. Away from the beach, you could get a whole lot more for your money.

The second house was bigger. It was private, with a big yard and hedges that screened the neighbors. There was a pool and patio out back, and beautiful landscaping in the front. It was also on a quiet street.

It had a white interior with lots of archways and some wrought-iron features. The floors were beautiful hardwood with scattered area rugs. Paned doors and windows into the backyard let in enormous amounts of light. And the kitchen was a dream, tons of counter space, cupboard space, and glass-fronted feature cabinets. An octagonal breakfast nook stuck out into the backyard. I could picture Jamie having coffee there in the morning.

The master bedroom was roomy and beautiful. But I couldn't bring myself to linger there. While I could picture myself in the bed with Jamie in the hotel room, here in what might be his new house, I could only picture faceless, nameless other women in his arms.

I pretended to check out the guest bedroom.

Marnie had assumed we were a couple, and Jamie hadn't corrected her. It made it worse when she talked like I'd be cooking in the kitchen or swimming in the pool, or showering in the en suite. But I tamped down my flailing emotions and played along. What else was I going to do?

The sun was setting by the time we made it to the last house. My first impression was of warm lights on the palm trees decorating the front yard. Around and above the front door were two stories of glass walls. The polished maple ceiling colored the glow from the entry hall.

The house was a roomy open concept. Walls were painted

white, but the maple trim and maple flooring warmed the atmosphere. The kitchen had stainless appliances and gray speckled countertops. It opened to a big, furnished deck with a built-in fireplace, barbecue and kitchenette. You could see the ocean in the distance.

I could imagine entertaining here. I could see friends and family—Jamie's friends and family, of course—spilling out from the family room and kitchen, onto the deck on a warm summer night.

The master bedroom had a peaked maple beamed ceiling and its own private sundeck. I told myself not to linger in it, but my toes curled into the plush carpet, and I kind of fell in love with the steam shower and gloriously huge bathtub.

"What do you think?" Jamie asked, coming up behind me.

"There's a lot to like," I said.

"Values in this neighborhood have steadily climbed for the past three years," Marnie said. "There's no end in sight."

"What do you like?" Jamie asked me.

"What do *you* like?" I said instead.

He glanced around. "It's the new me."

I told myself Jamie deserved this.

Whatever came his way next, he wasn't the James who'd been left at the altar. He was confident and decisive, great looking and a very exciting man. He had a new job, soon a new house, all his new clothes and hobbies. I was sure they had rock climbing in California.

The world was his to enjoy.

I had to be happy for him.

"I think you'll love entertaining on the deck," I said.

"Do *you* love the deck?"

"I do," I said. "And the yard. There's room out there to garden and to lounge. And you can't beat that en suite." I gestured to the attached bathroom.

"Is it a buy?" he asked.

"It's pretty expensive." It was also really big for one person.

"That's the beauty of short-term trading," he said. "What was unaffordable two months ago is now completely within range."

"I have you to thank for that." I was thinking I really would go condo shopping back in Seattle. It would give me something to focus on for the next few months.

I was going to get through this.

I knew I was going to get through this.

I'd refuse to do anything else.

"We'll take it," Jamie said to Marnie.

She looked shocked, but she recovered quickly. "I can help you write up the offer. Did you have a price in mind?"

Jamie looked at me. "Should we start low?"

"Do you want to dicker?" I wasn't a fan of the negotiating process.

Maybe Tasha would like to bargain. I didn't really know. It was getting hard to tell what the Tasha me would want versus the Nat me.

"Not really," Jamie said.

"If you go twenty-five thousand below asking, I can pretty much guarantee they'll accept."

Jamie looked at me.

I shrugged my shoulders. The game was over. It was his decision, his money, his life.

"Done," he said to Marnie. "Write it up."

"Subject to financing?" she asked.

He smiled and shook his head. "No need. I'm sure I can arrange the financing."

Marnie beamed. "Then congratulations. I'm guessing you want an early closing date."

Jamie squeezed my hand. "The earlier the better. They want me to start in the LA office on Monday."

I forced myself to smile, to keep up the facade for Marnie's sake.

I wanted to cling to Jamie and never let go. At the same time, I wanted to get the heck out of LA and never look back.

I knew in that second that I couldn't stay the night. I couldn't make love to Jamie one last time in that opulent hotel suite. It would kill me.

"I'll get started." Marnie dialed a number as she left the bedroom.

"This is terrific," Jamie said to me.

I pretended my phone buzzed and pulled it from my purse. "I should take this," I said.

"Sophie?" he asked.

I nodded. I don't know why I thought a silent lie was better than a verbal lie, but I did.

I moved a couple of paces away. "Hi," I said into the phone.

I waited a minute, feeling terribly, utterly awful about what I was doing.

I scrambled for a viable reason to leave.

"She did?" I said into the phone. "Uh, okay." I looked at Jamie to find him watching me. "I can. If you think so."

"What?" he mouthed.

I held up one finger, trying to stall as I solidified my plan. It was shameless. It was probably unforgivable. But I didn't have a better idea, and I was running out of time.

"As soon as I can," I said into the phone. "Bye."

"What?" Jamie asked.

"It's Brooklyn," I said. "I don't know what's going on, but Sophie wants me to come back to Seattle."

Jamie clamped his jaw.

I knew he wouldn't ask about Brooklyn. It was the one thing he'd stay miles away from.

"I'm sorry," I said.

"Don't go."

"I have to." I wanted to cry. I wanted to collapse into a puddle of guilt. But mostly, I wanted to throw myself into his arms for as long as he'd have me.

We could hear Marnie's muted voice outside the room.

"You don't need me for this part," I said.

He opened his mouth, but I kept on talking.

"I'll book a flight in the cab."

"You're going *now*? Right now?"

"I'm sorry," I said again.

"How soon can you come back?"

"I don't know."

"You'll come back as soon as you can."

I nodded, another silent lie. I'd come up with more excuses later if Jamie pushed it.

He might not push it. He probably wouldn't push it. He'd get settled here in this great new house, with his great new job, and a great new girlfriend within a week or a month, surely not longer than that.

He'd have the life he'd wanted, just like we'd planned.

"My assistant has started on the paperwork," Marnie said brightly as she came back into the master bedroom. "We can swing by the office and sign, and I'll present the offer tonight."

"Good luck," I said to Jamie. I was already calling a cab.

Twelve

Five days, thirty texts and seven missed phone calls later, I decided I had to bring Sophie in on my deception. Jamie was more persistent than I'd expected, and I was afraid he might reach out to Sophie. If he did, he'd discover my lie.

I didn't want him to know I'd lied. For some reason, that was important to me.

I poured Sophie and me each a glass of merlot.

"We got another big order today," Sophie was saying.

She'd kicked off her shoes and curled up on one end of my sofa.

"Congratulations." I thought about recorking the bottle, but I had a feeling we'd finish it off before the evening was done.

"Japan was for sure the place to go. Cash is starting to flow in, and we've gone into actual production. Ethan's looking at expanding the facility to the space next door."

"I'm so glad it's working out." I really was.

Sophie's success was a bright spot in my dismal-feeling life.

"I'm not ready to quit The Blue Fern yet. Neither is Bryce. But we're talking about approaching the general manager with a proposal to job share. We'd each work half-time, and hire another person to take up the slack. That way, we don't need to take a full salary from BRT, but we'll have more time to devote to building up the company."

"That sounds like a good idea." I wished I could focus on Sophie's company, but I was painfully distracted.

I handed her one of the glasses and took the other end of the sofa.

My shoes were already off, and I turned sideways to face her, leaning my back against the arm.

"What about you?" she asked.

"What about me?" I told myself to take the opening and plunge right in, but I didn't know how to start.

"What's going on?" She took a sip. "Oooh. That's good."

"It's not too expensive," I said, taking a drink myself.

Inwardly I was kicking myself for being a coward. I had to speak up already.

"I did something," I said.

Sophie's brows went up, and she stilled. "Do tell."

"I lied."

She looked surprised by that. "To me?"

"No. Not *to* you. But it was about you."

"What did you say? Something good, I hope. Did you tell some guy I was really smart and rich and hot?"

I knew I shouldn't smile, but I did. "No."

"Too bad. I could have faked that, at least for a little while."

"You are smart and hot."

She coughed out a laugh. "Maybe a little smart. And maybe a little hot. I'm sure not rich."

"Not yet."

"No, not yet. But back to your lie…"

"Right." I'd been framing up my words for the better part of a day. I didn't know why I was trying to rephrase them on the fly right now. "I lied to Jamie about you calling me to say Brooklyn had a problem."

"Who's Jamie?"

"James. I mean James."

Sophie looked completely baffled. "What are you talking about?"

I took another drink. "I've been seeing James." Okay, that had come out all wrong. "I mean, not seeing him, as in seeing him. Just, well, with Brooklyn leaving him, and Henry leaving me, we kinda got to talking one day, and we've done a few things together."

"What kind of things?"

"Rock climbing, for one."

"You?"

"Yes."

"And James."

"Yes."

"*Rock* climbing?"

"We did. We took lessons and everything."

"Why didn't you tell me? How is that a secret? Was it illegal rocks? Were you trespassing? Did you steal something from... I don't know... Olympic National Park? A treasure or something?"

"We didn't steal anything."

"Well, that's a relief."

I knew I had to get to the point. "While we were in California, I—"

"You and James went to California?"

"Last weekend."

"Okaaay..." She drew out the word. "Did you, like, climb some California rocks?"

"No. He has that new job. We were house hunting."

Sophie sat back. She took a drink of her wine. "You do know you're not making any sense at all."

"I know."

"Tell me more about the lie."

"In California, in LA, I pretended you phoned me. I pretended Brooklyn had a problem. I knew he wouldn't ask any questions about Brooklyn, so I thought I'd get away with it."

"Did you get caught?"

"No. Not yet."

"I don't know, Nat. You're acting like this is a big thing. It doesn't sound like a big thing to me. I'll lie for you if you want me to. I'll tell him anything you say."

I knew she would, and I loved her for it.

"But why did you lie? What did it get you?"

"Out of there."

"Out of LA."

"Yes."

"You needed an excuse to leave?"

"I...thought I did in the moment."

Sophie sat forward and stared at me straight in the eyes. "What happened?"

I shook my head. "Some things I can't tell."

I wasn't sure if Jamie wanted to keep our makeover plot a secret. It didn't seem like such a big deal if we told people at this point. But I didn't want to break my word without getting his permission.

"What things can you tell me?"

"Jamie and I became friends."

"Jamie? He's Jamie now?"

"It's a nickname."

A knowing light came on in Sophie's eyes. "Like Tasha is for you. What *have* you two been up to?"

"Nothing... I mean..." I couldn't look at her.

There was awe in her tone. "Holy cow."

I could feel my face heat up.

"You slept with James Gillen? Nat, you slept with Brooklyn's fiancé?"

"They weren't engaged anymore. And it was nothing. It was a friends thing, friends with benefits thing."

"You have benefits with James?"

"Only a couple of times."

"Is that what happened in California?"

"No. It didn't happen in California. It would have. If I hadn't left."

"And you didn't want it to."

I wasn't sure how to answer that question, so I moved on. "And now he keeps texting and calling."

"Hang on," Sophie said, holding up a finger. "It sounds like you're saying you *wanted* to have benefits in California. So why did you leave?"

An ache formed in my stomach. "I didn't mean to tell you all this."

"Of course you meant to tell me all this. You must have been dying to tell me all this. Why did you wait so long to tell me all this?"

"It was a secret. It was a thing. It was a secret thing."

"James wanted to have a secret affair with you?"

"It wasn't an affair. Neither of us is with anyone."

"You were kind of dating Ethan."

I gave her a look. "Please."

"Okay. I guess you weren't really dating Ethan."

"It wasn't romantic," I said.

To my embarrassment, my voice cracked.

Sophie's eyes filled with sympathy.

"Oh," she said. "You mean it wasn't supposed to be romantic."

I struggled to breathe. I was afraid to try to talk. The heartache I'd been suppressing was fighting to get out of my chest.

"But it got romantic."

A whisper was all I could manage. "Only for me."

I blinked against the threat of tears. I wasn't going to cry. I wasn't going to let this make me cry. That would be a whole other level of pain.

"Oh, Nat."

I shook my head, and I swallowed hard. "I'm fine. I just…

I didn't want Jamie to ask you about the phone call and have him find out I made it all up."

"Yeah, because *that's* the biggest problem here."

"I'd be embarrassed," I said.

"He's the one who should be embarrassed. What was he thinking? Sleeping with you, swearing you to secrecy. What kind of a man does that?"

I realized I'd mischaracterized our relationship. I hadn't been fair to Jamie. This wasn't his fault. It was my fault for letting it get out of hand.

I should have pulled the plug earlier. I recognized the signs. I'd have to be an idiot not to recognize the signs that I was falling for him.

A knock came on the door.

I wasn't expecting anyone.

"Do Bryce and Ethan know you're here?" The last thing I wanted was to deal with anyone else right now.

"Maybe it's Brooklyn," Sophie joked.

I couldn't find the humor in it.

"Too soon?" she asked.

"I think it is."

"Tasha?" a voice called.

It was Jamie.

Sophie's mouth dropped open. Her voice dropped to a whisper. "I'm guessing nobody else calls you that?"

"Tasha, open up. I can hear you're in there."

I looked to Sophie for advice.

She cringed and shrugged at the same time.

"Tasha?" Jamie sounded frustrated. "This is ridiculous."

"She's coming," Sophie called out.

I shot her a look of astonishment.

"You can't hold him off forever."

I opened the door.

"*What* is going on?" Jamie asked.

"Sophie's—"

"You don't pick up the phone. You barely answer my texts. You said you were coming back. Why didn't you come back?" He barged into the apartment. "There were papers to sign."

He spotted Sophie.

"Hi, James," she said.

He clamped his jaw and glared at me.

"I can leave," Sophie said.

"No," I said.

I wasn't ready to be alone with Jamie. Okay, that was a lie. I was dying to be alone with Jamie. But that was a bad thing, a very bad thing.

Seeing him now, I wanted to grab him and hold on to him. I wanted to be wrapped in his arms...like...forever.

It was worse than I thought.

I was in love with Jamie.

"We need to talk," Jamie said to me.

I backed away from him. "She knows most of it anyway."

"What do you mean she knows most of it? What does she know?"

"*She's* right here," Sophie said. "Listening."

Jamie ignored her. "What does she know?"

"That we slept together."

"You told her that?"

"I pretty much guessed," Sophie said. "And why would you ask her to keep that a secret anyway?"

The question seemed to stump Jamie for a second. When he spoke, it was to me. "I didn't think you'd want to tell people. I don't care if anyone knows."

The conversation felt surreal. "Well... Sophie knows."

"Fine," he said. "Why didn't you come back? What did I do?"

I found the question more than absurd. "You moved to California."

He seemed puzzled. "Yeah...and I asked you to come with me. You said you would."

I almost laughed at that. "You asked me to help you *buy a house*."

"Uh-huh. A house. That we both loved. That we could live in. Together."

"Whoa," Sophie said. She came up on her knees and watched over the back of the sofa.

"You did not," I said to Jamie.

If he had...well... I would have... I didn't really know, but it would have been something different than what I had done.

Now my brain and my heart started fighting again, trying to work out what Jamie had meant, what Jamie meant now.

He took a few steps toward me. "Tasha, what did you think was happening between us?"

"Makeovers," I said. That much I knew for sure. "We wanted to attract the opposite sex."

"Really?" Sophie asked.

"We did attract the opposite sex," Jamie said. "We attracted each other."

I waved my hand. "You know what I mean. We were friends."

"With benefits," Sophie said.

We both looked at her.

"Should I go now?" she asked.

"Don't bother," Jamie said.

He took another step toward me. "I don't know how it went off the rails. I wish I'd said or done something different." He came closer. "I don't know how you feel about me, Tasha. But I have to think there's something there. I can't be in this all alone. It doesn't make sense. I'm wild about you, *wild* about *you*, intellectually, physically, romantically." He leaned in. "I want to be your best friend. I want to be your lover. And I want to do it all forever. Rock climb with me, dance with me, skydive with me, buy tuxes with me. It can be in LA. It can be here. It can be anywhere. I don't care about any of that." He took my hands. "I'm in love with you, Tasha."

"Swooning over here," Sophie said.

"Marry me," Jamie said.

My brain—which was already struggling to process his words—fogged completely over. "Huh?"

Jamie grinned at my baffled expression. "I think you have to give me a yes or no to that."

"Yes," Sophie said. "Say yes already."

Jamie cocked his head in Sophie's direction. "I like her. I always have."

"Yes," I said, barely believing it was happening. "I love you, Jamie. I love you so much."

He pulled me into a hug, and then a kiss, and then a deeper kiss.

"I'm out of here," Sophie said.

This time she didn't wait for either of us to answer.

Ours was going to be the simplest wedding in the history of weddings.

We both wanted it that way.

And we tried, we really did. But Sophie insisted Layla had to be there.

It was hard to argue that Jamie's sister shouldn't attend.

And if Layla was coming, Max had to be included. If Max and Layla were going to be there, it seemed churlish not to invite Brooklyn and Colton. Especially since Jamie was adamant that he didn't hold anything against Brooklyn.

He told me if it hadn't been for Brooklyn breaking up with him, he never would have found me. And he realized now that what he'd felt for Brooklyn had been puppy love. He'd hung on to it for so many years, he didn't know how to let it go, even when they grew apart.

He also said if it hadn't been for me, he wouldn't have grown from James into Jamie.

I believed him. I felt the same way. I wasn't Nat anymore. I wasn't only Tasha either, but I had a lot of Tasha in me, and I loved it.

Our parents had to be included, of course. Mine had traveled up from Houston.

Jamie's parents spent the winters in Fort Lauderdale now, but they were happy to put off their travel plans for a wedding.

Me, I just wanted to be married to Jamie. I didn't much care where or how.

We found a rustic resort on Waddington Island, an hour's boat ride from Seattle. It had a chapel overlooking the ocean, a five-star dining room, and cottages for everyone to spend the night.

I wore a short white dress, with a lace overlay and a scalloped hem. The lace neckline was scooped and detailed, while the underdress was strapless. I wore a little diamond pendant that Layla had lent me. Jamie had once given it to her for her birthday. I matched it with diamond stud earrings.

I felt pretty. I didn't think I'd ever felt this pretty in my life.

My shoes were sleek, heeled pumps, white with blue soles. Something blue. I liked that, too.

When the music came up, Sophie started down the aisle in front of me. She wore a simple aqua dress that let her beauty shine through. She looked amazing, as she always did.

I saw Jamie at the front of the chapel. He wore the tuxedo we'd bought together.

I smiled, and he grinned back, gesturing to the suit.

Yeah, I'd take a guy with a perfectly cut, perfectly fitting, owned tuxedo any day of the week—especially this guy.

"Nice touch," I whispered to him when I got to the front.

He took my hand. "Not as nice as you."

"Brookswood Bridal Department."

"Seriously?"

"Where else would I shop?"

"Friends..." the preacher began.

I sobered and stopped talking.

We said our vows, promising love and laughter and adventure forever.

When we kissed and made our way down the aisle, I thought my heart would burst open with joy.

In the garden out front, Layla hugged Jamie. Then she pulled me to her.

"I can't believe it," she whispered. "I'm *so* happy to have you as a sister."

"I love Jamie very much," I told her.

"I know you do. And I can see how much he loves you. You're perfect for each other."

Brooklyn was next.

I hesitated in front of her. We hadn't spoken since she'd left Jamie at the altar.

"Congratulations," she said. It was clear she was as nervous as me. I thought of all the platitudes I could offer.

"This is so weird," I said instead.

Her expression relaxed. "Isn't it?"

"I don't know how it happened this way. But I'm so glad it did." I pulled her into a hug.

"I do love James," she said into my ear. "Just not in the right way."

"I love him in exactly the right way."

She hugged me tighter. "I'm so happy for both of you."

"Thanks for leaving him," I said.

We both laughed.

"Do you think he wants to talk to me?"

Her question was answered before I could say anything. Jamie was there beside us.

"Hello, Brooklyn."

She looked up at him and stepped back from me. "Hi."

"Thanks for coming," he said.

"Thanks for inviting us."

They both fell silent.

"I'm sorry," she said.

Jamie shook his head. "I'm not. You were braver than me. I'd have gone ahead and made a mistake for both of us."

Brooklyn looked startled.

"You were right to walk away." He paused. "Okay, maybe you could have done it a day or a week or a month before the wedding. But at least you did it." Jamie took my hand and drew me to his side. "And I'm the big winner."

"I'm so glad you feel that way," Brooklyn said.

I caught movement out of the corner of my eye as Colton approached.

I couldn't tell the twin brothers apart, but from the expression on his face, I was pretty sure this one was Colton, not Max.

He firmly stuck out his hand for Jamie. "Congratulations," he said.

"To you, too," Jamie said. "You have an amazing wife."

"I hear you lucked out, too." Colton looked to me.

Jamie wrapped an arm around me. "She's the best. I'm not sure I deserve her."

No one seemed to know where to take the conversation from there. I didn't want to leave it at this. Brooklyn was one of my best friends, and I was deliriously happy at how things had turned out.

"Thank you," I said to Colton. "I appreciate you stealing Brooklyn."

It was clear he had no idea how to react.

I let him hang for a second.

"I...uh..." He gamely stepped in. "It was my pleasure."

I looked around the circle. "We all agree it turned out right?"

Everyone enthusiastically nodded.

"Great. Then let's quit being so weird about it."

Jamie leaned in. "Way to go, Tasha."

"Tasha doesn't mess around."

"Yes," Brooklyn said with enthusiasm. "I'm through being weird."

"Okay by me," Jamie said.

He gave Brooklyn a hug.

They were both smiling when they pulled back.

Colton looked happy, too. He looked relieved and happy.

Other people came forward with their congratulations. We cut the cake, threw the bouquet and danced the night away under a full moon and the scattered stars.

Later, at our cottage on a point of land overlooking the rolling ocean, Jamie carried me across the threshold. An open window had the sea breeze flowing into the pretty room.

Jamie set me on my feet, his arm staying around my waist. He smoothed my windblown hair. "I love you, Tasha Gillen."

My heart was big and full in this perfect moment. I touched his face, stroking the rough whiskers that shadowed his chin. "I adore you, Jamie Gillen."

He smiled as he leaned in for a kiss. "I'd point at you across any old room."

* * * * *

Friend, Fling, Forever?

Janice Lynn

Books by Janice Lynn

Harlequin Medical

Christmas in Manhattan
A Firefighter in Her Stocking

Flirting with the Doc of Her Dreams
New York Doc to Blushing Bride
Winter Wedding in Vegas
Sizzling Nights with Dr. Off-Limits
It Started at Christmas…
The Nurse's Baby Secret
The Doctor's Secret Son
A Surgeon to Heal Her Heart
Heart Surgeon to Single Dad

Visit the Author Profile page
at millsandboon.com.au for more titles.

**Janice won the National Readers' Choice Award
for her first book,
*The Doctor's Pregnancy Bombshell***

Dear Reader,

Sometimes volunteering for something good can get us into hot water. That's how Dr. Gabriel Nelson feels when an ex-girlfriend plans to buy his charity auction date package. Gabe is determined to convince good friend nurse Kami Clark to win the bid instead.

Good thing Kami knows better than to be drawn in by Gabe's charm, big heart and good looks. Women are disposable to men like Gabe, and she has no intention of being just another has-been. Only, Gabe is unlike any man she's ever known and her heart keeps forgetting he's off-limits when he says he wants more than friendship. Can a fling with Gabe lead to forever? Or just repeat what she'd watched her mother go through time and again?

I had so much fun writing Gabe and Kami's story. Gabe is such a fun hero and I loved watching him get under Kami's skin. I hope you enjoy their story.

Janice

To Samantha Thompson, who puts together the best fundraisers ever! Thanks for your big heart and all you do for others.

Praise for
Janice Lynn

"Ms. Lynn has delivered a really good read in this story where emotions run high and the chemistry was strong and only got stronger."
—*Harlequin Junkie* on *The Nurse's Baby Secret*

One

"Buy me at the charity auction."

Nurse Kami Clark didn't look up from the computer screen where she keyed in vital signs on the patient in bay two of the Knoxville General Hospital's emergency department.

Doing her best not to let her eyes veer in Dr. Gabriel Nelson's direction, she made a nurse's note on the normal results. "Not happening."

Wearing his favorite blue scrubs, Gabe moved into her peripheral vision. She didn't have to look to know the color paled in comparison to the brilliant hue of his eyes.

"You know you want me, Kam. Here's your chance."

"Right," she snorted, keeping her voice flippant despite how his accusation almost sent her into a choking fit. "Keep dreaming, lover boy."

Most straight women did want Gabe. Not that he typically encouraged their desire. He didn't have to. Not with his looks, personality, and quick intelligence. The fact he was a successful emergency-room physician didn't hurt. Women flocked to him.

But not Kami.

Oh, she thought he was all that and more. The man had the biggest heart of anyone she knew and seemed to always be able to make her laugh. But she knew better than to get caught up in his revolving-door love life that left a long line of broken hearts. She was immune to his love-'em-and-leave-'em charms. Mostly.

"More like I'm trying to escape a nightmare in the making." He gave a frustrated sigh that was almost believable as he plopped down into the chair next to hers. "Debbie is planning to buy my date."

Ah. Debbie. The latest ex-girlfriend who didn't want to admit it was over and had been finished for a month or so.

No wonder Gabe was in such a tizzy. Debbie had stuck like glue even after he'd told her point-blank on several occasions that their relationship was finished. The poor woman must be hoping to rekindle a spark. Good luck with that.

Gabe never dated the same woman for more than a couple of months and never went back to the same one. Not once. He was a move-on-and-never-look-back kind of guy.

"You have to rescue me."

"Says who? You got yourself into this mess," she reminded him, fighting back a small smile at her friend's overly dramatic tone. She could almost buy into his angst. "It's only right for you to face the consequences."

"I was roped into this charity fund-raiser and you know it. Not only do you know it—" he leaned close enough so that his words were just for her "—you're the one who convinced me to say yes."

"I meant the Debbie mess, not the auction," she clarified, fighting the urge to look his way. Better not to look into Gabe's eyes when he was trying to convince you to do something. Staring into those dazzling blues got women into trouble. Immune or not, she wasn't taking any chances.

"Besides," Kami continued, "even if you had to spend a *week* with your beautiful and persistent ex, if it raised money to help Beverly's family and others like her, then so be it."

Anything any of them could do to raise money for their coworker's seriously ill infant daughter needed to be done. Although their medical insurance was covering many of the expenses, there were still co-pays and deductibles. Not to mention Beverly had been out of work since giving birth, as had her husband, most of it as unpaid leave of absence. Even after Lindsey got her heart transplant, months would pass prior to Beverly leaving her baby's side to return to work. Their friend had enough worries without having to be concerned about how she and her husband were going to pay their bills.

"Easy for you to say," Gabe pointed out. "You aren't on the auction block."

Yeah, as one of the fund-raiser's organizers she'd dodged that bullet.

"I'll be working the night of the auction, but not by being auctioned." Thank goodness. Kami would have been a statue. Not her scene at all.

"Not the same," he pointed out.

"You love the attention and you know it," she accused, closing out the patient's chart. Fun-loving Gabe would work the stage and have a blast.

She glanced at him for the first time since he'd barged into the nurses' station located across from the patient bays.

Her incorrigible playboy friend actually looked a little frazzled.

"Fortunately for you, it's not a week, just one night where you have to show Debbie—I mean, whoever wins your date—a good time."

Okay, that was bad but she couldn't resist teasing him. It was so rare to see him off his game. Actually, she couldn't recall having ever seen him off his game. Not during any crisis that came through the ER doors. Given he was such a goofball at times, Gabe was one coolheaded dude.

Plus, she wasn't buying his woe-is-me-buy-my-date-package-so-Debbie-can't act.

"You're real funny, Kam."

"Come on. That was a good one." Kami had thought so. He didn't look convinced. "I'm sure you'll manage one night with Debbie if needed."

After all, he dealt with situations and people a lot more intense than the Z-list television actress he'd been involved with still obsessing over him. Debbie might be crazy over Gabe, but the woman didn't have any real psychiatric problems.

"And risk encouraging her nonstop calls and texts continuing?" He winced. "Thanks anyway."

Kami raked her gaze over his six-foot frame. "You're not *that* bad, Gabe." She patted his hand as if reassuring a small child. "There will be other bidders." Faking a look of uncertainty, she shrugged. "Well, hopefully."

One side of his mouth cocked upward. "Gee, thanks for the compliment, *friend*."

"Anytime," she assured him, her lips twitching. "What are friends for?"

Eyes sparkling, he gave a pointed look. "To rescue each other when one's relentless ex plans to buy her way back into your social life."

He had a point.

If Kami believed he was in real need, she'd probably empty her house-deposit fund to bail out his butt. Good thing he wasn't because she'd been hoarding every spare penny for years, had a hefty down payment saved, and would hate to have to start over to make her dream of owning a home come true just as she finally had enough saved to actually start looking for the perfect house.

"Just because Debbie plans to bid doesn't mean she'd be the winner," she said on a more serious note. "Stop worrying."

He didn't look assured. "Debbie doesn't like to lose."

Kami gave a semi-shrug. "Who does?"

He raked his fingers through his hair. "Come on, Kam. Place

the winning bid and I'll show you the night of a lifetime." He waggled his brows. "We'd have fun."

Kami laughed. As if. "You must have me mixed up with one of the other women running around the hospital who actually wants you to show them a 'night of a lifetime.' I've better things to do than mess with the likes of you."

Looking as if she'd said exactly what he'd expected her to say, he chuckled. "Or maybe I want you to buy my bid because I know I can ask this huge favor and not worry about you freaking out down the road when I break things off."

Yeah, there was that. She wouldn't freak out over a man. Never had. Never would. She'd watched her mother do that one time too many.

This time it was she who gave the pointed look.

"If I ever gave you the privilege of dating me—" she stared straight into his blue eyes, held her chin a little higher than normal "—who says it would be *you* to break things off?"

Although she adored his friendship, his arrogance irked. Then again, was it arrogance if it was true he'd been the one to end every relationship he'd had during the time he and Kami had worked together? Probably his whole life?

Gabe chuckled, then surprised her by tweaking his finger across the tip of her nose. "You might be right, Kam. Only a fool would break things off with you. Speaking of which, how is Baxter?"

Ha. Talk about turning the table.

"Our breakup was a mutual decision," she reminded him, not that she hadn't already told Gabe as much a dozen times previously. "We aren't talking much these days, but he's fine as far as I know."

Just as she was. Baxter had been sweet, only she'd realized continuing their relationship was pointless. When he kissed her, she felt nothing. No sparks. No butterflies. Nothing.

Kami wasn't so delusional she thought someone would come

along, sweep her off her feet, and give her a fairy-tale romance. But she wasn't going to settle for *nothing*, either.

Good friendship and sparks—it could happen.

Not that it had, but she was only twenty-seven. There was plenty of time for someone special to come into her life.

And, if not, she'd rather be alone than like her mother and with the wrong man over and over.

"Keep telling yourself that he's fine. Dude was devastated last week when I bumped into him."

Baxter hadn't been devastated. When she'd broached the subject of their relationship not working, he'd seemed relieved. Obviously, he hadn't felt any sparks, either. On paper they were a good match. In reality, there had been little chemistry beyond their initial attraction.

"When did you run into my ex?" Baxter, an accountant for a law firm, and the usually laid-back man in front of her didn't exactly move in the same social circles.

"At the gym."

Kami's jaw dropped. "Baxter was at the gym?"

She shook her head to clear her hearing because she couldn't have heard correctly. Not once during the time she'd known Baxter had he ever gone to the gym. To her knowledge, he'd not even had a membership.

"Pumping the iron in hopes of winning you back." Gabe's eyes twinkled with mischief. "Too bad you aren't up for grabs at the auction 'cause he could buy a night to remind you of all you're missing out on. You, him, Debbie and me could go on a double date and reminisce about the good ole days."

Kami rolled her eyes.

"Baxter is a great guy," she defended the man she'd dated for over six months. He truly was. He'd been steady, quiet, dependable. She'd wanted to feel something, had tried to convince herself she did because he'd make a good husband and father someday, but *nada*.

"Just not the guy for you?"

"Exactly. Now, was there a reason you interrupted my work other than to whine about Debbie?"

"As if she isn't enough of a reason." He gave an overly dramatic sigh that should have put him up for an award or two. "I can't believe you're refusing to help, Kam. You know I'd do it for you."

"I wouldn't want you to." She curled her nose and shuddered at the mere thought. "Can you imagine the rumors that would start around the hospital?" She gave a horrified look. "Uh-uh. No way. I can, however, put out word you're hoping someone outbids Debbie at the auction. I'm sure there'll be a few takers."

He shook his head. "I'm disappointed in you, Kam. I was sure I could count on you to save me."

"You have the wrong girl, but no worries. You'll find someone over the next few weeks to outbid Debbie."

Gabe disagreed. He had the right girl. The perfect girl.

Kami wouldn't get happily-ever-after ideas. He always had fun when she was around. And, best of all, she already knew the real him. The him who had no intentions of settling down anytime in the near future.

But he changed the subject instead of pursuing the topic further. As she said, they had a few weeks before the fund-raiser. A lot could happen during that time.

Like his convincing Kami to buy him.

Not that he couldn't deal with Debbie. He'd just rather not have to.

She was great, but had gotten too clingy too fast and he'd started feeling claustrophobic in their relationship by the end of the first month. At the end of the second, he'd been done. Too bad Debbie hadn't been.

"How is Racine Mathers tonight?" he asked to change the subject.

Apparently, the fragile elderly woman had arrived by ambulance in hypercapnic respiratory failure earlier that day. Yet again. She'd been admitted to the medical floor, which neither Gabe nor Kami had anything to do with, but he knew Kami would have checked on the woman prior to clocking in for her shift. She cared about people and that big heart was one of the things he liked most about the perky little blonde who'd quickly become one of his closest friends.

At the mention of their patient, her green eyes filled with concern. "Her arterial blood gases are still jacked up. Her CO_2 level remains in the upper fifties."

"I was hoping once they got her on BiPAP her numbers would improve." He logged in to the computer, began scanning messages in his inbox.

"That makes two of us, but apparently she hasn't wanted to keep the mask on and the day-shift nurse caught her with it off several times."

He shook his head. "Racine knows better than that."

Kami nodded.

The woman did. This wasn't her first respiratory failure rodeo. Then again, Gabe suspected the elderly woman was tiring of her inability to breathe and the medical community's failure to do much more than Band-Aid her back together until the next episode.

"I'm going to swing by and see her. If I'm needed before I get back, page me."

She arched a brow. "You think I wouldn't?"

Gabe grinned. No, he never doubted that his favorite nurse would do the right thing and get him where he needed to be when he needed to be there. Kami was an excellent nurse. There was no one he'd rather spend his shift working with. Fortunately, their schedules were on the same rotation and he got to spend several nights a week in the emergency department with her.

Whether it was busy, slammed, or on the rare occasion slow, he was never bored. Not with Kami around to keep him entertained with her quick wit and sassy mouth.

Which was yet another reason she should be the one to rescue him from Debbie. Not only would Kami not get the wrong idea, but Gabe would truly enjoy their "date." Not that they'd ever gone anywhere just the two of them, but when the work gang gathered, he gravitated toward Kami and they almost always ended up paired off.

There was just something about her that made him feel good on the inside.

She needed to buy his auction package and he intended to make sure she did.

"That is the most exciting thing I've heard in weeks."

While dropping in a urinalysis order for bay one, Kami curled her nose at the woman who'd been her best friend since they'd bonded during nursing school. "You would say that."

Mindy gave her a *duh* look. "The man is gorgeous and I saw that once-over you gave him. I think you should go for it."

Kami shook her head. "You misunderstood. That once-over was a joke and Gabe doesn't want me to buy his date so we can go on a *real* date. He wants me to save him from having to go on a date with someone else. Either way, no, thank you."

Mindy leaned against the desk. "I'm just saying, the most eligible bachelor in the hospital asked you to buy him at the fund-raiser. I think you should see that as a sign and go for it."

Go for it? Her friend had lost her mind.

"A sign of what?"

Mindy waggled her brows. "Your good fortune. Do you know how many women would kill for Gorgeous Gabe to ask them to buy his date package?"

Kami made a bleh motion with her tongue. "They can have him. He's too stuck on himself for my taste."

Mindy didn't look convinced. "That's not how I see him."

Kami didn't, either. Not really. Gabe was gorgeous, but he didn't seem to get caught up in his looks other than that he took care of himself and worked out regularly. Nothing wrong with trying to stay healthy.

Gabe was the picture of good health.

Great health.

Health at its finest, even.

Yeah, yeah. The man was easy on the eyes. No big deal.

"He's got a big heart and you know it," Mindy continued, oblivious to Kami's wayward thoughts—thank goodness. The last thing she needed was Mindy pushing her toward doing something she knew better than to do. She might be immune, but you didn't rub your face in germs to tempt fate, either.

"He doesn't mind getting his hands dirty. He's the first to jump in and help when someone needs something. I've never known him to pull the doctor card." Mindy gave a pointed look. "I'd be hard-pressed to name someone, male or female, who didn't like him."

"Since you're a walking, talking advertisement of his virtues, you bid on him," Kami suggested and wondered at the slight twinge in her belly at the thought of her friend buying Gabe's date.

Her two friends getting together would be a good thing, right? Well, except that Gabe would eventually break Mindy's heart and then Kami would have to bust his chops for hurting her bestie. That was what the issue was. She didn't want to have to dislike him for breaking Mindy's heart.

But Mindy's eyes lit at Kami's suggestion and a smile slid onto her face. "I might do that."

Kami's brow shot up. Her mouth opened, but she didn't comment as Gabe came strolling back into the emergency department.

"What have I missed?"

"Not much. Been a slow one so far," Mindy told him, all smiles and looks of all sorts of possibilities.

"Bite your tongue," Kami and Gabe said at the same time.

"Listen at you two," Mindy said, giving Kami a mischievous glance that said maybe her friend hadn't really veered from her original mission after all. "So in sync."

"Not wanting you to jinx our evening is common sense. Nothing in sync about that," Kami corrected, hoping her friend caught her warning tone. "Now, Dr. Nelson." She turned her attention to Gabe, ignoring his curious looks between her and Mindy. "Bay one is a urinary tract infection. Onset earlier today. Her urinalysis results are in her chart. Bay two is a fever and sore throat. I've swabbed for strep, but the results are pending. Both are pleasant, stable, and accompanied by their significant other. You want me to go with you while you examine them?"

Bay one was given an antibiotic, a bladder antispasmodic, a handout on the preventions of UTIs, and was sent on her way. The woman in bay two, however, looked worse than she had a few minutes before when Kami had last checked.

Her temp was just over one hundred and three, her throat beet red, and her conjunctivae injected. The woman was also now complaining of a severe headache, which she hadn't mentioned during triage or when Kami had done her nursing assessment.

The woman shivered as if she were freezing and looked miserable.

"Can you get her a blanket or something?" her husband asked, looking frustrated that his wife was getting worse.

"She doesn't need to cover up," Kami reminded him. She'd intentionally not given the woman a blanket. She directed her next comment to her patient. "It'll hold heat to your body and you're already too warm. We have to get your fever under control before we can even consider giving a blanket or doing anything that might make you worse."

Wincing with discomfort, the woman tightened her arms around her body. "I'm so cold."

They had to get her fever down and stable. Once they did, then she could possibly have a lightweight blanket. Certainly not before.

"When did the headache start?" Kami asked.

"She had a headache when she got here. It's just gotten a

lot worse," the husband clarified. "It wasn't bad enough to mention."

Apparently not even when Kami had directly asked about a headache. Ugh. She really didn't like when patients said something completely opposite when the doctor was present than what they'd told her during their assessment. It happened almost nightly.

Gabe ran through a quick examination of the woman. "Some swelling in the cervical nodes and neck stiffness. I want a blood count and a comprehensive metabolic panel on her STAT, and has that strep finished running?"

"Should be. I'll log in and check." Kami signed in on the in-bay computer and the test result was back. "She's negative for strep."

"Ache all over," the woman told them, her eyes squeezed tightly shut. "Cold."

Gabe gave some orders, which Kami turned to do, but stopped when the woman said, "I'm going to throw up." Then did exactly that.

Gabe was closer than Kami and got an emesis pan in front of Mrs. Arnold just in time.

"Give her an antiemetic IM now." He named the one he wanted given and the dosage. "Then let's get a saline lock on her."

Kami drew up the medication and injected the solution. The woman was shaking and looked much worse than she had when they'd entered the bay.

"Do something," the husband ordered, sounding worried, as he hovered next to his wife's bed, gripping the woman's pale hand.

Gabe sent Kami a concerned look. "Get phlebotomy to draw blood cultures times three and the previous labs I mentioned. It's off season, but run an influenza test, just in case. Let's get a CT of her head, too. I'm probably going to do a lumbar puncture."

He was thinking a possibility of meningitis. Rightly so, given how rapidly her status was changing.

"Let's put her in isolation. Just in case," Gabe continued in full doctor mode.

The husband was talking, too. Kami didn't want to ignore him, tried to answer his questions while she worked, but he continued to fret.

Gabe gave an order to get IV antibiotics started and told her which he wanted. Kami rushed around making things happen. Although she'd really not looked like more than a typical sore throat patient, Mrs. Arnold had gone downhill scarily fast. In case she continued on the decline, they needed to act fast to get an accurate diagnosis as quickly as possible.

Linda Arnold's blood count came back showing a significantly elevated white blood cell count with a bacterial shift. Her headache and neck pain had continued to increase and the woman refused to even attempt to move her neck. Her strep and influenza were negative.

Lumbar punctures weren't Gabe's favorite things to do as there was always risk, but his concerns over meningitis were too high not to test her spinal fluid. As soon as he had the CT scan results back, he'd pull the fluid so long as the scan didn't show any reason not to. He didn't want to risk brain herniation by not following protocol.

From all indications, the woman had meningitis. Gabe needed to know the exact culprit.

He cleared out two other patients who'd come into the emergency department. Then, protective personal equipment in place, he went back to Mrs. Arnold.

The woman was now going in and out of consciousness and didn't make a lot of sense when she was awake.

Also wearing appropriate personal protective equipment, Kami was at her bedside. She'd already gathered everything he'd need for a lumbar puncture. They needed to move fast.

Hopefully, the antibiotics infusing into her body via her IV line would be the right ones for whatever caused her infection, but if they weren't, waiting around to see could mean the difference between life and death.

That wasn't a chance he was willing to take.

"Dr. Nelson?" Mindy stopped him from entering the area where Mrs. Arnold was. "Dr. Reynolds just called with her CT results. He is concerned about meningitis and recommends proceeding with lumbar puncture."

This was the call Gabe had been waiting for giving him the safe go-ahead.

Checking to make sure his respiratory mask was secure, Gabe nodded, then entered the area where Mrs. Arnold was isolated.

From behind her clear plastic glasses, Kami's eyes were filled with worry when they met his.

"She has gaze palsy and mild extremity drift now," she told him. "I thought you'd prefer her husband not be in here for this as he was getting agitated. I sent him to the private counseling room to wait for you to talk to him after we get this done."

That was one of the things he loved about Kami. She was always one step ahead of him.

Except when it came to the auction.

On that one, he planned to outstep her. Not planned to—he *would* outstep her, because the more he thought about it, the more he wanted to go on that "date" with Kami.

Two

"What a night," Kami mused at the end of her twelve-hour shift that had turned into over fourteen. She couldn't wait to get home, shower, eat whatever she could find in the fridge, and crawl into bed to pass out until it was time to come back and do it all again for night two of her three in a row.

"You look tired."

She glanced toward Gabe. "You don't look like a bowl of cherries yourself."

He laughed. "Not sure if that was meant to be an insult or not, but I'll go on record saying I'm grateful I don't look like a bowl of cherries."

Kami shrugged. "Too bad. Cherries would be an improvement."

"A cherry fan?"

"They're my favorite," she admitted with a quick sideways glance toward him.

"You one of those talented people who can knot the stem with your tongue?" he teased.

Kami had very few silly talents, but tying a cherry stem

into a knot was in her repertoire. Rather than admit as much to Gabe, she shrugged again.

"I'll never tell."

"Because you prefer to show me?" he joked, not looking tired at all despite the fact he had to be exhausted.

It really had been a long night.

"Okay." He gave a dramatic sigh. "I'm game. There's a pancake house a few blocks from here where you can get whipped cream and cherries."

She frowned. "You know this how?"

"A man has to know where he can get whipped cream and cherries twenty-four hours a day."

Kami scrunched her nose. "Ew. Spare me the details because I don't want to know."

Looking intrigued, he chuckled. "Your mind went to the gutter, Kam. I'm surprised, but I think I like it."

"Nothing to like about you grossing me out."

His brow arched. "My liking whipped cream and cherries on top of my pancakes grosses you out?"

She ran her gaze over his broad chest, down his flat abs that his scrubs failed to disguise. "Yeah, I can tell you regularly chow down on pancakes with whipped cream and cherries."

"You might be surprised."

Not really. She'd seen him put away a lot of food during their shift breaks. The man could eat. Not that it showed. Whether because of good genetics or his time spent in the gym, Gabe truly was the picture of good health.

"Doubtful," she tossed as she clocked out and grabbed her lunch bag. "Not much about you surprises me."

His brow rose. "Oh? You know me that well?"

"As well as I want to." She gave him a look that said she was well aware he had fallen into step beside her as she exited the emergency department. "Bye, Gabe."

"You have to eat, Kam. Let me take you to breakfast before I hit the gym."

Her brows knitted together. "You're going to the gym this morning after working over and having to be back here this evening?"

His eyebrows lifted. "Why wouldn't I?"

Kami stared at him as if he were the oddest anomaly. "Do you not need sleep?"

He grinned. "Not when I'm properly motivated."

"You that excited at the prospect of running into Baxter again?" She glanced at her watch. "You should hurry or you may miss him. Wouldn't want that to happen."

Gabe burst out laughing. "Okay, I'll take a hint and a rain check on the pancakes with whipped cream and cherries."

That evening, Kami glanced at her cell phone and winced. Her mother. Should she answer? Guilt hit her that she considered not doing so. Her mother knew it was time for her to be at work. If she was calling, something must be wrong, right?

"Hi, Mom. I'm about to clock in at work, so I can't talk but a second. What's up?"

"I'm headed out of town," her mother answered. Then a male voice spoke in the background and, muffling the phone, her mother said something back. Then she said into the phone, "Can you feed my cat while I'm gone?"

Why her mother had gotten the scruffy cat, Kami had no clue. Most days she couldn't take care of herself, much less a pet. But at least she'd not left without making arrangements for the stray she'd taken in. Then again, her mother should have been an expert at taking in strays.

Fortunately, her mother didn't make a habit of asking Kami to feed them. At least, not since Kami had moved out the moment she'd graduated from high school and escaped the constant chaos of Eugenia's life.

"I'll swing by in the morning and feed her." Then she couldn't hold back asking, "What's his name?"

"Bubbles. You know that."

"Not the cat. The guy."

"Oh." Her mother giggled and the person in the background said something else, which elicited another giggle. "Sammy. He's a drummer in a band and so good."

Her mother tended to be drawn to artistic types. Especially unemployed ones who needed a place to crash while they waited on their big break. Not that any of them ever stuck around long. They stayed. They used. They moved on. Another arrived to fill the vacancy. It was the story of Kami's childhood and was still ongoing. Would her mother never learn?

"Okay, Mom," she sighed, putting her lunch in the breakroom refrigerator. "I'll feed Bubbles. Any idea when you'll be back?"

"A couple of days. I'll text to let you know for sure. Don't forget to love on Bubbles."

"Right." Because she wanted to stick around at her mother's apartment longer than she absolutely had to. Not. "Well, I'm at work, so I need to go. Bye, Mom. I'll feed Bubbles."

She'd probably love on the scrappy cat, too. Goodness knew that if her mother had a new man in her life, the cat would be ignored until his departure.

Kami had a lot of empathy for Bubbles.

"I was disappointed I didn't see Baxter this morning," Gabe teased as Kami came over to where he sat reviewing chart notes. Gabe loved his job, loved being a doctor, and loved knowing that, if the need arose, he could do everything humanly possible to save someone's life. Knowing he'd see Kami made the prospect of going to work all the sweeter. He never knew what was going to come out of that sassy mouth of hers.

"Maybe he's already given up his exercise kick," Kami mused, not looking as if she cared one way or the other.

Actually, she looked distracted and he wondered who she'd been on the phone with earlier. He'd been coming back into the department from the NICU, where Beverly and her husband had been sitting with their baby. He couldn't imagine the stress they were going through as each day was a struggle for their tiny baby girl to live. He'd been thinking on the fund-raiser, hoping it raised enough money to cover the couple's out-of-pocket medical expenses, not to mention all their day-to-day expenses that still had to be paid despite their being at the hospital instead of their jobs. Whomever Kami had been on the phone with, it hadn't been a pleasant conversation.

"Doubtful." Gabe leaned back in his chair and eyed the petite blonde nurse standing a few feet away. Were there problems with the fund-raiser? Or had the call been personal? "My guess is he was already there and gone by the time I got there. He's determined to buff up for you."

"Yeah, yeah." She didn't sound impressed. "Someone should tell him I'm not into buff."

Gabe arched a brow. "I thought all women were into buff."

She rolled her eyes. "Men are into buff. Any intelligent woman would rather have a man of substance than bulgy muscles."

"Can't a man have both substance and muscles?"

Kami shrugged. "Apparently not."

"You're overlooking the obvious."

Her forehead scrunched. "What's that?"

He waggled his brows. "I'm substance *and* bulgy muscles."

Giving him a critical once-over, she seemed to be debating his claim. "You're not that gross. You don't have that no-neck, bulgy-muscles look I can't stand."

Gabe wasn't sure if she'd insulted or complimented him. "That means I don't count?"

"You don't count, anyway," she said flippantly, handing him a piece of paper she'd jotted patient vitals on.

Ignoring the paper, he asked, "Why's that?"

"We're talking muscles and *substance*, remember?" she said matter-of-factly and gestured to the paper she'd handed him.

Gabe laughed. "Right. I forgot. Disqualified on all counts."

"Exactly. Now, are you going to go see the poor lady in bay three? Her blood pressure is crazy high at two hundred and fifteen over one hundred and thirty-seven."

"Slave driver," he accused, glancing down at the numbers on the paper she'd handed him as he headed toward the bay. "But rightly so."

Connie Guffrey's EKG was normal, as were her cardiac enzymes. Fortunately, after Kami administered IV medication, her blood pressure decreased to closer to the normal range, but Gabe decided to admit her for overnight observation due to her having developed some shortness of breath and mild chest pain just prior to plans to discharge her home.

Kami agreed doing serial cardiac enzymes overnight was in Ms. Guffrey's best interest and arranged the transfer to the medical floor.

"Don't look now," Mindy advised, "but you know who has been watching you all night. I think he really does want you to buy his date."

Kami immediately turned toward where she'd last seen Gabe. He was busy talking to a respiratory therapist who'd just administered a breathing treatment on an asthma patient.

"I told you not to look," Mindy reminded her.

"Doesn't matter that I looked because you're imagining things."

"Not hardly. And you know what?" Mindy looked absolutely smug. "He's not the only one who's been staring."

Realization dawning as to her friend's meaning, Kami frowned. "I have not been staring."

"Sure you haven't."

"The only time I've looked at the man is when we're discussing a patient or treating a patient." She scowled at her friend. "Don't you have something better to fill your time than making up stories?"

"You just looked at him, Kami."

She gave a *duh* look. "Because you told me not to."

"Exactly, and you immediately seized the excuse to look at him." Mindy bent forward and whispered, "I think you like him."

"Of course I like him. He's a nice guy who I work with. We're friends."

Mindy shook her head. "Not buying it. You should be more than friends."

Kami's gaze narrowed. "Says who?"

"Me." Mindy leaned against the raised desk area that provided a divider for the nurses from the examination bays. "Apparently he thinks so, too, or he wouldn't have asked you to buy his date."

"The reason he asked me to buy his date is because we're just friends and I wouldn't get the wrong idea."

"Which is?"

"That there could ever be something between him and me." Kami outright glared at her friend. "This isn't some television show where doctors fall for nurses and harbor secret feelings. This is reality and the reality is that he and I are just friends and that's all we want to be. Don't make this into something it's not."

"Maybe you should make it into something it's not."

"You sound like a broken record. Let it go," she ordered, then, frowning, added, "Besides, I thought you planned to bid on him."

Mindy crossed her arms, regarding Kami. "I should."

"Good. Buy him. He's taking his date to Gatlinburg for a fun-filled Saturday of visiting the aquarium, playing laser tag and putt-putt golf, riding go-karts, and topping the night off with a dinner show. You'd have a great time."

"I should hire you as my press agent. My bid might break records."

Kami jumped at Gabe's interruption. "I didn't hear you come up. I was...uh...telling Mindy she should bid on you."

"I heard." He grinned at Mindy. "She convince you?"

"I'm saving my pennies, Dr. Nelson."

He laughed. "Good to know."

Mindy looked back and forth between them, smiled as if she was in on a secret, and gave Kami a you-should-go-for-it look. "I hear the receptionist talking to someone. I'm off to see if it's a new patient and they're ready to be triaged."

Kami frowned at her retreating friend. She hadn't heard anyone registering. Her friend had purposely left her and Gabe alone. Mindy had a distinct lack of subtlety.

"Good to know that since you don't plan to buy my package, you at least plan to save me by convincing others to bid."

"What are friends for?"

He met her gaze. "I've already answered that question."

"True." Still feeling irked at Mindy's comments, she gave him a tight smile. "And we've already established that I'm not bidding on you."

"I'd spot you the money. Imagine—you'd get a fun-filled day in beautiful Gatlinburg, my company, and you wouldn't even have to save your pennies."

"You're wasting your breath."

"Talking to you is never wasted breath."

"Don't try sweet-talking me, Gabe. I know you better than to buy into that garbage."

He held his hands up. "Hey, I was making a legitimate observation, not trying to woo you into bidding on me."

"Right."

He laughed. "Okay, you're right. I was trying to woo you into winning my bid. Can you blame me?"

She gave him a look she hoped said she sure could.

"Fine," he relented. "But I do enjoy our conversations, Kam. You make me smile."

He made her smile, too, but she wasn't convinced that was what he'd meant.

"How is Ms. Guffrey?" she asked to redirect the subject to work. "Any news of how her cardiac tests are holding?"

"She's stable. We're thinking she just panicked and that's where the new symptoms came in. I sure didn't want to send her home and her have an MI."

"Agreed. I'm glad she's doing okay."

He glanced at his watch. "Only another hour until the end of our shift. You want to go for pancakes with me?"

Surprised at his repeated offer from the day before, Kami frowned. "Why would I do that?"

"Because you didn't go yesterday and you have me curious."

"About?"

"You know what." He waggled his brows.

It took her only a second to realize what he referred to.

"Puh-leese. That's what this is about? You want to know how talented I am with my mouth?"

As the words came out of her mouth, Kami realized how her comment could be interpreted. Her cheeks flushed hot.

"That's not..." At his laughter, Kami's face burned even hotter. "You know what I meant, Gabriel Nelson, and what I didn't mean."

"Do I?"

She narrowed her eyes. "You know you do."

He crossed his arms and leaned against the desk. "Maybe, but saying I don't might be a lot more fun. Why are your cheeks so red, Kam?"

Deciding that ignoring him was the best approach, Kami grabbed a brochure and fanned her face. "It is hot in here, isn't it?"

Which was a joke if Kami ever heard one. The emergency department was notoriously cool—purposely so to help keep germs down.

But, for once, the area felt blazing.

"Not particularly." His grin was still in place. "Even better than you going for pancakes with whipped cream and cherries with me would be if you did that *and* went to work out with me. That would send Baxter the message that he was wasting his time, for sure."

"If I ate pancakes then tried to work out, I'd be sick, so, in that regard, you're right about sending a message."

He laughed. "We could have breakfast after we work out."

She looked at him as if he was crazy. "Again, wrong girl, Gabe. I'm not a gym rat and I'm not a girl who would work out on an empty stomach."

His gaze ran over her. "You look like you could be."

"Is that a compliment?"

One corner of his mouth slid upward. "It wasn't an insult."

Kami fought to keep heat from flooding her face again. "Either way, I'm not going to the gym."

"You don't want to see the new and improved Baxter?"

Not that she could go anyway since she had to go feed Bubbles, but Kami pointed out, "You don't even know he'll be there this morning."

"Then you do want to see him?" Gabe sounded surprised.

"No, I don't want to see Baxter. That's why I broke things off."

Gabe immediately seized on her comment. "I thought your relationship ended due to a mutual decision."

"It did. Mutual means I told him things weren't working and he agreed." She glared at Gabe. "Would you stop twisting what I'm saying?"

Feigning innocence, he put his hands up in front of him. "I'm doing nothing of the sort. I'm just trying to buy you breakfast. Quite friendly of me, I'd say."

"You just want to harass me into buying your bid," she countered, knowing it was true. Gabe was her friend, but he was a guy and guys had ulterior motives, right?

"Perhaps," he agreed. "But I was serious about buying you breakfast. We could discuss the fund-raiser."

"What about it?"

"I could help in ways besides the auction."

"Uh-uh." She shook her head. "You're not getting out of the auction, Gabe. We're auctioning off five men and five women and you're the big-ticket item."

Grinning, he asked, "You think so?"

Despite all her efforts to prevent the heat, her face went hot again.

"Women seem to think so." At his pleased look, she added, "Especially Debbie."

That ought to simmer his arrogance down. If not, the brilliant idea that hit her would.

"I'm thinking of asking if she'll use her television connections for local publicity to raise awareness of the fund-raiser."

Rather than look annoyed, he looked impressed. "That's brilliant. You want me to check with her?"

A bit floored he'd be willing since he was making such a big deal of the woman planning to buy his date, Kami nodded. Garnering as much free publicity as possible was important and she should have thought of Gabe's connection to the local television station sooner. "Would you?"

His eyes danced. "For you?"

"For Beverly and her baby," she corrected.

"If it would help Beverly's baby get a new heart, I'd talk to the devil himself."

Kami didn't recall Debbie being anywhere near that bad, but she'd only met the woman a couple of times when she'd shown up at the emergency department to bring Gabe a late dinner or a cup of his favorite coffee. On television, she smiled often as she made over homes in the Eastern Tennessee area and seemed nice enough.

"Great." Kami rubbed her palms together. "Encourage her to pay plenty when she wins that Gatlinburg getaway. Sounds like fun."

"Obviously not fun enough. I can't convince you to bid."

"Can I go without you?"

He gave an offended frown. "That appeals more than the total package?"

Rolling her eyes, she clicked her tongue. "You're hardly the total package, Gabe."

Later that morning, Kami hit the drive-through and ordered a coffee to keep her going long enough to get to her mother's when all she really wanted was to go home and crash.

Within a few minutes, she was sitting on her mother's sofa, Bubbles walking back and forth next to her while Kami stroked the cat from her head to the tip of her tail.

Silly cat. Often, Kami wondered if the cat was happier to see her during her short visits than her mother was. She glanced around the tiny, messy apartment. No family portraits lined the walls. No memorabilia from Kami's childhood. Instead, the walls were bare except for a Red Hot Chili Peppers poster. If there had been a photo, Kami wouldn't have expected it to be of herself, but of this latest guy.

Kami emptied the litter box, bagged her mother's overflowing trash, put in a fresh bag, and picked up the empty food containers and drink cans scattered around the apartment.

Making sure the cat had food and water, Kami grabbed the trash and headed out of the apartment to go home. Sleep had her name all over it.

Only, when she got back to her place and finally crawled into bed, sleep refused to make an appearance.

Perhaps she should have skipped the coffee. She didn't need anything interfering with her rest prior to going into the third night of her three-in-a-row work schedule.

Especially not thoughts of her mother, a silly cat who was home alone, and Gabe.

Why was Gabe even on the list of things running through her mind?

He was a friend. Nothing more.

Ugh. Sleep was not happening.

She reached over and grabbed her phone off her nightstand. Ten a.m. Still early enough that if she dozed off she'd get plenty of rest before going back to work. Not that sleep seemed anywhere near.

Maybe she should get up for an hour, then try again later to go to sleep.

Sometimes after the first night of her three-in-a-row, she struggled to get to sleep the next morning, but never after the second or third nights.

Ugh.

Gripping her phone, she hit the text emblem, then Gabe's number from her contacts.

So, was he there?

Why she asked, she wasn't sure. She didn't care if Baxter had been at the gym or not. She just couldn't sleep. It made no sense, but deep down she knew talking with Gabe—even via text— would take her mind off her mother and off Bubbles, whom she'd considered packing up and bringing home with her. She might have, had her apartment not had a restriction against pets.

Who?

You know who.

Ah, the ex. He was there. Looking better every day.

Good for him.

There was a long enough pause that Kami wondered if Gabe was going to respond again.

Come on, Gabe. I need you to take my mind to a better place so I can close my eyes and stop my brain from racing because I feel sorry for a cat who has my mother as a caregiver.

Want me to take a picture for you next time I see him?

The idea of Gabe snapping a shot of Baxter working out had Kami laughing out loud.

People might get the wrong idea, think you had a man crush on him.

Yeah, well, I'm the kind of guy who would risk it to help a friend.

Good one. i'm still not bidding on you.

She lay back, head sinking into her pillow as she stared at her phone screen.

So you keep saying.

You think I will?

Hoping you will. Spoke to Debbie this morning. She's talking to her producer about the fund-raiser, see what they can come up with to help.

He'd already talked to his ex about the fund-raiser? Then again, Gabe had said he would and she'd never known him not to follow through on something he'd said he'd do.

Awesome. Hope it wasn't too painful. Thank you.

Thank you for all you're doing to help Beverly and her baby girl. If it wasn't for you and Mindy putting so much into this the fund-raiser wouldn't even be happening.

Ha, I'm not sacrificing nearly as much as you. She was only doing what she thought needed to be done to help with the overwhelming expenses that come with having a seriously ill baby. I'm not the one being auctioned off.

So you admit you feel badly for me?

That you're going to have women fighting over you with their wallets? Sure, I'm heartbroken. Poor, poor Gabe.

You're a funny girl, Kam.

She could picture his smile.

Something like that.

Why aren't you asleep? You were clamoring to get home to bed when I asked you to have pancakes with me.

Yeah, she had been. Too bad sleep continued to elude her.

I had errands to run. I may or may not have drunk coffee. Just saying.

It's not too late for those pancakes.

Sure it is. I'm in bed.

Nothing wrong with breakfast in bed. You want syrup or cherries and whipped cream? I recommend the cherries and whipped cream, but I admit I'm biased.

Kami stared at her phone screen and shook her head. The man was incorrigible.
Good thing she knew better than to take him seriously.
A smile on her face, she snuggled into her covers and began typing a response worthy of his outrageous suggestion.

Three

Gabe stared at his phone. What was he doing?

Flirting with Kami, that was what. It didn't take a genius to figure that one out.

Question was, why?

He and Kami were friends. So why had he typed out the message and hit Send as if flirting with Kami were the most natural thing in the world?

They often bantered back and forth and he enjoyed their conversations a great deal. Talking with Kami was mentally stimulating. They'd texted before but always light or something about work.

This felt different, not quite all in fun and games.

How about both, Gabe? We can use the whipped cream and cherries for after the pancakes.

Gabe's eyes widened and he wondered if he'd fallen asleep while sitting on the sofa messaging with her. Not once during their friendly banter had Kami ever flirted. Usually she came back with something sassy to put him in his place.

Her comment had his throat tightening; had him swallowing to clear the knot that formed there; had him fighting to keep the image of Kami, cherries, and whipped cream out of his head.

Why did her comment have his heart picking up pace?

Have his breath hitching in his chest?

Have his... This was *Kami* texting him. His friend Kami. His coworker Kami. What was he thinking?

Obviously, he wasn't.

Because if he was he wouldn't be considering calling in a to-go order for pancakes with whipped cream and cherries.

His phone buzzed and he braced himself, drawing on all his willpower not to run out of the door to grab that order.

Only, can you just set them inside the front door? I'll let you know later what my company thinks of your thoughtfulness in delivering breakfast.

Her message dumped a mental bucketful of cold water over his being.

Sitting up straighter on the sofa, Gabe tensed. His teeth clenched and his heart pounded as he typed.

There's someone there? In bed with you?

Why did that bother him? She'd dated Baxter for months, had probably spent many mornings with the accountant. What did it matter who Kami spent her mornings with? It wasn't his business.

You didn't think I meant to share pancakes in bed with you, did you? Ew, Gabe. Get real.

Ah, there was the Kami he knew and expected. Still, for a minute she'd had him going.

Then again, the gutted feeling in his stomach that at this very moment Kami was in bed with some Joe Blow, well, he didn't like the thought at all.

Which didn't make sense. They were just friends, right?

"So, who is this mystery guy?"

Kami flinched. She'd hoped Gabe would have let her ridiculous attempt to cover her comment go. She'd been meaning to take him down a peg, have him backtracking, but he'd taken her comment seriously and clearly hadn't known what to say back.

To which she'd been flabbergasted with embarrassment and had done what needed to be done to ease the tension crackling over the phone.

She'd made up a boyfriend.

No big deal. Women had been doing it for centuries. Not that Kami ever had, or even fully understood why she had that morning. Not with Gabe. It wasn't as if it mattered what he thought.

"No one you know." She refused to look at him, just kept staring at the computer monitor.

"Does Baxter know about him?"

"Shh." Kami glanced around, hoping Mindy didn't overhear their conversation. The emergency department had been slow since they'd arrived, and her friend was chatting with a paramedic who'd brought in a non-emergent patient for direct admission just prior to shift change and had stuck around afterward.

"Your best friend doesn't know about a guy you're having sex with?" Gabe tsked, pulling up a chair next to hers.

"Would you keep it down, please?"

Gabe gave her a suspicious look. "What's wrong with this guy that you don't want anyone to know of his existence?"

"Nothing is wrong with him," she defended. There wouldn't be a thing wrong with him. If he actually existed, she thought. Too bad he didn't. She'd like to throw him in Gabe's face right about now.

"How long have you known him?"

She swiveled her chair to face him. "Since when do you have the right to question me on my love life?"

His expression didn't waver. "Since you invited me to breakfast in bed."

"I didn't invite you to breakfast in bed," she hissed, not bothering to hide her outraged horror at the mere idea.

"Technically, you did."

Technically?

Kami's temples throbbed as she thought back over their conversation. Technically. Ugh.

"This is the most ridiculous conversation I've ever had." She pushed back her chair, stood to walk away, but he grabbed her hand, his hold gentle but firm enough to stop her.

She glared at where he touched her. Anger. That was why her skin burned there.

"Be careful, Kami," he warned. "Don't jump into something so fast on the heels of your breakup with Baxter."

Kami didn't know whether to burst out laughing or to cry. That Gabe would say not to rush into a new relationship when he usually had a new girl on his arm the week following a breakup was comical. She and Baxter had called it quits five, no, six weeks ago. Had she been in bed with another man, she still would have logged more getting-over-it time than Gabe put in prior to jumping into another bed. She was sure of it.

Men were so hypocritical.

"Take note, Gabe." She pulled her hand free. "My love life is none of your business."

"I am one hundred percent positive I'd rather have been in on this conversation than the one I just had with Eddie Pruitt."

Ugh. Mindy would have to overhear that. No doubt her friend would jump to all sorts of wrong conclusions, but at the moment Kami just wanted away from Gabe. Far away.

"Then you're welcome to this conversation, because I'm done with it."

With that, she left Mindy and Gabe staring after her.

* * *

"You want to tell me what you said to my best friend that upset her?"

Gabe wasn't sure what he'd said that had put Kami on the defensive. He'd been concerned and her hackles had stood at full attention. Even if he had known why she'd gotten so irate, he doubted he'd discuss it with Mindy.

If Kami hadn't told her friend about this mystery guy, then Gabe wasn't going to be the one to spill the beans.

Mindy studied him a moment. Then her expression softened. "You trying to get her to buy your date again?"

"No." If Kami was involved with another man, she wouldn't be buying his date. Nor would he ask her to. That went beyond the call of friendship.

Only, something didn't feel right about the whole conversation.

Then it hit him.

"Excuse me, Mindy. Kami might have been done with our conversation, but I wasn't."

He found Kami restocking bay one despite the fact that the shelf wasn't low.

He wasted no time in asking, "If you were in bed with another man this morning, why were you texting me?"

Letting out an exasperated hiss, Kami turned toward him, pursed her lips, crossed her arms, and glared. "Fine. I wasn't in bed with another man."

He let that sink in, let the wave of emotions wash over him and sought to label the one beating him down.

Relief. Why was he relieved that she hadn't been in bed with someone?

Because they'd been flirting and he'd liked it?

"Why did you lead me to think you were?"

An annoyed sigh escaped her lips. "Because you shouldn't have said what you did about breakfast in bed."

Now she wasn't meeting his eyes, which made him all the more curious. "Why not?"

"Because you didn't mean it." She gave him a disgusted look. "No wonder women like Debbie don't let go if you make comments like those when you don't mean them."

"First off, I don't make comments like those to Debbie or any other woman. Second, who says I didn't mean my offer?"

She rolled her eyes upward. "Right."

"Right, what?"

Her hand went to her hip and she stared him down. "Right, you meant it when you offered to bring me breakfast in bed."

He had. It floored him as much as it did her.

He cocked a brow. "You're saying I didn't?"

Looking flustered, she huffed out, "Quit being ridiculous, Gabe. Of course you didn't."

He held her gaze, refusing to look away or back down. "Want to bet?"

"You'd lose," she returned.

The challenge in her eyes had Gabe knowing he'd do nothing of the sort.

"Guess we'll find out when I bring you breakfast in bed tomorrow, won't we?"

She let out a huff of air. "You aren't bringing me breakfast in bed tomorrow or any other day."

"You'll see. Tomorrow morning." He glanced at his watch, saw it was after midnight. "Technically, *this* morning. You're going to eat every bite and you're going to like it."

Annoyed at him and herself, Kami gawked at Gabe, not quite believing that she was arguing with him about breakfast in bed.

That he was arguing back.

Had they ever argued? Or raised their voices with each other? Never.

That they were now, over breakfast in bed, was the most ludicrous thing she could imagine.

So ludicrous that, despite her tension of moments before, she burst out laughing.

His face tight, Gabe's gaze narrowed. "What's so funny?"

"You."

He frowned. "I see nothing funny about this."

"Really? You don't find the fact you just threatened to make me eat every bite of my breakfast and that I was going to like it hilarious?" Another round of laughter hit her and she grabbed her stomach. "Oh, Gabe, I thought you had a better sense of humor."

His expression easing, a smile twitched at his lips. "Okay, so maybe a little hilarious, but don't think that gets you out of breakfast. You are going to eat up. Mmm…good."

"Yeah, yeah," she mocked, grateful the tension inside her had dissipated. "Keep threatening me and I'm going to report you to my nearest supervisor."

"I am your nearest supervisor," he reminded her, his tone back to its usual teasing.

"There is that."

"Hey, you two, we have incoming." Mindy stuck her head into the bay. "Motor vehicle accident. One dead at scene, two critical on their way here."

Their slow night morphed into total chaos as at the same time as the first ambulance arrived, so did a private vehicle with an overdose victim requiring multiple doses of Narcan administration prior to them being able to revive the woman and transfer her to the ICU.

The night flew by with one patient after another. By the time she'd given her report to the day-shift nurse taking her place, Kami was exhausted.

She clocked out, visited with an even more exhausted-appearing Beverly in the NICU for a few minutes, stopped by to feed and water Bubbles, fought guilt over leaving her mother's cat home alone while she drove home, showered, and was about to crawl into her bed when she heard knocking.

"Who in the world?"

Glancing down at her shorts and well-worn Ed Sheeran T-shirt, Kami headed toward the apartment door. She wasn't wearing a bra, but she wasn't overly endowed and doubted anyone would be able to tell.

"Who is it?" she called through the door at the same time as she stretched on her tiptoes to peek through the peephole.

Gabe!

Carrying bags displaying a local pancake house logo.

He hadn't.

He had.

"Delivery boy."

Heart pounding against her rib cage, she leaned her forehead against the door. Gabe was at her house. With breakfast.

Why?

Why was her pulse pounding in her ears?

"Wrong address. I didn't order anything," she called back.

What was he doing there? Why did she suddenly feel the need to go put on a bra after all? And a dozen other layers? Why was her heart racing as if something really good was happening?

"It's a special delivery."

"Sorry, I don't open my door for strangers."

"What's wrong, Kam? Someone in there with you?" he teased. "I could always leave the bags by the door."

Undoing the lock and dead bolt, she flung open the door. "That, Dr. Nelson, was a low blow."

He grinned. "You'd have done the same had the opportunity presented itself."

He had her there.

"Invite me in," he reminded her when she kept standing in the doorway, glaring at him.

"Because you're a creature of the night and can't enter unless invited in first?" She stepped aside, motioning for him to come in.

"Something like that," he tossed back, entering the apartment and glancing around. "Where do you want these?"

"Not in my bed." She closed the front door and followed him, not quite believing he was there, inside her home. With breakfast.

He laughed. "Ah, now come on. You're spoiling my fun."

"Right." She glanced around her mostly clean living room, thinking it wasn't in too bad shape for the end of three nights on at the hospital.

"How about you set them on the coffee table?" Then, thinking it might be easier, she suggested, "Or on the table over there?"

The apartment, although not really big, had an open floor plan so that the kitchen, dining area, and living room were all visible to each other. It was one of the features Kami had fallen in love with when she'd first walked into the place. That and its close vicinity to both the hospital and the university. She'd started out there with a roommate, but the woman had married and moved away several months ago. Kami had never bothered to replace her since she'd been mere months from reaching her house-down-payment goal and would hopefully be buying her first home soon.

Someday soon she would own her own home and no one would be able to take it away from her. A place where she'd never have to move from because it would be hers. A place where if she wanted to bring her mother's cat to her home, she could.

With her next paycheck, she'd hit the target she'd set for herself years ago and she'd start the search to make her homeowner dream a reality.

"Either way is fine," she rushed on.

"Let's do the coffee table." He set the bags down on the laminated wooden table. "Less formal."

Still way more formal than her bedroom.

Her cheeks heated at the thought.

She stopped moving. "Why are you here, Gabe?"

"I'd think that was obvious."

She arched her brows and waited.

"I promised you breakfast."

"Actually, you threatened breakfast in bed."

He picked the bags back off the coffee table. "Point me in the right direction."

Kami had thought her cheeks had been hot before, but the heat coming off them now could melt the polar ice caps.

"You goofball. I ought to take you up on that." She rolled her eyes, trying to ease the twirling in her stomach. "That would teach you."

At his mischievous look, she shook her head.

"Or, more likely, not teach you anything at all." She sighed. "You're not going in my bedroom, Gabe. Not now or ever."

"Now who's threatening who?" he teased, putting the bags back down and unpacking the plastic containers. "Jeez, Kam, you're grumpy in the mornings. Now I know why you work night shift."

Eyeing the numerous containers he was pulling from the bags, she asked, "How is it that you're so cheery when I know you were up all night?"

He waggled his brows. "What man isn't cheery when he's been up all night?"

Rather than respond, Kami gave in to the smell coming from her coffee table. "Why do you have three drinks?"

He pulled out a milk carton and a plastic orange-juice container from one of the bags.

"Five drinks?" she corrected.

"I wasn't sure what you'd want, so I got a variety of choices. I aim to please, so I'll drink what you don't want."

"That was thoughtful of you."

He grinned. "I'm a thoughtful kind of guy."

Kami sank onto her sofa, suspiciously eyeing the man unpacking a third bag. "It's been my experience that when a man does something thoughtful he wants something in return."

He shot her a serious look. "Baxter has a lot to answer for."

Kami shook her head. "I wasn't referring to Baxter."

He continued unpacking plastic containers and setting them on her coffee table. "What was the guy's name before him? Kent or Kenny or something?"

Surprised that he recalled her previous boyfriend's name, Kami nodded. "Kent, but I really didn't mean him, specifically, either. Just was making a comment about men in general."

"I'm not like other guys."

"Sure you aren't," she said, although secretly she agreed. Gabe was unlike anyone she'd ever known. Although he never stuck around, just as her mother's numerous boyfriends hadn't, Gabe never made promises that he would. Plus, he was genuinely a likable person. She didn't recall liking any of the men her mother had brought in and out of their lives. "You delivered breakfast." She gave as mean a look as she could muster. "If you brought whipped cream and cherries, I'll know for sure you're up to no good."

Eyes sparkling with mischief, he popped the top off a plastic container. Sure enough, inside was a big dollop of thick whipped cream with six or seven long-stemmed cherries to the side.

Kami's breath sticking in her tight chest, she lifted her gaze to Gabe's. "Oh, my."

He laughed. "Am I in trouble?"

"I'm beginning to think you're always trouble," she mused, tempted to reach for a cherry. They really were her favorite, but no way would she stick one in her mouth while Gabe watched. Besides, as difficult as it was simply to breathe at the moment, she'd likely choke if she did.

"There goes my knight-in-shining-armor image."

"I've never thought you were a knight in shining armor," she scoffed.

"There is that." He placed the now empty and folded bags on the floor. "Which is one of the reasons I like you."

Ignoring his comment, she eyed the multiple containers as he popped off lids. "Which of those did you get for me?"

"The ones I knew you'd like."

She started to ask how he'd begin to know what she liked for breakfast, but asked instead, "What if I told you I didn't like pancakes?"

"I'd know you were lying." He scooted a plastic container toward her. "These are yours."

She eyed the contents. "Are those pecans?"

He nodded.

Rather than digging into the delicious-looking pancakes, she wrinkled her nose. "What if I told you I had a nut allergy?"

As if he knew she was purposely being ornery, his eyes twinkled. "I'd know you were lying," he repeated.

"Lots of people have nut allergies," she needlessly pointed out.

"But you don't." His smile said it all.

"How can you be so sure?"

He laughed, shaking his head at her obtuseness. "How long have I worked with you, Kam? Nuts are your favorite snack. Pecans, almonds, walnuts, cashews. I've seen you eat them all and don't recall a single hive ever."

He had her there.

"But if you suddenly develop an itch, I promise to scratch it."

Um, no. Gabe would not be scratching her itch.

"I don't have a nut allergy," she conceded, wondering that he'd paid attention to what she ate for snacks. Who knew?

"Or an aversion to pancakes," he added in case she went back to that.

She sighed. "Do you really have to hear me say it?"

He nodded.

She glanced upward, as if asking for help in dealing with the likes of him. "Fine. I love pancakes. They're amazing. My favorite carbs. Especially hot pancakes, which these aren't going to be if you don't quit talking and let me eat."

He laughed and popped the lid on another container, revealing bacon and sausage links, and held the tray toward her. "Help yourself."

She shook her head, then reached for a tiny bottle of syrup, unscrewed the top, and poured a generous amount over the plastic tray of pecan pancakes. Taking a bite, she couldn't contain the pleasure her throat emitted at the fluffy cakes coated with sticky sweet syrup.

"Mmm...you're forgiven for being a pain. That's good."

"Apparently."

Kami opened the eyes she hadn't even been aware she'd closed, met his gaze, and smiled. "Don't go being all smug just because this is amazing."

"Would I do that?"

"In a heartbeat."

He laughed and, rather than sit on the sofa next to her, he sat on the floor.

"You could have sat up here. I wouldn't have bitten you."

"Which is why I chose the floor."

"Seriously, Gabe, you need to quit that." She took another bite, enjoyed every morsel as she chewed, then added, "Someday it's going to get you into trouble."

"Possibly," he agreed, munching on a piece of bacon. "But life sure is fun in the meantime."

Still working on her pancakes, Kami eyed him. "It must be good to be you."

In between bites of the omelet he'd ordered for himself, Gabe stared from across the coffee table. "Why's that?"

She waved her empty fork in the air. "Women just let you do whatever you want and you get away with it."

His brow arched. "You're referring to me bringing you breakfast and you letting me?"

When he put it like that...

"Don't make yourself sound normal and me sound like the psycho."

"You said it, not me."

She laughed.

"Okay, so this was nice." It only hurt a little to admit that. "But I didn't really expect you to show with breakfast. I'd actually forgotten you'd threatened to do so."

"Good to know I'm so easy to forget."

She doubted any woman in the history of the world had forgotten him. Take Debbie, for instance. Had Gabe showered her with such attention—more, since they'd actually been dating—no wonder the woman was so desperate to get him back. Giving up a man like Gabe couldn't be easy even when one knew it was inevitable.

"Had you shown up fifteen minutes later, you'd have been stuck eating this all by yourself. I was about to go to bed."

He nodded toward her clothes. "Like your pajamas."

She glanced down at her T-shirt and loose shorts. It could have been much worse. "You should catch me on a good morning."

"That an offer?"

Good grief. If Mindy ever heard him making such over-the-top comments, Kami would never convince her Gabe was just teasing.

She shook her head. "No, Gabe, that's not an offer. Quit saying such things."

Kami was right. Gabe did need to quit saying such things. But teasing her, getting a rise out of her, sure did tempt him. "Afraid you'll get weak and say yes?"

She arched a brow. "Are you saying a woman saying yes to you is a sign of weakness?"

Gabe chuckled. "Never."

"For the record, you're leaving that whipped cream and cherries for me to eat later, at my leisure, without you."

"If I say yes does that make me weak?"

She laughed. "I'd say it makes you a smart man for not coming between a woman and her dessert."

"Point taken."

They ate in silence for the next few minutes. Then Kami stood and stretched, drawing Gabe's gaze to the expanse of skin on display, making him realize that he'd never seen her legs before.

Not unless they were covered by scrubs. But that couldn't be right because he would have seen her at the Christmas party and she wouldn't have had on her nursing uniform then.

He racked his brain.

"A black pantsuit."

Her brows veed. "Huh?"

"It's what you were wearing at the Christmas party."

She stared blankly. "What does that have to do with anything?"

"I was looking at your legs, and—"

"Hold up. Why were you looking at my legs?"

"I was thinking that I had never seen you out of scrubs," he continued, ignoring her question. "But that isn't right because you weren't wearing scrubs at last year's Christmas party."

"Which doesn't explain why you were looking at my legs," she reminded him.

"You have great legs, Kam. You should show them off more."

"Oh, yeah. I'll just roll up in the emergency room wearing a miniskirt."

He waggled his brows. "I wouldn't complain."

"I'm sure you wouldn't." She snapped her fingers and waved them in front of her face. "Eyes up here, Gabe. Not on my legs."

"You're such a party pooper, Kam."

She laughed. "You're crazy and did you really just call me a party pooper?"

"If the shoe fits."

Shaking her head, Kami gathered her leftover pancakes and

the trash, using the empty bags to store them. "You're lucky I'm not wearing shoes or I might be throwing them at you."

His gaze immediately fell to her bare feet. "Are those emojis on your toenails?"

Kami's gaze dropped to her toes and the most secretive smile he'd ever seen lit her face. "Smiley faces, Gabe. Those are smiley faces."

"Now you've gone and done it. I'm never going to be able to look at you the same."

Her gaze lifted. "Because I have painted toenails?"

"Legs that go on forever and smiley faces on your toes. A man could do worse."

"Just you forget you ever saw my legs or my smiley faces."

He stood and helped gather the remaining food and drinks. "Not going to happen."

"They're burned onto your retinas for life? Like tragic scars?"

He followed her into her kitchen, took in the brightly colored walls and multicolored dishes on the counters. What was it called? Festive ware? That didn't sound quite right. Fiesta ware. That was it.

The room fit the barefoot woman opening a cabinet and tossing trash into a hidden bin.

"There's enough left for me to have breakfast tomorrow," she mused when she put the leftovers in the fridge.

"Or I could just bring you breakfast again in the morning."

She spun toward him and pointed her finger. "No."

"Now that I've seen those toes, I'm not going to be able to stay away, Kam," he teased, enjoying the color that rose in her cheeks. "You had to have realized that when you opened the door bare-legged and laid-back sexy."

"Yeah. Yeah. I have that problem all the time." Her gaze hit the ceiling, then came back to his. "Don't fool yourself, Gabe. I opened the door because you had food. No other reason."

He laughed. "I won't ever have ego problems with you around to keep me grounded."

"You don't need me to fluff your ego," she said. "You have a whole slew of women for that without me joining the fan club."

Something about the way she said it struck Gabe. Not that he had a fan club or that many women fluffing his ego. He'd always been blessed with an abundance of dates, but he had never seen himself as she was making him out to be.

"But you are a fan, aren't you, Kam?" he asked, curious as to her answer.

"Your fan?" she asked, turning from the refrigerator and leaning against it to stare at him. Her eyes flashed with something he couldn't quite read. "Yeah, Gabe. I'm a total groupie. You know it."

Her tone and expression were flippant, but something sparked in those green depths that he couldn't quite read, as if maybe there was a spark of attraction there, too.

"But, seriously, breakfast was nice. You'll understand if I throw you out because I'm ready for bed." When he started to say something, she jabbed her finger in his direction. "Don't even go there. Not if you value your life."

Yeah, his former thoughts had been nothing short of ridiculous. Gabe laughed. "So what you're saying is breakfast in bed with you doesn't start or end in your bed?"

She bared her teeth in an exaggerated smile. "Exactly."

"Anyone ever told you that you're a party pooper?"

"A time or two," she admitted with a small laugh. "Now, time for you to go so I can get some beauty sleep."

"You don't need it."

Her brow arched. "Pardon?"

"Beauty sleep. You don't need it."

She didn't. There was something inherently attractive about her air-dried hair pulled back in a braid with a few escaped strands framing her face, her brightly scrubbed skin with its faint spattering of freckles across her nose, her loose T-shirt and shorts, and those long legs and happy toenails.

"Right," she scoffed at his beauty claim, shaking her head. "What was in that milk you drank, anyway?"

"Calcium and vitamin D."

"Hallucinogenics, too, perhaps?"

Perhaps, because, looking at Kami, he was definitely seeing things he hadn't in the past.

She really was beautiful. Funny, he'd never thought about that before. Sure, if asked, he'd have said she was an attractive woman, but he'd never really looked at her before. Not in that way.

Not as he was looking at her. Not with the idea that he'd like to run his hands over those legs and...

"It's the toenails. They've cast a spell on me."

Kami wiggled her toes. "Lay off the toenails, dude. They make me happy."

"Since you didn't seem to think the bare legs thing would jibe, I could put in a motion to allow open-toed shoes."

Kami shook her head. "Yep, that'll go over so much better than the bare legs. Nothing like exposed toes, sharp instruments, and bleeding patients."

"You have a point," he conceded. "Maybe we just need to spend more time together away from the hospital."

Her smile slipped and she stared at her feet. "You really shouldn't say things like that."

She kept reminding him of that.

At first, he'd agreed. But the more he teased her, the more he wondered why he had to stop when their conversations usually made her smile and come right back at him. When she made him smile.

"Why shouldn't I say things like that?"

Seeming taken aback at his question, she pushed off from where she leaned against the countertop. "Because we both know you don't mean them."

She rubbed one foot across the other in what was likely a

nervous gesture. The motion drew Gabe's attention, had him wanting to touch her there, kiss her there and work his way up.

"That's where you're wrong," he admitted to her and to himself. "I've had a great time. So much so, I want to do this again. Same time tomorrow morning?"

Her eyes widened. "No. Not tomorrow morning or the morning after that, either."

"Why not?"

She looked flustered, as if she wasn't sure what to say. "Because you being here is insane."

"What's insane about us having breakfast together?"

"We're not that good friends."

Did she not think so?

"We will be."

Four

Gabe didn't show at Kami's house the following morning, but he did text a photo that made her burst out laughing and eased the tension she'd fought all night.

She texted him back.

That does it. You're officially a creeper.

Some things a woman just has to see to believe.

Some things a woman should never see.

Hey, you were the one who dated the guy.

Not for his gym skills.

Which leads me to wonder what skills you were dating him for. Do tell, Kam.

Never.

A girl who kisses and doesn't tell, eh?

You'll never know.

Keep flashing those smiley-face toenails my way and I'll prove you wrong.

   Kami gripped her phone a little tighter as she reread his message. There went the butterflies in her belly again, so she reminded herself Gabe was just being Gabe and she shouldn't read anything into his comments.
   She texted again.

Ha. Ha. I see you had your morning dose of calcium, vitamin D, and hallucinogenics.

A full glass. Want to meet me for breakfast?

Nope. I already ate.

   Her heart wasn't racing because part of her wanted to say yes. Really, it wasn't.

A pity. What did you have?

Whipped cream and cherries.

   Now, why had she gone and admitted that? She was as bad as him.

Forget the toenails. I want to see your knotted stems. Show me.

   She shouldn't do it, but she was going to anyway.
   Feeling completely giggly, she held out her phone toward the seven perfectly knotted cherry stems she'd left on a napkin

because she'd not been able to bring herself to toss them. Silly. What was she planning? To save them as a keepsake?

A keepsake of what? Gabe bringing her breakfast? They were only friends. Had only ever been friends.

Would only ever be friends.

Yet, here she was sending a picture of her knotted cherry stems and grinning like a complete idiot.

Someday you're going to show me how you do that in person.

Keep dreaming.

I am. Of smiley toenails and talented tongues.

Pervert.

Leaning back against her kitchen countertop, she typed on.

Obviously you aren't working out nearly hard enough if you're able to keep up your end of this conversation.

Keeping things up has never been a problem for me. Nor working hard. I'm talented that way. Want me to show you?

Kami took a deep breath. She and Gabe had always gone back and forth at work, had occasionally texted each other funny little snippets, but this...this they'd never done.

This had blatant sexual overtones. It was a kind of sexual energy bouncing back and forth between them.

She didn't understand it, and the more she reminded him he shouldn't say such things, the more determined he seemed to say them.

Then again, how could she fuss at him when she'd been the one to bring up the whipped cream and cherries?

Gabe was a gorgeous man, a successful doctor. He had beautiful, successful women chasing him. His last girlfriend was a local television celebrity, for goodness' sake. What was he doing carrying on this conversation with Kami as if their relationship were blossoming into something beyond friendship?

He was just playing with her. Nothing more.

Why, she didn't know, nor did it matter. What mattered was her keeping things in perspective. Otherwise, she might get caught up in their play and end up hurt. Hadn't she learned anything from her mother's many mistakes? From the constant whirlwind of men who'd come in and out of her mother's life?

Gabe didn't run into Kami's ex at the gym the following morning.

Usually he put in an hour or so on his days off work, but today he had an excess of energy he needed to burn and he was hitting it hard.

Probably hard enough that he'd be sore, but he didn't slow his pace on the rowing machine.

Not even when his phone buzzed, indicating he had a text message. Hoping he'd be pleasantly surprised, he glanced down at his smartwatch, saw the name, and kept right on rowing.

The number hadn't been a pleasant surprise.

Although he didn't want to deal with Debbie's incessant efforts to get back together—efforts that had intensified since he'd contacted her about the fund-raiser—she wasn't the source of his restlessness.

Kami was.

He liked her, had liked her from the moment they met when he'd joined the emergency department in Knoxville the year before. She was dependable, fun, had a quick wit, and a sharp mouth that didn't mind putting him in his place.

And often.

He'd always found working with her refreshing, had always found himself seeking her company at the hospital and at the occasional work get-togethers they'd both been at.

Obviously, none of these had involved cherries as he wouldn't have forgotten had she tied a knot in a cherry stem.

An image of a knotted stem between her full rosy lips had a fresh trickle of sweat running down his forehead.

Now, where had that come from?

He didn't think of her that way. Not that Kami wasn't an attractive woman. With her sandy hair, heart-shaped face, big green eyes, and full lips, she was. Gabe had just always preferred tall, curvy brunettes or willowy blondes to petite women with smart mouths.

Since he'd seen that picture of those seven cherry stems with their perfect knots, his thoughts of Kami had changed.

Or maybe it had been the legs that went on and on.

Or the bare feet with their happy toenails.

Or the way her eyes danced when she countered him tit for tat and never let him have the last word.

Or the little happy bop she sometimes did when she put him in his place.

Or the...

Slowing his pace, Gabe wiped the sweat off his brow with the back of his hand and forced himself to begin cooling down.

He'd had enough for the morning. Time to go shower, eat, and not think about cherry stems, long legs, happy toes, or little dances anymore.

He liked their relationship, the camaraderie they shared at work. Why would he risk messing up a great working relationship? A great friendship? There were dozens of women to date, to fantasize about.

He wasn't willing to risk losing a friendship he valued.

Kami was off-limits as anything more than his friend, so maybe she was right to tell him he shouldn't say certain things and he needed to start heeding her advice.

Now, if he could only convince his body to go along.

"You didn't answer my text yesterday," Gabe accused the first moment he and Kami were alone during their next emergency-room shift together. He'd just finished suturing a fifteen-year-old kid who'd cut his hand on a broken glass and he'd followed her to the supply closet.

"I was busy." Rather than look at him, she kept gathering the supplies she'd come for.

Gabe frowned. "Too busy to answer my text?"

She glanced his way, arched her brow. "Did I answer your text?"

"No."

She gave a pointed look. "Then I was too busy to answer."

Right. Gabe studied her, taking note of the tension pouring off her. The unusual tension. Kami rolled with the punches. Nothing ever got to her too much. She was usually all smiles and sass. He knew he'd made the decision to back off from their flirting to preserve their friendship, but someone had put a bee in her bonnet.

Or had their flirting been the culprit and he'd not checked things soon enough? Regardless, he'd contacted her about business, not pleasure.

"Then you don't care that Debbie's producer wants to meet with us about the fund-raiser?"

Kami's dour expression took on new life, sparking her into her usual excitement. "That's awesome."

Glad to see the light back in her eyes, he wasn't quite ready to ignore her former cold shoulder. "But since you didn't answer my text, I wasn't sure when to tell her we could meet them."

Her eyes narrowed suspiciously. "We? Them?"

"Me, you, Debbie, her producer."

Her brows veed. "Why are you and Debbie going to be there? Couldn't I just meet with the producer?"

As if she didn't know. "You tell me, friend-who-refuses-to-bid-on-my-charity-date."

Okay, so he probably needed to quit with the poking comments, but he was irked that she'd ignored his message the day before and him for most of their shift thus far.

Kami's nose scrunched. "Oh."

"Yeah, oh," he agreed, then returned her sharp look. "Have I mentioned that you owe me?"

A tolerant smile twitched at her lips. "A few times."

"I'll expect you not to forget."

"I never forget when I owe someone something. You're doing this because you're a good man and want to help our coworker raise funds to help cover her baby's heart-transplant expenses. This has nothing to do with me, so I owe you nothing."

Her comment had put him in his place and he couldn't argue with her, not even teasingly.

"Way to make a guy feel bad." He hung his head in mock shame, then looked up and winked.

She smiled, this time for real, and the tension within Gabe eased.

"I was complimenting you," she pointed out. "Can I help it if you had a guilty conscience?"

Eyes locked with hers, he took a step toward her, stared down into her wide green eyes. "First compliment that ever left me feeling reprimanded."

"That's because you don't get reprimanded nearly often enough," she countered, her gaze dropping from his scrutiny and landing on his mouth.

She sucked in a tiny sharp breath, then glanced away to stare at something behind him. He wanted to touch her face, to brush his fingers over the stray hairs along her face that had escaped her clip, to place his thumb beneath her chin and lift her mouth.

To his.

Gabe swallowed. "You volunteering for the job? Because I'm willing."

Her gaze cut back to his. "Gabe, I can't do this."

"This?" he asked, knowing the gap between them had somehow shortened because he was so close she had to feel his breath against her face. He could feel hers; he wanted to feel more.

"You. Me. This."

She closed her eyes, but rather than take advantage of the moment, he waited.

"We can't do this. We'd regret it forever."

"What would we regret forever?" He knew what she meant, but asked anyway. He needed to hear her say it out loud. Maybe then it would drive the message home because what she'd closed her eyes to hide hadn't been regretting what they might do, but what they wouldn't.

"Oops." Mindy opened the tiny supply room's door and spotted them. "Sorry. I didn't realize you were in here. Together. Alone."

Kami's eyes had popped open, had filled with guilt and so much more he couldn't label. Gabe wanted to pull her close, tell her it was okay, that he was positive Mindy would celebrate if she'd actually seen anything physical happening.

Gabe had wanted something physical to happen. Had wanted to kiss her. Maybe he shouldn't have hesitated. Maybe he should have covered her mouth with his and settled his curiosity of what Kami's mouth would feel like.

But probably not.

Her hackles were back up and she refused to look at him.

"Very alone," Mindy continued, looking quite pleased at what she'd interrupted. "I can come back later."

"No. Don't do that. I'm finished here." Kami stepped back, bumping against a shelf, then blushing at having done so. "I have what I need."

"I'm sure you do," Mindy teased, looking back and forth between them with a smile.

Kami winced. "As for Dr. Nelson, he was telling me good news about promoting the fund-raiser. Great news about the fund-raiser," she corrected, sounding breathy. "You should ask him about it, since you're the event's cochair and are going to have to take my place on this one because I'm done."

With that, Kami rushed from the room.

* * *

"What did you do this time? And why do I have to keep asking you that?"

"Good question."

Mindy's hand went to her hip. "What's she done with?"

Gabe shrugged. He wasn't sure of the answer to that, either, but suspected she'd meant him and whatever was happening between them.

Mindy let out a long sigh and shook her head. "You convinced her to bid on you yet?"

He glanced toward his coworker. "You think I have a chance of changing her mind?"

Mindy shrugged. "I'd say you have a chance at anything you set your mind to, including my best friend buying that date package."

"I guess we'll see."

She sure didn't seem to have any problems pushing him away.

Or not answering his text.

Plus, the last thing he'd call the way his body had responded to her closeness, to her staring at his mouth, to the sparks that had been flying between them, was safe.

Unless playing with fire was safe, because he felt that hot under the collar.

"I'm sorry."

Not wanting to acknowledge Gabe, but knowing she should, Kami nodded and took another bite of the sandwich she'd packed for her after-midnight "lunch." They'd finally gotten a slow moment and she'd clocked out for her break.

Gabe had been tied up with discharging an asthma-attack patient who had settled down perfectly with a steroid injection and breathing treatment.

He sat down at the break table. "I don't want to lose your friendship, Kami."

"I feel the same," she admitted, wondering if it was already too late. She'd felt something in that room. Something that had been hinted at and building for days, maybe longer, but that she'd been able to tamp down.

Now she wasn't sure she was going to be able to safely tuck it back away. *It* being the chemistry she'd felt with Gabe as he'd zeroed in on her mouth.

She'd wanted him to kiss her.

To run his fingers through her hair and hold her to him and devour her mouth; to press his body to hers and... Ugh. Her brain had to quit going there.

"Good," he agreed. "As much as I love to tease you, I don't want to do anything that undermines our friendship."

Not sure what to say, she nodded again.

He sat next to her, quiet for a few moments. "Something's changed between us, hasn't it?"

She turned to him. "Do you really need to ask me that?"

He eyed her for long seconds before asking, "Are we going to be okay?"

Did he mean individually or together? Because for all her mind slips since their supply-room episode, she really couldn't see there ever being a "together" between them.

"We're going to be okay." They would be. He'd forget whatever this little blip of attraction was and move on to the next hottie who caught his eye. She'd go on being happy with her life, and if the right guy, a safe guy who wouldn't use her or leave her, came along, then she'd get involved again.

Baxter had been safe.

Now, where had that thought come from? Baxter didn't count. There had been no magic when Baxter had kissed her, touched her.

Gabe hadn't touched her or kissed her and yet the supply-room incident felt surreal.

"Well, as long as we're going to be okay. I really don't want to lose you, Kam." With that, he reached over and patted her hand much as an adult might pat a child's hand, then pushed back his chair and left her to stare after him.

Nothing awkward about that conversation, she thought as he left the small break room. Nothing at all.

Maybe she needed to stay away from Gabe for a while. At least until she got her head wrapped around what had happened.

Almost happened.

Because nothing had happened.

She closed her eyes, recalling the moment. Nothing physical might have happened, but something had happened.

Something intense and she didn't like it.

Gabe was messing with her immune system.

Maybe she needed to avoid him and pray her mother hurried home so she'd get another inoculation of all the reasons why messing with a man like Gabe was nothing but heartache waiting to happen.

Five

Kami successfully avoided Gabe for the rest of that shift and most of the next night's. Unfortunately, she couldn't completely avoid him as there were times patient care demanded their interaction.

She was polite. He was polite. Everything was awkward.

A heart-attack patient came in by ambulance and coded minutes after arrival.

Under any circumstances Kami hated working codes.

Not that the medical demands were more than other emergency situations she encountered, but because a code meant someone's life was on the line, and if the code team failed, that person was gone forever.

And everyone who knew and loved that person would forever be changed.

The current code she was working, happening right at the end of her night shift, was no different and she silently prayed for the man and his family.

Gabe was doing compressions on the man's chest, while she delivered breaths via an air bag.

A unit secretary recorded the events and Mindy readied the crash cart for Gabe's instructions to defibrillate the man in hopes of shocking his heart into beating again.

"On the count of three, all clear," Gabe instructed, keeping the compressions going. "One. Two. Three. All clear."

Kami and Gabe both stepped back as Mindy pushed the button and the man's body jerked from the electrical impulse.

Nothing.

Putting his interlocked hands back on the man's chest, Gabe went back to compressions and Kami to delivering precious air, watching the rise and fall of his chest from each squeeze and relaxation of the bag.

When the defibrillator had reset, Mindy motioned that it was ready.

"On the count of three, again, all clear," Gabe ordered. "One. Two. Three. All clear."

The man's lifeless body jerked. A bleep appeared on the cardiac monitor then went back to nothing.

Kami expected Gabe to call the code.

But he just kept compressing the man's chest in rhythmic pushes as the rest of the team did their jobs.

Gabe had Mindy defibrillate the man again. Nothing.

Still, rather than call the code, Gabe went back to his compressions.

Wondering why he hadn't called an end, why they were still trying to revive the man when too long had passed, she studied Gabe in between keeping a close check on their patient in hopes of a miracle. What did Gabe know that made him keep this code going so much longer than was usual?

"Want to swap places?" she offered.

He had to be exhausted. CPR took great effort.

Not glancing up from the man's face, Gabe shook his head, called for the defibrillator yet again.

Kami's gaze met Mindy's; she saw the same questions in

her eyes that she was sure were in her own. She shrugged and stepped back when Gabe called all clear.

Nothing.

None of the crew hesitated to jump back into their spots, but they all knew the code had failed and were also all wondering why it was continuing. Still, Gabe was in charge and it was his place to decide when to stop.

"Time?" he asked, his voice sounding slightly off to Kami, but maybe she'd imagined it.

The recorder told them how long they'd been doing CPR.

Gabe winced, gave one last chest compression with arms that seemed to buckle, then called the code and hung his head.

Kami had worked codes with Gabe in the past, but wasn't sure she'd ever paid attention to him immediately after a code came to an end, when the adrenaline rush subsided and that deep sense of failure set in.

At least, that was how she always felt when a code hadn't worked. Unfortunately, statistically, few codes were successful, but the few that were made going through the many failures worthwhile.

Was that how Gabe viewed codes, too? As emotionally, physically, and mentally exhausting, but worth it if you revived a single person?

She studied the fatigue etched on his handsome face, the way his head bowed forward ever so slightly, the way he slumped making him seem several inches shorter than his six-foot frame actually was.

He looked defeated.

Vulnerable.

Very unlike the man who was usually teasing her.

He looked unlike any Gabe she could recall ever having seen before.

Emotion pinched her insides, making her want to do something to put his usual smile back on his face, to put that mischievous twinkle back into his eyes. Which didn't go along at all with her goal to avoid him for a while. Still, a man had just died and Gabe looked wiped out.

Despite all her crazy emotions, he was her friend. She cared about him as a person. She couldn't just walk away.

"You okay?"

Briefly glancing her way, he didn't make eye contact, just nodded. "Fine."

He didn't look fine. His eyes were watery, red, and her insides twisted up even more.

She wasn't sure what she should do, but knew doing nothing wasn't an option. Not for her. Not when Gabe looked so devastated.

What she wanted to do was grab hold of his scrub top, drag him somewhere private and make him tell her what had upset him so about the code.

Other than the obvious, of course.

What right did she have to do that? None. They were friends, but she couldn't demand he tell her what had upset him. Not really.

Full of tension, she moved about the emergency bay, doing her job, while Gabe disappeared to go tell the family of the man's death.

That she didn't envy him.

Maybe that had been the issue. Maybe the deceased patient had been someone he knew, the family he was about to sit down with a family he was familiar with. If so, that couldn't be easy.

The rest of the night was busy and she never got a chance to corner Gabe.

Giving report to the arriving day-shift nurse, Kami was glad to see the shift end. She clocked out, but before leaving searched out Gabe.

She'd seen him a few times after the code, but he'd been busy with patients. No smiles, no jokes, no silly puns, no waggles of his brows, no...

Kami shook her head to clear her thoughts. Suffice it to say, Gabe hadn't been himself.

It didn't take long to find him.

He sat in the small dictation room off the emergency room that served as an office for the emergency-room physicians on staff.

First making sure he wasn't in the midst of recording a chart note, Kami poked her head in. "Rough night, eh?"

Turning toward her, he nodded.

Something didn't feel right. Not about how he looked. Not about how her gut wrenched. Not about anything that had happened since that stupid code. Why did she want to wrap her arms around him and hold him until whatever was bothering him subsided?

Because he'd messed with her brain in that closet.

Before then, too.

"I'll show you my toes if you'll smile."

As she'd hoped, Gabe smiled. It wasn't much of a smile, but he did smile and the gesture did funny things to her insides.

"Okay, but remember you smiled for it," she warned, bending and untying her shoe.

His eyes gaining a little spark of light, Gabe laughed. "Keep your shoes on, Kam."

She put her hands on her hips and pretended to be miffed. "So much for you implementing an open-toed shoes policy."

"Not one of my better ideas."

"Perhaps not, but I was willing to do my part." When he went quiet again, she couldn't stand it. "Want to go eat pancakes with me?"

Surprise lit his eyes. "You're kidding?"

Yes. She was. She did not invite men to breakfast. Especially men like Gabe, who went through women as if they were disposable.

Then again, she'd already eaten breakfast with Gabe once, so what would it hurt if they went to breakfast again?

As friends, of course. She had a cat to feed, but she'd go by to feed and love on Bubbles after breakfast.

"I'm hungry and I don't want to eat alone." Her stomach growled to confirm her comment.

At first she thought he was going to refuse, but, standing, he nodded. "Let me tell Dr. Williams I'm out of here."

Out of here with her.

Because she'd asked him and he'd said yes.

Which made her uncomfortable.

But not nearly as uncomfortable as his forlorn look had left her feeling.

A teasing, flirty Gabe was one thing. A lost-looking Gabe quite another and not one she could turn her back on without doing what she could to help him.

That was what friends did, right?

They said everyone had a doppelgänger. Gabe had just performed CPR compressions on a man who could have passed for his father.

His father on whom he'd been too young to perform CPR and had watched die, helpless to do anything other than cry and wait for the paramedics to arrive and do what he should have been able to do.

Logically, he knew he'd only been eight years old. A kid. He'd known to call for an ambulance, but hadn't been able to do one other thing but sob while he watched his father take his last breath.

Even now the moment played through his mind as if it had just happened.

He wasn't dense enough not to have realized long ago that his drive to become an emergency-room doctor had been seeded in that experience. Nor was he foolish enough to think that had he been able to perform CPR he'd have likely made a difference in his father's outcome.

But he *might* have, and because he'd been a kid with no skills, he'd never know what might have been.

Roger Dillehay, the man Gabe had done a code on that night, had been his shot. He'd failed again.

Maybe that was a sign, an assurance that he'd done all that could medically be done and it still hadn't been enough to save the man who looked so much like his father.

That had his eight-year-old self had skills, then the outcome would have been the same and he'd still have grown up without his dad there to cheer him on, would still have had to listen to his mother's tears.

"In all the time I've known you, not once have I ever accused you of being quiet."

Gabe blinked at the woman sitting across the table from him. Her big green eyes held a softness he'd seen as she cared for her patients but of which he'd yet to be the recipient.

He'd never had a reason to be the object of her empathy.

Nor did he want it now.

She'd been avoiding him and he'd let her because he'd waffled back and forth between thinking he needed to step back rather than risk their friendship versus giving in to what he was feeling and kissing her until they were both breathless.

"I'm sorry, Kam." He raked his fingers through his hair. "I should have skipped breakfast. I'm not good company."

"Which is exactly why you shouldn't have. We're friends." Had she really put emphasis on that last word? "Something is bothering you and I want to help."

Kami was a fixer. She wanted to fix her patients and now she wanted to fix him. He didn't need to be fixed. He wasn't broken, just...

"Want to talk about it?"

"You were there."

"You're right. I was. You went above and beyond with that code."

Gabe gave a low snort. "Let it go for too long, you mean?"

Her brows veed in disapproval of his comment. "As long as you had medical reason to believe there was hope of resuscitating him, then you were right not to call the code."

"I'm not sure that was the case," he admitted, unable to look into her eyes for fear of what she might see in his. "It was more a matter of the code patient reminding me of someone I once knew."

Now, why had he admitted that? He didn't need to go spilling his sob story to Kami, didn't need the sympathy that people had always given to the little boy who'd been alone with his father and had watched him die of a heart attack.

He was a grown man and didn't need sympathy or anyone knowing his past.

He hadn't talked to anyone about his father in years. He sure didn't want to start back today.

Especially not with a woman who was already getting under his skin.

"Oh," Kami said, then reached across the table and touched his hand. "I'm sorry."

Kami's touch carried the intensity of a defibrillator machine, so much so that Gabe was surprised when his body didn't jerk from the electricity in her fingertips.

His heart certainly jump-started as if it had been struck by a bolt of lightning.

He stared at where her hand covered his. "It's no big deal."

"One of the things I've always admired about you is that you are bluntly honest," she said. "Now I know why you're usually truthful."

Gabe glanced up, met Kami's gaze in question.

"It's because everyone would know," she continued. "You're a terrible liar."

He'd been called worse. One corner of Gabe's mouth lifted. "You think?"

"After that big whopper you just told? I know."

Gabe gave an ironic chuckle. "You're right."

"You could've just said you didn't want to talk about it."

"Would you have let me get away with that?"

"Probably not," she admitted with a sheepish grin. "I know things have been strained between us lately, but I don't like seeing you without a smile on your face."

Her admission warmed Gabe's insides. "Why's that?"

"Because we're friends."

He'd had enough of his wallowing in the past and focused on the woman across the table.

"You're a good person to have as a friend, Kam." As if to prove his point, he shifted his hand, laced their fingers.

Holding Kami's hand felt right and did make him feel better.

"Who did he remind you of?"

Gabe winced. "It was a long time ago."

"Sounds like the beginning of an interesting story."

"It's not."

"I'll be the judge of that."

He frowned. "You're sure pushy, lady."

She arched a brow and gave a *duh* look. "You're just figuring that out?"

He gave a low laugh, then lowered his gaze. "If it's all the same, I'd rather not talk about it anymore."

"Okay." She squeezed his hand. "But know I'm here if you need me."

"Thank you, Kami. You really are a good friend."

Her expression tightened for a brief moment. Then she seemed to shake it and teased, "Don't think buttering me up is going to change my mind about bidding on you."

Giving her hand a little squeeze, he laughed. "Maybe if I'd been on my game I'd have taken advantage of the moment."

"Too bad you missed your chance." Her gaze dropped to their bound hands.

"I'm not so sure I have," Gabe said half under his breath as their waitress set their plates in front of them. A loaded omelet for Gabe and a stack of cinnamon pecan pancakes for Kami.

"Pardon?" she asked, freeing her hand to reach for her utensils.
"Missed my chance to butter you up, I said."

Before Kami had the chance to question Gabe, he reached across the table, took her knife, and slathered her pancake with butter.

She rolled her eyes.

"Now you can say I have literally buttered you up."

"My pancakes don't count."

As his comment hit Kami, she glanced up, met his gaze, saw that the mischievous twinkle was back.

"That an offer?"

"You know it isn't."

"Why do I know that?"

"Because we're friends. Nothing more."

"Who better to slather butter on each other with than a friend?"

"Maybe that's something you do with friends, but that's not the kind of friendship I usually have."

"So you don't rescue your friends from their exes and you don't slather them in butter. What else do you not do with your friends, Kam?"

Rather than answer, she dug into her pancakes, grateful for the delicious bursts of flavor that practically melted in her mouth.

"I think I ordered the wrong thing."

Kami glanced up at Gabe.

"You make that look as if it tastes amazing," he clarified.

"It does."

"Prove it."

Kami started to tell him to be quiet and eat his omelet, but instead forked up a generous bite of her pancakes and extended the fork to him.

His eyes locked with hers, Gabe's mouth closed around her fork, then slowly pulled back. After eating the bite, he nodded.

"You're right. That is good. I'm going to have to do double time at the gym if I keep having breakfasts like these." He chuckled.

The sound warmed Kami's insides. She much preferred Gabe's smiles and laughter to the solemn man he'd been after the code. Not that it would have been appropriate for him to be all smiles after someone had died, just that she wanted him to bounce back into his normal self and he hadn't.

That had gotten to her in places she didn't want him or anyone to reach.

Good thing she knew his revolving-door history with women or she might fall for his brilliant blues, quick intelligence, and smile that encompassed his entire face because, as much as she'd like to think herself immune to his charms, she was quickly realizing that her heart had taken up a mind of its own and was feeling all kinds of awareness it had never bothered to feel with Baxter.

Or anyone, for that matter.

Just Gabe.

Six

"What's up with you and Gorgeous Gabe?"

Kami frowned at Mindy. "What's that supposed to mean?"

"I've caught you looking at him more than a dozen times tonight, and don't think I've forgotten walking in on you two the other night."

Yeah, it was best her friend didn't find out she and Gabe had gone to breakfast that morning.

"So what?" She made light of the incident because she wasn't admitting to Mindy that something had shifted in her relationship with Gabe. Something had shifted? Something had been shifting for a while. The supply room had been a landslide. "I was getting supplies."

"And Gabe?" Mindy pushed. "What was he getting?"

Kami's face heated. "Not what you're implying."

"Not even a little smooch?"

"Get serious. He's not my type."

Much.

Well, not her brain's type. Her body and heart seemed to have come out of a lifetime of hibernation with a vengeance.

"Smart and sexy as all get-out?"

She couldn't deny her friend's claim. "A total playboy. We both know he never stays in a relationship more than a couple of months."

Mindy shrugged. "Maybe he just sees no reason to keep a relationship going once he realizes things aren't going to work long term. Maybe he's just being efficient in searching for the right one rather than wasting time with women he's realized aren't for him."

"Or maybe he gets bored once the chase is over and can't commit."

"I doubt Gabe had to chase any of them."

Probably not, but her friend was missing the point.

"Okay, so maybe he gets bored once the shiny newness of the relationship is over."

Mindy shrugged. "I like my theory better."

"Because you're planning to bid on him and want to think the best of him?"

"I don't have to *want* to think the best of him. I *do* think that and so do you." Mindy's expression dared Kami to deny her claim. "He's a good guy."

Kami started to reply, but halted her words when Gabe came over to the nurses' station.

"Bay one is ready for discharge home."

Kami gave Mindy a warning look not to say anything inappropriate to Gabe, then said, "I'll get her IV taken out and get her discharged. Any scripts you need me to send?"

Gabe shook his head. "I'll get them in the computer record and send them. Thanks, though."

"I'd be happy to do that for you, Dr. Nelson," Mindy offered, a big smile on her face.

Looking a little uncertain at her overly bright expression, Gabe glanced back and forth between them.

"Uh, sure. Go ahead." He told her the scripts and to which pharmacy. "Thanks."

"Anything for you, Dr. Nelson."

Gabe looked confused and Kami rushed to discharge the patient rather than stick around for whatever else was said.

The best thing that could happen would be if Mindy did make a play for Gabe. Dating one of her friends would no doubt kill this unwanted awareness of him. Mindy was welcome to Gabe.

Kami had even encouraged her to bid on him, would even donate to the cause.

Only... No, she wasn't jealous at the thought of Mindy with Gabe.

She just didn't want her friend to get hurt when Gabe moved on to his next conquest.

Unless Mindy was right and Gabe just went through women so quickly because once he knew the relationship wasn't going to work out, he ended it, and moved on to someone who might.

That didn't make him sound like a player, but someone who was smart.

Gabe was smart and efficient. He was also a player. Wasn't he?

He'd had dozens of girlfriends during the short time Kami had known him.

She'd had two boyfriends during the same time.

Two boyfriends she'd known weren't her forever guys but she'd stuck around with longer than she should have. Why was that?

Because she didn't want to be like her mother, so she stayed to prove she could hold on to a man if she wanted to? Because they'd both been safe, hadn't made her heart step outside its comfort zone?

Ugh. She so wasn't going to psychoanalyze her motives in staying with Baxter or Kent.

Nor did it matter why Gabe went through women so quickly, because Kami wasn't interested, regardless of the reasons for his revolving-door love life.

If Mindy believed her theory, then she could bid on his date, or, better yet, save her money and just ask Gabe out.

They could have breakfast together.

As a couple and not just as friends.

That would be wonderful.

Great.

Awesome.

So why did her blood turn a little green when she glanced back and saw Mindy and Gabe laughing?

"Debbie wants to meet with us tonight."

"Tonight?" Kami asked Gabe as she finished last-minute cleanup prior to shift change. "It's Friday night."

"You have other plans?"

"I'm off work. Of course I have plans." Not that she was admitting to Gabe that her evening plans consisted of vegging out in front of the television while she caught up on her favorite reality show. "Don't you?"

"Even if I did, I'd cancel them. The charity auction is just a few weeks away. Any promotion Debbie helps with is going to have to be put into motion quickly. If we wait, it might not happen."

Guilt hit. He was right. Still...

"It's a television station. They're used to reporting on things as they happen. Promoting a charity event to raise money to help a sick baby shouldn't be outside their capabilities."

"Does that mean you want me to have Debbie reschedule the meeting with her producer?"

If the producer couldn't meet at a later time, she'd feel horrible that the event might not reach its potential. Especially since she didn't have any grand plans.

"Did you check to see if Mindy could go?" After all, she'd implied he'd have to take her co-organizer. Had he forgotten?

A stubborn expression took hold, tightening his jaw. "No. Either you go or everything's off."

Kami frowned. "Fine. I'll put off my plans so we can meet with your ex and her boss."

He studied her a moment, then seemed to have a change of heart of his own. "If your plans are that big a deal, I can see if Mindy wants to go."

Kami bit the inside of her lip and tried not to look addled. Did he want to take Mindy instead? Was he hoping she'd say she wouldn't cancel her plans so he'd have an excuse to invite Mindy? Had their laughter earlier in the week been bonding toward a more personal relationship?

No, Gabe was a man who would ask a woman out if he wanted to ask. He wouldn't play games. If he wanted to take Mindy to dinner, he'd take her to dinner.

"Someone special?"

Kami arched her brow. "Who?"

"Whoever you have plans with."

"I didn't say I had plans with someone," she countered, refusing to slide back into that untruth.

"Baxter's workout program softening you up?"

"I don't have plans with Baxter, and if I did, it's not your business."

He looked duly reprimanded. "You're right. I shouldn't tease you."

"No, you shouldn't." Not that she minded his teasing. Not really. Just, she didn't want him to know that she had no plans for the first weekend she'd had off work in close to a month other than working on the fund-raiser.

"I'll pick you up at six."

"If you'll tell me where to meet you, I can drive myself," she countered.

"I'll see you at six," he repeated and walked away before she could pry more details from him.

What did one wear to a Friday night dinner meeting with a television show hostess, her producer, and a coworker who was just a friend but that your body had become painfully aware of in beyond friendship ways?

Especially when you didn't know where the meeting was being held?

Okay, so, logically, they'd meet at a nice restaurant.

She'd had no chance to find out the location so she could drive herself. Him picking her up from her house seemed too much as if they were a couple going on a double date.

Quit being ridiculous, she ordered herself. Friends picked each other up for meetings. It was no big deal.

Still, what was she going to wear?

She could text him, but stubbornly didn't, just studied the contents of her closet. Her gaze repeatedly settled on a blue dress that was the right mix of casual and dressy. No way did she want to feel overdressed for the meeting, but she also didn't want to feel frumpy while with Gabe's beautiful ex.

Debbie was a knockout.

Kami put her hand to her forehead. What was wrong with her? What Debbie looked like did not matter. Not in the slightest. She was not competing to take Debbie's former place in Gabe's life. Far from it.

Kami needed to get her butt into bed and get a few hours of sleep after being up all night. That was what she should be worrying about.

Not about what she was going to wear or how she was going to look in comparison to Gabe's ex.

On her best day she couldn't compete with the television personality and, seriously, she didn't want to. This was a business meeting to discuss advertising a charity event for a coworker's daughter. Nothing more. Nothing social. Nothing. Nothing. Nothing.

That evening, Kami was still telling herself that when Gabe drove them to an upscale restaurant and her nerves were getting the best of her.

She wasn't a nervous person. This was ridiculous.

Glancing his way didn't reassure her.

He was too good-looking for his own good in his dark trousers and blue button-down dress shirt with the sleeves rolled up to reveal a generous glimpse of his forearms.

His manly forearms. Strong and skilled. The urge to reach out and run her fingers over them hit her.

Yeah, that urge didn't help her nerves, either.

Obviously, tossing and turning in her bed half the day hadn't done a thing to rest her brain because she was delusional. Sleep deprivation had to be the cause of this insanity.

"You look great, by the way."

Gabe's compliment didn't lessen her unease but she murmured a thank you.

"I like your dress."

"Because my legs are showing?" Now, why had she asked that? Just because he'd made a big deal of her bare legs the morning he'd brought breakfast didn't mean she had to point out her exposed limbs.

Putting the car into Park, he glanced toward her, then lower, letting his gaze skim slowly down her body, going lower to inspect her legs. Then, lifting his gaze to hers, he shook his head. "Nope, that's not why I like your dress."

With that, he turned off the motor and got out of his car.

Still trying to figure out his comment, Kami was even more stunned when her car door opened and Gabe extended his hand.

"You didn't have to open my door."

"My mom taught me good manners."

"Good to know, but this isn't a date, so you don't have to do things like that."

His brow rose. "Treating a lady right doesn't just extend to the woman you're dating. Ask my mom."

Good thing one of their mothers had taught good behavior. Kami's sure hadn't. Nor had she come home yet. Poor Bubbles.

Kami put her hand in his and got out of the car. She immediately pulled her hand away and straightened her dress.

After Gabe closed the passenger door, his hand settled low on her back and he guided her toward the restaurant entrance. Kami wanted to pull free, to push away his hand, but would doing so be making a big deal out of nothing?

His palm burning into her flesh through her dress material didn't feel like something that was nothing.

It felt so not nothing it was a little scary after all her nothing relationships.

"I still think we could have done this with a phone conversation," she mumbled, feeling more and more self-conscious as they made their way into the upscale restaurant.

"No doubt, and you're preaching to the choir." He pierced her with his blue gaze. "I'm not the one who insisted on a dinner meeting."

"Right." Guilt hit her. He probably didn't want to be here any more than she did. "Debbie seized the excuse to spend time with you."

He feigned surprise. "You think that's what this is?"

"I only know her through things you've said. What do you think this is?"

He sighed quite dramatically. "Foreplay for my charity auction date."

Despite her nerves, Kami laughed. "You're crazy."

"Apparently or I wouldn't be here."

She paused. "Thank you, Gabe. I'm not sure I've thanked you for setting this up, but I do appreciate it. I know Beverly appreciates everything being done to help ease the burden of Lindsey's expenses, too."

A genuine smile slashed across his face. "You're welcome, Kam, and so is she."

"Worth the sacrifice you're about to make?"

He grimaced. "Ask me again after dinner."

Seven

If Gabe wasn't enjoying himself, he was putting on a good show.

However, his attention wasn't focused toward the model-perfect woman who left Kami in awe of her beauty, grace, and poise.

Gabe's focus was on Kami.

Overly so.

As in, if she didn't know better, she'd think she and Gabe were a couple. She knew better and her head was still spinning.

Was that what he was trying to make Debbie think?

His little smiles, winks, and frequent touches of her hand and arm were getting to her.

To the woman sitting across from them, too.

She'd gone from super friendly to regarding Kami with suspicion.

Not that she wasn't nice.

Kami believed the woman was inherently pleasant and that was part of her television viewer appeal. She had a wholesome goodness that shone as brightly as her beauty. Plus, intelligence glimmered in her big brown eyes.

The woman wasn't buying that Gabe would be interested in Kami. What sane man would be when Debbie wanted him?

Tall, willowy, blonde, smart, successful.

"Gabe says you work with him at the hospital?"

"I'm a nurse." Kami took a sip of her water. She'd ordered a glass of wine but had yet to take a sip. She needed all her wits for this meal and didn't want to risk lowering her inhibitions even the slightest bit.

Especially not when Gabe gave her a fond look and said, "My favorite nurse."

"Every female nurse is your favorite nurse," Kami countered, knocking her knee against his leg in hopes he'd take the hint and stop with the cheesy comments.

"You know there's no one like you," he came right back, his leg brushing against hers. Only, rather than a cut-it-out knock, the grazing of his leg against hers was more an awakening of her senses as the material of his pants teased her thigh.

"You mean someone who doesn't fall at your feet?"

"Something like that." Gabe's expression said Kami had fallen at his feet a time or two despite her denials.

She decided to ignore him and finish this meeting as quickly as possible before she made a complete fool of herself over Gabe's attention.

"We appreciate your offer to help with the Smiths' fund-raiser." There, see, that sounded competent. "As your show is about home improvements, I don't know a possible angle for us to promote the fund-raiser for Lindsey's medical expenses. What were you thinking?"

Eyeing Kami and Gabe closely, the woman slid into professional mode.

"That's where Jerry comes in." She turned to her producer and smiled.

The slightly overweight man's entire persona brightened.

In that moment, Kami realized the producer was totally besotted with the woman. As in, head over heels. He'd probably jumped at the offer when Debbie had requested he meet with them just so he'd have an excuse to spend time with her outside work.

"He's going to arrange a segment on our late-night news that will run over a few days. Then—" Debbie's smile conveyed real enthusiasm "—we're going to do a home improvement for your coworker."

"The baby needs a new heart, not updated curtains and carpet," Gabe pointed out.

Debbie tsked. "There's going to be medical equipment and such, so it'll be a renovation to make their transition from hospital to home easier."

"I don't know if Beverly and her husband want their home renovated, but it's a generous offer. Certainly, I'll discuss it with them," Kami assured them, thinking the new family might need a lot of things. She didn't know. "I'll admit I worry the added stress of a home remodel during all the craziness of Lindsey's medical issues isn't a good idea."

"Obviously you've not watched my show," Debbie scolded with a pout of her full pink lips. "There will be no lengthy remodel. We'll time the remodel for while the baby is having her heart transplant. Everything will be done and waiting on them when they bring Lindsey home from the hospital." She glanced at Jerry, excitement practically seeping from her barely existent pores. "It'll be an amazing show."

"It sounds wonderful," Kami admitted. "But they don't have the money for a remodel."

Debbie smiled again. "There's no cost to them. This is our pleasure. We'll just want to film their story, of course, and especially when they return to the home the first time after the remodel, and maybe a quick shot or two of them in their new, improved home."

"I don't even know if they own their home," Kami confessed. "They may rent... We should have had them here with us."

"I'm sure Gabe can arrange a meeting."

Of course he could.

But he immediately passed. "Kami is organizing the fund-raiser, not me."

"Gabe, darling, the remodel has nothing to do with the fund-raiser," Debbie corrected. "We'll do a news piece for that, something we'll refer back to in the episode for their home improvement."

"It's a great idea for a show and ratings." Kami could have bitten her tongue when the words came out of her mouth.

However, Debbie didn't look offended. Instead, she and her producer nodded. "It's a win-win all the way around. Your co-worker gets a renovated, state-of-the-art home free of charge. We get a phenomenal episode. Right, Jerry?"

The man beamed at his hostess. "It's rather brilliant."

"I'll give your information to Beverly," Kami assured them. "Anything beyond that will be up to them. Our purpose is to generate awareness of the fund-raiser so we can raise as much as possible. Everything will need to be between you and Beverly and her husband directly."

"Sounds perfect. Now—" Debbie flashed a smile that truly was Hollywood-worthy "—let's set aside shoptalk and enjoy our meal."

Kami looked at Gabe, gave him a look that hopefully conveyed for him to get her out of there as quickly as possible, then said, "Let's."

The meal was delicious. The conversation not too horrible as Debbie came across as a genuine, albeit ambitious, person. Jerry was probably a killer businessman, but this softened whenever he looked at Debbie—which was all the time.

Something she seemed oblivious to as she zeroed in on Gabe.

Who in return zeroed in on Kami in a move to deflect Debbie's attention.

Kami was exhausted from it all.

"Are you two seeing each other?" Jerry asked after their entrées arrived.

"Yes," Gabe answered at the same time as Kami said, "No."

"I see," Debbie said.

Kami was glad the woman saw, because Kami didn't.

Ignoring the couple, Gabe asked, "What was breakfast this week?"

Kami glared at Gabe. What was he doing?

Actually, she knew what he was doing and that was what irritated her.

"A meal because I was hungry."

His gaze searched hers. "Both times?"

Kami's glare intensified. He was purposely trying to make them think breakfast had involved a lot more than food.

Gabe wanted Debbie to think they were a couple so it would deter her from bidding on him during the auction.

He didn't mind using Kami in the process.

"Sorry, Gabe. I shouldn't have used my status as your favorite nurse to get a free breakfast," she said in an overly sweet tone, all the while shooting mental daggers at him.

"True, but since you paid the second time, it all balanced out."

Ack. She should have known he'd point out that she'd paid when they'd gone to the restaurant on the morning of the code. Not that he'd liked it, but she'd insisted since she'd invited him. Eventually, after she'd snagged the ticket and refused to give it to him, he'd relented.

His expression was smug. "Guess that makes me your favorite doctor."

She rolled her eyes. "Don't count on it."

Debbie and Jerry watched them curiously and Kami became more and more self-conscious. This was ridiculous.

"Don't let Gabe fool you." She leaned toward Debbie. "He's not my type and I'm not his. We enjoy our friendship and being coworkers. This is all a game Gabe plays. Nothing more."

There. That should settle any doubts and teach him not to trifle with her.

But rather than look repentant, he put his fork down on the

table and stared at her, a confused look on his handsome face. "Who says you're not my type?"

Kami turned toward him and willed him not to have this conversation in front of the couple. "I'm not."

"Says who?" he persisted, oblivious or not caring that she didn't want to continue.

"You've never dated anyone like me," she pointed out, very aware of their curious audience.

"That doesn't mean I wouldn't like to."

He was laying it on thick for Debbie's sake. Kami didn't like it.

Then again, who liked being used?

Besides her mother, who seemed a glutton for punishment, that was.

"Thank you so much for meeting with us about Lindsey's fund-raiser," she told Jerry and Debbie, ignoring Gabe's last comment. "I'll give Beverly your business card." Despite only having eaten about half her meal, Kami pushed her chair back. "Now, if you'll excuse me, I've recalled that I had other plans tonight that really can't wait, after all."

When Gabe went to rise, Kami shook her head. "You stay and enjoy your meal. I'll catch a taxi."

Gabe joined Kami on the sidewalk outside the restaurant. "You didn't really think I'd let you take a taxi home, did you?"

A crowd had gathered, waiting for their turn to be seated inside the restaurant, but Gabe had had no difficulty spotting where Kami stood near the curb.

"You didn't really think I'd let you get away with using me like you were, did you?" she hissed without looking his way.

That had Gabe pausing.

"I'm sorry if that's what you thought. Let me take you home."

"What I thought?" she scoffed. "You know you were acting as if we were an item to put on a show for your ex."

"Aren't we an item?"

Risking escalating her wrath, he put his hand on her lower back and guided her toward his car. Whether out of a desire to get away from the waiting restaurant patrons or as a testament to how upset she was, Kami let him.

"You know good and well we aren't," she insisted, turning on him as they stopped at the passenger side of his car.

"We have a good relationship, have been flirting with one another, have had breakfast twice this week, and dinner together tonight. It's not illogical of me to imply there's something between us when there is something between us."

"Friendship," she spit at him, her eyes a vivid green. "That's what's between us."

"Yes. We're friends."

"Nothing more." She opened the car door, slapped his hand when he tried to help, climbed inside, and slammed the door.

Gabe stared down at her through the passenger-door window.

Friends. Nothing more, she'd said.

They were friends.

He drove her home, contemplating the night and what she'd said. He had flirted with Kami heavily during the meal. Had he been doing so to deflect Debbie?

Flirting with Kami had felt right.

Not because Debbie had been there, but because he enjoyed the back-and-forth between them. Enjoyed the chemistry he felt when he was with her.

He pulled into Kami's apartment complex parking area and turned off the motor. "I'm sorry, Kam."

She stared straight ahead. "Because you know I'm right?"

"Because I don't want you upset with me."

She sighed, touched her temple. "What does it matter?"

"Because you really are my favorite nurse."

She closed her eyes. "Fine, but don't use me ever again."

"Okay."

Kami was obviously surprised at his quick acquiescence, judging by the way her gaze shot to him.

"I won't ask you to rescue me at the auction again, if that's what you want." He crossed his heart.

"You won't ask me to rescue you from a beautiful woman? Oh, thank you," she said with great sarcasm and an eye roll. "Thank goodness I won't have to go through that."

He didn't come back with anything, just got out of the car, went around and opened her door.

She got out without taking his offered hand. Stubborn woman.

Gabe stared after her as she headed toward her first-floor-apartment building entrance, watched her fumble with her keys, then unlock her front door.

She was going to go inside without saying another word. Life was too short to let her go that way. He knew that all too well.

He sprinted after her.

"Kami?" he said from right behind her as she pushed open her door.

Standing half in, half out of the apartment, she turned.

"Why are you so upset with me over this?"

Rather than answer, she looked away.

Needing to know, Gabe lifted her chin, trying to get her to meet his gaze.

Finally she looked up, staring for long moments with her big green eyes, then dropping her gaze to his mouth.

"I don't like you pretending we have a relationship that we don't. It's as confusing to me as it was to our dinner companions."

Gabe was confused, too. He'd admit that. How could he not when Kami staring at his mouth had his brain turned to mush?

Obviously that was the case.

Because Gabe gave in to what felt like the most compelling thing in the world, but might be his most foolish move ever if she never forgave him.

He leaned forward and pressed his mouth against Kami's warm, sweet lips.

At the contact, her eyes widened.

One light kiss became two.

Still, she didn't push him away, nor did she tell him to stop.

Instead, she searched his eyes as his mouth explored hers, tasted her, and grew hungry for more.

Lots more.

Gabe wasn't holding her. She could pull away at any time.

She wasn't.

Quite the opposite.

She was kissing him back.

Slowly at first, uncertain and unsure, then with a mounting urgency that fueled his own.

He moved forward, bringing them both inside the doorway, and closed the door behind him as he pulled Kami against him so he could kiss her more deeply.

Her fingers went into his hair and she pulled him closer, her body now flush with his.

Her amazing body that still wasn't close enough.

He brushed his hands over her back, lower, cupping her bottom. Lifting her against him, he kissed her deeper, his tongue making its way into her mouth.

A soft sound emitted from her throat. She shifted against him, her fingers massaging his scalp, pulling him toward her as the kiss went on and on. As their bodies melted together.

He wasn't sure how long they kissed, touched, how long their bodies pressed so tightly against each other, moving, feeling. He wasn't even sure which one of them pulled away.

It had to be Kami. Only a fool would stop kissing her.

Kami's kiss had been tender, passionate, hot.

Had demanded his all, that he hold nothing back, but give everything he was to her.

He wanted to kiss her again. To sweep her off her feet and carry her to her bedroom and kiss her all over until she cried out in release.

Until he felt her release. His release.

Nothing pretend about that or his body's very obvious reaction to their kiss.

But Kami's mind and body obviously weren't at the same place as his.

She pulled away and stared up at him with confusion shining in her eyes.

"Kami, I..." he began, not sure exactly how to explain to her since he didn't fully understand himself what had just happened between them, not wanting to say the wrong thing, but wondering if there even were right words he could tell her.

Shaking her head, she held up her hand and pushed against his chest. "How could you? You promised not to use me again."

"Use you?" he asked, puzzled by her accusation and still more than a little dazed by their kiss.

"As a substitute or just someone handy or whatever it was that possessed you just then."

"What possessed me just then," he admitted, "was you."

That was when it hit Gabe.

What probably should have hit him months ago. He'd sought out Kami's company, laughed with her, flirted with her. They were friends, but he wanted more.

Lots more.

He'd been wanting more for months. Why hadn't he seen his feelings for what they were?

Because she'd been in a relationship with Baxter.

When Kami had ended things with the accountant, Gabe's interest in anyone other than her had dissipated. He'd wanted Kami.

Correction—he wanted Kami, and now that he'd admitted that to himself, he wasn't sure he could go back to how things were. He didn't want to.

Kami looked thrown off kilter by his claim, her eyes narrowing. "I did no such thing."

He raked his fingers through his hair, over the spots on his head that still tingled from her touch, and fought the stunned feeling in his brain, his body. "I think you did."

She shook her head as if to deny his claim. "What are you talking about?"

"This." He leaned forward and pressed a gentle kiss to her parted lips again.

Immediately, she softened against him, kissing him back.

Sometimes words just didn't cover what needed to be conveyed.

"That is what I'm talking about," he whispered against her mouth. "What I want and what I hope you want, too. You say we're just friends, Kam. I think you're wrong. We're so much more than that. But if not, then you're the only friend I want to date, to spend time with, to have sex with, and those things I want more than you might believe."

Eight

Despite her racing thoughts, Kami had finally settled into sleep and crashed for a good ten hours before rousing the next morning.

Upon waking, she assured herself the events of the night before had been a dream.

Reaching up to touch her lips, she knew better.

Gabe kissing her hadn't been a dream. It had been real.

Gabe had kissed her, had said he wanted to date her and have sex with her.

How crazy was that?

How crazy was his kiss?

A fervent, hungry kiss that was like the wildest spice she'd ever tasted. Something so good, so addictive you had to keep tasting even when it was setting your mouth afire.

Gabe's kisses had lit infernos, had melted her down to the core.

His had been the most amazing kiss of her life.

Comparing Gabe's kisses to Baxter's or Kent's or any of the men she'd dated was like comparing a firecracker to a stick of dynamite.

Being anywhere near something so explosive was dangerous.

Kami got out of bed, went about her normal day-off routine, spent an hour at her mother's playing with Bubbles, then headed toward the hospital where the board had volunteered the use of a conference room to store the donated items that would be auctioned off at the fund-raiser.

Kami and a few others were inventorying everything, gathering the smaller items, and making up baskets to be auctioned.

Working on the fund-raiser would hopefully distract her from the night before.

Or not.

The first person she saw when she walked in was Gabe. Gabe in a blue T-shirt and jeans that outlined his body in an oh-so-yummy kind of way.

Or maybe it was his smile that was yummy.

He was laughing with Mindy and didn't look as if he'd given her a second thought since she'd thrown him out of her apartment.

Of course he hadn't. If he wanted, he could crook his finger and have any number of women running to do his bidding.

Something gripped her belly.

Good grief. She was not jealous. Not of Gabe crooking his finger and women doing his bidding. Not of Gabe laughing with Mindy. Not of Gabe or anything he did.

She had no claim.

Despite the fact they'd kissed and he'd destroyed her brain circuitry with the way his hard body had felt.

That hard body, she thought, not able to pull her gaze away from how his T-shirt stretched over his chest, his shoulders. Not too tight, not too loose. Just right.

Like what was beneath the material.

Heat flooded at the memory of running her hands over those shoulders, of pulling him toward her as he kissed her.

At how he'd leaned down to press one last kiss to her mouth, almost as if he'd had to have one last touch, told her to think about what he'd said, and then he'd left.

As if she'd needed him to tell her to think about what he'd said.

She'd thought of little else.

She was surprised she'd slept at all considering the emotional surge his lips against hers had caused.

A tsunami of adrenaline and emotions had flooded her senses and knocked out all common reason.

Getting all worked up over Gabe was a mistake.

He ate women's hearts for breakfast and yet they invited him back for lunch and dinner and said, "Here you go," handing their entire beings to him on a platter.

She didn't want Gabe gobbling her up, even if his kiss had been out of this world. She didn't want to be so desperate for a man that nothing else mattered. Hadn't she learned anything from her mother's mistakes?

He turned, met her gaze, then smiled. One of those smiles that was uniquely him and encompassed his whole face, lit up his eyes, and made the room brighter. Like the sun coming out from behind a cloudy sky.

Listen to her, thinking sappy thoughts.

Gabe was not a man she needed to have sappy thoughts about.

As if nothing monumental had happened the night before, he winked and went back to what he was doing.

Her heart took that moment to skip a beat.

Oh, good grief. If she weren't careful she'd be hand-feeding Gabe her heart for breakfast, too, and asking if he'd like the rest of her for lunch, dinner, and dessert.

No, no, no. She was not on the menu.

There were more than a dozen volunteers making inventory lists and baskets for the fund-raiser. Kami had expected to spend the biggest portion of her day working on the project, but, thanks to everyone's enthusiastic efforts, they finished after only a couple of hours that had felt more like fun than work—

aided by the fact that Gabe had been on his best behavior and kept everyone smiling, her included despite all her attempts to avoid and ignore him.

One by one the volunteers left.

All but Mindy, Gabe, and herself.

"You want to go to lunch?" Mindy invited Kami as they put away the last of the baskets.

Thank goodness. Going to lunch with Mindy meant no opportunity to be alone with Gabe. It would happen, but she wasn't ready for that this afternoon. Not when she felt so rattled from his kiss.

"Sure." She beamed at her best friend. "That would be great."

Lunch with Mindy sounded like heaven and gave her the perfect excuse not to stick around to talk to Gabe—assuming that was why he had stayed until the end. No doubt, despite his smiles and friendly behavior, he wanted to reiterate that what had happened the night before meant nothing, that he didn't look at dating and sex the same way she did.

As if she needed him to tell her that.

It wasn't *her* bedroom door that was in a constant spin from the women going in then being pushed out.

Gabe cleared his throat.

Mindy glanced his way, her brows lifted, and then with a barely contained smile, she recanted. "Oh, wait. Sorry, I can't go to lunch with you today. I forgot I'd made other plans."

"Um...maybe we can get together tomorrow," Kami suggested, not quite sure what Mindy had seen in Gabe's face that had her changing her mind about lunch. Regardless, it didn't take a genius to know what had taken place.

Mindy's smile broke free as she said, "You should take my bestie to lunch, Dr. Nelson. She deserves it after all her fantastic work this morning."

"I could do that," he agreed, all innocent-looking.

Ha, neither of them were innocent. She was going to have to

have a serious talk with Mindy. The last thing she needed was her friend playing matchmaker.

"I thought you might be able to." She gave him an approving look, then glanced toward Kami. "You have to go to lunch with Gabe. Otherwise, I'm going to feel guilty for bailing."

Rather than wait for Kami to answer, Mindy hugged her and promised she'd talk to her later.

"Go," she ordered, "have lunch with Gabe, and have fun."

When her friend was gone, the conference room seemed a lot smaller than it had when filled with Mindy and the dozen or so volunteers. Or maybe Gabe's presence just seemed that much larger than life when she was alone with him.

She'd been alone with him before. This was no big deal.

Just because he'd kissed her the night before didn't change anything.

Not really.

Just everything. Because before she hadn't known what all the fuss was about.

Looking at Gabe, she recanted. Well, yeah, she'd known he was a great guy and that women were crazy about him. It was just that she hadn't personally experienced that greatness on a physical level.

Gabe on a physical level changed things.

Changed her.

Changed how being alone with him made her feel.

How could it not when every cell in her body throbbed with awareness of him?

Snap out of it, Kami.

She glanced around the room at the baskets and items that filled the table and that were pushed up against the wall. "I need to lock up."

He moved closer. "Anything I can do to help?"

Disappear so I don't have to deal with this right now.

Ha. Somehow, even if she had spoken her thoughts, she didn't think he'd comply.

Forcing a smile, she shook her head. "Thanks, but this is it for today. Later, we'll finish putting together items donated between now and the fund-raiser and move all this stuff to the convention center the day of the event."

Gabe nodded, followed her out of the conference room, then stood beside her as she locked the exterior door. Pheromones exuded from his pores. Had to. How else could she be so aware of him?

They walked down the hospital hallway.

"I didn't realize you'd be here today." She glanced toward him, then quickly refocused on watching where she was walking. The last thing she needed was to trip over her own two feet in front of him.

"There was an open call for volunteers. I volunteered." He sounded nonchalant, as if it had been no big deal. Why wasn't she buying it?

"The more help, the better, right?" Kami smiled at a couple of nurses they passed in the hallway, then walked through the hospital door Gabe held open for her.

When they were headed toward the employee parking lot, he asked, "Can I take you to lunch, Kam?"

She supposed they needed to talk, to work past this awkwardness, because she didn't like this new apprehension she felt being near him.

This underlying nervousness.

This awareness of just how hot he was. How was she ever going to look at him and not remember what his body had felt like pressed up against hers?

"Okay, so long as it's not something heavy." She imagined their conversation would be heavy enough when she told him that, although she hoped to date again soon, she didn't plan on him being the one she dated.

Or kissed.

Or pressed her body up against as if it were a contest to see just how much of her could be touching him.

Sure, he'd been a great kisser. Would be great at other things, too.

Of that, she had no doubt.

But she wasn't going to have sex with someone she didn't envision herself having a long-term relationship with. Someone who would be no different than one of the guys who came in and out of her mother's life. Gabe wasn't a long-term relationship kind of guy. She wasn't a quickie relationship kind of girl. Better to nip whatever this was in the bud.

"Dinner date?"

As she stepped off the sidewalk, she cut her eyes toward him. "What?"

His blue eyes stared straight into hers. "Not wanting to eat heavy with me because you have a dinner date?"

She'd let him think that there was someone else when he'd offered to bring breakfast, but she wanted to be honest. Their friendship was tense enough without throwing in deceit.

"You know Baxter and I broke up some time ago," she reminded him. "I've not been on a date since."

Her response put a pleased expression on his face.

"Not counting me."

"You don't count as a date," she corrected and took off toward her car.

Falling into step beside her, he pretended offense. "Says who?"

"Me."

"I want to count."

She frowned. "Because you kissed me and have decided you want to do more than that with me?"

"I find you attractive and want to have sex with you. Is that so terrible?" His expression was full of mischievousness, one that said if she was smart she'd want to kiss him, too.

She did want to kiss him, but wouldn't risk being just another woman who came in and out of his life. More than that, she wanted to protect their friendship. Gabe meant more to her than just a good-time romp in the sheets. She didn't want to lose the special bond they shared. Sex would change everything.

Giving him a look of challenge, she asked, "I don't know. You tell me. Is sex with you so terrible?"

"I've not had any complaints."

Kami wasn't sure whether to laugh or groan at the way his cocky grin slid into place. "I bet not."

Although the sparkle was still in his eyes, so was something more, something that hinted that, despite his teasing, Gabe cared about her response. "Because you enjoyed my kiss?"

She wasn't going there. Not in the hospital parking lot where anyone could overhear. "I didn't say I enjoyed your kiss."

Not looking one bit fazed, he grinned. "But you did."

"What makes you so sure?"

"You walked to my car rather than yours."

Kami blinked. He was right. She'd walked right past her car and gone to his. Heat flooded her face.

"That only means I planned to conserve gas by taking one vehicle instead of two." After all, she had planned to go to lunch so they could talk. "Not that I enjoyed you kissing me."

He opened the passenger door and she climbed into the car.

She glanced up at where he stood, his hand on the open door. The sun shone on him, making his eyes dance with light, making his hair glisten, and his skin glow. No woman in her right mind would have not enjoyed his kiss.

He was a kissing Adonis. Beautiful and talented.

He closed her door, came around and got into the driver seat.

She sighed. "You make me want to say just forget this."

He glanced her way. "Lunch, you mean?"

Although she wasn't sure she just meant lunch, she nodded.

"Because you want to go straight to your place and kiss me all over?"

Images of doing just that, of stripping his T-shirt off him and trailing kisses over his chest, his abs, filled her mind.

Yeah, so a part of her, a carnal, feminine part that probably had something to do with good old-fashioned nature at work, did want to go straight to her place and kiss him all over. Fortunately, she'd evolved enough to have the good sense not to give in to those urges.

Rolling her eyes, she shook her head. "Not what I meant and you know it."

"Sorry." But he didn't look repentant. Not with one corner of his mouth crooked upward and his eyes searching hers for things she didn't want him to see. "Wishful thinking."

"Truly?" she asked, frustrated that he wasn't taking her seriously and that her good intentions seemed to have come to a screeching halt, because all she could do was look at his mouth and wonder if those lips had really felt as good as she remembered. "If I said yes, I want to go to my place and have sex, you'd drive us there and go at it? Just like that?"

"Sounds crude when you word it that way," he complained, his smile slipping. "But yes." His gaze locked with hers. "If you told me you wanted to have sex, we'd be having sex just as fast as I could get you somewhere alone. But make no mistake—there won't be anything quick about it when we do and it won't be just me enjoying every touch of our bodies."

She pressed her fingertips to her suddenly pounding temple and contemplated what he said.

Part of her said, yes, yes, she did want to forget lunch. Another part kept reminding her that any involvement with Gabe beyond friendship was emotional suicide.

They rode in silence, but it didn't matter. Gabe didn't go far from the hospital, and when he stopped the car, Kami looked at him in surprise.

She wasn't sure what she'd expected, but certainly not a trip to the park.

"I thought we were going to lunch."

Grinning, he looked quite proud of himself. "We are."

"At World's Fair Park?" Not that she'd expected anything fancy, but they were at a park, not a restaurant. Whether it was nerves or hunger, her stomach gnawed at her and she wanted food.

She'd not had much of an appetite and had only eaten a few bites of her breakfast. No wonder she was starved.

"There's a couple of vendor trucks not far from here."

"Vendor trucks?" Well, she had said she didn't want anything heavy. She guessed hot dogs and hamburgers fit the bill. Still, eating at the park didn't quite jibe with their previous conversation. If he was trying to seduce her, surely he'd have chosen somewhere more impressive?

"You want me to take you somewhere else?" he offered as they got out of the car.

She shook her head. "Since I'm in jeans, a T-shirt, and tennis shoes, this is fine. I'm just surprised. I didn't think about you bringing me to a park for lunch."

"Never say I'm predictable." Stepping beside her, he closed her car door before she could. "It's Saturday. There's always something going on at Performance Lawn on the weekends. I thought we could walk along the waterfront, eat, and just hang out and enjoy being outdoors. No pressure."

"No pressure?" She eyed him suspiciously.

"I'll be on my best behavior. Scout's honor." But rather than hold up a scout's sign, his fingers made a space travel television show character's instead.

"I don't think Scout was his name," she mused.

"Probably not, but, either way, let's relax and enjoy the beautiful weather and the fact that we aren't at the hospital or having to sleep away a stressful night."

Tempting. And it fit with why she'd agreed to lunch to begin with. Gabe was her friend. She wanted to maintain that friendship. Maintain it? She cherished his friendship.

"Say yes, Kami." His tone was low, his smile full of temptation, his eyes mesmerizing. "Play with me this afternoon.

I'll deliver you safely back to your car whenever you say the word, I promise."

The twinkle in his eyes, so familiar, so warm, eased some of the tension that had been bubbling just beneath the surface all morning.

"Okay," she agreed and meant it. An afternoon playing in the park with Gabe. Wide open spaces. Lots of people around. Sounded safe enough.

Plus, the early spring sunshine and gentle breeze combination felt great. She'd always thought the park was beautiful and being outdoors really did feel awesome.

Already she could hear a great band playing, probably a local one, on the Performance Lawn and they were good. When she and Gabe reached the area, there was a small crowd spread out over the grass on blankets and some type of festival was going on.

A festival with food vendors.

Kami took a deep sniff of the afternoon air and her stomach rumbled in protest of how long it had been since she'd eaten. "Something smells good."

"I remember hearing about a Beer and Barbecue Festival this weekend. I think it was John from work telling me."

"Ah, now I know why you brought me here." She laughed. "Beer and barbecue."

"Not a beer and barbecue kind of girl?"

"Surely you know I'm a champagne and caviar kind of woman," she replied flippantly. She enjoyed a sip of celebratory champagne occasionally, but didn't recall having ever tried caviar. Wasn't really something on her bucket list to try, either. "But since we're here, I want to go find whatever smells so good and then find a place to sit and listen to the band while we eat. If that's okay with you?"

"Fine by me," he agreed, then, "Champagne and caviar, eh? I'll keep that in mind for future reference. For now, we'll make do with grabbing a bite of something here and listening to the band."

Nine

The relaxed atmosphere of the park and the gorgeous spring weather promised a perfect afternoon in spite of any lingering nerves Kami might have about their shared kiss.

At least, that had been Gabe's plan when he'd opted to go to the park. She'd been uptight from the moment she'd walked into the hospital and seen him. Not that he didn't understand, but rather than let her apprehension fester, he planned to knock it out of the ballpark. What better way to get her to relax than to take her to the park, surrounded by people, sunshine, and an overall air of well-being and happiness?

From a vendor he bought a small orange-and-white throw blanket emblazoned with the University of Tennessee's logo. From another, he got drinks and barbecue. Kami carried the blanket and spread it out on the grassy knoll, sat, then took the food and drinks from him while he joined her on the blanket.

They ate, chatted, then lay back on the blanket to listen to the band and soak up some vitamin D.

Gabe reached for Kami's hand, filled with pleasure when

she didn't pull it free, but laced her fingers with his. It wasn't much, but holding her hand felt pivotal.

Her warm, small yet capable hand clasped within his made his insides smile much brighter than the brilliant sunshine.

Yep, a perfect afternoon.

Which was why it made no sense for him to go and ruin it, but he opened his mouth and risked doing so anyway.

"The code the other night," he began.

Kami turned her head to look at him and he considered stopping, but pushed on anyway, because he needed to tell her. Perhaps it made no sense, but the thought that he'd kept that from her nagged at him and wouldn't let up.

"The man reminded me of my father."

Kami's eyes widened. "Oh, I'm sorry. That couldn't have been easy." She squeezed his fingers. "I've never heard you mention either of your parents before."

"Yeah, neither one of us talk about them much, do we?"

Kami's nose crinkled. "There's a reason for that on my part, but let's not talk about mine. Tell me about your parents."

"My mom is great, always showered me with love and attention, and you'd probably say she spoiled me rotten."

Smiling and looking a little wistful, Kami tsked. "The woman has a lot to answer for."

Gabe smiled. "She tried her best."

"And your dad?"

Gabe's lungs locked down, refusing to budge to pull in much-needed air. "He died."

"Oh, Gabe, I'm sorry. I didn't know."

"How could you? Like you said, I never talk about him."

"How long ago did he die?"

"I was eight."

Kami rolled onto her side to stare at him. "That's young."

He nodded.

"How did he die?"

"Heart attack."

"So working a code on a man who reminded you of your father..." Her eyes watered. "Oh, Gabe."

"I don't want your sympathy," he rushed out. "I just wanted you to know."

She stared at him a moment, then surprised him by lifting their interlocked hands to her mouth and pressing a soft kiss against his. "I'm glad you told me."

Feeling awkward and more exposed than he'd felt in years, Gabe nodded, then rolled back over to stare up at the sky. Next to him, Kami did the same.

He wasn't sure how long they lay listening to the music, lost in their own thoughts—probably about another thirty minutes—but when the band took a break, Kami sat up and stretched.

"I feel lazy, like I could doze off," she admitted, smiling sheepishly down at him. "I need to move or I might."

"You didn't sleep well last night?"

"I slept great," she countered.

Glad she wasn't dwelling on their earlier conversation, he laughed. "So much for thinking you might have lain awake thinking about me."

"I slept like a log." Although her cheeks were a little rosy, she didn't look repentant and fortunately her shoulders didn't tighten back up with tension.

He didn't like Kami tense. Not when their relationship had always been the opposite, when being together had always made the world a better place no matter what was going on around them.

"I'm never going to get a big ego while you're around, am I?" He picked up their trash.

"You don't need me to inflate your ego." Kami dusted off stray bits of grass and foliage and folded the throw blanket.

"A little ego boosting now and again wouldn't hurt, though."

Laughing, Kami followed him toward the trash bins. "I'll keep that in mind."

"You do that." After he'd tossed their trash, he brushed his hands over his jeans. "Want to walk the waterfront? We can drop the blanket off at the car."

"Sure."

They put the blanket in his car, then strolled along the waterfront.

At one point, they stopped to stare out at the water. Then Kami turned and looked up at the Sunsphere.

"She's beautiful, isn't she?"

Yes, she was, but he didn't mean the big gold structure she referred to.

Still looking at the woman rather than the twenty-six-story-high Sunsphere, Gabe shrugged. "It's made up of real gold, so I guess it would appeal."

She furrowed her brows. "What's that supposed to mean?"

He shrugged. "Women like jewelry, and since the Sunsphere's glass panels contain twenty-four-karat gold dust, you'd be more prone to appreciate it."

Giving him a look of pity, Kami shook her head. "That, my friend, might be the most sexist thing I've ever heard you say, and that's saying something."

He gave a *who, me?* look. "I meant no harm."

She held up her ringless fingers and wiggled them. "You shouldn't lump all women into the same category."

"Especially not present company," he added, grinning.

"Exactly." Because she did not want to be lumped in with all the women he'd known. What all that meant, she wasn't sure, just that she knew she didn't want to be like the others.

"I'm not like other women," she said, to be sure there was no doubt.

"Amen."

Obviously surprised at his affirmation, she cut her gaze back to him. "What's that supposed to mean?"

"You're different."

Her eyes narrowed. "As in good different or as in weird different?"

"Definitely weird different," he assured her, grinning, but inside feeling a bit sober at just how true saying she was different was. He'd never told any woman about his father, had never wanted to. And, as vulnerable as it left him feeling, he was glad he'd told her.

Kami playfully slapped his arm. "Tell me why I'm here with you, again."

"Because you like me."

"Lord only knows why."

That she didn't deny his claim reverberated through him. Finally.

Smiling, Gabe gestured toward the golden globe in the sky. "You want to go up?"

She glanced up at the iconic gold ball that had been built for a World's Fair decades before. "Seriously, you'd want to do that?"

"It's one of the first things I did when I moved to Knoxville. Amazing views of the city and the mountains."

"I've never gone up," she mused, staring up at the Sunsphere with a bit of longing on her face.

"You've never gone to the observation deck?"

"I was supposed to once, on a school field trip…" She paused, stared up at the golden globe with a glimmer of sadness in her eyes. "…but I ended up not being able to go."

"That settles it." He grabbed hold of her hand and was once again grateful that she didn't pull free. "We're going up."

Gabe was right. The views from the Sunsphere were spectacular. So was the man beside her.

When she let herself forget everything she knew about Gabe and allowed herself to glory in being the recipient of his attention and smile, it was easy to smile back, to give in to the chemistry between them.

When that little nagging voice reared its ugly head and reminded her of all the women Gabe had been through just during the time she'd known him, nervous energy boiled in her belly. They needed to establish that they were never going to be more than just friends, but she kept putting off the conversation.

She probably should've done that when he'd held her hand while lying on the blanket.

She'd been so relaxed, had been enjoying the music, the sunshine, the peacefulness of the afternoon so much that she hadn't pulled her hand away when he'd taken it.

Gabe's hand holding hers should have wrecked her peaceful feeling, but to her surprise, despite the electricity in his fingertips, it hadn't. Lying on that blanket next to him, eyes closed, the sun warming her face, lacing her hand with his had felt natural. Like just another part of what felt like a perfect afternoon, a happy afternoon.

Because she was happy.

Hanging out with Gabe at a city park made her happy.

That he'd shared with her what had happened to his father made her happy, too. He'd been too hesitant, his voice too raw, for her to believe that it was something he'd talked about much in the past. That he'd shared that with her made the afternoon all the more special.

"Just think, if you bought my date, you and I could explore those mountains."

So much for her peaceful, happy feeling.

She cleared her throat. "You promised you weren't going to ask me to bid on you again."

"I didn't ask you to bid on me. I was just making an observation. While on the observation deck." He winked and gestured to where they were.

She rolled her eyes. "Ha ha. You're so clever."

He grinned. "It's about time you noticed."

Ignoring his comment, she didn't point out that she'd noticed a lot of things about him, and, instead, smiled. "Are these panels really made of gold?"

He chuckled. "That got your attention, eh?"

Apparently when Gabe had previously visited the Sunsphere,

he'd done his research because he launched into the history of when the iconic structure had been built and why.

"You sound more like a tour guide than a doctor," she teased, impressed at his knowledge of the architectural wonder and the World's Fair that had prompted it.

"A man of many talents."

"So I'm learning."

"You've barely begun," he assured, wagging his brows.

She rolled her eyes. Again. "There's that ego."

"Waiting for you to pop it."

She shook her head. "Not this time."

"What? No denials about my talents?"

"Like you said," she conceded, "I barely know what your talents are, so denying them seems a bit foolish."

He studied her a moment, then, eyes twinkling, said, "We need to remedy that."

His gaze dropped to her lips and any lingering sensations of peace dissipated into awareness. Awareness of the very maleness of the man holding her hand, of how he was looking at her, of how her insides trembled at the brevity of his touch, of his words.

Stop this, Kami. Stop flirting with him. You're supposed to tell him that you can only be friends, nothing more. That's why you came to lunch. Not to have a mini-date.

Mini-date? This afternoon was better than her last dozen dates. More than that.

"How do you suggest we do that?" That wasn't what she was supposed to say. Nor was she supposed to be staring back at his mouth, at those wonderful lips that had caressed hers not even twenty-four hours ago.

"You need a crash course in my many talents."

She suspected the course would be fabulous, full of pleasure and good times. It was the crash that worried her. "Sounds dangerous."

"Don't like to live dangerously, Kam?"

"Nope. I'm a safety first kind of girl." Although, if that were true they wouldn't be having this conversation, nor would she still be staring at his mouth and wondering if it had felt as good against hers as she remembered.

"I can appreciate that about you."

"Good thing, because I don't plan to change for any man." She'd watched her mother do that to no avail whenever a new man popped into her life. No, thank you.

"That why your previous relationships haven't worked out?"

"Why's that?"

His gaze lifted to hers. "Your unwillingness to change?"

"Are you saying you change to make relationships work?" she challenged, not believing he did.

He considered her question. "That's a good question. My initial response would be yes, but the truth is, probably not."

Interesting that he'd given such a thoughtful answer.

"A person shouldn't change to make a relationship work." Which was why she needed to point out that she had no desire to join the ranks of his has-beens. No way would she and Gabe ever work. He was a pro with women at his command and she was an amateur with really high checklist standards. They were a recipe for disaster.

"Sure they should."

Surprised at his comment, she frowned. "You just admitted you hadn't changed for past relationships."

"You're right. I did." Holding her gaze, he took a deep breath and said, "Which is why those relationships are in the past. For a relationship to work, both parties have to care enough about the other to give and take, to change. Otherwise, the relationship is doomed before it's started."

That was a good lead in to why a relationship between them would never work. And why they should stop this before they irreparably damaged their friendship.

Yet, she didn't. Instead, she turned back to stare out at the mountains just beyond the city limits and let her mind wonder. *What if?*

She'd had such a great time with him today. Thrilled at the tingles his hand holding hers shot through her entire being.

What if they *could* have a relationship and still be friends afterward?

"Safe and sound, as promised," Gabe reminded her as he pulled into the empty parking place next to Kami's sedan.

"Thank you for a lovely afternoon."

"You're welcome. We'll have to do it again sometime." The sooner the better as far as Gabe was concerned. He'd truly enjoyed the day.

Silence hit them and then Kami reached for the car door handle.

"I'd like to see you again, Kami." Surely she knew that, but he didn't want there to be any doubt.

Grinning, she pointed a finger. "Lucky for you, you get to work with me three to four nights a week."

There she went popping his bubble again.

"Not what I meant."

Although her hand toyed with the door handle, she didn't make a run for it. "I enjoy our friendship."

So did he.

"You'd enjoy dating me more," he promised. He'd make sure of it.

Her lower lip disappeared into her mouth. "I—I don't know."

"I'm attracted to you and want us to explore what's happening between us."

She stared at where her fingers perched on the door handle. "Which is what exactly?"

"Something worth taking our time to figure out."

"I really don't think I need to be here for this," Kami insisted as she got out of Gabe's car the following afternoon and stared at the faded white-framed house where Beverly Smith and her husband lived.

Debbie was a fast worker. She'd arranged a meeting and insisted on Kami and Gabe attending as well. Or maybe she'd just requested Gabe and he'd embellished to say Kami had to be there, too. She'd tried to plead out, but he'd insisted that if he had to spend the afternoon with Debbie, then so did she.

"That's because you're heartless and have no qualms about throwing me to the wolves." Gabe came around to her side of the SUV and led her across the paved driveway.

"So dramatic. You really went into the wrong profession, Gabe. You'd have been great on prime-time television." Pausing on her way up the porch steps, she feigned a light-bulb moment. "Hey, I bet Debbie could introduce you to a few of her friends. You could be the latest and greatest thing since sliced bread."

"And deprive all our emergency-room patients of my tender, loving care?" He clicked his tongue. "No, thank you. Besides, you'd miss me."

"You have a point," Kami conceded, knocking on Beverly's front door. She gave Gabe a nervous look. "I hope this works out for Beverly. I can't imagine everything she and her family are going through right now. I'm going to feel terrible if it doesn't or adds to their stress."

"If Beverly and her husband don't want their story to be an episode of Debbie's show, then all they have to do is say no." Gabe touched her arm in what was meant to be a reassuring gesture.

Only his fingers against her bare arm added to the swirling in her belly.

She arched one brow. "Just like all you have to do is tell Debbie no?"

He chuckled. "Good point. Maybe we should bar the door and not let Debbie anywhere near the Smiths." Then his expression grew more serious. "But, really, whatever they decide is what they decide. Debbie can't force them to do anything they don't want to do."

"I know." She did know but felt protective, as if she'd be responsible since it was through her that the opportunity had presented itself.

The front door opened and a tired-looking twenty-five-year-old nurse and her husband of the same age stood on the other side.

"I wasn't sure if you'd both be here," Kami admitted to her friend, as they joined the couple on their sofa.

"My parents are with Lindsey while we're here," Beverly said, her face filled with guilt. "I wanted to meet at the hospital, but because of the show Debbie wants to do, she insisted upon meeting at the house. Leaving the hospital was hard, but...but Gregg says that we need to do this." She gave a little shrug. "I know he's right."

Lifting her hand to press a kiss there, her husband nodded. "If nothing else, you needed a few minutes away from the hospital, a shower in your own bathroom, a minute alone with your husband."

The two exchanged looks and, despite their horrid current circumstances, Kami felt a stab of envy.

That was how a relationship should be, she thought. Not the way her mother's relationships had been. Not the way her own relationships had been. But the deep abiding love that shone in the couple's eyes as they looked at each other, even while they dealt with great financial and emotional burdens with their new baby's health needs.

Debbie and her producer arrived moments later, along with a cameraman, who sat in a chair awaiting further instructions with his camera ready to go at a moment's notice.

Debbie asked Gabe's opinion several times and she threw out comments left and right to her producer, but, other than a few smiles and polite pleasantries, she didn't have much to say to Kami.

Truly, Kami was unneeded. Other than answering a few questions about the event, she didn't say a word.

Jerry was pleasant enough, but, again, he only had eyes for his show's star.

Motioning to the cameraman, Debbie led the Smiths through a series of questions about their relationship, Beverly's pregnancy, when they first found out about Lindsey's heart problems, and what her status was now.

The cameraman moved about, getting different angles.

Her hand locked with her husband's, Beverly's shoulders slumped as she looked at the television producer. Her voice quavered as she said, "Do you know how difficult it is to pray for a heart for your baby, so your child can live, when it means someone else's baby has to die to give that heart?"

Kami's eyes watered at the implications of what her coworker said, at how heavy Beverly's heart ached for what her baby and family was going through, but also for what another family would have to go through for the Smiths to get their miracle.

Within minutes, Jerry presented the Smiths with a contract giving the television station the rights to the footage shot that day, permission to film their upcoming big moments, to have behind-the-scenes shots, and to completely renovate their home any way Debbie saw fit.

Neither of the Smiths looked nervous or hesitant.

No problem—Kami was nervous enough for them. "Are you sure?"

Without batting an eyelash, the Smiths both nodded.

"We talked about this before everyone arrived. Our biggest hope is that this will raise awareness of the need for organ donation. If us signing these—" Beverly gestured to the papers "—helps achieve that, helps one person sign their donor card, then it's worth sharing our story."

Her heart full of admiration for her coworker, Kami watched as the Smiths signed the contract.

Debbie made arrangements to meet with the couple at the hospital to film them with Lindsey. Then she, the Smiths, Jerry, and the cameraman went through the house.

Which left Kami and Gabe sitting in the living room. Alone.

Gabe's gaze met hers.

"They can always say no, you said," Kami mock whispered, but with a smile on her face and her eyes a bit watery.

"You think they should have?"

She shook her head. "How could I when their reasons for saying yes are so powerful?"

Gabe nodded. "If Debbie's cameraman is worth his paycheck, he got Beverly on film and they'll use that. If I wasn't already an organ donor, I would be after the emotion Beverly just poured into this room."

Feeling much better about the whole ordeal than when they'd arrived, she nodded. Maybe the story would help the Smiths and other families, too.

"You ready to leave?"

"Before we got here," she admitted, but was glad she'd come, was glad that she'd gotten to hug her friend, witness the love the couple shared, and was even more glad that she and Mindy had initiated the fund-raiser.

He grinned. "Me, too."

"Yeah, yeah. I saw you making googly eyes at Debbie," she teased.

"Any googly eyes I was making were meant for you, not her."

"Um...right." She was saved from having to comment further as the others rejoined them in the living room.

Kami hugged Beverly again, making her promise to call if there was anything she could do to help, even if it was just running errands or picking up something to bring up to the NICU as this was one of the few times Beverly had left the hospital since Lindsey's birth.

Within minutes, Kami was back in Gabe's car.

"You hungry?" he asked.

She was about to say no, but her belly growled, making any denial seem petty.

"Champagne and caviar?"

She smiled that he remembered her quip from the day before. "You planning to ply me with expensive food and drink?"

"Would it work?"

She shook her head.

"I didn't think so." He grinned. "How about we hit my favorite steak house instead? No caviar on the menu, but they have a wide variety of options and I've never been disappointed."

"Sounds good."

The steak house was good. Gabe ordered a cedar plank salmon and Kami ordered a shrimp pasta. Both were delicious.

"Only a few more weekends until the fund-raiser," Gabe mused. "Everything ready?"

Kami shrugged. "As ready as we can be. There are still some last-minute donations coming in, which is great. The more that come in, the better."

"Anything I can do to help?"

She gave him a pointed look. "Don't forget to show up the night of the fund-raiser."

He laughed. "As if I could."

Kami set her fork down next to her plate. "You know, I don't understand why you're so worried about Debbie. She's beautiful, talented, and successful. A guy could do a lot worse."

From across the table, he arched a brow. "Are you trying to sell me on my ex? I may not let you order dessert for such treachery."

Kami laughed. "You mean, like you trying to sell me on the new, improved Baxter?"

"Definitely not trying to sell you on him. Just trying to make sure you weren't interested in getting back together regardless of how buff he becomes."

She shook her head. "His physique had nothing to do with why he and I weren't working."

Eyeing her, he leaned back in his chair. "What were the reasons? Besides the fact that he wasn't me, of course."

"Of course," she agreed with a great deal of sarcasm, trying to decide if she really wanted to go there with Gabe, whose kiss made her feel everything Baxter's had lacked. "Let's just say our chemistry wasn't right."

Gabe studied her for a moment. Then to Kami's surprise, rather than push for her to elaborate, he accepted her answer.

"I'm glad."

"Because?"

"If you'd had the right chemistry with him, you wouldn't be here with me."

"This isn't a date," she pointed out.

"It doesn't make my comment any less true. If you and Baxter were still together, you wouldn't be with me regardless of how we labeled the meal."

She conceded his point. If she'd had the chemistry with Baxter that she felt with Gabe, she'd not have wanted to be with anyone but Baxter, would have wanted to spend all her spare moments, all her meals, with him. That wasn't the case.

Baxter had been ideal on paper, but in reality, not so much so. What he'd been was safe.

Gabe... Gabe was not safe, but that didn't seem to stop her silly mind from wondering *what if?* What if she gave in to the chemistry and told him she wanted him?

No matter what happened between them, friendship or something more, she would not make a fool of herself over him.

If, and that was a big if, something did happen between them, she'd not get attached and she'd be the one to walk away. She'd keep control.

She wouldn't chase him or hold on to unrequited feelings the way women tended to do where he was concerned.

She knew better.

Not that she planned on anything happening, but still...

Forcing herself not to stare at his mouth, she swallowed.

"Now, about dessert," she said, picking up the menu and studying it. "I'm more of a cake than a pie person, so if you're planning to share, I hope that's okay."

Ten

Gabe hadn't meant to share dessert with Kami, but watching her eat the sweets was more enjoyable than eating the carrot cake he'd ordered would have been. Not that she didn't let him have a bite here and there.

"This is really good."

"Better than your Death by Chocolate?"

Looking ecstatic, she nodded. "This could be Killed by Carrots."

Gabe laughed. "I don't think that's going to catch on."

"Probably not," she admitted, her lips wrapping around the fork, her eyes closing as she slowly pulled the fork out.

When she opened her eyes, realized he was watching her and that what she was doing was affecting him, she winced. "Sorry. I keep forgetting."

"Forgetting?"

"Nothing."

"You really think I'm going to let you get away with that?"

She shrugged. "You can only make me tell what I'm willing to."

He thought on her comment a moment. "The only thing you're willing to tell me is nothing?"

"Maybe."

"I never took you for a tease, Kami."

"Yeah, yeah. I've been teasing you for months. It's what you and I do. What we've always done. It's safe and fun and, despite your momentary lapses, it's probably all there should be between us."

Elated at her "probably," Gabe studied her, trying to decipher if she was serious or testing him, wanting him to correct her.

"My momentary lapses? Are you saying you didn't have a lapse when you kissed me back?"

"Oh, I had a lapse, all right. A big one."

"Meaning you regret having kissed me back?"

As if she was trying to keep them from spilling her secrets, her lips pressed tightly together.

Gabe smiled. He couldn't help himself. She couldn't admit that she'd enjoyed their kiss, but she couldn't lie and say she regretted it, either.

Whatever her reasons were for not wanting to move into a more physical relationship, Kami wasn't immune to the chemistry between them. Not by a long shot.

"Okay, you refuse to tell me if you regret kissing me. I can live with that. But what I really want to know," he mused, picking up his fork and feeding her a piece of his carrot cake, "is when are you going to let me kiss you again?"

Kami choked on the cake. Coughing, she cleared her throat, took the glass of water Gabe offered, then coughed some more.

"Not exactly the reaction I was going for," he said wryly, his lips twitching.

"I imagine not." She took another drink of water and this time the cool liquid went down correctly. "Don't do that."

"Don't do what?"

"Say things that catch me off guard."

Gabe laughed. "That caught you off guard? You who always have a fast comeback for anything I say?"

"Yeah, well, I didn't just then."

"Apparently."

She put her water glass down and pushed what was left of both cakes toward him. "I'm finished. You eat the rest."

Gabe motioned for the waitress, asked for a box and the check.

"I can pay for mine."

"You could, but you're not," he corrected. When she went to argue, he reminded her, "It's my turn. You paid last time."

"Actually, Jerry paid last time."

"I imagine the television station reimbursed him." Gabe got the check from the waitress and paid while Kami boxed up her leftovers.

When they exited the restaurant, the sky was streaked with yellow, orange, and red hues as the sun made its final splash of the day.

"Wow. Beautiful sunset," Kami exclaimed as they made their way toward the car.

"It is. Seems a shame to call an end to such a great evening. You want to go downtown and throw back a few?"

She started to ask him to bring her home. He could see it on her face. But then she took on a determined look.

"Sure. Let's throw back a few," she surprised him by saying. Her eyes glittered with challenge. "Why not?"

Gabe hadn't thought she'd agree, but then, Kami had been surprising him from the moment they'd met. Everything about her kept him on his toes. He drove them downtown to a place he knew, then paid for a parking spot.

He took her hand and they walked to the club, found two vacant seats at the bar, then ordered drinks.

An hour later, they were both laughing at anything and everything.

Gabe wasn't drunk, but he was feeling good. Too good.

Not because of alcohol, but because of the woman smiling and laughing with him.

Kami went to order another round, but Gabe shook his head. "No more for me. I've got to drive us home. You go ahead, though."

Her mouth made an O, and then she changed the order to one. "You doing okay, still?"

Smiling, she nodded. "Since I never do this, surprisingly, yes. What about you? You come here often?"

He glanced around the club. "I've been here a few times."

"With Debbie?"

He frowned. "No."

"Some other woman?"

"Be careful, Kam," he teased, watching her closely. "You almost sound jealous."

She glanced away. "I'm not," she quickly denied, her voice not feisty. "I know you've been with lots of women. That's why you kiss like the devil."

"The devil, huh?" He laughed. "Since I think you're giving me a compliment, thank you."

"You're welcome." She half turned on her bar stool to watch as a dance instructor called for more to join in the fun. A country song was playing and there were a bunch of regulars line dancing and a few watching the instructor and doing their best to keep up. "I never could line dance. No rhythm and two left feet."

"I thought line dancing was for people who had two left feet and no rhythm?" he ragged.

She turned, stared him straight in the eyes, and challenged, "I suppose you're an expert?"

She was beautiful, Gabe thought. Absolutely beautiful. Her eyes sparkled, her chin jutted forward, and her lips parted just so. It was all he could do not to lean forward, cup her face, and take her sassy mouth for another "devilish" kiss.

"I've been known to scoot my boots a time or two," he said with an exaggerated drawl.

Leaning on her bar stool, she peered down, her gaze dropping to his shoes. "Too bad you aren't wearing boots. I'd make you put your feet where your mouth is."

Gabe's lips twitched. "Not having boots has never stopped me before."

Her brow arched. "Is that a backwoods way of asking me to dance?"

Grinning, he slid off his bar stool and held out his hand. "You want to dance, Kam? I promise not to step on your toes any fewer than a dozen times."

He wanted her in his arms, wanted to embrace every moment because life was short—just look at how young his father had died. It should be lived to its fullest. Still, he'd settle for whatever she'd give him until she realized they belonged together.

Like what his parents had. That was what he wanted, what he'd been searching for and never found. Looking into Kami's eyes, his chest inflating, Gabe couldn't help but smile as he thought, *Until now.*

Placing her hand in his, she laughed. "Oh, this is going to be good. Especially since if you're stepping on people's toes while line dancing, you're way worse than me."

Gabe wasn't way worse than Kami. Not that Kami had expected him to be. He was one of those guys who excelled at everything, so of course he line danced with ease, quickly picking up the routine for whatever tune played if it wasn't one he knew.

Kami, on the other hand, decided she was just going to go with it and not worry about her two left feet. She probably misstepped more than she grapevined or ball-changed, but she was having fun and was keeping time, mostly, with the other dancers.

Then again, it might be the alcohol making her think she wasn't doing too badly.

Either way, she was laughing, spinning, and having fun.

With Gabe.

In a completely different way than they'd ever spent time together before. She liked it.

A lot.

When the dance instructor announced she was taking a break, a slow number came on.

Kami started to head back toward where she and Gabe had been sitting at the bar, but he grabbed her hand and pulled her toward him.

"Not so fast, my little do-si-do. This might be my favorite song."

Putting her arms around his neck, she fell into rhythm with him. "Might be?"

He grinned. "Ask me when the music is finished."

"Deal." Kami rested her head against Gabe's chest, marveling at his heartbeat against her cheek, at his arms around her, his hands at her waist.

Why had she been fighting this? Pushing him away? This felt so good, so right.

Unbidden, she giggled.

"What's so funny?"

She smiled at him. "I feel like I'm in high school dancing with the cutest guy in school."

His eyes crinkled at the corners. "How'd you know I was the cutest guy in school?"

Kami laughed. "Just a hunch."

"I wasn't really, you know."

"Weren't what, the cutest guy in school?" She leaned her head back to look up at him. "I don't believe you."

"I wasn't," he admitted. "Tommy Smithson had all the girls after him. The rest of us guys were just there to collect his leftovers."

"Tommy must be amazing," she cooed, her fingers toying

with the soft hair at his nape. "When's your class reunion? I want to meet him."

Gabe shook his head. "You think I'd risk introducing you to Tommy? No way. I'm already struggling to convince you to be more than my friend. You meet Tommy and I'm not even in the ballpark anymore."

"He's an athlete? No worries. I'm worse at sports than I am at dancing. Not my thing."

"For whatever it's worth, I think you're a wonderful dancer."

Her heart skipped a few beats at his compliment.

"Ha," she countered, her insides feeling warm and mushy. "You must have drunk more than you realized."

"Nope, but it might be that you fit into my arms so perfectly that I don't notice anything else. Not sure I'd care if you stomped my toes so long as I get to hold you."

She couldn't argue. She did fit into his arms perfectly.

At least, from her perspective it felt perfect. Just to be sure, she snuggled closer and laid her head back against his chest.

Yep, pretty perfect.

Gabe moved to the slow music, Kami in his arms, her head nestled beneath his chin, and decided that this really was his favorite song.

But then the next one came on and the next, and as long as the music kept playing and he got to keep holding Kami, he'd keep on loving the songs.

Because he knew when the music stopped, he'd take her home, and he'd leave.

Not that he'd want to leave.

What he wanted was to make love to the sassy woman in his arms.

But he wouldn't.

Not tonight.

Not when she'd been drinking and might have regrets. As

much as he wanted her, he didn't want her to think this was just physical, didn't want her to think he'd taken advantage of the first opportunity her guard was down.

He wanted more than just sex. Lots more.

So, he'd hold her, breathe in the sweet scent she attributed to soap, water, and lotion but that he was convinced was some aphrodisiac blend all her own, and he'd enjoy the moment.

In the moment, he was holding Kami.

And she was holding him back.

The line-dance instructor came back out and announced she'd be doing her last set of instructions for the night.

Full of enthusiasm, Kami jumped back in. Despite her fairly frequent incorrect moves, she seemed to be having a great time, which made Gabe happy.

Over the moon. Giddy drunk. But not nearly as giddy drunk as when he drove her home and walked her to her apartment and she kissed him.

He'd meant to just tell her good-night, but before he could say a thing, she'd stood on her tiptoes, wrapped her arms around him, and pressed her lips to his.

Fully, wholly, no holding back, hands in his hair, body grinding against his, enthusiastically kissed him.

His libido skyrocketed.

His willpower went to hell.

"Kami," he groaned, wondering how he was going to untangle himself when all he wanted was to lose himself in her arms and tell her all his crazy thoughts. "I have to stop."

"Why?" she breathed as she traced her mouth over his throat and spread her fingers over his back, holding him tightly to her. "I don't want you to stop."

"You're drunk."

"Not that drunk."

"Drunk enough."

Her hands slid down his back, pulled his shirt from his pants, and slid beneath the material.

Goose bumps prickled his skin.

Kami's fingers on his bare back undid him. His groin hardened. His jeans constricted to the point of pain.

Having to pull away from Kami caused pain, but he managed, instantly feeling defeat at the loss of contact.

"No," she told him, her green gaze locked with his and fire sparking to life. "You can't stop. Not now. Not when I want you."

Gabe groaned, then took a deep breath and cupped her face. "You have no idea what hearing you say you want me does to my insides."

"Apparently not what's happening to my insides," she complained. She moved against him, as if to show him.

"Worse."

"Impossible." She glared at him. "You're going to leave, aren't you?"

He nodded. "It's the right thing to do."

She let out a long sigh.

He was trying to do the right thing, but Kami wasn't making it easy. Not with her take-me eyes and pouty, kiss-me lips and with how she couldn't stand still, but instead swayed ever so slightly as if dancing to a song of seduction.

Gabe swallowed, fought for willpower. "What is it you think I should do right now, Kami?"

She stared at him a moment, then closed her eyes. "I think you should get back in your car and drive home. Alone. Without me. To a cold, lonely bed, knowing I would have rocked your world."

Knowing he was doing the right thing, Gabe leaned forward, kissed her forehead, then finished unlocking her apartment door and opening it for her to step inside. "For the record, you rock my world every single day."

With that, he picked her up, set her inside the apartment,

reached around to make sure the lock would catch, then pulled the door closed.

With him locked on the outside of her apartment because, heaven help him, he was already questioning his decision to leave.

Eleven

"Go to breakfast with me?"

Having almost reached her car in the employee parking lot, Kami spun toward Gabe, not bothering to hide her surprise that he'd followed her out of the hospital and obviously jogged to catch her.

She'd seen him several times throughout the long night, had worked next to him, had talked to him in regard to patients, but she'd fought humiliation and felt the tension.

Not just on her part.

So his breakfast invitation truly did take her by complete surprise.

When she didn't immediately answer, he continued. "Your pick on where we go."

She bit the inside of her lower lip, then acquiesced. "Sure."

Why not? How much more could she embarrass herself than she had the other night?

"I tried calling yesterday. The day before, too," he said after they were settled in his car.

"I didn't feel like talking," she admitted, checking to make sure her seat belt was secure.

"What about now? You feel like talking about what happened the other night?"

"Nothing happened the other night," she reminded him, crossing her arms. Why had she agreed to this?

He shot a quick glance her way. "I wasn't sure how much you remembered. If perhaps that was why you weren't answering my calls."

"If you're implying something happened that I don't recall, I'm not buying it." She'd know if something more had happened between them. It hadn't.

"Sorry, that's not what I meant." He raked his fingers through his hair. "You're not upset with me because I left, are you?"

She wasn't. Much.

"I wanted to stay," he continued, staring straight ahead at the road. "But I didn't want you to have regrets, but now I think you do anyway."

She cut her gaze toward him, took in his profile, the tense way he gripped the steering wheel. Gabe didn't want her upset. He was trying to make things right between them.

She leaned back against the headrest and inhaled deeply. They were friends. Nothing had happened. This awkwardness was ridiculous.

She sighed. "I'm sorry I didn't answer your call or text. I needed some space."

"Understood." He glanced her way, then back at the road. "You still feel that way?"

"That I want space between us?" She shook her head, then admitted the truth. "I value our friendship, Gabe. I missed talking with you last night the way we usually do at work. I don't want to lose that. That's what scares me about what's happening between us."

"Me, too. I should have been more persistent in calling, should have pulled you aside last night to clear the air, but

I didn't want to put you on the spot or beg forgiveness at the hospital."

Beg forgiveness? Realization dawned. "You thought I was mad at you? That's why you were standoffish last night?"

His brow arched. "Weren't you?"

Only that he'd left her when she'd wanted him to stay.

"I was more upset with myself than you. I acted very out of character on several counts. But it's okay, Gabe. I understand."

He slowed the car at a traffic light, looked her way. "Unbelievable. You thought I left because I didn't want to have sex with you, didn't you?"

His eyes were so blue, so intense, it was like looking up into the sky and losing one's self.

"I think you want to have sex with lots of women," she admitted, then sank her teeth into the soft flesh of her lower lip.

"You make me sound like I've no scruples and have sex with anyone."

"Don't you?"

"No." His answer was immediate and brooked no argument, almost as if he was offended that she'd thought he might.

"If you want to have sex with lots of women, it's not my business."

"I want to make it your business, Kam." He glanced to make sure the red light hadn't changed back to green.

The light changed and Gabe accelerated the car, driving in silence until he pulled into a restaurant parking lot and into an empty space near the entrance.

He didn't kill the engine, just turned to her and waited for her to say something.

She'd known the conversation wasn't over. She'd been able to feel the wheels turning inside his head as he drove them. She'd even known what he was going to say when he spoke next, so she'd prepared her answer in her mind.

She took a deep breath. "Despite what you might think from my behavior the other night, sex is a big deal to me."

"Sex is a big deal to me, too."

"No, it isn't," she countered. "You're casual about sex. I'm not."

"You're making assumptions about me that aren't true."

She turned in the seat, stared straight into his eyes, which shouldn't even be real they were so blue. "You've never had casual sex, Gabe?"

He didn't flinch but Kami read the truth on his face even before he said, "I didn't say that."

She reached for the passenger door handle so she could get out of his car. She'd gone from tense to her belly being in a tight wad to where she wasn't even sure she could eat. She should have asked him to take her back to her car.

"Sex between us wouldn't be casual, Kami. If you believe that, then you're fooling yourself and denying us both something that would be amazing."

"What's amazing is my friendship with you to begin with and why I want to hang on to that relationship when you're determined we completely destroy it."

"Is that what you believe would happen if we had sex? That we can't be friends and lovers? That's the real reason you won't have sex with me? Because of our friendship?"

"At the moment, I'm not sure we can be friends," she threw back.

"Then what's stopping you from closing your car door and asking me to drive us to my place right this very moment?"

Hand still on the handle, she glared at him. "What? So you can reject me again? I don't think so."

"Is that what this is about? I left because I didn't want to take advantage of you. Rather than see the truth, that I left because I care about you and want things to be right when we take that step, instead, all you see is that I left."

Kami's heart pounded in her chest. Her hands shook as she dropped them back into her lap.

"Take me home, Gabe."

"Fine." His movements full of frustration, he restarted the engine and backed out of the parking spot.

He drove in silence, pulling in at her apartment complex. When she went to get out, he gripped the steering wheel and leaned forward.

"I'm sorry, Kam."

"Me, too." She gave a resigned sigh, then a little shrug. "Because even though I asked you to take me home, well, my car is still at the hospital and, short of walking to work tonight, I'm going to need a lift back there."

"Oh! You're here!"

Startled by the woman stepping into the apartment, Kami glanced up from the worn sofa where she'd fallen asleep while petting Bubbles. The cat had apparently dozed off, too, and, yawning, stretched.

"Someone has to take care of your cat," Kami reminded her, sitting up on the sofa and staring at her, obviously shocked to see her mother.

"Hey, babe, where do you want me to put these?" A long-haired free-spirited man came into the apartment behind her mother carrying some grocery bags.

Ah, so that was why she was so startled at Kami being at her apartment. Eugenia had company.

Kami's mother glanced the man's way, then blushed. "In the kitchen is fine, Don."

Her mother didn't bother to introduce them. Why bother? None ever stuck around long.

The man nodded in her direction, then carried the bags to the small kitchen that was open to the living area and began unpacking the bags.

Don. Hadn't the guy her mother left with been named Sammy? Maybe Kami had misunderstood her. Then again, probably not.

"Hello, my Bubbles, did you miss Mommy?" her mother

crooned to the cat as she picked her up and kissed her nose. The cat actually licked her mother's nose, so maybe the cat had missed her after all. "Mommy missed you, but it looks like Kami has taken care of you."

Had her mother thought she wouldn't? *She* wasn't the irresponsible one.

"You didn't mention you were going to be gone for so long," Kami said, watching as her mother continued to love on the feline.

It was more of a greeting than Kami had ever gotten, so maybe her mother really did care about the cat, just wasn't responsible enough to actually take care of the poor girl.

"I didn't know I was going to be," her mother admitted, then gave Kami a semi-annoyed look. "Was it that big a deal to stop by and feed Bubbles? I can find someone else next time if you're too busy to help your own mother with something as simple as feeding her cat."

Ugh. How had her mother turned things to make her feel guilty?

Kami sighed. "It was no problem."

"I didn't think so."

Don came back into the living area, stood quietly in the doorway and gave Kami's mother an expectant look.

Eugenia gave a nervous giggle, then said to Kami, "Then I guess you can be on your way since I'm back. Bye."

Kami's jaw dropped. Maybe not literally, but figuratively, it definitely fell. Just like that, her mother was kicking her out of her apartment. No *thank you*. No questions about Bubbles. No explanation of where she'd been, what she'd been doing, why she'd been gone longer than expected.

Then again, why was Kami surprised? Her mother had been pushing her aside for whatever man was in her life for years.

Kami worked her three on, had Friday and Saturday night off, then worked Sunday, Monday, Tuesday, and Wednesday nights.

She and Gabe hadn't found a happy medium.

They hadn't found a happy anything.

Because she wasn't happy at the way they were walking on eggshells, talking to each other without eye contact, and talking without saying anything at all beyond work.

"Bay two's CT scan shows a non-obstructing renal calculus in the right kidney."

Glancing up from where she stripped the bedding off in the next bay, Kami met the eyes of the man toward whom all her thoughts were directed.

"I'm going to print off some scripts," he continued, not meeting her gaze, "then discharge with instructions to see Urology tomorrow."

"Okay."

He stood watching her a moment, then left. Kami quickly made up the bed with fresh sheets, wiped the countertops down with an antibacterial cleanser, then went to get the scripts and discharge orders from Gabe.

"Thanks," he said as he handed the scripts to her, their fingers touching. Her breath caught. His gaze jerked to hers as if he'd felt the jolt that shot through her at the contact.

Kami hesitated a few moments, wanting to say more, wanting him to say more, then berated herself for her idiocy.

She discharged the patient, then went back to do her nurse's note. Gabe still sat at the station, leaned back in a chair, with his eyes closed and a strained expression on his face.

Her heart squeezed. "You okay?"

He opened his eyes, nodded.

Again, she wanted to say more, but didn't know what. Maybe with time the tension between them would ease. Hopefully.

"I hate this."

Had he read her mind or what?

"Me, too," she admitted, sinking into the chair next to his.

Glancing around to make sure no one was close enough to

overhear their conversation, he leaned close. "I miss you, Kami. I miss everything about you."

She bit her lower lip.

"I don't know what else to say. You know how I feel, what I want, that I don't like where things are between us. I'm trying to give you time and space to figure out we're worth taking a chance on." His gaze was intense. "I don't want to push you into something you don't want, but I don't understand why you refuse to give us a chance."

Oh, how easy it would be to give in, to tell him how much she wanted him. To tell him how she dreamed of his kisses, of knowing what it felt like to wrap her legs around his waist and...

Stop it, Kami, she ordered herself. *Just stop it*.

"You and I want different things out of life."

Seeming to understand her turmoil, he still refused to back down. "Are you so sure about that? Because I'm not."

She found herself wanting to believe, wanting to forget a lifetime of lessons and just give in to her heart's desires.

"Need I remind you that you're the one who left me?"

"No, you've reminded me often enough." He held her gaze. "Invite me again, Kam, because I assure you I won't make that mistake a second time."

Twelve

Gabe's challenge haunted Kami for the remainder of her shift.

Even now as she gave report to the day-shift nurse taking her place, his voice echoed through her mind.

Inviting Gabe into her bed wouldn't change what would ultimately happen.

She couldn't fall into the same pit her mother willingly leaped into time and again. She was smarter than that.

Only, maybe she wasn't.

Because before she left the hospital, she yielded to her need to see Gabe and found him alone in the dictation room. When he looked up and her gaze met his, she saw the question in his eyes.

She didn't look away.

Couldn't look away.

She stared into his beautiful blue eyes and let herself be mesmerized, knowing she was about to change everything between them.

Who was she kidding? Everything was already changed between them. She might have been denying it, but they'd been in a relationship for weeks.

She was tired of denying that truth. Reality was, she was a woman. A woman with needs and wants and hopes and desires.

A woman who wanted Gabe more than she'd ever wanted anyone.

Scary, but also exciting.

Cocking her hip to the side, she gave what she hoped would pass for a seductive look.

"You're invited. Don't make the mistake of disappointing me a second time."

Gabe had been waiting for this moment for weeks. Longer. Now that he was here, in Kami's bedroom, he wasn't going to rush.

At least, he was going to do his best not to rush.

What he really wanted was to rip off her scrubs and taste every inch of her.

But part of him was enjoying letting her set the tone of what was happening.

Another part of him was still stunned that he was here, that Kami had invited him to her apartment, that she was taking this step. With him.

He wasn't a fool. He knew what being with her meant.

Finally, Kami realized how much she meant to him, was embracing what was between them.

Anticipation building, he'd followed her home from the hospital, parked next to her car, stood next to her while she unlocked her door, then followed her to her bedroom.

Calm, controlled, as if his insides weren't shaking in eagerness of finally making love to her.

Now he waited to see what was next with this lovely woman who monopolized his every thought.

Similar to his own bedroom designed for daytime sleeping, her window shades were drawn, leaving the room dark despite the morning sunshine.

Rather than raise the heavy shade, she flipped on a lamp, casting a low light around the room.

Pillows. Lots and lots of pillows registered first.

Then yellow. A pale yellow, the color of moonlight. And grays.

There was only one photo in the room and he didn't catch sight of who it was because the moment his gaze landed on it on the bedside table, she turned the frame face down.

"This wasn't preplanned, so I don't have protection." She shrugged a little self-consciously. "I am on the pill, though. I just kept taking it even after Baxter and I broke things off."

Gabe didn't like the thought of her with Baxter or any other man, but the past didn't matter. What mattered was that she was here, with him, and that she was finally accepting that they had a future together.

"I have protection."

She nodded, as if she'd thought he might.

Rather than say anything more, she lifted her hair from her nape. At first Gabe just stared, then realized she was waiting for him to undress her.

With hands that trembled from the significance of what was happening, he slowly pulled up her scrub top and the T-shirt beneath it, revealing her creamy flesh as he lifted the material over her head.

He intentionally kept his fingers from touching her skin, but did his best to take it slow, to savor every second of this moment he'd wanted for so long. One touch and he would be a goner.

He was already a goner.

Unable to resist, he slid his fingers inside her waistband and pulled down her scrub bottoms, placing a soft kiss on each thigh as he did so.

Her flesh goose bumped and her fingers went into his hair.

His knees almost buckled.

Yet he still had to pause, look up at her and ask, "You're sure this is what you want?"

***

"If you leave me now, I'll never forgive you." Kami wanted this. Wanted him.

If he changed his mind, she really might curl up and cry.

She wanted her phenomenal sex experience even when she knew she'd pay the price later. She'd decided the price was worth what she'd get in return: Gabe. For however long they lasted, Gabe would be hers. Her friend and her lover.

"I'm not going anywhere," he assured her.

Kami trembled as his fingertips brushed over her skin. Wearing only her bra and matching panties, she stepped out of her scrub pants, waiting on his next touch.

She wasn't disappointed.

Gabe kissed her knees. Soft, delicate kisses. Then he stood and kissed her neck as his palms trailed down her shoulders, her arms.

Taking her hand, he stepped back and took her in. His eyes deepened to a dark blue as his gaze skimmed over her from head to toe.

"Mercy."

A smile spread across her face. She didn't have to ask if he liked what he saw. She saw it on his face, felt it in his touch, in his kiss, as he possessed her mouth in a blistering kiss. Gabe really did want her as much as she wanted him.

She wanted to touch him, to see him; her hands found their way to his waistband and tugged his shirt free, but he stopped her by taking her hands into his.

"No." She pulled her hands free.

Surprise darkened his eyes.

"You aren't going to deny me touching you back," she told him, not willing to be a passive participant in what was happening. "I get to touch, too."

Rather than argue, he took her hands and placed them back at his waistband and helped her undress him. "I'm all yours."

She wished.

Which scared her.

But now wasn't the time for such thoughts. Now was time for enjoying the here and now because what was happening would be fleeting.

She planned to enjoy it.

Every touch of her hands over his body. Every touch of his hands over hers.

His lips, his mouth tasting.

Hers replying in kind.

"Gabe," she moaned as he pushed her back on the bed and tossed a half-dozen pillows to the floor.

He stared down at her as he donned protection, then joined her on the bed, his body poised over hers.

His eyes were dark, turbulent. "I've wanted this for so long."

"Me, too," she admitted, knowing the time for denials had long passed. "I want you, Gabe." She gripped his shoulders, lifted her hips to push against him, ready for everything his eyes, his body, promised. "I want you now."

"Kami," he groaned, shifting his hips to join their bodies.

She kept her eyes locked with his as he stretched her body to accommodate him, as his hips rocked against hers, creating a rhythm that melted her insides into a hot, quivery mess.

Until she exploded beneath him and had to hold on to keep from shattering into a million pieces.

Then he did it all over again.

Blown away, Kami stared at the ceiling, tracing patterns in the tiles as she caught her breath.

Ha. She'd never catch her breath. Not after what she'd just experienced.

She'd never be the same.

Not her body, her mind, or her heart.

She turned to look at Gabe, to see if he was as affected as she was. Instead, her gaze landed on the face-down photograph.

A photo of her and her mother that had been taken at her nursing school pinning.

A day on which she'd felt empowered because she'd checked off another important step in her life. Graduate from college with honors.

Her next big life goal had been to get her dream job. Most nights, she believed she'd checked that one off, too.

Up next was buy a house—a goal she'd been saving for from her very first paycheck.

Because, as much as she loved her, she didn't want to be like her mother.

She didn't want to get so caught up in a man to the exclusion of all else and make bad decision after bad decision.

Taking her hand into his, Gabe gave her a little squeeze, drawing her attention to where he lay next to her.

"You have to go."

Okay, so her voice had sounded strained, but surely that could be chalked up to the vigorous activities she'd just engaged in.

With Gabe.

Sex with Gabe was a marathon. A marathon with orgasms around every bend. Who knew? Who knew her body could have such a meltdown of pleasure? Could shatter into a million pieces and yet still be whole?

She'd had sex with Baxter, with Kent. Pleasant enough, but no meltdowns. How did one live without meltdowns once one had experienced them?

How was she going to live without Gabe now that she'd experienced him?

"You want me to leave?" He rolled onto his side and stared at her. Confusion shone in his blue eyes. "Why?"

"Because *I* can't. *I* live here."

"I'm not leaving you, Kam. Not after what we just shared."

"This is my apartment," she reminded him, surprised that he wasn't leaping at the out she'd given him.

"You're overthinking, going back into that shell you hide behind. What we just shared was amazing. I know you felt it, too. So, again, I ask, why are you telling me to go?"

Kami closed her eyes. "Because you will leave, Gabe. It's what you do. What men do."

She waited, waited for him to say whatever he was going to say, but only silence met her ears. Slowly, she opened her eyes, looked into his.

His brows furrowed. "You dumped Baxter. I know you did. He told me himself one day at the gym."

He'd talked to Baxter about her at the gym?

"And that Kent guy, too," he continued. "I don't know about the men in your life beyond that, but I do know that the two guys you've dated since I've known you didn't leave you. You left them."

"What does that have to do with this?"

"Because this is about you. Not me. You're the one who always leaves in your relationships. The one telling me to leave now. Why is that?"

What he said hit her hard.

"What?" She scooted up in the bed and glared at him. "You want me to wait a couple of months? Wait until you get bored, then you'll leave? Is that it? You have to be the one to make that call?"

He stared at her as if she'd grown two heads, then calmly reminded her, "A very smart woman once pointed out to me that if she ever gave me a chance it wouldn't be me who left. Perhaps she's forgotten that, but I haven't."

How dared he quote her to herself?

"Yeah, well, she was bluffing because you were so full of yourself and needed to be taken down a peg or two."

He studied her. "Is that what this is about?"

"No," she denied, shaking her head and feeling very exposed. She flipped the comforter up, covering her vital parts, yet still felt vulnerable. Reaching over, she grabbed one of the few throw pillows still on the bed and hugged it to her.

"Then what?" he pushed.

Why couldn't he have just said okay and left? Why did he have to question everything? Make her question everything?

She didn't want to admit the truth.

She didn't like the truth, didn't like how naked she felt.

"I don't want to be like all the others, Gabe. Nor do I want to admit any of this to you." She hugged the pillow tighter to her chest. "If you leave me and I care, it makes me...weak."

He scooted up beside her, took her hand in his, and studied their interlocking fingers. "You're the strongest woman I know."

Fighting the emotions threatening to overwhelm her, she shook her head. "I'm not strong."

"Because you're with me?"

She didn't answer.

"Kam, I don't want to leave you. Not now or this afternoon or even tonight. But at some point, I will go home. What I don't want to happen is for you to question how I feel. Nothing has changed."

She scowled at him.

"Okay, so some things have changed. Obviously. But not how I feel about you."

"Which is what?"

She waited for him to answer, curious as to what he'd say. Would he feed her a bunch of crock?

"I care about you."

His voice was too sincere to be crock and she heard herself admit, "I care about you, too."

He lifted her hand, kissed it. "That's a pretty good start, I'd say."

Her insides trembled at what was happening between them. "A good start to what?"

"That's what time will tell us. For now, I'm not leaving because I plan to sleep with you in my arms and make love to you again this afternoon."

***

"You're quiet this morning."

Turning to look at Gabe in the driver seat of his car, Kami forced a smile. What could she say? Over the past twenty-four hours, the man had made her smile. A lot.

"You were there," she reminded him. "The ER was swamped last night."

Looking unfazed, he nodded. "It did get a bit crazy for a while. So crazy, in fact, that I failed to execute my plan to woo you into the supply room for a kiss or two."

Kami's eyes widened. She wouldn't have put up much resistance had he done any wooing. "There's always tonight."

He laughed. "Want to swing by and get breakfast before we go to your place? I don't think either one of us took time for a break and I can't have you weak from starvation."

She was hungry.

"Breakfast sounds great." An idea hit her. "Pancakes, please. Wherever you got those the morning you first showed at my place."

The corner of his mouth twitched. "Whipped cream and cherries?"

"That's the one."

"You going to show me?"

Although Gabe had no doubt that Kami knew exactly what he referred to, she played innocent. If you could call her toying with the long-stemmed cherry innocent.

"Show you what?"

"I think it's time."

She sighed, put the cherry in her mouth, then, a few seconds later, pulled a de-cherried knotted stem from between her lips.

Gabe grinned. "Such a talented tongue."

"You should know."

Oh, he knew.

"You might need to show me again."

She glanced down at the remaining cherry on her plate. "If you insist."

Eyes locked with hers, he laughed. "I didn't mean tying knots. Although that might be an interesting twist."

Her eyes widened. "Oh."

"Yeah, oh."

She pushed her plate away. "Think we can get an order of these to go?"

Gabe brushed stray hairs away from Kami's face. "I'm crazy about you."

Wondering where his comment had come from, Kami smiled up at him. "You are pretty crazy," she teased, turning her head to where her lips brushed against his fingers so she could press a kiss there. "For the record, I'm rather fond of you, too."

She'd expected him to grin or to say something silly back. He didn't, just stared down at her with a look in his eyes she couldn't quite read.

The longer he stared, the more unease filled her and she found herself babbling just to be saying something.

"I have an appointment with a Realtor next week." Now, why had she told him that?

"You moving?"

"Maybe." She shrugged. "I've been saving for a while so I could put a down payment on my own place and I've finally reached my minimum-down-payment goal. I'm not in a rush, but I don't want to miss it when the right place comes along. I'm meeting with the Realtor so she knows exactly what I'm looking for and can be on the lookout."

Propping himself on his elbow, Gabe regarded her. "What is it you're looking for, Kami?"

"In my dream world or what I'll most likely end up with?" She gave a little laugh. "I dream of a place of my own, not too far from the hospital, but far enough out that I can have a decent-sized yard. A yard with trees," she added. She'd never lived in a house with trees before. Just apartment complexes with a few decorative trees in front occasionally. "And I think I'd like a pet."

His brows rose. "A pet?"

She nodded. "I've never had a pet."

"Never?"

She shook her head. "We moved a lot while I was growing up. Most of the places we lived didn't allow pets, so it was easier not to have one, even when we lived at the few places where we could."

Odd that her mother had Bubbles now. Kami remembered many a time begging her mother to keep some stray she'd found and brought home. Her mother hadn't once even considered letting her, demanding Kami get rid of the animal and not dare bring it into their home.

"What about you? Did you have pets growing up?"

"A few. Dogs mostly, but a few cats along the way, too. My mother liked a full house."

"Sounds heavenly."

"It wasn't really. Mainly, she just liked a lot of things to keep her distracted from thinking about my father."

"She must have missed him a great deal."

Gabe sucked in a deep breath and waited so long to answer that Kami didn't think he was going to. Then he said, "She did. We both did. For years I had nightmares about him dying."

"Oh, Gabe."

"I watched him die, Kam." Gabe wondered why he was still talking, why he was admitting the horrible truth to her. "I watched him take that last breath and didn't do a thing."

"You were eight years old. What were you supposed to do?"

"Logically, I know you're right, but it took me a long time to accept that."

She hugged him. "I'm sorry, Gabe."

"It was a long time ago." So long ago, he wondered why he'd

been thinking of his father so much over the past few weeks. Why he'd had to tell her that day at the park. Then again, after working the code the other day, no wonder thoughts of his father had haunted him.

"At least you were old enough to remember him."

What would she think if he admitted that he'd likely be better off if he'd been young enough not to recall? Gabe closed his eyes. No, not true. Because prior to the heart attack that had claimed his father's life, Gabe's memories of the man he'd helplessly watched die had all been good.

"What about you?" He changed the subject. "You talk about your mother, but never a word about dear old dad."

Kami snorted. "My father was just some guy who came in and out of my mother's life. Not anyone special or amazing. Just another in a long string of failed relationships."

"That's sad. Tell me she found happiness eventually."

"Oh, she finds happiness a lot. He just never sticks around."

Gabe rolled over, took Kami's hand into his, and stared up at the ceiling. "Guess that's why you're so adamant that men don't stick around even when you have no personal basis for thinking that way."

Kami pulled her hand free. "No personal basis for thinking that way? Did you not just hear everything I said? Every man who came into my mother's life used her, then left. That's a pretty strong personal basis for thinking that men don't stick around."

"Not all men are like that, Kami."

"I didn't say they were."

"I'm not like that."

Kami didn't comment. Next to her, Gabe sighed, then, after a brief silence, lifted her hand and pressed a kiss to her fingertips. "Good luck with the Realtor next week. If you want someone to go with you to look at houses, I'm your guy."

"Unless she just has something perfect, I won't start looking until after the fund-raiser."

"Makes sense." He closed his eyes; his breathing evened.

"Guess we'd better get a little shut-eye before having to be back at the hospital tonight." She leaned over, kissed his cheek. "Sweet dreams, Gabe."

"Unfortunately, I'm going to have to take a pass this morning," Kami told Gabe at shift change a few mornings later.

Gabe glanced up from the computer where he made notes regarding a patient, his expression concerned. "What's up?"

"My mother."

His eyes darkened. "Something wrong?"

Kami shrugged. Where did she begin to explain about her mother's frantic phone call? A call during which her mother had been crying so profusely she'd barely been able to understand her pleas for Kami to come to her apartment.

"Let me finish here and I'll go with you."

Kami shook her head. The last thing she wanted was for Gabe to meet her mother. Especially as her mother was already so upset. Kami hadn't asked over the phone, but past experience told her what the problem would be.

"Sorry, but now isn't the time for you to meet my mother." She gave a look she hoped conveyed she'd much rather spend the morning with him and didn't reveal that she didn't expect him to ever meet her mother. Her heart squeezed and she fought back the panic that rose in her chest, reminding herself that it was the call from her mother making her antsy, not Gabe. She forced a smile. "I'd say to call me when you wake up, but, truth is, who knows what time I'll even get to go to sleep?"

"Then you call me when you wake up. We'll go somewhere for dinner."

Leaning against the doorjamb of the small physician's area, she eyed him and smiled for real. "Sounds perfect."

When she got to her mother's, Kami found her mom was a bumbling mess, as was the apartment. How someone could accumulate so much trash in the short amount of time since Kami had cleaned the apartment, she couldn't fathom. The place was a wreck, stank of the stench of the cat litter box and old food.

Ugh.

"Where's Don?" she guessed. Although was it really a guess when she had years of experience of seeing her mother all to pieces over whichever guy had just walked out on her?

"Gone."

Kami sighed and stared at the woman who'd raised her; the woman who fell in love at the drop of a hat and left herself vulnerable to any Tom, Dick, or Harry. Or in this case, Don.

How was it her mother continued to put herself out there after all these years? Didn't she ever learn to protect her heart?

"He didn't deserve you," she offered, trying to comfort her mother. How did one comfort a woman who'd been through more men than stars in the sky? When none of them had ever stuck around and most had taken everything they could and then some from the pitiful woman hunched over on the sofa with her cat cradled in her arms?

Why did her mother keep diving into relationships with her heart wide open?

Amid another big tearful bout, her mother cried, "That doesn't stop me from giving my heart."

Frustrated at her mother's reaction to the man leaving when surely she'd expected it, Kami reminded her, "Mom, you hardly dated Don for any time at all."

"What does time have to do with anything? I loved him."

Hardly any time at all. That's how long you have been "dating" Gabe. What if it was her who'd been dumped? Would she feel any different than her mom?

Of course she would. Unlike her mother, she knew Gabe would leave. For some reason, her mother believed Don, and all the others, was actually going to stick around.

Kami sighed, moved closer. "I'm sorry. It's just that he didn't seem so different from any of the others."

Her mother blew her nose. "Maybe not to you."

True. To her, he hadn't.

"To me, he was the one."

"You think that with every man you date."

Her mother looked up at her with sad eyes. "Is it so wrong to believe that I'm lovable? That this man is finally the one who will love me back and won't do me wrong? Just because you've never been in love and don't know how it feels, don't you judge me."

Kami opened her mouth to correct her mother, to say she had been in love, that she *was* in love, then, stunned, bit her tongue, instead.

Shaken to her very core, she tried to comfort her mother the best she could.

Finally, her mother drifted off to sleep. Unable to walk away from the messy apartment, Kami emptied the litter box, picked up the trash, then sat in the chair opposite the sofa where her mother slept.

Bubbles jumped up into Kami's lap for some attention, purring in pleasure when she got it.

"I don't love him," Kami told the cat. "Well, as a friend, but I'm not in love with him."

Bubbles ignored her and circled back around for another head-to-tip-of-tail stroke.

"But if I'm not careful that's what's going to happen."

Her gaze focused on her pitiful mother, who had nothing in life because she'd given away what little she had to useless men.

For the rest of the morning, Kami's insides felt rattled.

That would be her. Someday soon. How much longer until Gabe lost interest? Until he moved on to someone new and left her brokenhearted like her mother?

Kami slept a little but was restless and finally got up to run errands and catch up on her laundry, all the while battling the demons in her head.

That night, when Gabe called, she apologized for not calling, begged off dinner, stating she'd not slept much and really just wanted to go to bed and catch up on her sleep.

When he called first thing the following morning, she declined breakfast under the guise that she'd fallen behind with her cleaning.

To keep her mind occupied, she pulled everything from her closet and began sorting through the items, culling out things she never wore and straightening favorites.

The knock at her apartment door startled her, but the person on the other side of the door wasn't really a surprise.

"Gabe," she said as she opened the door and stared at the smiling man. "What are you doing here?"

"Two sets of hands are better than one."

She eyed him suspiciously. "You're going to help me sort my closet?"

He gave a suspicious look of his own. "If that's what you're doing."

"See for yourself." Grateful she'd dug out a ton of stuff, she led him to her bedroom.

He eyed the stack of clothes on her bed, then turned to her with a dubious look. "Maybe I can give a thumbs up or thumbs down while you try those on."

Kami suppressed a laugh. "Sorry. You're too late. That's the bye-bye stack I'm donating to charity."

"Want me to load them into your car?"

She shrugged. "I can do it later."

"Or I could do it now and you wouldn't have to."

He had a point. "Fine."

While Gabe loaded the stack into her car, she stored the keep items back into her closet, and was waiting in the living room when he came back into the apartment.

"What next?"

She shook her head. "Nothing. I'll finish up later."

"I didn't mean to interfere with what you were doing. I wanted to help."

"You did. Thank you for carrying the load to my car."

He studied her a moment. "Everything okay?"

"Fine."

Not looking convinced, he eyed her. "That's what you said on the phone, too. So why don't I believe you?"

She shrugged but had to glance away.

He sighed. "You're never going to trust me, are you?"

She lifted her gaze to his. "What do you mean?"

"No matter how long we're together, you're always going to be waiting for me to leave just like all those guys did to your mom."

She shrugged. "It's what men do."

Staring at her for a long moment, he nodded. "I can't deny that it's what I've done in the past."

"And what you'll do in the future."

He didn't deny her claim, just sank onto the sofa and looked defeated.

"I knew something wasn't right when you canceled dinner. I thought something had happened at your mother's, so I stayed away last night. But it's just this same old thing, isn't it? You not trusting in me, in us."

She didn't answer. Something had happened at her mother's but she wasn't telling him that.

"Kami, the past couple of weeks have been wonderful."

They had.

"But, even after everything we've shared, you don't trust me any more than you did that first morning."

Going on the defensive, Kami lifted her chin. "Don't pretend you plan to stick around, Gabe. We both know that isn't your style."

He studied her. "Is that what you want me to say? That I'm never going to leave you? Would you believe me if I did tell you?"

Pain shot through her at what she saw in his eyes. This was it. What she'd been dreading.

She shook her head in denial.

"I didn't think so." He raked his fingers through his hair. "I care about you, Kami. If you haven't figured that out by now, then you're never going to."

Was this how he did it? Tried to convince women that it was their fault that he was leaving?

Heart breaking, she crossed her arms.

Face gaunt, he added, "I came here because I wanted to be with you. Too bad you can't believe that."

He got up and walked out of her apartment, quietly closing the door behind him.

Thirteen

"I heard a dirty rumor that you and Gabe had broken up."

Kami shrugged without looking at her best friend. She was at the hospital to work, not gossip about her nonexistent love life.

"This is the part where you tell me I shouldn't believe dirty rumors," her friend persisted.

"That particular rumor is true."

Mindy slapped her hand against her forehead. "What happened?"

"Nothing."

"Couples don't break up over nothing." Mindy frowned. "Did you have a fight?"

"Not really." How could she explain to Mindy what she didn't want to acknowledge? What was easier to ignore? "It was just time for us to end."

"Kami, you and Gabe are perfect together. Why would things ever end?"

"Because that's what he does."

Mindy looked taken aback. "He broke things off with you?"

"Yes. No. I think so." She thought back over their conversation for the millionth time. "He left. He hasn't called or texted." She shrugged and kept her voice monotone. "So, yeah, he broke things off."

"You don't sound too upset."

Was that what her friend thought? Tears didn't change anything. She would not cry at work. Would not break down. Would not carry on as her mother did.

She refused.

"I knew before we started that we weren't going to last."

"Because you wouldn't let it."

Mindy's staunch defense of Gabe irritated Kami.

"Why do you always take his side? You're supposed to be my friend."

Mindy put her hands on her hips. "I am. Which is why I'm pointing out that you refused to give this relationship a chance."

"Where have you been? I gave this relationship all I had to give."

"Not your heart."

"I gave him all I had to give," she repeated. "It's not my fault that all I had wasn't enough."

She spun to walk away and almost collided with Gabe. A red-faced Gabe.

"We need to talk."

"I can't. We're at work."

Gabe glanced at Mindy.

"I'll come get you if I need either of you," Mindy assured them.

His grasp on her arm firm, but not painful, Gabe marched Kami to the tiny dictation room and shut the door behind them.

"All you had wasn't enough? Seriously? That's what you think?"

"You shouldn't have been eavesdropping on my conversation."

"You shouldn't have been talking about me if you didn't want me to overhear."

"This is ridiculous. We have nothing to say to each other."

"Wrong." He put his hand on the door, preventing her from being able to open it. "We have a lot to say to each other. Perhaps this isn't the best place to say it, but hell if I'm going to just let you walk away without explaining your comment."

"I don't have to explain myself to you. I owe you nothing and you can't make me stay."

Her words hit their target and seemed to deflate him. His hand fell away from the door.

"You're right. I can't keep you here."

Kami reached for the door.

"But you're wrong, Kami."

She hesitated.

"All you had was enough. The problem was—*is*," he corrected, "that you never gave all you had. Not even close. Maybe it was me who wasn't enough."

The rest of the night passed in a blur. They had a couple of wrecks come in, several upper respiratory infections, an overdose, and a chest pain.

Kami worked side by side with Gabe, pretending that there was nothing between them.

Pretending that her heart wasn't breaking.

Pretending she hadn't lost something, *someone*, special.

"Oh, Kami! We got the call."

At Beverly's breathy, nervous tone, Kami didn't have to ask which call that was. A heart had been located for Lindsey.

Even as excitement filled her for her friend, she felt a stab of pain for the family who'd donated the heart.

"When?"

"The transplant team is prepping her for surgery now. I'm so scared and can't believe this is happening," her coworker gushed over the phone line. "Gregg and I wanted you to know that she's going into surgery."

Kami glanced at her fitness watch. She'd had a half-dozen

things on her to-do list for the day, most of them picking up donations for the fund-raiser, but none of them mattered in light of what was happening in the Smiths' lives. She could pick up the items later.

"I'll be there."

"The surgery is going to take hours and hours. I don't expect you to sit here with us. I just wanted you to know Lindsey is getting a new heart. You did so much for my family and we love you."

Kami's chest squeezed. "I want to be there. See you soon."

Gabe winced when the first person he saw in the transplant family waiting room was Kami.

He should have known she'd be here.

Of course she would.

If Beverly had called him, she'd certainly called Kami.

He'd been out with friends on the lake when the call had come and, after they'd returned from their water-skiing trip, he'd showered, then headed to the hospital.

Several hours had passed, but Lindsey was still in surgery and would be for some time.

Kami averted her gaze.

Anger and frustration filled Gabe. Anger that she'd not given them a fair shot.

If she couldn't freely care for him, they were just wasting their time.

Ignoring Kami, he went to Beverly, hugged her, then shook Gregg's hand. He chatted with them for several minutes, then joined the others in the waiting game.

As luck would have it, the only empty chair in the small, crowded private waiting area was next to Kami.

He'd almost rather stand than take it, but to do so for who knew how long was ridiculous.

With a nod of acknowledgment her way, he sat and pulled out his phone, skimming through his text messages.

Five, then ten, then fifteen awkward minutes went by, during which he was acutely aware of how near she was, of how much he missed her.

But she'd made her choice. Her choice wasn't to open herself up to him, wasn't to give them a chance, to trust in what was between them.

Maybe he didn't even blame her. Lord knew he had enough issues of his own without digging into hers.

On the Friday night before the fund-raiser event, volunteers had worked hard finishing the baskets and organizing the donated items. As he'd promised, Gabe came, helped, and made several of them laugh when he finally got his ribbon to curl just right after several failed attempts.

Not that Kami laughed.

Or even looked his way, but he refused to let that dampen his spirit.

Over a week had passed since Lindsey's heart transplant. The first few days were the most critical, but Lindsey had gotten through them with flying colors. She still had a long road ahead, but the tiny baby was holding her own.

When they'd finished the last basket and had each auction item to be listed, labeled, and numbered, Kami thanked them all for their dedication to their friend and her family.

"Well, I don't know about everyone else, but I'm parched. Anyone up for drinks?"

Kami's gaze narrowed and he realized how she might take his comment. Too bad. He wasn't going to walk on eggshells just because she'd bailed on their relationship.

"Unwinding for a while before the big event sounds perfect." Mindy spoke up. "Hope that's okay with you, Kami, since you rode here with me. We won't stay late, I promise."

Kami looked as if she wanted to argue, but when all the other volunteers said they were going, she just nodded.

Gabe and Kami ended up next to each other in a large round booth with their friends bookending them on each side.

No one commented on the sitting order, but Gabe doubted it had been accidental. Although few of their friends had commented on their personal relationship, or recent lack thereof, they all knew something had transpired between him and Kami; knew and were obviously playing matchmaker by trying to throw them together.

Good luck with that.

Kami ordered water and Gabe ended up doing the same.

She didn't speak directly to him, but conversation was going on all around them.

The chatter was loud, fun and varied from the fund-raiser to an upcoming marathon several of them were running. There were lots of laughs.

Except nothing felt right.

Not to Gabe.

He needed to forget her and move on. Fine, he could do that. He would do that.

He turned and started talking to Eddie, the paramedic who'd volunteered with them, asking if he'd caught any of the Stanley Cup playoff game the night before.

Fortunately he had and they launched into a discussion regarding their winner predictions.

Saturday morning, the day of the fund-raiser dawned bright and early. Kami leaped out of bed and rushed about, getting her day started. It was going to be a long day, but a good one.

At least, she hoped so. What they had raised from selling raffle tickets and dinner tickets would more than pay for the few expenses for the event and would be a nice addition to the Smiths' funds. Hopefully, before the night was over the coffer would be overflowing and they wouldn't have to worry about how to pay the bills for months to come so they could focus on Lindsey.

Kami, Gabe, and a handful of other volunteers moved the baskets and donated items from the hospital conference room to the convention center where the event was being held.

When they got there, Mindy and other volunteers were setting up the tables.

"Here, let me get that for you," Gabe offered when Kami went for a particularly heavy basket.

"Thanks." She stepped aside and let him effortlessly grab the basket and head into the building.

She watched him go and was filled with such frustration she wanted to scream. Frustration at him. At herself. At the whole world.

Frustration that had interfered with her sleep and had her edgy as she'd dreamed of stomping his toes under the table and demanding he talk with her the night before. He'd totally humiliated her, turning his back to her and publicly shunning her in front of their friends.

Then today, he showed up and was all nice. What was with him, anyway?

Not that it mattered. It was just as well that he'd turned his back. Maybe their friends would take a hint and quit with the cupid.

When the fund-raiser was over and she didn't have that worry hanging over her, she'd go back to feeling like her old self. Not this uptight, frustrated, on-edge woman who couldn't stop overanalyzing everything that happened.

Sighing, she grabbed a lighter basket and followed him inside the hotel.

"Where do you want me to put this one?" he asked when she walked up beside where he stood in front of one of the display tables.

"All the items are numbered. We're going to auction them in numerical order to make it easier for the emcee and the recorders to keep up with what's what during the auction." She realized she hadn't really answered his question and he was still holding the basket.

"Here." She pointed to the right area on the display table. "It goes here."

Gabe set the basket in the appropriate spot, then turned back toward her. "Everything looks fantastic. You've done an amazing job."

"Mindy and the other volunteers have done most of the decorations and taken care of the food. I was in charge of donations and we won't really know until tonight how that went."

He gestured to the numerous items on display. "I'd say you did good."

"For the Smiths' sake, I sure hope so."

"Are they coming tonight?"

Look at them making small talk. Kami's heart hurt from the brevity of it. This was her friend whom she'd teased and laughed with on so many occasions, her lover who had wowed her time and again. Now carrying on a simple conversation that was nothing but a farce.

Not able to bring herself to look him in the eyes, she answered, "As long as there are no changes with Lindsey at the hospital, they plan to. She's doing great, but everything hinges on her, of course."

"Kami, where does this artwork go?" one of the volunteers asked, joining where they stood by the table.

"Somewhere around here is a display stand for that piece. We're going to put it at the end of one of the tables. It's the first item up for auction."

Gabe stuck his hands in his jeans pockets and shrugged. "Guess I'd better get back outside. There's still several things to be carried inside."

"I...uh... I'm going to help position the painting," Kami said needlessly since he hadn't waited on her response. He'd just walked away.

When they'd finished arranging everything on the tables and

had double-checked to make sure everything was lined up numerically, Kami and her volunteers joined in on setting up the guest tables and their decorations.

When mid-afternoon rolled around, Kami glanced at her fitness watch and gave Gabe a pointed look.

"Don't you need to head home to shower? We need you looking good so you'll bring top dollar."

"You make him sound like a piece of prized meat," Mindy accused, having overheard Kami's comment.

"What about you?" he asked. "Won't you and Mindy need to be heading out to clean up, as well?"

"I'm heading out in the next five," Mindy said, then winced. "Except the band's not arrived yet to set up their equipment and I promised I'd wait around so they could."

"I'll wait until they get here," Kami offered. "I'm planning to stay until the rescue squad arrives anyway. They had some last-minute donations to be auctioned off tonight and I'll need to get them labeled and on the recorder's list."

Mindy offered to stay, but Kami declined. "Go," she ordered Mindy. "Just get back as soon as you can in case I'm still here."

Her friend gave her a quick hug and promised to do just that.

Kami turned to Gabe, who was still standing next to her. He looked so good her heart hurt.

"You should go, too," she told him, keeping her voice light. "It's going to be time to get started before you know it."

He hesitated, then nodded. "You're right. The night of the big auction."

"I really do appreciate all you've done."

His gaze met hers. He raked his fingers through his hair, took a step toward her. "Kami, I..."

She wasn't sure what he'd planned to say as at that moment a long-haired kid twirling a drumstick came walking into the ballroom and asked if this was the Smith party.

She stared up at Gabe, wondering what he'd been going to say, wondering what, if anything, words could change.

"Looks like the band is here." Not what he'd been going to say, but whatever had been on the tip of his tongue was gone. She could see it in the way his expression had hardened.

"Looks like it." She waved at the guy who'd been joined by a few others. "Over this way."

When she finished showing them where to set up, she glanced around the room and noted that Gabe had left.

Good. He had to be back soon.

So that he could be auctioned off to the highest bidder, because she'd asked him to.

Not just because of that, she assured herself. He wanted to help the Smiths.

She understood. She wanted this night to be all it could be, for as much money to be raised as possible to help the sweet family.

She'd hoped to make it home in time from the setup to leisurely get ready for the big event.

No such luck.

Still, she got a quick shower, styled her hair, and put on more makeup than she usually wore, so she figured she was doing well.

When she got to the convention center and saw Gabe already there, looking like a zillion dollars in his tuxedo, her breath caught. Right or wrong considering the state of their relationship, she wanted Gabe to think she looked good, too. For him to look at her and feel the same *vavoom* her lungs had undergone when she'd caught sight of him.

Was that why she'd donned a splashy short dress that showed off her legs? She'd be on her feet too long for heels, but her comfy sparkly slip-ons weren't bad. Either way, she was showing leg.

Gabe had said he liked her legs.

Only, when he turned her way, caught her watching him, his gaze didn't drop to her legs. His pale blue eyes locked with hers for a brief moment, and then he averted his gaze.

Because he was no longer interested in her legs. Or anything about her.

Kami couldn't avoid Gabe all night, and it wasn't long before she got drawn into a conversation with the volunteer running the sound system.

The volunteer he'd been talking to gushed for a few minutes, then was called over to double-check the equipment.

Which left Kami alone with Gabe.

He glanced around the room. "Everything looks great."

Ah, there went the small talk.

She responded with more small talk. "There have been dozens of volunteers. Everyone has worked hard."

"True, but without you and Mindy putting it together, I doubt tonight would be happening, so, again, great job."

"Sometimes it just takes someone getting a project started to have lots of volunteers jumping in. Certainly, this is one of those cases where we've been blessed by so many helping out from the hospital and from the community." A blonde in a flashy red dress stepped into Kami's periphery. "Speaking of volunteers from the community…"

Gabe turned, frowned a little. "Let me brace myself."

"I don't know why you say such things. She seems nice."

"She is."

Kami started to say more, but instead smiled as the television hostess descended upon them.

"Everything looks perfect," Debbie praised. "My cameraman and I are going to do a few commentary pieces as everyone arrives."

Kami nodded. "We really appreciate all you're doing to help the Smiths."

"When we run the piece on tonight's news, there should be more money raised via the online donation page. Especially with the shots we have of that adorable baby girl." Debbie gave a heartfelt sigh. "Seriously ill babies pull on people's heartstrings and make for great stories."

Kami would take the woman's word for it on the great story part as she didn't find anything great about her coworker's baby having been born with a defective heart. Thank goodness a match had been found, the transplant had been a success so far, and Lindsey was getting stronger every day.

"If you'll excuse me, I need to make sure everything is going smoothly with the food preparation." Kami was pretty sure she had made the woman's night by leaving her and Gabe alone.

Good. More power to them. Kami didn't care.

Much.

Fortunately, everything was going smoothly. The volunteers from the rescue squad and the fire department were ready to serve the five hundred guests who'd bought meal tickets.

"Do you feel as crazy as I do?" Mindy gushed as she came up and hugged Kami.

"Crazier. Thanks for letting me sneak away long enough to get cleaned up."

"Cleaned up? Girl, you did more than that." Mindy gave her an up and down. "You look great."

Kami's cheeks heated at her friend's praise. "Thank you. I feel a lot more presentable than when I headed out of here earlier, for sure."

A feminine laugh rang across the room. Both Kami and Mindy turned toward where Debbie chatted with Gabe.

"Please tell me you're all dolled up for him."

"I wouldn't hold your breath."

Mindy eyed Debbie with Gabe, and her nose crinkled. "Surely, you aren't going to let her win him."

Kami fought to keep an I-don't-care expression. "It's an auction for a single day's date. What he does beyond that is up to him."

She eyed how the hostess brushed an imaginary speck off Gabe's tuxedo jacket. An excuse to touch him, no doubt.

She'd touched him, had her arms around those shoulders

while he held her close when they'd danced, when they'd kissed, when they'd made love.

Mindy sighed. "Just seems such a shame for you to let this opportunity pass you by."

"What opportunity is that?"

"To win Gabe back."

"As if I'd buy a date to try to win him back," Kami scoffed. Buying a man was even worse than the things her mother did.

"Your loss." Looking disappointed, Mindy shrugged. "Maybe you'll get lucky and Debbie won't win him back, but I think you're a fool to risk it. That woman has talons she's dying to hook into him."

Kami's gaze cut to the couple. Despite his woe-is-me antics, Gabe didn't appear to be in any hurry to get away from his beautiful ex.

Quite the opposite.

No, she wasn't jealous. Kami rubbed her pounding temple. She wasn't jealous. Only…she averted her gaze from the couple and met Mindy's curious eyes. Rather than launch into another spiel about why she should bid on Gabe, Mindy just gave her a look of pity.

"What?"

Her friend sighed. "Whatever your reasons are for not hanging on to that man, I hope you don't live to regret that decision."

Glancing back toward where Debbie smiled up at Gabe, Kami agreed. Yeah, she hoped she didn't live to regret that decision, too, but for her long-term sanity and heart, she'd made the right choice.

Not that she'd really made the choice. He'd been the one to leave her apartment. He'd been the one to stop calling and texting. He'd been the one to step out of her life.

Why her friend acted as if it were all Kami's fault was beyond her. He'd left. Just as she'd always known he would. She'd let him, but he'd been the one to leave. End of story.

The dinner went off without a hitch and the band played while everyone ate. Both the food and the meal were a hit.

After the meal finished, the auctioneer relieved the band, taking command of the stage.

Time for the auction.

Prior to the date packages being auctioned off, the baskets and donations were being auctioned. One after another, prizes were sold.

Kami won a basket full of body, hair, and bath products donated by a local hair salon and felt quite proud of herself.

"Practicing?" a male voice whispered close to her ear.

Turning toward Gabe, she caught a whiff of his spicy scent and fought inhaling and holding the scent of him inside her forever.

Her heart sped up at his nearness, at how his whisper in her ear toyed with her equilibrium. *He left you, remember?* her heart whispered. *Sure, you kind of pushed, but he left.*

Pulling herself together, she smiled. "You wish."

"I like that your sass is back."

She cut her gaze toward him, thinking a more handsome man had never lived. "It never left."

His dark brow rose. "Just wasn't pointed my way?" He scanned the room, spotted the television crew at a table near the front of the venue. "Pretty sure Debbie plans on picking out china with me in the near future."

"Poor Gabe. It's so hard to be you and have to fight off beautiful women."

Rather than smile back or make a quip, he turned, searched her eyes a moment, then said, "The only beautiful woman I'm interested in won't give me the time of day."

Kami's heart thundered in her chest. He shouldn't say such things, but her silly body responded full throttle that he had. Unbidden, her eyes closed. She wasn't sure she could deal with him making such comments, not when her heart ached so.

"Kami?"

Opening her eyes, she flashed her teeth at him in a semblance of a smile and glanced down at her fitness band. "It's almost eight."

Looking as if he'd seen more on her face than she'd have liked, he asked, "You going to bid?"

"Only in your dreams."

He studied her a moment, then softly said, "You'd be surprised what you do in my dreams."

Kami wanted to ask, wanted to know what he dreamed of her doing, but what would be the point? She was not going to act on anything Gabe said.

Been there, done that, and had a lost friendship and tearstained pillow to prove it.

Fourteen

The night's take was going to be awesome even before Gabe's date came up for bid. Kami had been keeping a mental tally of what the different items and dates were going for and the Smiths must have been relieved.

She glanced toward the couple sitting at the front of the room. Despite the stress of the past few months, her friend was smiling and enjoying her evening with her husband.

That Lindsey was doing so well so quickly after her heart transplant went a long way in causing those smiles.

The emcee who was doubling as their auctioneer introduced the last package to be auctioned before Gabe's.

Gabe was next.

Kami's stomach knotted and she suddenly wished he'd never agreed to the auction, that she'd never asked him to take part in it.

Which was silly.

Several of the others had gone for four figures. His date would raise a nice amount for the Smiths.

She needed to shove aside her selfish thoughts. They'd had

their time. He never went back to the same woman after he'd left her. He had left Kami. Sure, he'd given some spiel about her not opening herself up to him, not trusting him, but he'd been the one to walk.

She had opened herself up to him. She had. Only...

Her blood doing a jittery dance through her veins, Kami shook her head to clear her thoughts.

"Please tell me you're shaking your head in protest of what is about to happen."

Kami looked at Mindy. "What's that?"

"You blowing what might be your last chance with Gabe."

"He left me. That was our last chance."

"Seriously? Is that pride speaking, Kami? Because I don't understand how you could just let him leave without putting up a fight to hang on to him."

"Isn't that what started all of this? Him asking me to bid on him tonight to keep one of his exes from trying to hang on?"

"Are you really so blind?" Mindy asked, shaking her head. "Did you ever stop to think that it's not Debbie buying his date that ever concerned him? That it's wanting you to buy his date that's important to him? That all of this has been about you from the very beginning? Not his ex or any other woman."

No, Kami hadn't considered that. Nor did she believe it.

Gabe hadn't teased her about buying his date package because he'd been interested in her and wanted her to bid on him. He hadn't.

The current auction ended and the emcee told the crowd about Gabe's Gatlinburg Getaway.

The bid started at a thousand dollars and quickly rose five hundred dollars at a time as Debbie immediately countered every bid anyone else made.

The others being auctioned off had smiled and flirted with the crowd, encouraging more bidders. Kami had thought Gabe would work the stage, too, but he wasn't. Then again, Gabe didn't need to do anything but stand and smile at the crowd.

It was good to be Gabe. To have women wanting you to the point of them thinking nothing of emptying their wallets for the opportunity to spend time with you.

Then again, she supposed it was the way of the world. Men emptied their wallets to impress women by taking them to fancy restaurants and driving fancier cars. Women emptied their wallets to buy the latest fashions and to try to preserve their youth.

Her mother had emptied her already rather pitiful wallet anytime a new guy came along, that was for sure. Even if it meant not being able to pay the rent or buy groceries.

How many times had they been kicked out of their home because they couldn't pay the rent—all down to her mother's foolish heart?

"Bid," Mindy stage-whispered.

Kami frowned. "Mind your own business."

"You're my best friend. Your happiness is my business. Fight for him. Let him know he matters, that your relationship matters, and that you want to date him."

"You have this all wrong, you know," she corrected her friend, her gaze going back and forth between the current bidders. "He doesn't really want to date me. He just wants…" Kami paused. What did Gabe want? To have sex with her again? Why? He could have sex anytime he wanted it. The room full of rabid wallet-wielding women was testament to that.

Mindy gave her a *duh* look. "Then why aren't you bidding?"

Kami's eyes widened. "You want me to have sex with him, knowing it won't last? That he's left me once and will leave me again? Knowing if I do this, he'll only end up hurting me? How is it that we're friends when you give such bad advice?"

Her heart was pounding so loudly it must be drowning out the emcee. She had life goals, and getting used by a man, even a man as fabulous as Gabe, wasn't on the list.

Only, what if he really had left because of her? Because she'd constantly been waiting for the ax to fall? What if she'd pushed him into doing exactly what she'd feared most?

She had done that.

"Bid, Kami. Do it now."

"Are you crazy? Or just deaf? The bid is way out of my budget." Financially and emotionally.

"He's worth it and you know it," Mindy prompted. "Bid now before it's too late. Blame me, if you must, but *bid*."

The stage lighting prevented Gabe from seeing where the bids were coming from, but it didn't matter. Debbie wasn't going to let anyone else win him. Even if a miracle happened and Kami had considered bidding, the bid was too high.

Who would have thought a day with him would go for so much?

Especially when he couldn't get the woman he'd wanted to spend that day with to admit she wanted him, to open her heart and trust in what was between them.

He'd thought... Never mind what he'd thought, what he'd wanted. It no longer mattered.

Kami wasn't willing to risk anything for their relationship. Instead, she'd kept up her defenses and in the end that had suffocated what was happening between them.

Perhaps he shouldn't have expected more. What made him think he deserved more in life? That he should get to have what few attained?

Love.

It was what his parents had had prior to his father's death. What he'd wanted with Kami, but that kind of relationship took two working at it.

"Going once," the auctioneer said, working the crowd. "Going twice... Wait—we have a new bidder!"

Gabe couldn't see where the new bid had come from, but his belly did a flip-flop because he instinctively knew who the bidder was.

The crazy thumping in his chest told him.

Kami had just bid on his date package. Why would she do that? Guilt? Pity?

He didn't want either.

Well, hell, this was unexpected and left him not quite sure what to think.

"Yes!" Mindy squealed in Kami's ear and did a happy dance next to her. "Yes. Yes. Yes."

Kami ignored her friend's antics and kept her gaze trained on Gabe.

Because if she looked away she might wonder why she'd just raised her number and bid on his Gatlinburg Getaway.

She'd just bid a lot of money. So much, her stomach hurt.

Of course Debbie immediately countered her bid, looking around the room to try to spot who her new competition was. She looked bored, annoyed, but resilient. She planned to take Gabe's date package home.

She planned to take Gabe home.

"You in?"

Swallowing the lump in her throat, Kami nodded to the auction volunteer who'd taken her initial bid and was waiting on her answer.

The man called her bid and the auctioneer ate it up that there was a new battle on.

Ha. Not much of a battle, she thought, as Debbie seemed to grow tired of the back-and-forth and raised the bid by a whopping four-figure amount.

Kami bit into her lower lip. What was she doing? Why?

"I'll toss in a few hundred," Mindy offered. "Bid again. Don't lose Gabe. This is important. You know it is."

Kami hadn't really seen this auction as winning or losing Gabe.

But suddenly it did feel that way.

That if she didn't win this bid she'd be losing him forever. That she'd never get another chance to show him he was important to her, that he mattered, that she regretted letting him walk away.

She had to risk this, had to put herself out there and bid. She didn't have time to analyze or to figure it out. The auctioneer was calling for another bid.

She couldn't.

But she had to.

Kami nodded to the volunteer and he called out to the auctioneer.

Again, Debbie turned to search the crowd and countered Kami's bid by going up another four figures.

Kami gulped. This was getting serious.

Getting?

It had been serious for a while now. They were talking figures that equaled long periods of work time for her to earn. *Long* periods.

Which was why raising her number and saying the exact amount in her house down-payment fund would be absolutely crazy.

Her down payment that she'd been building for years in order to buy the house which was the next big item on her life list.

Her down payment that would give her the security of knowing she owned her home and that she'd never be homeless again.

Her down payment that proved she wasn't like her mother, that she didn't throw away everything she had on a man.

If she bid on Gabe, she'd literally be throwing away everything she had on a man.

But the bid was for a good cause, right? She remembered the emotion in Beverly's voice when she'd talked about why they'd agreed to the television bit.

What was making a down payment on a house compared to helping pay for the medical expenses of a precious baby?

Or bidding on the only man to ever make your belly do somersaults because you didn't want him to go on a date with his ex?

Or anyone else.

Ever.

Just you.

Or bidding because you had to prove to him that you did trust in him, in what was happening between you. What had happened between you.

Bidding on Gabe and emptying her savings would be something her mother would do.

It would be stupid in so many ways.

It would be the antithesis of everything Kami had always held important.

So her next move made no sense.

She raised her number and kept it held high as she quoted the amount in her down-payment fund.

"What?" Mindy gasped from beside her, reaching out to take hold of her arm, trying to pull it back down.

The bid taker repeated the amount to be sure he'd heard her correctly.

Number still held high despite Mindy's tugging on her arm, Kami nodded and repeated the amount.

Looking impressed, the bid taker called out her new bid to the emcee.

This time Debbie's gaze collided with Kami's and she stared at her for what felt like an eternity but could only have been a few seconds.

Myriad emotions shot toward her like daggers meant to knock her off her feet, no doubt.

No matter. Not Debbie, nor any other woman, could have Gabe without a fight. Without Kami telling him, showing him, how much he meant to her. If he couldn't forgive her stupidity, then she only had herself to blame.

But until she'd tried, she wouldn't give up.

Hand high with her number on display, Kami held her breath, waiting to see what the television hostess would do. Gabe had said she didn't like to lose.

One penny higher bid and she'd have Gabe.

His date package, at any rate. Because even if the woman bid higher, Kami had gone all in. All she had for Gabe—her heart and very being, her dreams, her future.

As they eyeballed each other, Kami was positive the woman knew she'd put all her cards on the table.

When the emcee pushed for a higher bid, the television hostess surprised the entire room, especially Kami, by shaking her head and saying, "I'm done. He's hers."

"Sold! To the pretty woman in the blue dress," the emcee announced, eliciting a loud round of applause from everyone in the room save three people.

Debbie, Kami, and Gabe.

She'd just bought a day in Gatlinburg. With Gabe.

By using her house-deposit fund.

By proving that she was her mother's daughter and the acorn didn't fall far from the tree no matter how many times she'd sworn she'd never be like her mother.

She'd lost her mind.

But maybe, just maybe, she hadn't lost Gabe, a small voice whispered.

Gabe watched as a shell-shocked Kami was pushed toward the stage by well-wishers giving her high fives and hugs. The emcee held out his hand and escorted her up the couple of steps onto the stage.

"Little lady," the emcee said into his microphone, "make sure this fella gives you your money's worth."

"Oh, I intend to," she assured him, garnering a few laughs from the crowd, as the emcee escorted her over to where Gabe stood.

Trying to make sense of the fact that Kami had just bid on him—had won his bid—Gabe bent, kissed her cheek, then clasped her hand.

She didn't look directly at him, just nervously faced the crowd and gave a thumbs-up with her free hand. The event photographer moved around them, snapping pictures.

Gabe felt dazed, and not from the flashes of light.

The emcee called for all ten couples to come back onto the stage for photos.

While they were waiting for the others to join them on stage, Gabe took advantage of the moment to lean down and ask, "What changed your mind?"

"I... You're my friend. I couldn't not rescue you."

"Pricey rescue."

Not meeting his eyes, she nodded. "Guess I'll be staying in my apartment longer than I once thought."

What?

"You used your house savings to bid on me?" Gabe must have misunderstood.

Only he hadn't. Then again, hadn't he thought earlier that the bid had already escalated far beyond Kami's price range, even if she'd wanted to bid? Never in a million years would he have guessed she would use her savings. For him.

Her face was pale, but she nodded, confirming what he'd guessed.

"Why?" When she didn't look at him, he touched her face, turning her toward him. "Tell me why, Kami."

"We're being watched," she reminded him through clenched teeth. "Smile, Gabe."

She was right. He'd forgotten where they were, that they were literally on stage being photographed at an event that was important to the Smiths.

He smiled as several photos were taken, then escorted Kami off the stage. As soon as they were out of the spotlight, he turned her to him.

"Why, Kami?"

One blue-spaghetti-strap-covered shoulder lifted. "It was for a good cause."

He'd wanted her to bid on him, had secretly craved her taking that step and admitting she wasn't ready for them to end, that she didn't want him with another woman, not even for a second or for charity. But he hadn't meant for it to cost her so much.

It had cost her so much.

It had cost her everything. He knew how important buying a house was to her, how long she'd been working toward that goal. Why would she throw her deposit fund away on him?

The only possible reason hit Gabe and he stared down at her in wonder.

No way could he let her give up her savings. "I'll pay for your bid."

Not quite meeting his gaze, she shook her head. "I placed the bid. Not you. Besides, I wanted to help Beverly and her family."

Gabe considered her a moment, trying to decipher if helping their coworker had actually been what had motivated her outrageous bid rather than how he'd taken her bid.

"Don't look now," she warned, "but we're about to be accosted. Will she hurt me?"

"You were the one saying how nice she was," he reminded her, squeezing her hand.

"That was before I snatched you away from her. Now I'm just plain scared."

Both Kami and Gabe had pasted-on smiles as they greeted Debbie and Jerry.

"I knew it," Jerry announced, sticking his hand out toward Gabe. "Congrats."

Staring at Kami, Gabe fought with the realization that she hadn't pulled her hand away from his even after they'd been out of the limelight, that she'd given up something she'd worked hard for to win him, something she held dear that gave her a sense of security. She'd gone out on a limb, for him.

Whether she'd realized it or not, Kami had made a monumental decision regarding their relationship.

Mainly, that they had one at all, and that it was worth sacrificing for, fighting for, changing for, that it was worth trusting in.

Which left him feeling exactly what?

Kami stared at the television producer, a bit baffled. She'd won Gabe's date package. Nothing more. Surely the man's enthusiastic pumping of Gabe's hand was overkill?

"I knew there was no point in raising my bid once I realized you were the new bidder," Debbie admitted while the men were distracted.

"I couldn't have gone any higher," Kami confessed, although she wasn't sure why she was making her confession.

"I knew you were all in," Debbie admitted, "that I could win if I raised the bid."

Kami regarded the woman. "Why didn't you?"

"Because once you were all in there was no way I could win what I was really after." The woman shrugged, gave a self-derisive smile, then surprised Kami with a hug. "Congrats. May you hold on to him longer than I did. Something tells me you will."

"I, uh… Okay. Thanks," Kami blustered, wondering if she should check herself for knife wounds or maybe even claw marks. Was Debbie really so nice that she'd just conceded and congratulated Kami on her win?

The next hour passed in a blur. A blur where Gabe didn't leave her side as the emcee brought the event to a close and a loud round of applause went up at the large amount that had been raised by the event.

"Need me to stay to help clean up this place?"

In a bit of shell shock at everything that had happened and not knowing exactly what would happen next, what she needed to do next to make sure Gabe knew how she felt, Kami shook her head at his offer. "No, a group from the medical floor agreed to break down the decorations and pack them in boxes to be donated. The hotel will do any cleanup beyond that."

His expression unreadable, he asked, "Any reason you have to stay?"

Kami's gaze cut to where Mindy was giving instructions to the volunteers on what to put where and what to trash.

She caught her friend's eye, read Mindy's expression, which seemed to say, *Get out of here now 'cause I have this and I'm so happy for you.*

Kami's stomach twisted. Her friend might be happy for her, but Kami wasn't sure exactly what she'd gotten herself into.

Just what did buying Gabe's date package mean? Other than that she was financially broke and wouldn't be buying a home anytime in the next few years?

Could he forgive her for how she'd refused to trust in him? Refused to let her guard down?

Not that it had mattered. She'd fallen for him the same as if she'd dived in headfirst with all the enthusiasm her mother did time and again.

Fighting the nervous flutter in her belly, she forced a smile. "I can leave anytime you're ready."

Gabe regarded her for long moments. "Does that mean you're leaving with me?"

Why didn't he smile or say something to let her know where his thoughts were? Where his heart was?

Kami mentally took a deep breath, assured herself that she was not making the biggest mistake of her life, but she was all in now, so what did it matter?

Only everything. He meant everything.

Sure, she'd be fine if he walked away. She wouldn't wallow, or go into some deep pit of despair. She'd work and keep moving toward achieving her life goals, would save up another down payment.

But nothing would shine quite as bright without Gabe to share her life with.

She looked straight into his blue eyes and knew that she wasn't going down without a fight.

"Yes, I'm leaving with you. You're mine, remember? Bought and paid for."

Gabe's eyes darkened and one corner of his mouth slid upward. "Is this part of getting your money's worth?"

Finally, a smile.

That smile was priceless.

"Only if it's what you want, too. Like I've told you from the beginning, your only obligation to the winner is your date in Gatlinburg. Beyond that is up to you." Kami took his hand, clasped their fingers, and hoped her eyes told him everything she was feeling. Then she realized that hoping wasn't enough. She needed to tell him. "But, just so you know, I will spend every day between now and our 'date' making sure you know how important you are to me and that I don't intend to let you walk away from me ever again without doing everything I can to convince you to stay."

"Is that so?" His eyes danced with mischief as he reached out and caressed the side of her face.

"Everything in my arsenal," she assured him, turning her head to kiss the inside of his palm. "And I'm not above playing dirty if I have to."

Gabe's smile made everything else in the ballroom fade away, everything but him and the way he was looking at her, the way his hand cupped her face. He stared into her eyes with more emotion than she'd ever had directed her way.

Her heart squeezed in her chest, racing and slowing down in the same beat, making her head spin.

"As intrigued as I am by the thought of you playing dirty, I have to ask—what if I want a lot more than a date in Gatlinburg?"

Reaching up, she wrapped her arms around his neck. "Good, because otherwise I might have to ask for a refund."

* * *

"I've missed you, Kam."

Kami's cheek pressed against Gabe's chest as she listened to the beating of his heart. "Not as much as I've missed you."

"You going to tell me what happened tonight?"

Toying with the light spattering of hair on his chest, she considered his question.

Her gaze went to the photo on her nightstand. The photo she'd stuck inside a drawer after that first morning with Gabe and hadn't pulled out until after he'd walked out on her. Somehow, looking at the photo had been a balm to her achy heart, a reminder that Gabe had only done what she'd expected him to do.

What she'd pushed him to do.

"I decided I wanted to be more like her."

Gabe turned and looked at the photo. "Your mother? You look a lot like her."

Kami nodded. "I've spent my whole life doing everything I can not to be anything like her. It almost cost me you."

"What's so bad that you didn't want to be like her?"

"She loves with all her heart and that makes her an easy target to be taken advantage of."

"She's been taken advantage of a lot, I assume?"

"Time and again. My whole life I've been waiting for her to finally learn, to finally realize, and not jump into love heart first. She never has. I thought that made her weak, foolish."

"Doesn't it?"

She rose up, propped herself on her elbow, and stared at him. "I thought so. Until I bid my entire house down payment at a charity auction."

"Let me at least halve the bid with you, Kam. Don't get me wrong. I appreciate what you did, what it meant, how it made me feel to know you'd do that for me, but I don't want being with me to cost you your dream."

She shook her head. "It didn't. That money bought me exactly what I need most. You."

He cupped her face, his thumb caressing her cheek. "Not just a Gatlinburg date?"

"As many dates as you'll have me."

He grinned. "Before this is all said and done, you're going to think you got a bargain."

She leaned down, kissed his lips. "I already do."

He wrapped his arms around her and hugged her close. "I'm never going to leave you."

"I know," she whispered back, knowing in her heart he spoke the truth. "Nor would I let you. Not ever again. Not now that you're bought and paid for."

He laughed. "I love you, Kam."

Her heart filled with joy, because Gabe wasn't just spouting off words. He meant what he was saying.

She knew because she recognized what she saw in his eyes, what she felt in his touch. It was what was in her own.

"I love you, too, Gabe."

Epilogue

"Okay, Gabe, you're freaking me out a little," Kami admitted, adjusting the blindfold he'd insisted upon putting on her prior to leaving her apartment.

"Oh, ye of little faith. Bear with me for a few more minutes."

"Yeah, yeah. Easy for you to say. You aren't the one being hauled around town blindfolded."

"You trust me, don't you?"

"With all my heart." She did. She and Gabe had been inseparable for the past six months and she was looking forward to their first Christmas together as a couple in just a few days.

"Good answer," he praised from the driver's seat of his car. Not that she could see him thanks to the heavy blindfold.

"Honest answer. Are we there yet?" she asked, wondering where he was taking her. A show maybe? Or perhaps he'd rented them a cabin in Gatlinburg for the holidays? They'd had so much fun in the idealistic little town on their "date."

He'd certainly given her her money's worth a million times over. Every time she looked into his eyes and saw the love there, she thanked her lucky stars that he was hers.

"Has the car stopped moving?" he teased.

"No."

"Then we aren't there yet."

"Is this like a Christmas surprise?" she asked, hoping he'd give her a clue where they were going and why he was being so secretive about it.

"I'm not going to tell you, so it's pointless to try guessing."

Kami sat back in her seat and quietly contemplated the wonderful man she was so desperately in love with.

How could she ever have doubted him?

He'd loved her so fully, filled her heart so completely, she couldn't imagine not having his love or giving him hers.

"Hey, the car stopped moving," she said, realizing that he'd turned the engine off. "Does that mean I can take this off?" she asked, reaching for the blindfold.

"Not yet..." He pushed her hands away from the thick material. "...but soon. No peeking."

He got out of the car, then came around and opened her car door. A swoosh of cold winter air filled the car.

"Brr. I hope we're going somewhere warm," she told him as she took his hand and got out of the car. Letting him guide her, she took a few steps away from the car, then stood while he shut the door.

She wrapped her arms around herself, pulling her coat tight. "Gabe, I'm freezing."

She felt him move in front of her, undo the blindfold and remove it from her face. He stood right in front of her, his body inches from hers.

A goofy grin was on his face. A goofy grin that was full of excitement.

"What are you up to?" she asked, staring into his gorgeous blue eyes. She went to lean in for a kiss, but he stopped her by pulling back.

Her gaze went past him.

"Gabe?" She looked back at him. If anything, his grin had widened.

"Where are we?"

He gave an address.

"I mean, why are we here? Who lives here?"

"What do you think?"

She looked at the house beyond him. It was a beautiful home surrounded by trees and a big yard. "It's gorgeous, but... Gabe?"

"Do you want to go inside and get out of the cold?"

"Um...sure."

When they got to the front door, Gabe pulled a key from his coat pocket and unlocked the door.

"Whose house is this?" she asked again, stepping inside. Then she realized there was no furniture. "Gabe?"

"Come on. Let's look around." He grabbed her hand, guiding her through the house.

Kami took in the gorgeous staircase, the large open-plan living room with lots of windows, the oversized kitchen with granite countertops and solid wooden cabinets, the master suite bedroom-bath combo, three other bedrooms, and then back into the living area.

"Wow, it's a beautiful house, Gabe." Her gaze went past him to a package on the fireplace mantel. A package that hadn't been there earlier. Had it?

He turned, saw what she was looking at, and, grinning, picked up the present and handed it to her.

"This is for you."

"That's not fair. It's still a couple of days until Christmas and I didn't bring your present."

"You are my present. Christmas and every other day of the year."

Leaning forward, she plopped a kiss onto his lips. "Thank you." She glanced down at the box she held. "I can wait until Christmas if you want me to."

"Open the present, Kam."

She laughed. "Well, if you insist…"

Carefully tearing off the paper, she eyed the velvet box inside. The small square velvet box.

Her breath caught and she lifted her gaze to Gabe's. Joy shone there. Joy and excitement and anticipation and perhaps a bit of nervousness, too.

Hands trembling, she lifted the lid, then swallowed at the diamond ring glittering back at her.

Before she could say anything, Gabe took her hand and dropped to one knee.

"Gabe…" Her voice broke as she said his name.

"Marry me, Kam."

Not quite believing what was happening, she nodded. "Yes." Tears streamed down her face. "Yes. Oh, yes."

Smiling, he took the ring out of the box, took her hand and slid the diamond onto the third finger of her left hand.

Kissing her finger, he stood, then kissed her with so much love she thought she might faint from the enormity of it.

"The house is ours if you want it. I told the Realtor what I thought you'd want, what your likes and dislikes were, what the things you once told me you wanted in a home were. I've been looking for weeks. When I walked into this one, it felt like you, like coming home."

Kami stared at him in amazement at the lengths he'd gone to.

"I've talked to your mother. As soon as they're old enough, you get first pick of Bubbles's kittens."

Kami's eyes widened further. "She's going to let me have Sunshine?"

"The runty little yellow kitten you love all over every time we visit?"

Kami nodded.

"I think she's hoping you'll take that one. House, pet, me," he ticked off items, then grinned. "I'm hoping kids are somewhere on that list of yours, because this house is way too big for just the two of us, and someday, if we have a son, I'd like to name him after my dad."

Kids with Gabe. Only in her wildest dreams would she have ever dreamed any of this possible once upon a time.

"A son named after your father sounds perfect. I love you," she whispered.

"I know." One corner of his mouth hiked up. "Any woman who uses her life savings just to spend a day with me must be in love."

"Yeah, well, you make sure I get my money's worth," she teased, wrapping her arms around his neck and smiling at him with her heart in her eyes.

"Every single day for the rest of my life."

And he did.

* * * * *

Keep reading for an excerpt of
Secrets And Speed Dating
by Leah Ashton.
Find it in the
A Patch Of Paradise anthology,
out now!

CHAPTER ONE

The Sophie Project (Project Manager: S. Morgan)
Task One: Find a boyfriend

'JUST SO YOU KNOW, I can't have children.'

Sophie Morgan watched her date's expression morph from a twinkly-eyed grin to slack-jawed surprise at her calmly delivered statement. She took a sip of her vanilla martini and met his wide eyes as she continued. 'I *really* can't. It wouldn't matter if I "stopped trying" or "went on a holiday" or "just relaxed".' She shrugged. 'It just won't happen.'

Her date had barely blinked, so she gestured vaguely at her flat stomach. 'Things down there just don't function properly... *reproductively* speaking, of course. I mean, I *can* have sex. That's all normal.'

The poor guy spluttered into his beer. 'Ah, isn't this conversation a bit...premature? We've known each other five minutes.'

He was being literal. A moment later the high-pitched chime of a small silver bell silenced the room.

The hostess of the speed dating evening—a depressingly stunning model-type who Sophie was sure would never need to attend such an event herself—waited until all eyes were on her. Unlike Sophie, her hostess looked completely at ease in the *über*-modern bar, with its black granite floor, chrome and glass furniture and leather couches. Back in Sydney, this type of place had been Sophie's domain. But now, in Perth, with her old life three thousand kilometres away, she felt like an impostor.

'Okay, gentlemen, time to say goodbye and move on to your next date.'

Her date still look dazed, so she tried to explain quickly, hopeful that she didn't sound like a completely unbalanced lunatic. She *did* know blurting out her infertility wasn't exactly normal behaviour. 'Look, everyone here wants a relationship, right?'

He nodded. In fact, this speed dating event was specifically for people seeking long-term relationships.

'So, when most people picture a relationship, they want the whole package deal—wife and kids. With me, that's not possible. I just thought it was only fair you should know.'

He shook his head. 'Not everyone wants that. I don't know if I want kids.'

Sophie smiled, but shrugged. 'I still think it's better to be up-front, get it out in the open. What you want now can change a heck of a lot in the future.'

People changed their minds. She knew that far too well.

Her date smiled at her. Reassuringly, he now looked more bemused than ready to run screaming away from her—that twinkle was even back in his eyes. 'Who knows about the future?' he asked as he stood. 'Why not let a new relationship just flow? Why worry about it now?'

She watched him sit down at the neighbouring table, his attention already on his next date. She envied his naivety. The ability to live a relationship in the moment, to pretend that all you needed was each other. But Sophie wouldn't do that again. She couldn't.

Not that she didn't want the fairytale happy ending. She did. She'd love to grow old with her perfect man—whatever that meant. Definitely someone who didn't want kids. And *really* didn't—although she really had no clue how she could unequivocally determine that. Maybe someone who'd already had his children? Or was older? Not that she really went for much older men.

She took another sip of her cocktail, a humourless smile quirking her lips. Clearly she didn't know what she wanted. She just knew that she wasn't about to waste her time—or risk her heart—on some guy who would dump her once he knew what she couldn't give him. Getting it all out up-front was definitely a good idea. An *excellent* idea, even.

Still, when she'd flipped over her date card she quickly circled 'No' beside her last date's name. As she had for the four dates before him, and probably would for the remaining five.

Wait.

No. She needed to—*had to*—think positive.

She wasn't ready to admit that speed dating was a mistake. After all, it was the first task on her list. If she couldn't do this, what chance did the rest of her project have?

And if she knew that dropping her bombshell was abnormal behaviour, she *certainly* knew that the very existence of her project tipped her over the edge into...well...a little bit nutty. Knew it—but was determined to carry on regardless.

After the amorphous, directionless mess of the past six months she needed a goal—needed a *plan*.

Reaching into the handbag hanging on the back of her chair, she ran her finger along the sharply folded edges of the piece of paper that had led her here this evening.

A single piece of paper. Flimsy—it could so easily be crumpled and thrown away. But she wouldn't be doing that. Instead, it gave her focus. Just as when she'd sat down at her laptop and methodically put the document together. Soothing lists of tasks and deliverable dates—familiar in their structure and yet so different in their type and intent from the project plans she was used to. For this time Sophie Morgan, Project Manager, was *not* implementing a major software upgrade, or rolling out new hardware, or co-ordinating a change management program.

No, this time the project was her life. Her *new* life.

Sophie took a deep breath. Straightened her shoulders.

It didn't matter that she didn't know who or what would make her circle 'Yes'. She just owed herself—and her remaining dates—her full attention, and at least the tiniest smidgen of hope. No premature circling of 'No'.

And definitely—*definitely*—still disclosing her...uh...situation.

So far the reaction to her announcement had been almost comically consistent, except for the beer-spluttering of her last date. That had been new—but then so had her rather graphic description. She grinned at the memory. She probably shouldn't have done that, even if her more than slightly sick sense of humour had always helped her deal with her problems, infertility or otherwise. She figured that was healthier than the total denial of her mid-teens to early twenties: *I never wanted kids, anyway. They're just snotty alien spew-makers. Yuk!*

Her next date settled into his seat. Middling height, with bright red hair, he beamed at her, and she couldn't help her grin becoming a smile.

'Hi,' he said, obviously about to launch into a well-practised line. 'Why on earth would a stunningly beautiful woman like yourself need to go speed dating?'

But she laughed anyway, determined to enjoy the next four and a half minutes.

And then she'd let him know.

After his third or fourth surreptitious glance, Dan Halliday decided to just give in and look. Something about the woman who'd stayed long after the other speed daters had left kept drawing his attention. Unsurprisingly, the appeal of polishing wine glasses or counting the night's takings really couldn't compete with the beautiful woman propping up his bar.

She was twisted slightly on her seat, so she could stare out of the window that ran the length of the Subiaco Wine Bar. He had the feeling she wasn't people-watching, though, as the one time he'd asked if she wanted another drink he'd felt as if he was interrupting, that she'd been lost in her own little world. He'd left her alone since then—surreptitious glances excluded.

If she *had* been watching she would have seen the constant stream of cars and the packed café tables of a few hours earlier transition into a rowdier, typical Friday night club crowd. The cafés and restaurants that spilled onto the busy city street were now mostly closed, and only the late-night pubs and clubs remained open. His bar needed to close too, and she was the last customer.

Her hair was long, dark blonde, and swept back off her face in a ponytail—which he liked. He'd never understood women who hid behind curtains of hair. This way he had an unrestricted view of her profile: pale, creamy skin with a touch of colour at her cheeks, a long, slightly pointed nose and a chin that hinted at a stubborn streak.

He couldn't tell her height, seated as she was, but he'd guess she was tall. She wore a deep red silky blouse that skimmed the swell of her breasts, and he could just see her crumpled, obviously forgotten speed dating name-tag stuck beside the V of pale skin her top revealed. But he was too far away to read it.

And then she turned her head and locked her gaze with his.

'Are you closed? Do you want me to go?'

Even from where he stood, a few metres away, he was caught momentarily by the intense colour of her eyes. They were blue—but unlike his own boring plain blue, hers were darker. Richer. More expressive.

He gave himself a mental shake. *Dan Halliday philosophising over the colour of a woman's eyes? Really?*

Dan cleared his throat. 'Yes to the first question, but no to the second. You're welcome to stay and finish your drink.'

'You sure? I must have been here for...' she glanced at her

watch '…almost *three* hours, and I've only had half of my cocktail. You could be waiting a while.'

He put down the glass he'd been not polishing while he'd stared—*leered, maybe, Dan?*—and walked to her end of the bar. 'Really, I don't mind. I'll tell you what—how about I give you a fresh cocktail on the house and you can get back to that serious contemplation you looked to be doing while I finish up?'

She shook her head. 'Thank you, but no. I'm sure you don't want me staring out of the window like a zombie any longer. I'll go.'

'So it's all figured out, then?'

Her brow furrowed. 'What is?'

'Whatever it was you were contemplating—it's all sorted? Done and dusted?'

She laughed, but it was a brittle sound. 'No. Not sorted.' She sighed. 'But, trust me, one more cocktail is not going to sort out the total mess of my life.'

Dan knew he should just let her leave. That right about now all his instinctive confirmed bachelor alarm bells should be ringing. This was a woman who had just attended a speed dating evening and had a self-confessed messy life. That was one alarm bell for 'wants a relationship' and another for 'has baggage'. The noise should be deafening.

Instead, he reached for a fresh martini glass, and didn't bother analysing why he didn't want her to go. 'Stay. Stare like a zombie all you like.'

A moment passed. Then another. But eventually she smiled, and nodded. 'Thank you.'

His gaze flicked to her name tag.

Sophie.

A deep aversion to her mother's inevitable requirement for a blow-by-blow account of her speed dating 'adventure', as her mum insisted on calling it, was the reason Sophie had lingered at the bar. At least that was the original reason. But hours had passed since she'd sent a 'Don't wait up' text message, fully aware she was only delaying the inquisition, and still she didn't go home.

At some point she'd stopped making up stories about the diners she could see through the bar's window. She'd stopped imagining which couples were on a first date, who was out for dinner for their birthday, or who was a tourist. The stories were a habit she'd fallen into over the past few months—an effective distraction from actually thinking. It was far easier to analyse and deconstruct a stranger's life than her own. Even her ill-fated plan had been all about striding forward. She hadn't been brave enough to look back.

But tonight she'd let her eyes unfocus, her vision blur, and for the first time in what felt like for ever had let the jumble of memories in.

Sydney.

Rick.

Rick's new girlfriend.

Rick's new *pregnant* girlfriend.

Lost in thought—in contemplation, she supposed, like the bartender had said—she hadn't noticed the other customers leaving. And somehow—remarkably, really—she hadn't noticed the fact her bartender was drop dead gorgeous.

She'd felt him watching her, but had expected a 'finish your drink and leave' type of glare when she'd looked up. He'd surprised her. He hadn't been glaring—not even close. There'd been undeniable interest in his hooded gaze.

She lifted the fresh martini to her lips and studied him over the rim of the cocktail glass as he methodically counted money from the till. He stood with his hip resting casually against the stainless steel counter, his long legs clad in darkest grey jeans and the breadth of his shoulders emphasised by his fitted black shirt. The sleeves were rolled up, revealing rich olive skin and arms that looked strong—as if he did a lot more than just pour drinks with them.

With his short cropped black hair and sky-blue eyes he was far more handsome than any of her speed dates that evening. Of course it hadn't been her dates' looks, intelligence, charm or even their reaction to her unsolicited medical announcement that had been the problem.

She twisted in her chair so she faced the window again, her back to the bartender. She watched a gaggle of young women spill, laughing, out of a restaurant across the road. Hmm—Maybe they were on a hen's night? Or maybe they worked together and were having particularly enthusiastic Friday night drinks?

No. Focus. Her free drink was for contemplation, not daydreaming.

Okay. The problem was that she'd been wrong. She just wasn't ready for a relationship.

Her bruised heart didn't care that she had a perfectly scheduled five-week plan practically burning a hole in her handbag. It turned out that, no matter how hard she tried, she wasn't able to self-impose a 'get over it' or 'move on' deadline.

So, sexy bartender or not, she'd take his offer at face value: continue her zombie-like staring out of the window, finish her drink, then leave.

'How's that contemplation going?'

Sophie jumped, surprised to hear him so close. She looked over her shoulder to see him wiping down the bar.

'Fine, thanks! Plus I've nearly finished my drink, so I'm almost out of your hair.' She held up her near-empty glass in demonstration, then turned back to her window.

'Anything you want to talk about?'

She spun around in her seat at that, ignoring the concerned look in his eyes. 'Nope!'

She gulped the rest of her martini and plonked the empty glass down a little too hard on the bar's polished surface.

The bartender raised his eyebrows. 'I've owned this bar for ten years. Trust me, I know when someone needs to talk.'

Sophie slid off the barstool, slung her handbag over her shoulder and headed for the exit. The click of her heels echoed in the near-empty room. A cleaner swept near the door, but he paused to open it for her.

She wasn't sure what she'd expected. That he'd follow her? Tell her to stop?

The fact that he did neither, and that of course he wouldn't—she was a total stranger!—made her pause.

She couldn't unload to her mother and sister. They were too quick to interject, to judge. Too desperate to give her a solution when all she wanted was someone to listen.

The temptation to talk to the bartender—a man who didn't know her, whom she was unlikely to see again—was too strong to ignore.

She turned and walked back to the bar.

He was calmly polishing a wine glass.

Sophie took a deep breath. 'My fiancé dumped me two months before my wedding.'

He didn't say anything for a moment. He just looked at her, as if he was thinking something over.

'Ouch,' he finally replied. 'Let me get you another drink.'

OUT NEXT MONTH!

Volume 1
in-store and online
March 2025

The Cahills of Gilt Edge, Montana — a family defined by pride and stubbornness. They stand united against trouble, but it's within the family where the real challenges lie. Now, more than ever, unity is their only hope.

Volume 2 available June 2025

MILLS & BOON
millsandboon.com.au